REBECCA MILTON

Mundane Magic

This book was professionally typeset on Reedsy.
Find out more at reedsy.com

Contents

For Stephanie,
who made me brave enough.

<h1 style="text-align:center">1</h1>

The truth of it was that Henry Oakley *hated* teaching.

It wasn't that his students were unruly – on the contrary, every one of them was exceptionally well-behaved, hard-working and highly intelligent. It was less about what the job entailed, and more that he had to do it at all. Over the past years, Professor Oakley had cultivated a great deal of respect for those who worked in espionage; it was not the spying that was exhausting, but holding down one's cover job simultaneously.

For though he really was a professor of philosophy, it was not Henry's true profession – he was, unbeknownst to all but a very small number of people who made up his true department, one of the foremost English researchers into various forms of magic.

During his mornings, he would lecture and teach his philosophy students, but in the afternoons he would sequester himself deep in a hidden part of the university and continue his research into the origins and manifestations of sorcery.

Contrary to what many people believed, magic was everywhere. It was hidden within a huge number of individuals – though to varying degrees – many of whom would never know of their exceptional nature. Though he and his colleagues had only been studying the modern resurgence of the phenomenon for a matter of years, history bore countless examples of the workings of magic, and Henry was quite certain that, with time, they would learn to use it to great effect. But unlike many others, Henry was not focused on understanding how magic worked so much as seeing what could be done with it.

As such, he had, until very recently, been entirely convinced that it would be best if they simply *told* everyone about magic – no more of this ridiculous and tiring subterfuge. Since his colleague and closest friend Vivalda had come into his office in a flurry of panic, however, everything had changed. Her words echoed hollowly through his mind even now, days after they'd been uttered to him. *There is a boy, a mage,* she'd said, *who has used his magic to kill another man. He claims to speak for all of us.*

The ensuing days had passed in a whirlwind of confusion. At first the police had come, interviewing everyone in his department with incredulity and scepticism – but it was not long before even the police had deemed the situation as one they were unable to cope with, and the army had been brought in.

And with the army, of course, had come the major general – Henry's father.

It wasn't that Henry disliked his father; the man was, like much of his family, a caring man who loved his children dearly. The problem was that this love was buried under several levels of stubbornness, arrogance and a constant expectation that he would always get his way.

Thankfully, Henry's mother was a good deal less troublesome, and he was often told that he got most of his mannerisms and personality from her – something he was rather grateful for.

As a result of being father to a mage, and of a high enough rank, the major general had for many years known precisely what it was his son really did, but had nonetheless remained as sceptical of its uses as the police who'd spent the previous days interrogating Henry.

Now, however, things had changed – and Henry's father suddenly viewed him as an expert on all things magical, who would surely have the answer to everything. It wasn't quite as if all their years of strained relations had been suddenly overturned, but Henry more frequently found himself in the position of being asked questions, and that, coming from his father, seemed simply incongruous.

At that very moment, for instance, his father had not only initiated a conversation – something that was rare in itself – but in doing so had asked for Henry's *opinion*. The professor was so floored by this that it took him several moments to stammer a reply.

"Ah – well, I am concerned about the notion of using Aunt and Uncle's household staff as the sole source. I mean, it's entirely possible that none of them will possess any magical ability at all. It's an awful lot to reveal to people, only to find nothing. Wouldn't it be better to use our existing contacts at the university? We could even, ah – contact my counterpart at Cambridge ..."

"Already done," snapped the major general, interrupting Henry as if it were the most natural thing in the world. "As if we'd entrust only one person with something as important as this. Professor Morley will be conducting his own search for a solution."

Edward.

No – no. He wouldn't think about that now. The rattling of the carriage around him seemed, for a moment, to echo the beat of his own heart.

"And if neither of us find anything? Even if we find mages, they may not have power like this Braddock's, or that can be used to counter it ..."

Henry's father levelled him with a stern look. "What else do you suggest we do, boy?" he snapped, causing Henry to flinch. "No weapon can pierce this murderer's armour. Even explosives have proven entirely ineffectual against him. And still he travels the land, converting people to his foul philosophy. If we find nothing amongst the staff, and if Morley finds nothing, we shall search another house. And then another. And then another. And we shall keep going until we bloody well find something!"

For a brief, wild moment, Henry wondered what would happen if they just asked the entire country to come forth – then realised that unveiling the secret of magic so abruptly would likely cause a mighty panic that would serve only to give Thomas Braddock, the young man responsible for all this trouble, precisely what he wanted. No, that was certainly not an option. Although it might seem a vain hope, starting small and branching out if necessary was the most sensible way.

"I don't suppose ..." Henry began hesitantly, "anyone has tried *talking* to Braddock."

"Talk? Of course they've talked – and gotten a damned headache for their troubles. The boy's mad; claims that mages are being silenced, oppressed, that their talents should be out in the open and used. Thank the blazes that most people have the sense not to believe him."

This was, in Henry's opinion, a rather unfair assessment.

For a start, the boy Braddock was not entirely wrong – any time Henry or his fellows in Oxford and Cambridge had suggested seeking out those with magical talent and helping to train them, the higher-ups had been staunchly against it. Oppression still occurred. Henry had even written a thesis on the very subject – for while great progress had been made over the past decades with the creation of the university departments, it was hard to argue that it had gone away.

All those who worked within the magical research departments were forced to hold down cover jobs, teaching additional courses within the university to justify their presence.

The *real* work was classified at the highest levels. They were ordered to take vows of silence on matters magical, and to never reveal their powers, even to help someone in desperate need. This was easier for some than others; Henry's powers could be used in less obvious ways, but he knew people who could do things so astonishing that no one would ever believe they were normal. Their magic might be mundane in many ways, might come from otherwise normal skills and talents, but it was nonetheless miraculous.

But this, of course, was not the time to convince his father of that. If he'd not managed in over a decade, he was not going to manage it now.

Resigned, Henry settled back into his seat, and the two of them fell back into their usual barely comfortable silence.

2

For as long as she could remember, Odette had been possessed of a terrible tendency to daydream at every possible opportunity. Even when she was working, she was always somewhere else in her mind.

Reading was like breathing. From a young age, she'd devoured books, having been lucky enough to learn to read and write – skills her employers had believed every young person should be taught, regardless of their rank or wealth. This had opened her mind up to a huge variety of fantasy worlds, from dragons and knights to great romances that were conducted in a few intense glances across ballrooms.

She had an uncanny ability to fantasise whilst appearing to be attentive to her duties, though there were those who could spot when she was less than wholly present. In her mind, Odette could imagine a million different stories – other lives that she could live, and the lives of other people, observed from above. Though she was trapped in a life that was often much the same from day to day, excitement only coming on those rare occasions when something out of the ordinary happened, Odette had a whole other existence in her mind.

That morning, she took herself into another world entirely – to London, which was not physically far away, but was far removed from the bustling household in which she lived.

Odette imagined that she was a delivery girl, rushing from place to place. She wove effortlessly between the sprawling crowds, her package clutched in her hands. She was tipped by one of the maids at the house. Doffing her hat to them, she returned to walking down the street – more casually this time, her hands in her pockets, a whistled tune on her lips.

In the real world, Odette ran her hand across the smooth mahogany of the banister, tilting her head slightly to listen into the corridor just ahead. She lingered on the penultimate step, her bottom lip worrying as she waited, wanting to be sure that none of the household were walking along the landing – she was, after all, meant to be neither seen nor heard unless called to service. It was a skill that all the servants developed quickly, usually after bumping into the earl once or twice and finding themselves at the painful end of half a dozen lashes with a ruler.

Her mind drifted for a moment to a beach drenched in blood, where a convict was slumped, strapped to a pole, several savage wounds on his back dripping at the whim of a uniformed assailant. Odette's vision zoomed out from the eyes of the whip-wielding army officer to view him from above as he raised his arm and cast down another lash on the deserter. But this was a strange and violent imagining, so Odette cast it aside quickly with a stray thought.

Sensing the coast was clear, she padded silently into the corridor. It was much easier to be quiet upstairs, where the thick carpet that ran down the middle of every walkway muted her footfalls; downstairs, the entire house was floored by thick oak planks that were liable to creak and click. Indoor shoes were one of the greatest expenses for the servants; they were made of a soft suede designed to make as little noise as possible.

Odette placed her palm down carefully onto the handle of the fourth door on the left and made her way into the chambers of the earl's eldest child. She'd served Lady Yasmin since she was old enough to carry linens, first as an assistant to her lady's maid and then taking the position herself as an adult when her predecessor, Valerie, had given birth to her first child and moved away from the household.

Yasmin was a kind mistress, with patience for mistakes and errors. Odette prided herself on making very few, though to say that she made none would be a lie – that was unusual amongst her family.

Indeed, Odette counted herself quite lucky that she'd been assigned to Lady Yasmin and not, like her mother, to the countess – who was renowned for her violent rages and tantrums if so much as a hairpin fell out of place.

She scurried across the carpeted sitting room floor, pushing her sleeves up to her elbows, and began to prod at the dwindling fire with a poker, coaxing the embers to spark as she added more wood. It was that late part of autumn when the afternoons were warm but the nights and mornings bitterly cold.

It was not that the family were bad employers; on the contrary, Odette's mother had assured her that they were far more generous than most. The countess would, for all her anger, give great speeches about how the wellbeing of the servants was reflected in the wellbeing of the house – and as such Odette slept not in the tiny, straw-filled beds that most servants enjoyed, but instead on a mattress filled with down soft enough to mould but hard enough to support. Sometimes, though, she forgot how lucky she was – despite her mother's constant reminders.

The fire was roaring again, and Odette rocked back on her heels, then replaced the tools into the copper bucket with only a few unavoidable clicks.

Stepping towards the bedroom, she could hear Yasmin's breathing as she approached, soft and rhythmic in slumber. It was earlier than she usually woke, but there was a good deal to get ready today with the arrival of the earl's brother and his family. Odette had been up for hours already, helping Mary, the cook, with all of the baking. Her arms ached from kneading, and by the end of it she'd been quite glad of the excuse to leave and help Yasmin dress.

Lady Yasmin was curled up on her side as Odette crossed the room to open the curtains and let in the pale light. Outside, an early frost had begun to form on the green grounds, making the rose garden seem almost crystalline. Odette turned and padded over to the cupboards. She took out the day's outfit and placed it onto the bench at the end of the bed. The light brought Yasmin to waking, her slender arms stretching out above her head.

"Ditty?"

Odette smiled slightly at the nickname. "Yes, my lady?"

"Is it that time already?"

"I'm afraid so," replied Odette with a small chuckle. "Your mother wants you ready for the day by breakfast, since the guests will begin arriving so soon after."

The noblewoman wriggled up to a sitting position, wrinkling her nose up in displeasure. Despite her reticence, she pulled back the quilt and stepped out of bed, where Odette stood with her dressing gown.

"Well, we might as well get it over and done with, then.

Take me through the delights that await us today, Ditty."

The slight drawl of sarcasm in her mistress's voice made Odette's lips curl at the corners, and she turned her head to hide the expression, waiting a moment to reply so as to hide as much of her amusement as possible.

"We must get you washed and dressed as quickly as possible," she explained, reaching up to ensure that none of Yasmin's braids had come undone in the night, "to be ready for breakfast at nine. There will be tea in the primrose room at eleven, before the arrival of your uncle and cousin at noon."

Yasmin's nose curled at the mention of her relatives. The major general was a stern and uncompromising man who'd never been fond of her demeanour. His wife, Yasmin's aunt, was far kinder – as was her cousin, of whom she was fond – but even they couldn't quite make up for the major general's domineering presence.

Unperturbed, Odette continued. "Lunch will be taken at one, and then we'll prepare you for the evening at five."

"So early?"

"The countess has insisted that you're all dressed for dinner in advance."

As Yasmin moved through to the bathroom to wash, Odette began preparing the ties on the corset that formed the basis of the daytime gown. It was her mistress's favourite, a deep peacock-blue that seemed to turn her eyes from misty grey to pale sapphire. Though the embroidery that ran up the corset and around the skirt was intricate, it was picked out in a thread almost the same colour as the gown itself; only up close could the outline of feathers be discerned, delicately raised from the silk. The days it would've taken to create didn't bear thinking about. Odette could sew, but only well enough to make repairs – her fingers shook too much to do such minute work. Abigail was much better at it than she was.

The two of them fell into a comfortable silence as Odette worked on dressing Yasmin and preparing her for the day. The braids that had been woven into her hair the night before were undone, creating a torrent of mahogany waves and curls that Odette carefully pinned into an artful style. Once done, Yasmin's face was powdered, her nails buffed and the final finishing touches put to her appearance.

It was a quarter to nine when Odette's mother appeared silently at the door, doing her best to look nowhere near as harassed as she clearly was.

"Oh, dear," sighed Yasmin, reaching over to pat the older woman fondly on the shoulder. "I can tell she's in a temper already."

To her credit, Odette's mother managed to conceal her agreement. "The countess has sent me to ensure that you're ready and bid you come down to breakfast," she said politely.

"Just one moment," Odette said, reaching over for a small bottle. She tilted the open top onto her fingers and tapped the tips against the hollow of Yasmin's throat and behind her ears and wrists. She nodded her head. "There, my lady. I'll be around to check on your hair and makeup during the day, but it should hold quite well."

Yasmin smiled, the expression lighting up her handsome face. "Thank you, Ditty, Nancy," she said, bestowing the smile upon Odette and her mother in turn. "Where will breakfast be?"

"The tulip room, m'lady," Nancy replied, holding the door open for her as she went through to the parlour.

"Thank you. Have a good morning, both of you."

As Yasmin swept out in a rustle of blue and the scent of lavender, Nancy finally allowed herself to sigh gently with fatigue. Odette wrapped her arms around her in a comforting hug.

"That bad?" she asked, and Nancy nodded.

"Oh, yes. She really does hate his brother, you know."

The two of them checked the corridor to ensure that the coast was clear in a mirrored gesture, then padded silently to the back stairs and headed down to the kitchens. Once they were well out of earshot, Nancy continued, "Though if you ask me, it was worse than normal. Oddly so."

Odette's brow dipped slightly in a frown. "Yasmin seemed fine," she said. "But I suppose if something was wrong they wouldn't have let the children know."

"No, and Abigail said that Johanna seemed perfectly happy, too. I was going to ask Kingsley if he'd spotted anything odd in the earl."

Johanna was the youngest of the earl's children, Abigail her lady's maid. Kingsley, the longest-serving of all of the staff, was the earl's valet. Abigail was the newest, having transferred from another household as soon as Johanna became old enough to require her own maid rather than a nurse.

"What was odd about the countess? It doesn't sound like it was just her temper."

They took refuge at the bottom of the stairs. Other members of the staff bustled quickly past them, rushing to finish the preparations for breakfast.

"That's just it," Nancy said, mirroring her daughter's frown. "I don't think she was as angry as I would've expected.

She almost seemed … if it was anyone else, you know, I would've said she was afraid."

Blinking widely, Odette let her confusion show. "I wouldn't even know what the countess's fear would look like," she said, and her mother chuckled in agreement. "Talk to Kingsley. I'll see if Robbie found out anything from Daniel."

The second oldest of their master and mistress's children, Daniel seemed the most likely to know what had spooked the countess, since he and his mother were very close. He was notoriously closed-lipped, though, and Odette held out little hope of enlightenment. Robbie was Daniel's valet now that he was back with the household, and Odette's closest friend.

Seeing that their moment of pause could continue no longer, Odette and her mother returned to their tasks – though Odette's mind was less on her chores than on what could be wrong with the countess. Her earlier daydreams were entirely forgotten.

She didn't have to wait long for her chance to speak to Robbie – he was in the laundry room when she entered with a basket full of silks.

At nineteen, Odette was the youngest member of staff – Robbie was the next youngest, being three years older. Both of them had been raised in the household, Odette because of her mother's position, and Robbie as a foundling who'd been taken from the local orphanage. The running of St Ethel's Orphanage was one of the many charitable works that the countess insisted on participating in – mostly through donations, but occasionally through grand gestures such as taking one of the children into her household staff.

Robbie was doing his best not to sweat over the shirt he was ironing as Odette placed her basket down next to the washing barrel. He looked up to flash her a crooked grin.

"Ready for the big event?" he asked, almost as sarcastically as Yasmin earlier.

Odette returned his grin. "You know I got everything ready in advance. Unlike some people, apparently," she added, nodding towards the dress shirt in front of him. "Leaving it to the last minute?"

"As always." He leant back against the cool stone of the wall and sighed. "Got to get it out of the way before the other staff get here though. You know they always like to feel they own the place."

"Well, they're guests. We ought to make room for them."

"Oh, surely. Just not *all* of the room." Robbie held his elbows out in a demonstration of just how much space the guest staff liked to take up.

Odette shook her head at him. "They're not *that* bad," she said, though she knew it was true – she just found it impossible to think too badly of people. Ignoring the blank stare Robbie was giving her, she changed the subject, remembering what her mother had told her. "You haven't heard anything odd lately, have you? Mum said the countess was a bit out of sorts."

Even from the other side of the room, Odette could see Robbie's eyes widen. "Really? I didn't realise she'd – well, I guess it makes sense."

"So there *is* something." Almost knocking over the box of detergent in her excitement, Odette leant forward and dropped the silks she was washing. "What is it?"

Robbie looked towards the open door cautiously. He placed the iron back on the hearth for a moment, then crossed the room. After glancing out into the corridor he closed the door.

Butterflies began to dance in Odette's stomach. She'd rarely seen him act so secretive – and though she'd guessed from the countess's concern that it was likely to be something quite serious, his strange behaviour confirmed it.

"I don't know all the details," began Robbie, wiping his brow with a handkerchief. "Daniel hasn't told me anything about it; I overheard a conversation between him and the earl last night. Did you read in the paper last week about the people who died in Cardiff?"

"I did," said Odette, though she had no idea what a couple of accidental drownings had to do with the countess being worried.

"They were talking about them – the people who died. I don't know what got them, but I heard the earl saying that it wasn't an accident. He and Daniel were arguing about something to do with it. Whatever it was, Daniel was convinced that they'd died because of something strange, but the earl wouldn't hear of it."

"I still don't see what this has to do with the countess."

His expression turning grave, Robbie hesitated before replying. "Whatever it is," he said, "the army's involved. That's how Daniel knew about it."

"The army?" Odette was becoming even more confused. "I guess that means the major general will know more about it – and that could be why the countess is worried, if it's something that might cause a fuss at dinner."

Robbie nodded but looked as unconvinced as Odette sounded. Whatever else there was to it, it almost certainly wasn't going to be likeable – the last time the earl and his brother had had an argument over dinner, the guests' stay had been cut considerably short, and the countess had spent the next month ranting about the amount of money they'd wasted on food as a result. Though that had been nothing compared to the fury that had been unleashed at the meal itself.

Lord Austin Oakley, major general, was the younger brother of the earl, and with little to inherit had joined the army as soon as he'd turned eighteen. He'd risen up the officer ranks effortlessly, and was now one of the most senior military advisors to the crown and Parliament. If anyone knew what could possibly concern the army regarding the Cardiff deaths, it was him. Given that Daniel held an opinion that countered his father's, Lord Oakley was likely to agree with it; Daniel was also part of the army, on the last of his leave following a battlefield injury that would see him transferred to administration for the remainder of his career.

The door opened, causing Robbie and Odette to scurry back to their work as Abigail entered. The older woman eyed the pair of them shrewdly, her raised eyebrows suggesting she'd clearly drawn an entirely different conclusion than the truth of the situation. It made Odette grin a little – a few years ago, the assumption would not have been wholly incorrect; it was almost inevitable, after all, that two children growing up together would at some point explore the boundaries of their friendship.

That had not lasted long, however – Robbie had been her first everything, but he and Odette had quickly realised that they worked far better as friends than as a couple. There was no mystery between them, and for all that she hated not knowing things, Odette could never have lived in a world where there was not more to learn.

With Abigail now in the room, their discussion halted, and

indeed there was no chance to resume it – for as soon as Odette had finished with the laundry and seen to tidying and cleaning Yasmin's chambers, it was time for her to check in on her mistress and ensure that all was well.

The elaborate hairdo sported by the young noblewoman was unlikely to come undone, but the rouge on her cheeks and black on her eyelashes would've faded by now.

As she collected the compacts from Yasmin's dressing table, Odette checked her own appearance in the mirror. It would not do to appear in front of any of the household looking untidy – especially not before the countess, who was notorious for needing everything *just so*. Luckily, it seemed she'd not made too much of a mess of herself during the cleaning – her auburn hair was still pinned tightly to her head, and the bun had not come askew. Her dress was not smudged or stained, and still retained enough of its crispness whilst also looking worked in; the countess would be as displeased with a perfect-looking servant as she would an unclean one – for how could the perfectly dressed one possibly have done any work?

As she slipped down to the primrose room, Odette could hear the arrival of the professor and major general's retinues. Professor Henry Oakley, the oldest of Lord Oakley's children, was a respected figure in his own right – a lecturer in philosophy at Oxford, and one of the gentler members of the family. His father, unfortunately, was not similarly minded – nor were his staff – and the sound of arguments drifted up the stairwell as Odette stepped out of the servants' corridors and into the house proper.

The primrose room was just the other side of the billiard room, which was empty as she padded softly through it. The sounds of breakfast had ceased, and as she lingered by the door to the tulip room Odette could hear quite clearly the low conversation from within. Yasmin's voice drifted out, confident and just a little wry. Odette waited until she heard the response, which was soft and youthful when it came – just Johanna. With no other voices forthcoming, Odette decided it was safe to enter, and took a careful step into the room.

Seated at the furthest end of the tea table, the two sisters were laughing lightly together, but there was a tension in their demeanour – each sat quite stiffly, and though she'd moved silently Odette was spotted by both as she entered, their senses clearly on edge. Yasmin raised one hand and waved her over.

"Oh, you're just in time," she said with a warm smile. "I'm afraid I've quite worn all of your handiwork away."

Odette knelt down next to Yasmin and immediately began to fix her makeup, first touching up the rouge on her cheeks before moving on to her thin lips, which had paled to their natural colour with the rigours of the morning. As she worked, she felt Johanna's eyes on her.

"Miss Odette?" the young woman asked, tentatively.

"Yes, m'lady?"

Johanna glanced at her sister surreptitiously, her usual timidity considerably exaggerated by nerves. "I don't suppose – you haven't heard anything *strange*, have you?"

"Han," Yasmin said with a note of warning, bristling slightly. "You know it isn't fair to ask such a thing."

It was a little embarrassing to Odette to have it acknowledged aloud, but her mistress was right – everyone knew that the servants gossiped, of course, but it was quite another thing to call them on it. Or, indeed, to ask for information!

But the funny feeling in Odette's gut, the impression that something was very wrong, had returned – and she found herself not minding the question, despite her blush.

"I couldn't say for sure, m'lady," she began carefully. "My mother said that the countess had been out of sorts, and I heard that your brother and the earl had a disagreement."

Yasmin's eyes narrowed slightly, and Odette could tell that her mistress knew there was more information to be had. Johanna, however, seemed content – or at least distracted enough not to press further.

"See, Minny! I told you," she said, a little of her nervousness disappearing in the face of victory. "Daniel wouldn't have argued with Papa over nothing. That's why they were both so sulky this morning."

"I'm sure it's nothing to worry about," said Yasmin soothingly, holding her eyes open wide so that Odette could replace the black on her eyelashes. "It's not as if they've never disagreed, and both can be very passionate."

Odette politely ignored their conversation as it continued, diverting into a discussion of past disagreements that gave her no new information about the deaths in Cardiff, nor how they could possibly concern several prominent members of the army. She cast her mind back to the article; had either of the victims been soldiers, or from army families? Alas, she couldn't remember, nor was it the sort of detail that she'd have been certain to note. Neither her father nor her siblings were in the army – indeed, her entire family was in household service – so it was simply not something that concerned her a great deal.

It didn't take her long to finish Yasmin's makeup, and Odette was about to quietly excuse herself when a hand settled on her arm.

"Just a moment, Ditty," her mistress said, stalling her exit. "I have some questions about tonight's outfit."

Rolling her eyes, Johanna stood up and brushed crumbs from her own gown. "Ugh," she said, shaking her head. "Why would you be excited about that, Minny? We're sure to be stuffed into something hideous to please Mama's standards."

Odette was reasonably certain that Yasmin didn't intend to ask her about the evening's gown at all, but it certainly encouraged her entirely uninterested younger sister to leave. Johanna flounced out with her usual mixture of timidity and poise, and Yasmin turned her attention back to Odette.

"Well, then," she said with an impish grin. "You had best spill the rest of that story you half told my sister."

Unable to conceal her grin, Odette blushed and looked down at the golden compacts clasped in her hands. Quietly, she explained everything that her mother had told her, and that Robbie had overheard – careful, of course, not to say who'd told her the latter. There was overhearing conversations and there was eavesdropping, and whilst one was expected, the other was significantly less well looked upon ... even though everyone did it.

"Goodness," sighed Yasmin when Odette had finished. "That does explain a great deal. And you really do feel like there's something worth the worrying about?"

"I do," said Odette softly, shaking her head. "Though I couldn't tell you why for certain."

Yasmin nodded her head, and considered this carefully for some time. "Well, there isn't much we can do for now," she said finally, her words interrupted by the chime of the bell as the front door opened. "Ah, that will be them. We'd best be about it, Ditty."

Nodding, Odette gathered her things and rushed back through the billiard room to the stairs.

The servants' corridors were a hive of activity when she entered, dozens of guest staff carrying boxes and cases through the narrow tunnels that ran underneath the manor. Because the house had been built on a hill, many of the servants' rooms actually had windows, as they were carved into the earth itself rather than situated in the rafters as with most houses. Odette's own room, which she shared with her mother, had large windows that overlooked the lake in the grounds. The window faced east, and so the two of them had no need of a wake-up call in the morning – the rising sun served as a much gentler awakening.

Tucking Yasmin's compacts into the pockets of her apron – she'd need them later, after all – Odette decided to find Robbie, since she had a little time before she was needed again. She had no more information to give to him, but maybe he'd heard some more himself. With quick, silent steps she made her way to the small servants' garden, where Robbie was most often to be found if he wasn't working.

At the end of the main corridor that ran the length of the servants' level were two large double-doors filled with glass. They led out into a small, secluded orchard enveloped on three sides by more of the hill. Odette had once been told that this sheltered corner of the grounds had been worn in by an old river, hundreds of years ago; now deep beneath the earth, it was supposedly the river that fuelled the well. Whatever the explanation, it had created a very nice meeting point – and was far away from the other, far busier end of the house, where the gravel path ran round for deliveries.

Robbie and Odette had come to the orchard for most of their breaks since they were children – until the time of year when it became too cold to do so, of course. But the sun had been up for some time now, and it was warm enough for Odette not to pick up her coat on the way out.

Sure enough, Robbie was seated outside on their bench under the pear tree. A cigarette dangled between his fingers. Odette plonked herself down next to him, stretched out and sighed tiredly.

"Oakley's lot are here, I see," observed Robbie, glancing into the house. The corridor was still full of people. "Hard to miss them. You can practically hear the sneering from here."

"They're not that b—" began Odette in protest, before shrinking slightly from his gaze. "Fine, Lord Oakley's might be, but the professor's aren't so bad. They're ... quieter."

"Oh, sure. But I bet they think they're cleverer than you, working for a professor."

"I've never really seen Lord Henry much," remarked Odette, glancing up at the now almost bare pear tree. "Though Lady Yasmin talks about him a lot. What's he like? You must've seen him much more; he's fast friends with Daniel, or used to be."

"Quiet, bit like his staff," said Robbie. "You can tell a lot about a man from his staff, and he's not got many, so you know he's more grounded than the rest of them. But get him talking about some things, he'll light up like a fire. It's like watching him turn into a totally different person. He and Daniel have some of the biggest rows – you'd never expect it from Henry – but somehow they always seem to come out of them liking each other more. Never really got that."

"I suppose it's a scholarly thing."

"Guess so. Anyway, he's all right. Definitely thinks he's above you and all that – intelligence-wise, I mean. Never because he's highborn as far as I can tell – but not as bad as some. Anyway, did you find out anything else about those murders?"

Shaking her head, Odette replied, "No, though Yasmin and Johanna had noticed something was wrong with their father and Daniel. I think they were out of sorts at breakfast."

"But no idea what's going on?"

"Not a clue," sighed Odette.

3

The remainder of the carriage journey had gone by without any more arguments; nonetheless, Henry was rather relieved to get out once they'd arrived. His father quickly marched up to the house, greeting Henry's aunt and uncle with a brusque nod before taking the countess's arm and following the earl inside. This left Henry, rather pleasingly, to be welcomed by his cousins – who though in many ways were like their parents were much warmer in their greetings.

"Henry! Good to see you, chap," called Daniel, walking forward with only a slight limp to greet him warmly. He'd traded his crutches for an elegant walking stick since Henry had last seen him. But of more concern was his expression – there was a tension in his demeanour that led Henry to believe that Daniel knew a little of what was really going on. "You survived the journey, I see."

"Barely."

Peals of tinkling laughter came from the women, who collectively caught him in a rather bruising hug. "Oh, Henry, it's lovely to have you here," enthused Yasmin, Johanna nodding emphatically at her side. "It's been far too long."

"It has," he agreed, leaning down to kiss the top of Johanna's head. "I see you've made it almost to lunchtime without getting charcoal stains on your dress, little one."

Johanna grinned and held up her right hand, which was stained ever so slightly around the index finger and thumb with ink. "I'm past charcoal now. You'll have to come and see!"

Henry smiled broadly. "I'd love to. You must meet one of my staff – her name is Isobel, and she produces the most wonderful paintings. I'm sure she'd love—"

He broke off suddenly, as a horrible realisation dawned upon him. It caused his cousins to look at him with alarm and ask if he was all right – but Henry couldn't answer. His mind had been suddenly filled with the image of a painting Isobel had once done. She'd told him it had simply come to her one morning and that she'd felt compelled to paint it. It was a self-portrait of her working to clean his office, the light streaming through her hair. The very day after she'd shown Henry it, he'd watched her take that exact same pose when she was cleaning.

How foolish he was to have brushed that aside as a stray coincidence! He, who knew that so many coincidences turned out to be magical occurrences. A mage in his very own staff and he'd never realised – he was certain of it now, of course. It was precisely the sort of talent he spent his life studying, looking for.

"Henry, are you sure you're all right?"

"My apologies, dear cousin," he said, shaking his head. "I'm just, ah, a little weary from the journey. Father can be trying at the best of times."

And these were most certainly not the best of times.

The three of them ushered him inside, weaving through the now-bustling corridors to Henry's favourite room in the house. The earl's library wasn't a patch on the Bodleian, of course, but it had a comforting ambience that Henry always enjoyed. He sat down, and the ladies bustled off to find refreshment, leaving him alone with Daniel.

"Well," Henry began, "you should probably tell me how much you know."

The younger man ran his hands through his hair and sighed, taking a seat. "I only knew bits and pieces before this past week. Every now and then, related things come across my desk; I get the censored versions, of course, or they're bound up above my security clearance, but over time you start to put things together. I confronted my father about it this week and he eventually told me everything he knows."

"I'm not privy to how much my father has told the earl."

"I know about – about *magic*. I know that the deaths in Wales weren't accidental, and that there's some mad boy out there trying to convince the country that people like him are being kept under wraps, and killing those who don't agree with him. I know that we've tried to take him down but his ... magic ... is stopping us. I know that you're here to see if you can find people who have the skills to help. And I know that you ... that you're ..."

"A mage."

Daniel flinched slightly in apology. "I don't mean to be rude, it's just – well, it's all a bit like something out of one of Johanna's stories."

This made Henry laugh, the rumbling sound easing the tension from the room. Daniel had soon joined him, and the two sat shaking their heads at themselves, at one another, and at the situation in general.

"It's quite all right," Henry said softly. "I'm aware that it's no small thing to ask people to believe; it's hard enough to realise that someone you know very well is not quite the person you thought they were, let alone try and understand the existence of something as fantastical as this."

"How did you find out? When did you find out?"

"A little after my thirteenth birthday. I was performing in a school recital, an old medieval drinking song – you know the type, all about clapping your hands and stamping your feet to celebrate the harvest, that sort of thing. I got quite into the performance, and halfway through the song, I realised the audience had too – indeed, they'd leapt out of their chairs and begun doing precisely as the song said to. Dancing in the aisles, stamping their feet, singing along with me. The school decided it was just an exceptionally good performance, of course. But there was someone in the audience who recognised what had happened, and came to tell me."

Daniel looked torn between amusement and disbelief. "God, what a thing to have to deal with at such a young age. But you told no one?"

"My parents were told, but I was otherwise sworn to secrecy. I kept training my power, but in secret – only when I got to Oxford did I finally tell someone else. I met a woman there named Vivalda Entwhistle, who also confessed to having some magical power. It was Vivalda who helped me petition the university and the crown to form the department we now work for."

"I remember now that you stopped singing for all of us," said Daniel. "I'd always assumed it was because your voice had broken and ruined it."

Henry grinned. "I was encouraged to allow you all to believe that. But yes – especially then, when I couldn't control my powers fully, it was imperative that I not accidentally expose you to them. I performed controlled experiments with my mother, and together we explored what I could and couldn't do with my voice. It was her political influence that helped us get the department started."

"What else can—" The library door creaked open to reveal Daniel's sisters and a number of servants. "Ah, tea! That which helps us recover from even the most hideous of journeys."

Yasmin took a seat next to Henry, and Johanna next to Daniel as the servants laid out the refreshments, including a delicious-looking selection of cakes and pastries.

Henry fell into a contented silence as the tea washed away the tension in his mind with a warming balm, and settled back to listen to Johanna talk enthusiastically about her new tutor and how he was teaching her all manner of different artistic mediums, but that her favourite was ink.

After a while his mind strayed back to poor Isobel. He'd have to speak to her as soon as possible about her paintings. The more he considered it, the more instances he could remember of her paintings being prescient. She'd always spoken of her paintings simply coming to her in dreams or in stray thoughts. There was no doubt in his mind that she had a gift, and a very precious one indeed. He cursed himself over and over for not having seen it before. If only he'd not had to keep his true profession a secret from her; she might've come to him before now.

Vowing to speak to Isobel as soon as the opportunity presented itself, Henry returned his attention to his cousins. Johanna had exhausted her enthusiasm and passed the conversation over to Yasmin, who was now entertaining them with a story about yet another of their mother's attempts to simultaneously hide and proclaim her generosity. Selecting another utterly sublime cake from the tray, Henry smiled and reflected upon how lucky he was to have such a delightful family.

4

For Odette and Robbie, knowledge was not as forthcoming as they'd hoped. Once their break was over, the day flew by as more staff and guests arrived, throwing the household into a frenzy of activity. Lunch came hot on the heels of the end of breakfast, and though there was a much longer break between lunch and dinner, the preparations for that evening meal were far more elaborate. This was especially true in the case of Yasmin, whose gown took half an hour and two assistants to get her into.

Unfortunately for Odette, there was no respite – she just had time to throw down some soup, bread and cheese before dressing to assist with the dinner service. Usually, the valets and ladies' maids wouldn't be needed, but with so many people to serve, the rest of the staff would be overwhelmed without the extra hands.

Waiting in the adjoining room to the dining hall, Odette shifted uncomfortably on the spot – the much fancier dress she was forced to wear was significantly itchier than her everyday one.

The first two courses had gone without event, despite her constant fear of tripping or spilling something, and the main course had just been served. Barring a sudden flurry of requests for more wine or other accoutrements, the staff could do nothing but wait for the next wave of activity.

Because of the tension between the household staff and the guest retinue, however, things were a little uncomfortable – and consequently an eerie silence hung over the group as they waited. This was in Odette's favour; it meant she could easily overhear the conversation in the dining hall.

"… not that I think you're wrong, Sylvia, it's just that we simply can't be seen to be making too much of a fuss." It took a moment for Odette to place the earl's voice – he sounded so much like his son at times. "If we did, it would be all over the county, the country even. Society at large does like to follow the tune of families like ours, you know – and that simply wouldn't do."

"Wouldn't do?" harrumphed the countess. "I'll tell you what will not *do*, Brandon, and that's sitting by whilst innocent young men and women are sacrificed on the altars of the greed of a few. And yes – a fuss shall certainly be made in Society if we do make a stand, and that's precisely the fuss I wish to create. I'll not be party to this hideous tendency of the English to ignore the painful truth in the name of *progress*."

It was one of the countess's most common rants, but there was something of an edge to it that evening that was not normally present. The earl's reply confirmed Odette's rising suspicions.

"That's enough, Sylvia," he said curtly, in an unusual display of authority. "I'm sure that Austin does not want to hear us besmirching his army's decisions at any time, let alone *these* times."

There was a rough laugh that probably came from the major general. "Not to worry, old chap. Don't blame Sylvia for thinking that – terrible loss of life, and she's right that too many overlook it. You can rest assured, though, that there are many of us who most certainly *do* remember the cost of these things – and whilst many may not be forced to weigh up the true value of war, I and my fellows face down that unfortunate topic every day. Take Cardiff, for instance—"

Odette's ears perked up, as did those of several others around her. She was clearly not the only person who'd heard mention of Cardiff during the day. When Oakley was interrupted, she had to strain to hear the response.

"Father," came a soft but firm voice that Odette took a moment to recognise as Henry Oakley's, "let's not bring that sort of thing up at the dinner table, please. You know as well as I that such things are best discussed in context."

"Quite," proffered the earl, who quickly diverted the conversation to another topic entirely – some point of economics that Odette had little interest in and even less understanding of. But the tension seemed to remain, both amongst the servants and the nobles, and the professor's staff quietly muttered about how strange it was for the major general not to have snapped back at his son's suggestion.

Odette wasn't to be starved of information for long though – just after dessert had been served, there came an almighty knocking at the front door. All of the servants jumped to attention, one or two letting out startled gasps. Roger, the butler, quickly composed himself and dashed out to the entrance hall to answer it. Even the conversation from within the dining hall stopped, the clamour at the door having been so fierce that the entire household had heard it.

The staff stepped to the side as Roger came through some moments later, holding a telegram and accompanied by the soldier who'd delivered it by horseback. The man was drenched in sweat, and several of the staff noted with disdain that he'd not even thought to scrape the mud off his boots before entering. Odette's mother clucked under her breath at the sight of him and quickly moved to offer the poor man a glass of water and a chair whilst Roger delivered the message.

"Are you quite all right, dear?" asked her mother, producing a handkerchief for the soldier's brow and shooting a glare at the maids who were now loudly complaining about the mud that had been tracked all over the floor.

The officer coughed, still catching his breath, and nodded. "Thank you, ma'am, I am," he managed after several gulps of water. "Never been sent anywhere in such a hurry. Came all the way from Bristol, too."

"Bristol? Goodness, but you must not have had anything to eat. Abigail?"

"I'll go see what Mary has left. I'm sure there's something about," she replied with a smile before dashing to the stairs.

"That's very kind of you," said the soldier with a genuine, though weary smile. "Not sure how long I'll be here though. They want the major general back as soon as possible."

"So soon? But he left just last night – he's barely been here half a day! Whatever could've happened so suddenly?" her mother said, sharing a curious look with Odette.

"I–I ..." The soldier looked uncertain. "I'm afraid I can't say, ma'am. It's top secret, though I'm sure you'll hear about it soon."

He had that same unsettled look that everyone in the know seemed to carry with them – a mixture of confusion and shock. It settled heavy on his brow, and he fell silent despite the staff's continued questioning – until the major general came through, a grave look on his face. The soldier jumped to attention.

"At ease, Corporal," said the senior man with unexpected gentleness, placing a hand on the soldier's arm. "You've done well, son. Now, is this all you've got for me?" he asked, holding up the telegram, "or is there more to it?"

The soldier looked either side of him at the gathered servants, who all began to do their best to look busy – even if simply turning away and brushing at the furniture.

"That's all we knew when I left, sir," he said, holding his voice as steady as possible. "But I expect he's made more of a fuss by now. Cardiff was the first of many demonstrations – 'just the beginning', that's what he said, sir."

Odette's ears perked up, and she tilted her head surreptitiously to listen.

"And it's just Br—, the one man?"

"Aye, that's what I've been told. Sure he's got something of a following already, else he wouldn't dare go so much more public. Talking to a handful of people's different to talking to the press. But he's the only one who can ... who can—"

Oakley nodded, cutting off the soldier's fumble for words. "I understand, son. Takes a bit of getting used to, doesn't it?"

"It does, sir. Sir, if I may ..."

"Go ahead."

The soldier shifted uncomfortably on the spot. "How do you *know*, sir? I mean, he says all sorts of us can – you know – but how do you *tell*?"

A warm chuckle came from the major general's throat. "For that, my dear boy, you'd have to ask my son. He's the expert. And speaking of which – he'll be staying here."

"But, sir, my orders were—"

"I know what your orders were, Corporal. But the professor was ordered to put his plan into action, and he can't do that without people – and the people he needs are here. I'll come straight back to it with you, of course, but Henry – he'll just have to stay and do his ... what he does ..." Oakley looked suddenly uncomfortable, an expression that did not sit well on him.

Odette tried not to be disappointed that the major general and the bedraggled corporal moved away before she could catch more of their conversation, and she could tell from the others' expressions that she wasn't the only one.

As the servants' talk turned to the logistics of a return journey to Bristol, and they hurried to ready the horses and luggage, Odette found herself amongst the staff left to wait on the somewhat disarrayed dinner party. Her mother was there, too, as were Roger and two valets.

Dessert passed more quickly than usual. Then the earl ordered a halt to proceedings until he'd spoken to Henry. The two men stepped out together for a moment, and Odette wished dearly that she could follow them. What could a professor of philosophy possibly have to do with what appeared to be several murders? The corporal had said that whomever was responsible had called it "just the beginning". Was it an act of war? But how, then, could Lord Henry be involved?

"Roger," said the earl. His return surprised Odette; she'd fallen deep into thought. She jumped to attention much like a soldier, holding her hands behind her back. "I need you to gather all the staff in the dining room. The guest staff, too."

The request stunned the butler, who swayed slightly on the spot. "M'lord?" he asked, confused.

"As many as possible," elaborated the earl, seemingly oblivious to the exceptional nature of his request. That he'd summoned the staff to the dining room was astonishing; that a meal would be interrupted was unheard of. "Leave the people needed to help my brother get away, but gather everyone else. As soon as you can, Roger. Thank you."

The earl turned on his heels and left, leaving a still-stunned Roger to order everyone to assemble.

He sent Robbie and Abigail down to gather the rest of the staff, and did his best to ensure that the already present staff were as smart as they could be. Odette thought this was less because he thought it was necessary, and more because there was little else they could do whilst they waited for the rest of the staff to arrive.

She brushed off her dress and checked her hair just as everyone else was doing, but it was not enough to stop her thoughts from roaming. What could possibly have happened? This wasn't the first crisis the family had faced, of course – their military and political activities subjected them to scrutiny often – but Odette could not remember such secrecy ever occurring.

The thought unnerved her deeply, and as she adjusted the pins in her hair she noticed that her hands were shaking. Biting her lip, she began to pray that her nerves wouldn't get the better of her this time. Remembering something her mother had told her, she focused on her breathing – taking in slow, languid breaths through her nose and out through her mouth. But this only made her all the more certain that she was on the verge of one of her fits – and though she tried to breathe as deeply as possible, it never seemed that she was quite getting enough air.

Her eyes darted about to see if Robbie had returned – his presence always made her feel calmer, even though he often had no idea how to help – but he was still away, collecting the rest of the staff. Clasping her hand to her throat, she felt for her pulse, which was fluttering as quickly as a butterfly's wings. Just as the panic began to overwhelm her, she felt a warm pressure in the small of her back, and a cool hand taking hold of her own.

"It's all right, darling," her mother whispered, and Odette felt her eyes go glassy with relief. "I'm sure it's nothing to worry about. Come on, now. Deep breaths – that's it, that's my girl."

The soft, soothing tones of her mother's voice brought a calming relief, and her breathing began to slow. She felt the strong grip of the fit passing, and leant into her mother's embrace with heartfelt gratitude. An undercurrent of panic still remained, but her mother continued to comfort her until the rest of the staff had arrived.

Once they'd gathered, they lined up in pairs to march through. Odette stood behind her mother, who kept glancing back to ensure she was all right, and next to Robbie, who was a little out of breath from rushing round to collect the rest of the staff. In silent confusion, the servants stepped through into the dining hall, where the gathered nobles sat waiting for their attendance – the novelty of which seemed not to be lost on anyone.

"Thank you, Roger," said a soft voice, and Odette was curious to see that Lord Henry appeared to have taken charge of proceedings. "I'm sorry to pull all of you away from your duties; I'm sure you have much to attend to. Unfortunately, the message that just arrived is ... I'd like to say unprecedented, but I've feared its possibility for some time, despite the disagreement of my peers. We must move up our schedule, and I don't think you should be kept in the dark any longer."

He rose to his feet, placing a hand on the back of his aunt's chair. Then he paced around the table towards the staff. "I'm afraid that what I'm about to tell you, many of you shall not believe. It took me several years to accept it myself. Indeed, only three others in this room are privy to the secret that I'm about to unveil." He nodded to the earl, the countess and Daniel, who, Odette now noticed, were the only people not looking wholly confused. "I refer," continued the professor, "to magic."

"Magic?" whispered Johanna, a little louder than she'd probably intended to. "Like in fairy tales?"

A small smile played at Henry's lips. "A little, dear cousin. In fact, much more so than in other stories. The magic of this world is not – has not been, at least – that of transmogrification and great fireworks."

"F–Forgive me, m'lord," stammered Roger, who was so astonished that he spoke quite out of turn, "but surely you're not suggesting that magic is real?"

"I am," replied Henry simply, and a stunned silence fell across the hall. Several of the servants let out small, nervous laughs of disbelief. Odette glanced over at Yasmin, who seemed surprised but also incredibly curious. She was looking up at her cousin as if seeing him for the first time, and was not alone in doing so.

Breaking the silence, Roger continued, "You will have to pardon me, m'lord, but I don't see how such a thing could be real without some of us knowing about it."

"Indeed! A fair point," said Henry, his smile broadening. His voice began to gain a little power as he spoke. "I'm so glad you made it. You're quite correct – and, indeed, this is not the first time that magic has been revealed to the world. It has simply done so under different names and guises before – miracles, the works of the saints, anything unexplainable – these things have all been magic making a step from the unknown to the known."

"How is this time any different?" asked Yasmin, leaning forward in her seat.

"An excellent question. This time, a man has come forth and used magic to kill. Now, this is not unprecedented in itself; there have been magically fuelled deaths before. But this man sees himself as something of a visionary. He wishes others to acknowledge their magical power, and is using his ... might, to put it one way, to demonstrate the possibilities."

"Is he the only ... what do you even call them? Magician?"

"Mage," corrected Henry gently, before shaking his head in response to Yasmin's question. "No, he is not."

There was an exchange of looks between Henry and the earl, which was broken by the countess's heavy sigh and a throwing up of her hands. "For God's sake, Henry," she snapped, "just show them. It's the fastest way to make them believe."

The professor flinched slightly at the command, but nodded his head. He'd now made his way to the other side of the table, and stood between the family and the servants in their neat lines. Brushing a hand over his dark hair, which had come slightly askew, he cleared his throat as if preparing to make another speech.

Instead of launching into a lecture, however, he opened his

mouth in song. He had a deep, resonant voice that Odette had never truly appreciated before – when singing, it came to life, simultaneously losing all of the soft hesitancy of his speaking voice and transforming into a redolent tenor. He looked at no one, singing instead to the portraits on the walls. Odette was so distracted by the beauty of his song, and was straining so hard to make out the words – which were, she concluded after some frustration, in Latin – that at first she didn't notice the effect.

It was her mother's gasp and pointed finger that drew Odette's attention to Johanna. The teen was gazing enraptured at her cousin, and as he continued her eyelids grew suddenly heavy. She swayed slightly on the chair, finally slumping into sleep, her head lolling against the table. Abigail rushed forward to catch her mistress before she fell wholly to the floor, and in doing so caused Henry to break off his song. Moments later, Johanna opened her eyes blearily, as if waking from a deep slumber.

"What happened?" she asked drowsily. Her question was met with silence; everyone was gazing, many open-mouthed, at Henry, who'd tilted his head down, a small smile catching at the corners of his lips.

In hushed whispers, Abigail explained to Johanna what Henry had done.

"I thought that was odd!" exclaimed the girl in response. "I would hope that I'd never be so rude as to fall asleep at dinner."

Nervous laughter rippled through the room. Henry regained his composure and resumed speaking.

"I'm sure that you're wondering what this could possibly have to do with all of you," he said, turning to address the staff. "The army have sought my expertise in working to bring down this murderer, and I've come up with a solution – or, at least, a potential route to one."

"Can you not just … sing him to sleep?" asked Abigail, returning to her place now that Johanna had settled.

"It's been tried," answered Henry with a sigh. "It didn't work. He has the power to weave something of a barrier around himself – against both physical weaponry and magic such as my own. I believe that the only possible solution is to find a source of magic that counters this barrier." He paused, clearly a little flustered by all the attention. "Now, my research has shown that magic is often found in unlikely sources – specifically, magic is far more likely to manifest in what we might call labourer's work."

"Are you saying," asked Odette softly, understanding dawning on her the fastest, "that we could all be mages, and not know it?"

A broad smile settled on Henry's features, making them seem suddenly incredibly handsome. "That's precisely what I'm saying, miss."

Odette wasn't quite sure what to say to that. She wasn't sure what to say to any of it.

5

Performing in front of so many people had left Henry incredibly weary, but he was determined to keep his promise to himself. Once the commotion had died down, and he'd answered the not inconsiderable number of questions posed by his family – the staff, it seemed, had retreated somewhat into themselves after the initial discovery – Henry took himself off to the library once more.

On his way he spotted Kingsley, his uncle's valet, and asked him if he wouldn't mind sending Isobel up to the library with coffee. Kingsley seemed a little skittish but was doing his best to conceal it, which Henry thought was rather more courtesy than he deserved. After all, he'd just told them that the world was entirely different from what they'd believed all their lives. It was a wonder they weren't exploding.

With a sigh, he settled down comfortably in front of one of the library's tables and waited for Isobel to appear. Her knock when it came was tentative, and Henry chuckled to himself before calling her in.

Isobel was a tall woman who'd been in his family's employ since her teens, and had moved to work for Henry when he'd attained his professorship. Until then, he'd had no need for staff, living as he had done in the halls of the university. But with his title came prestige enough to establish his own household, and his parents had generously sent several of the family staff over to join him.

"Will there be anything else, Professor?" asked Isobel softly, placing the tray down upon the table and pouring him a cup.

Clearing his throat, Henry sat up a little straighter. "Actually, Isobel, I wonder if I could speak to you."

She looked for a moment like a rabbit caught in the headlamps of a cart, but sat down quickly as instructed.

Henry took a sip from his own drink before pouring one for Isobel, who was clearly too disconcerted by the evening's revelations to take account of the strangeness of her master serving *her*.

"I feel, first of all, that I owe you an apology," Henry began. "I wished very much to tell all of you the truth about who I am and what I do, but I' m afraid I was not permitted to. Whilst I think a level of secrecy is needed, it always discomforted me that I was not allowed to tell the people who have served me so generously and kindly."

Isobel shook her head. "Professor, we always knew there was something else going on, and we never minded one bit. We trusted you to tell us if it was necessary or when you could. And now you have." She smiled softly, taking a sip of her drink. "Though, I'll admit, we were expecting to find out you were a spy of some sort, not ... this."

"A spy? Good grief. I'd be an abysmal spy."

"It was George's idea," said Isobel with a laugh. "He had this elaborate tale about how you were recruited as a boy and trained up, and that your – forgive me – outward appearance was all an act. I think he's not sure whether to be disappointed or even more amazed by the truth."

"Either way, I'm still sorry to have lied to you all. I'm rather relieved to have told everyone now, to be truthful. But I didn't ask you here to speak about me; I'd actually like to talk about you, Isobel."

"Me, sir?"

Henry saw worry flicker back into her eyes, and wondered how many times he'd have to repeat this conversation, and whether it would get any easier. "When did you first start painting?"

This was clearly not the question she'd expected, and Isobel was so discombobulated by it that it took her a moment to answer. "I suppose I've always painted, sir," she said. "My father was an artist, as you know, and I was always encouraged to follow in his footsteps. By the time I was working for your family I'd found that I liked painting most of all, though."

Henry nodded. "And did you always paint things you'd dreamt, or did you sometimes paint things you'd seen?"

"I'm afraid I honestly don't remember. I suppose I must've painted things I'd seen, sometimes – it's one of the first things they do in classes, give you a bowl of fruit and ask you to draw it – but certainly for as long as I've been painting things for enjoyment rather than study, I've always felt drawn to paint certain things. Often it's people I know."

"I remember you painted an excellent portrait of yourself," Henry remarked. "Tidying my study. Do you recall it? There was a beautiful effect as the light fell through your hair, like a golden curtain."

Isobel blushed slightly and nodded. "I remember it, sir."

"The strangest thing happened with that painting, you know. For shortly after you'd completed it, I saw you in that precise pose, the afternoon sun lighting up your hair."

"Oh," said Isobel, laughing. "How very strange! George once told me the exact same thing. I'd painted him standing to greet guests, I think the first time Professor Entwhistle came to visit your new house. It was ever so strange, for I'd never met her before then, and had no idea what she'd be wearing, yet I picked precisely the right colours for her hair and suit."

Henry couldn't help but sigh. "Isobel," he said softly, "I don't think it's strange at all."

She hesitated then, her brow dipping in confusion. "...Sir?"

"Magic is one of those things thought of as being omnipresent, but it's not quite everywhere, my dear. It hides within the talents of individual people. That's how it survives without our noticing; no one would think it strange to view the work of a master crafter of any sort, and be amazed by it. Yet they may not notice those properties that make it not simply an incredible creation but a magical one."

Isobel had frozen in place, her hands around her cup. Henry continued, knowing that the only way of offering some sense of catharsis was to tell her what she was beginning to fear.

"You paint things that will one day come to pass," he continued. "They come to you in what feels like perfectly normal inspiration, but I believe it's more than that. I believe it's the magic within you that guides you to paint these prescient works. I believe you've been a mage all of your life, but not known it. No, dear, it's all right – put the cup down; don't spill it."

He quickly took the coffee from Isobel's hands and moved to her side. Placing a hand on her shoulder, he knelt beside her as she processed the revelation. Her eyes darted back and forth, and he could almost see the thoughts speeding through her mind.

"Oh," she managed after a moment. "Professor, I ... I don't really know what to say."

Chuckling, Henry patted her shoulder fondly. "Nor should you! I don't believe there is anything one can say at this point."

"Will I be able to help you, sir, with what you're doing?"

Henry was gripped with a sudden pride and fondness for Isobel, who, in the face of uncovering such a great secret about herself, seemed immediately concerned about whether she could help someone else.

"Absolutely," he said, smiling warmly at her and returning to his seat. "But, first, I'd like to explore what you can and cannot do. You're relieved of all your duties, and I shall have the equipment that you'll need sent for. For now, you can borrow my cousin Johanna's supplies, I'm sure. She is a budding artist herself, though not in quite the same way."

"What do you mean by explore, sir?"

Henry sat back in his seat and considered her for a moment. "When you're painting," he asked thoughtfully, "do you ... do anything in particular? Hum, perhaps? Tap your feet?"

Blinking widely in confusion, Isobel replied, "I have no idea, sir. I've never really thought about it. I suppose I do tend to move about quite a lot – I prefer to stand when I'm painting. Sitting down feels so confined."

"Often, people with magical powers have an almost ... ritualistic approach to whatever it is they do. It's one of the ways to spot magical power over simple talent. Whatever that behavioural tic may be, it's the manifestation of your casting."

"Like how people say their spells in stories?"

Henry nodded. "Precisely so."

"What do you do, sir, if you don't mind my asking?"

"I don't mind at all – you really must feel free to ask me any questions you need to. Mine is a slightly strange one; you see, what I choose to sing seems to inform the manner of my casting. This is only logical to an extent – one can hardly expect to send someone to sleep by singing a revel – but it's additionally impacted by the language in which I sing."

"So if you sing a lullaby in Greek, it's different to the same lullaby in Latin?"

"Indeed. I find that different languages do different things. Latin, for example, makes things fast-acting – that's why I used it earlier to sing Johanna to sleep. Additionally, I rock back and forth slightly whilst singing, but I've never been quite sure if that's part of my casting or simply because I'm generally the restless type."

Isobel laughed softly, nodding. "I suppose my moving about could be something to do with it, then. And ... I do like the colours I'm painting with to be placed in a particular arrangement around me. It used to drive my father batty because he always liked things to be a different way around." She paused, thinking. "Do you ... do you think my father is magical too?"

"I couldn't say. Due to the secrecy involved we've not yet been able to study whether magic is an inherited trait – it makes it very difficult to find enough test cases. I can tell you that neither of my parents are so inclined, nor are any of my siblings. But I do know people who have familial links to magic. We simply haven't been studying long enough to observe such a thing as of yet."

This seemed to relax Isobel somewhat, and the two of them fell into comfortable conversation. Henry was pleased to see that, once settled, Isobel had a great number of questions. He stayed with her and fielded them late into the night, pausing only to answer the occasional caller at the door with arrangements for the following day.

6

The house remained a buzz of activity well into the night. The professor had explained that his investigation into their potential powers would involve a brief interview with him prior to conducting experiments if he thought that they were likely candidates. Though there were many more questions, he'd promised to answer them all individually, not wishing to interrupt the dinner any further.

Still, the staff couldn't help but ask one another once they'd returned to their business; Odette suspected that most of them would be up late into the night discussing it.

For her part, she was too stunned to engage in the gossip. Everyone else seemed to be far too quick to accept this new reality. It was not that she doubted Lord Henry's claims – he was supported by the British Army, for goodness sake, and had offered a clear demonstration of his power. But her mind was whirring with all of the possibilities. What other sorts of magic were there? The professor had made it clear that there wasn't just one type of magic, as in books and fairy tales, and she doubted that the reality reflected these stories in any way. If people had the ability to turn one another into swine, for example, then one surely would've heard about it by now. Besides, he'd said that transmogrification wasn't part of real magic.

Real magic. Ha!

So she went about her duties deep in thought, keeping busy and quiet until it was time to go up and help Yasmin get ready for bed. Doubtless her mistress would've had more of an opportunity to ask her cousin questions about this revelation, and would be sure to share some of it with her if she asked.

It was late by the time Yasmin was ready to retire, however, and Odette found herself beginning to fret somewhat.

What if she had magic? What if she *didn't*? What if her mother did, or Robbie? What if it turned out to be horrible magic – if she had the power to make people feel terrible pain, or if there was some sort of price? Odette considered fairy tales – they always seemed to have a cost, some hidden extra payment required of the characters in return for the power gifted to them, or a trap for them to stumble unwittingly into.

All these questions and more swirled about in her mind as she headed upstairs to Yasmin's rooms. The weight of her thoughts made her feel grumpy, and she entered Yasmin's rooms with an uncharacteristic frown set deep in her brow.

"Goodness, Ditty," exclaimed Yasmin upon seeing her. "You look terribly out of sorts. But with such exciting news, how could you possibly be so?"

Odette did her best to give an encouraging smile, but suspected it looked much more like a grimace. "Oh, I'm sorry, m'lady," she said with a blush. "It's just that there's an awful lot to think about. I can't say this was what I expected when I got up this morning."

"But that's the most wonderful part," said Yasmin enthu-siastically. "I only wish I'd known sooner! Ditty, you must've realised now that cousin Henry is not a professor at all – oh, at least it's only a front. He is a mage, Ditty – my own cousin!

And so many other people that we know could be. Isn't it terribly exciting?"

Despite all her reservations, Odette couldn't help but feel some of the excitement creeping into her belly. Yasmin's enthusiasm was infectious, and drove her to smile more convincingly.

"I suppose it is," confessed Odette, a little of her fear drifting away. She continued wrestling Yasmin out of her dress. "There's just still so much I don't understand."

"Well, you shall have the chance to ask Henry tomorrow," Yasmin pointed out as she stepped over the hoops of her gown to finally escape its clutches. "When is your interview?"

"Mum and I are just after lunch," said Odette. The list had been drawn up alphabetically by Roger, and posted by the kitchens downstairs. "She's before me."

"Oh! But that's not long to wait at all. Things are still continuing tomorrow, albeit a little differently without Uncle around, so you shall be swept off your feet until it's time, I'm sure." Yasmin patted her comfortingly on the arm. "Hardly any time to worry about it at all."

This was a lie, of course; for Odette had the whole night to fret about the possibilities. And what little support Yasmin had given her faded in the wake of several restless hours, staring at the ceiling in the moon's dim light. She must've slept at some point, for she woke to find the sun blearily shining in through the window, and her mother already up and moving, but Odette barely remembered sleeping at all.

The two of them washed and dressed quickly before heading up to their respective mistresses' rooms.

And with that, the morning did indeed pass as swiftly as Yasmin had promised. So busily, in fact, that Odette didn't even get a chance to ask Robbie how his own interview had gone – neither of them had been able to stop long enough to meet in the orchard. All that she'd managed to glean from the other staff was that one or two of them had indeed been considered to have "potential". Foremost amongst them was Mary, the cook, who was known the county over for the quality of her food. But there was also Abigail, whose knack for embroidery turned out to be much more than that, and Roger, who'd been a stable boy in his youth and still had an uncanny ability to calm horses.

When it came to lunchtime, and her mother's time to be called into the study that Professor Oakley was using as his office, Odette began to feel her anxiety pricking at her hands and feet as well as roiling her stomach. Restless, she hovered about the conservatory like a moth, grasping desperately at the times when the countess would call for more tea, as if they were a lifeboat keeping her from drowning in her own thoughts.

Half an hour passed, and it was time for her to make her own way up the stairs. Relieved from her station by Abigail, who was still puffed with pride at having been selected as having potential, Odette rushed up with no real care for how loudly her suede slippers thwapped against the boards. Her mother had just exited the study when Odette rounded the corner, and she smiled wearily at her daughter.

"It looks as though your old mother is simply that," she said cheerily, hugging Odette as she approached. "I have no great talents, hidden or otherwise."

Odette gave her mother a level stare. "You're an excellent maid," she stated with a small huff of indignation that Nancy might possibly have considered herself, "and an even better mother. I shall have none of these talentless claims."

Dropping a fond kiss on her daughter's head, Nancy smiled warmly. "Professor Oakley is waiting for you. Be sure to answer all of his questions honestly, now."

She left Odette blinking widely in confusion – why on earth would she ever lie? – and returned to her post.

Unable to do anything but face the inevitable, Odette turned to knock cautiously on the door, doing her best to swallow the lump in her throat and hoping it would envelop the butterflies in her stomach.

The study was one of her favourite rooms in the house – its walls could hardly be seen for the bookcases that towered from floor to ceiling, filled with all manner of delights. Odette had been told that the earl's private collection of books was the largest in the county, and indeed it took up not only the study but the adjoining office and another library beyond, too. Occasionally, Yasmin would borrow books from her father's study so that Odette could read them, often calling on her servant to read aloud in the evening or even on less busy afternoons.

When the command to enter came in response to her rap, Odette took a deep breath and opened the door. She bobbed a small curtsey, head lowered, before closing the door behind her. Only then did her eyes drift up to meet Henry Oakley's. She always remembered him as much older than he was, perhaps because of his profession – or, at least, what she'd thought was his profession. Who knew what he was more invested in now.

He'd lost some of the radiance present during his demon-strations of power the previous evening, and Odette was struck by how normal he looked – though tall, seated on one of the settees he looked much more … human, she supposed.

"Come, have a seat," Henry said in a soft, low voice, gesturing to the chair opposite.

Odette faltered – sit in one of the family's chairs? Good grief! – but Oakley didn't seem to notice; his attention was focused on a list in his hand.

"You must be Odette," he said simply. "That was your mother, I suppose?"

At a second gesture from him, Odette managed to sit in the chair, perching awkwardly on the edge as if she were likely to be snapped at for doing so at any given moment.

"Yes, m'lord," she said hesitantly, her nerves almost overwhelming her speech.

"And what is it that you do, Odette?"

"I'm L–Lady Yasmin's personal maid, m'lord."

Henry nodded, and made a note on the sheet in front of him, which was supported by a thin wooden board. "How long have you served my cousin?"

"Seven years as her personal maid. I … I've been in service to the family since I was old enough to work." Odette felt some of the tension leave her shoulders. This wasn't so bad; simple questions she could certainly manage.

"Ah, because of your mother's position. I see. The rest of your family is also in service, up in London, I understand."

For the first time since he'd begun speaking, Henry glanced up at her – and though Odette was not accustomed to making eye contact with people, she found herself doing so. He looked at her piercingly, critically, and she was able to hold his gaze for only a moment before lowering her eyes again.

"Do you have any special duties, Odette?"

"No, m'lord. But I can serve in whatever way my lady

requires, of course," she added hurriedly, suddenly realising that she might come across as inept, which was certainly not something she wanted to do. "I try to do my best in everything. I don't think there's any one thing that I'm especially good at – not like some of the others."

A small smile tugged at Henry's lips. "Ah, you must've been speaking to some of the other staff. Of course, I expected as much."

Somehow, his comment left Odette feeling rather small, though its tone hadn't suggested anything accusatory.

"It's true that magic as we know it is largely hidden under the guise of talents – Miss Abigail, for example, is an exemplary seamstress. Yet no one would ever consider that more than a natural gift."

Odette frowned. "Is magic not a natural gift?" she asked, before looking a little sheepish for the interruption.

Henry, for his part, did not look concerned; indeed, he seemed pleased by the question. "Oh, certainly," he said, "but what you think of as a natural gift, and what I would think of as a natural gift – there are differences, you see?"

At her nod, he continued, his soft voice gaining a little power. "There are ways to spot these. Miss Abigail, for example, says her prayers whilst she's sewing – have you ever noticed? This little sign, this tiny signifier, is what suggests to me that there could be more to this than simple needlework. Has she ever repaired anything for you?"

"Not for me, sir. She mostly just sees to Miss Johanna's things – oh, but I know she repaired one of the countess's cloaks once," said Odette, casting her mind back. "It was beastly to repair, and mother was ever so busy that day. Abigail helped her in return for doing some of Lady Johanna's laundry."

"And has that cloak broken since?"

Odette blinked widely. It had not, not to her knowledge, but then she herself had repaired plenty of things that had not broken again. But was it not that cloak that the countess had been wearing when she'd fallen from her horse last year? She remembered thinking how strange it was that the stitching hadn't come loose – the countess had landed on it and the rest of her clothing had torn terribly. As the realisation dawned on her face, she heard a small chuckle.

"I take it from your expression that it has not," Henry said smugly. "That's the sort of thing I mean – seemingly ordinary skills that have extraordinary effects. Effects that are unnoticed until they're closely scrutinised."

"I'm afraid I don't have any special skills," Odette said, shaking her head. "I've never been terribly exceptional."

"Have you ever tried other things? Other skills unrelated to your profession. Painting, perhaps."

Odette wrinkled her nose. She'd tried painting once but her hands had shaken so terribly that she'd simply splattered paint all over herself. "I suppose I can sing as well as most," she said thoughtfully, "and my father taught me to play some simple tunes on his violin once. I liked it a great deal. But I've never had the time to spend on either."

Henry let out a *hmm* under his breath and made another note. "Usually, those who possess magic are drawn to its manifestation – that's not to say that they feel they couldn't live without that thing, but that they might derive more enjoyment from it than others – it naturally becomes a large part of their life."

A slightly wistful smile settled on Odette's face. "Then

I'm afraid I don't have any such thing," she said simply. "At least, not that I yet know of."

"I believe that magic manifests in people as they transcend into adulthood," explained Henry, running his hand over his curly hair to smooth it back into place. "It's highly likely that if such a skill were to appear, it would've done so by now."

Finally, the last of the tension left Odette's body, and only then did she realise just how terrified she'd been that there'd be this great secret that she'd not known about herself – something so hidden that she'd never realised it. She'd not be called upon to assist in capturing – or worse, killing – a murderer, nor would she have to leave her home, her mother or her friends. The relief must've been visible on her face, for Henry laughed again.

"Yes," he said, a rare warm smile lighting up his eyes as he looked at her, "it's certainly something to feel grateful for – sometimes I wish ... ah, but no matter. You're correct in your assessment, I think. Now let me see ..." He consulted the list before him. "I believe it should be Matthew next. We're a little earlier than expected, however – if he's not there, please wait for him and send him in when he arrives."

"Of course, m'lord," said Odette, standing and bobbing a parting curtsey. She might've cared that she was fleeing his presence so soon but for the fact that she was so relieved to be getting away – and her relief had offered him some amusement, at least, so she wasn't wholly without grace. Almost rushing to the door, she gave a small, shy smile before exiting into the hallway.

Matthew wasn't there, which didn't surprise her – she'd barely managed to get away on time herself, and Matthew worked in the stables, where they were still recovering from the sudden departure of the major general.

She waited the few moments until he appeared, and then gladly passed on the message that Professor Oakley was done with her and ready to receive him. With a smile that – to Matthew, at least – was probably quite confusingly happy, she practically flew down the stairs and back to the conservatory, just in time to assist with the clearing of lunch.

The interviews continued late into the afternoon, but it was a little after four when Odette finally managed to corner Robbie. It was too windy to sit outside, so they holed up in the servants' dining room, clustering about the hearth for the chance to warm their hands a little. Having quickly explained her relief at finding that she was not, in fact, possessed of any great ability, Odette asked how Robbie's interview had gone.

"Funny thing," he said, laughing a little nervously. "He thinks I might, actually."

"Really?" Odette said, then immediately felt bad for lacing her intonation with quite so much surprise. "W-What does he think it is?" she asked quickly to cover up her fumble.

"It's weird," said Robbie, whose affront was seemed tempered by the knowledge that she hadn't meant that he was without talent. "I didn't think of it myself. He spotted it – we were talking about what I do, and my skills and so forth, and I was fiddling with this." He reached into his pocket and pulled out a small piece of wood that was in the process of being whittled and buffed into a fine sculpture of some sort. "He asked if I'd made it myself."

"You make them all the time," said Odette, realisation dawning on her. "Oh, Robbie, that sounds exactly like it – like all of the others, too. Abigail's sewing, and Mary's cooking – something you do all the time, out of habit, and have always been naturally good at."

"I guess," he said, looking a little sheepish. "But, I mean, whittling. How's that magic?"

Odette grinned. "How can you sing a person to sleep?"

"Fair point. But what am I ever going to do with this? Abigail said that the professor was talking about her sewing armour for the soldiers, or having Mary cook at important diplomatic events to ensure the discussions go well. What can I do with a bit of wood?"

An answer came to her mind instantly, and Odette stumbled over her reply. It seemed so obvious, but at first she couldn't bear to offer the suggestion – magic was exciting, yes, but it was dangerous too, and the idea that Robbie could be drawn into it reignited the ill feeling in her gut.

But he was her dearest friend, and Odette couldn't lie to him, nor hide the truth. So, hefting a sigh, she answered. "Arrows. Or guns that can't be broken. If Abigail can sew armour, there's no reason you can't make weaponry. Have you ever tried working with more than little bits of wood? Maybe it's just wood, or maybe you're good at sculpting all sorts of things, Robbie. You simply don't *know*."

A tense silence hung between them for a moment; both stared at the previously innocuous carving still resting in Robbie's hand.

"I don't want to," he said after a long moment, tucking the wood away into his pocket. "I want to know whether this is magic, but – I wouldn't want to hurt people, Det, you know that."

She couldn't help but smile. "I know," she said, putting all of her feeling and conviction into it in the hope that he'd believe her. "And no one can make you. Let them help you work out what it – what this – is and then it's yours to do whatever you want with. No one's going to force you to do anything, I promise."

Grasping her in a sudden and fierce hug, Robbie almost knocked the wind out of Odette – who though not tiny was far smaller than him. "This won't change anything," he said, his cheek scratchy against her ear. "I swear."

7

Six of the staff had shown promise as potential subjects for Henry's project. Isobel had been joined by five of his aunt and uncle's staff: Abigail, a talented seamstress; Roger, excellent with animals; Mary, the cook, whose creations were famous for uplifting the spirits; Robbie, who whittled wood almost constantly; and Matthew, a stable hand adept at climbing. It took two days to interview everyone, and just after dinner on the second day Henry called all his potentials into the library to talk over what lay ahead of them.

"Thank you all for coming to speak with me," he said softly, his smile warm. "I hope you've not felt too overwhelmed by the revelations of the past few days – I know from my own experience that it's an awful lot to take in. Please remember that you're not alone in this; use one another as support during the transition. The earl and countess have been kind enough to offer us the use of this room and the adjoining studies for the duration of our stay."

"The duration of our stay, sir?" asked Roger, the oldest of the potentials. "This is our home – well, for most of us."

"I'm afraid we're rather at the whim of the army to an extent. They've allotted me a week from tomorrow to ensure that your powers are indeed manifest, after which we'll move to join them in Bristol."

This caused a murmuring to ripple through the staff, which Henry allowed to swell and pass before he continued speaking. "I'm aware that this will mean abandoning your posts for a time, and, for some of you, leaving your families – it's my hope that we'll be able to find a quick solution to the situation and you shall then have the option of returning or moving on to make new lives in light of your powers. But – really, don't worry about this for now."

"How can we be sure our magic is real, sir?" asked Isobel, and Henry gave her a grateful look. He'd been feeling rather flustered by having to turn these poor people's lives upside down.

Smiling, he settled down a little more comfortably. "Ah, well, that's quite simple – we will practise, and we will analyse. Each of you tends to practise your craft or talent naturally; you feel drawn to it. It's one of the hallmarks of magical talent. But, now, we'll be able to look at that practice with a keener eye, and spot the other signs of your powers."

Mary shook her head. "Well, sir, I'm sorry to say I ain't got time to do more than I already tend t' as par' of my duties. It migh' only be yer own household here now, but tha' still means a lo' more work."

"Oh, my apologies," chuckled Henry. "You're all immediately relieved of your normal duties, of course. As a matter of fact, I believe there are arrangements being made to section off a portion of the kitchen for your own use."

Looking both delighted and affronted, Mary fell silent again.

"I'll be available to assist you and answer questions at any time, of course. I do have some ideas for things that you might do to practise and explore the breadth of your powers

– Robert, for example ...”

With a small cough, the young man said, “Begging your pardon m'lord, but it's Robbie.”

“My apologies. Robbie – you've only ever worked with wood, I assume?”

“That's right.”

“One of the things I'd like you to try and do,” continued Henry, “is experiment with some other materials. I've ordered a number of things for you, Abigail, Mary and Isobel to use. All the canvas and paint you could possibly want, countless reams of fabric, and plenty of ingredients for everything from cakes to bread.”

The four crafters' faces lit up with excitement, and Henry could see their thoughts immediately begin to race with all the things they might do. Isobel in particular had drifted off into thought, and her fingers twitched slightly as if needing to occupy her.

“What about us, m'lord?” asked Matthew, looking a little left out of the celebrations.

“For you, Matthew, a portion of the gardens has been sectioned off – not only trees, but indeed the very walls have been allocated for your use. Please do your best not to damage the walls, however. I don't look forward to a conversation with my father about having to foot a bill for such a thing.”

This earned a chuckle from everyone, which Henry hoped would relax them all further. Turning to Roger, he added, “And the staff in the stables have been instructed to accommodate you in their work. Hopefully, there should always be at least one horse for you to work with. But I'd also like to see what you can do with other animals – birds and the like.”

“Thank you, m'lord,” replied Roger in an oddly gruff voice.

Henry wondered whether the man was displeased at having been singled out for magical talent. Or, no – his eyes had pinched slightly, as if he was trying to push away a feeling. It was noticeable only for its strangeness upon the butler's normally unreadable face.

Lowering his voice and leaning over to the valet, Henry said softly, "If this is at all difficult for you ..."

Roger's eyes flicked over to the other staff, but they'd devolved into a conversation about the various things they were going to make and do. Turning his attention back to Henry, he murmured, "It's quite all right, sir. Just that my late wife was ... fond of the horses here. It's thanks to her that I kept going to see them, to be quite honest with you. Otherwise I might've stopped long before now – not through lack of wanting to, you understand, but it's hard to make time."

"I imagine my uncle is a very demanding master," remarked Henry wryly, and Roger chuckled. "If it's ever too much, take a break. You don't even need to tell me you're doing so – I'll trust your judgement and your work."

To Henry's surprise, Roger leant over and patted him on the arm. "You're very kind," he said, looking a little more like himself. "Thank you. I hope we can repay you for your generosity."

Returning to the others, the two men joined in the discussion about the various things that were to be cooked, whittled, painted and sewn – the trees to be climbed, and the tricks to be performed. Surveying his charges with a pleased eye, Henry couldn't help but feel buoyed by their enthusiasm and passion. It might not feel like he'd quite found what he was looking for – none of their skills seemed an obvious counter to Braddock's – but in that moment, he he didn't really mind at all.

8

Run off her feet in an attempt to prepare both Yasmin and Johanna for bed in Abigail's absence, Odette was especially grateful for the patience and kindness of her mistress – who'd quietly tended to many things herself whilst Odette was absent.

When she returned, she felt herself bristle initially at the suggestion that she couldn't do all of the work – but, of course, she truly couldn't be in two places at once, and so after some mental arguing she concluded that it was not a comment on her abilities that Yasmin had located her own nightclothes and dressed herself, nor that she'd plaited her own hair.

Little did Odette know that this was only the beginning: the next day, Lord Henry announced to the household that the six servants showed a great deal of promise – and that he'd need them to enter immediately into a fierce period of study to develop their abilities sufficiently to explore the potential of their powers. This, of course, meant that Johanna was entirely without her own maid, and Odette was left to take Abigail's job on in its entirety. Her mother helped when she could, but the countess took up a great deal more of her time than Yasmin did of Odette's, and so for the days that followed Odette was without a single moment to herself.

She didn't even get to see Robbie, though now and then

she spotted signs of his activity – a large delivery of various materials, from different woods to metals, came two days after his interview. Odette eyed it with suspicion, renewing her concern that he'd be forced to make a weapon that would kill the man Lord Henry hunted. But with no time to speak to him, Odette could neither confirm nor deny her suspicions, and that left an uncomfortable roiling in her stomach.

Luckily, Johanna was a quiet and polite mistress – in many ways like Odette herself, though she often felt that this was more detrimental than useful. Having so much in common, they'd naturally fall into uncomfortable silences, neither possessing the extroverted nature necessary to spring conversation onto one another with any frequency. Abigail, she knew, was much better at coaxing a conversation out of her mistress – and Odette loathed being inadequate. She did her best to make several attempts at it, but Johanna simply wasn't comfortable enough with her, and so eventually Odette ceased her ineffectual social blunders.

Odette finally managed to catch a few moments with Robbie three days after he'd begun his studies. It was the brief time between the end of lunch and the preparation of dinner, and her mother was covering the few chores she had to attend to before the run-up to the evening meal. As soon as she was free, Odette rushed out to the orchard – where, with much relief and gratitude, she found Robbie sitting on their bench. He was whittling away at a long piece of wood clearly much finer than his usual scraps from the log pile.

"I was hoping you'd manage to get out here," he said as she approached, placing his tools down to draw her into a warm hug.

"Mum's covering for me," Odette explained, settling down

next to him on the bench. "How's magic?"

"I'm pretty sure the blisters on my hands have blisters," replied Robbie with a wry grin, opening his right palm to display the calluses and red-raw patches created by too many hours holding his knife. "But it's – it's amazing, Det. He had me make something, just a silly little sculpture, and then he took an axe to it. It didn't break. Roger and Mary had a go too, and they couldn't get the thing to so much as dent."

Odette's eyes widened. "Really?" she asked, picking up the piece of wood between them. It was long and thin, and it looked as though he'd been carving intricate patterns into the side. "So you're saying that if I try and snap this, nothing will happen? It's not that thick; it should break easily."

Robbie shrugged. "I guess so," he said. "Try it."

Taking one end of the stick in each hand, she bent down on it. The wood bowed, then buckled with a loud noise. "Huh," said Odette.

"Maybe it's because it wasn't finished," suggested Robbie, taking the two broken halves from her. "I don't know how all this works, really. No one does, not even the professor."

"Or maybe I've secretly got super strength," said Odette with a laugh. "But it's all right? They're not pushing you too hard or anything? I mean, this could still be rubbish."

Letting out a soft sigh, Robbie reached over and took her hands. "It's not, Det. I know you still think it is, and I don't blame you, but … I've seen Abigail sew a vest that couldn't be cut with a sword. I've seen Isobel paint things and then watched them come true hours later. These things aren't normal, no, but … they're real. And I'm part of it. That's … that's pretty amazing."

Odette sagged, the truth of how terrible a friend she'd been sinking into her. Robbie was so excited about this, and yet trying so hard to conceal it from fear that she'd – what? Hate him for this strange and inexplicable gift that he'd been given? And all that she'd done in return was play down the amazing things that were happening around her. Odette had loved reading since she was little, and always felt most drawn to those stories that were fantastical. Now she had a chance to watch one play out before her, and she was denying it.

"Hey," said Robbie, breaking her out of her reverie. He reached up and brushed the pad of his thumb across her cheek, swiping away a tear she hadn't realised was escaping. "What's wrong?"

"I'm – I'm really proud of you, you know," she replied after letting out a small cough to make sure her voice didn't crack on the words. "I'm sorry I didn't say that before."

"You didn't have to, Det. I know you well enough."

Odette laughed; it was true, so true, though in a way it made her feel all the worse. She shuffled up on the bench to lean against him, but just as her head touched his shoulder her mother's voice came calling from the door. Was it time to go back inside already?

"Go on," Robbie said, dropping a kiss on the top of her head. "I'll see you soon."

She managed to flash him a small, brave smile before dashing inside to her mother, who explained that Yasmin had rung the bell to ask for assistance. Flattening her skirts out and brushing away the damp from the bench, Odette slipped up the stairs to attend to her mistress.

Oddly, Yasmin was not in the conservatory as Odette had expected, but seated upstairs in the library that adjoined the studies – one of the rooms that had been set aside for the professor's students. There was a plush chaise longue on which Yasmin was perched demurely, examining a book in her hands.

Odette slipped in silently through the open door and knelt down next to her mistress to ask what was required of her, barely noticing that Yasmin was not alone.

"Oh, Ditty," said Yasmin with a warm smile, looking up from her book as if waking from a delightful dream. "Thank you for coming. I was wondering if you wouldn't mind getting some tea for Henry and me."

Only then did Odette notice the second figure in the room, shadowed in the far corner. "There really is no need," he said, his low voice soft. Odette noticed that his hair had come loose, falling slightly to cover his eyes. His shoulders were hunched and his spine curled.

"I insist," said Yasmin, in the tone of voice learned from her parents that brokered no agreement. "You've not taken a break for days, cousin, and I'll take advantage of these brief few moments of your presence to ensure that you're suitably cared for. Ditty, if you would?"

"Of course, m'lady," replied Odette, dipping a quick curtsey before rushing downstairs to prepare a tray.

It didn't take long – Mary's need to test her newfound magical skills had resulted in a constant and somewhat copious supply of freshly baked goods in the house – and soon Odette was setting the tray carefully down upon the coffee table.

As she began to serve, her mistress set her book aside and let out a soft sigh.

"And how long do you expect this to continue?" Yasmin asked, clearly continuing a conversation that had begun prior to Odette's entry. "The household cannot go on indefinitely in such a manner, as I'm sure you know."

"We'll be gone by the end of next week," replied Henry, though the tiredness in his voice weakened some of its conviction. "I've had to negotiate an extension on our original time from my father. What these few have – their powers – are unique. A week is not enough time to explore their potential. And to find so many …"

"Six hardly seems a groundbreaking number."

"But from two households alone, Yasmin!" Henry said. "From a combined staff of forty. If the ratio of mages to not holds true, imagine how many there could be in England. In Britain. In the world!"

A small, cat-like smile curled across Yasmin's lips. "You have grand dreams indeed, cousin. But these are but men and women. You, yourself are but a man. Possessed of incredible powers or not, all of you are still fallible. No, Ditty, please stay. I may need you again."

Stopping halfway to the door, Odette nodded her head and took up a standing position nearby. She felt Henry's eyes on her, and couldn't stop herself from glancing up to meet them. His gaze was intense and scrutinising, just as before, and Odette felt herself growing hot with embarrassment. It was not as if she was anything to look at – for what reason could he possibly be staring?

"I cannot fault your wisdom," he said, turning his attention back to his cousin. "But things are escalating. Braddock killed two police officers last night."

Both Yasmin and Odette let out small gasps, though Odette's was better concealed. "Lord preserve us," murmured Yasmin. "And you wish to send our staff up against them? No, Henry, this is surely foolish."

"Sometimes I think that it might be. My father certainly agrees with you at times. But I'm not a martial man, cousin – and this solution is all I have to offer. I'll continue with it, even if it proves fruitless, for not to try …" He looked away. "If people really begin to believe what Braddock is saying, if it continues to expand beyond a scant few groups, it will be so much harder, if not impossible, for those like me to hide our powers. I might agree with many of his ideals, but … imagine what could happen if we were taken, our powers used for ill deeds. I have great faith in the people of Britain, but one can only too easily imagine how some of its darker members would seek to use this for their own ends."

There was a pause; Yasmin couldn't fault that logic. "I cannot blame you for your fear," she said, tapping her slender fingers against her teacup. "But *my* fear is that you've not found the solution you were looking for. Great power, yes, and great potential – but it did sound like you were looking for something in particular."

"None of their powers are obvious … counters to Braddock's, save for in the application of weaponry."

Odette felt her anger awaken and prickle.

"But I'll strive to keep from asking that of them for as long as possible."

As he made his statement with gentle conviction, Odette felt her shoulders relax slightly – and a flicker of his eyes towards her told her that it hadn't gone unnoticed. She thought she saw a tiny twitch of amusement in his face, but it was concealed as he lifted his cup to his lips.

"For that, I'm glad," said Yasmin, who though had not noticed Odette's reaction was all too aware of her fears. "Is it possible you'll need to continue your search elsewhere?"

"Very possible," Henry said. "There's another search continuing right now, but I don't know how it's progressing. The issue with widening our search further – well, imagine the scale it would need to be on, the uproar it would cause. At present, the majority of the public don't believe Braddock's claims – save for those who've seen his power demonstrated, and he's going to great lengths to ensure as many do as possible. To begin a larger search, we'd have to reveal the truth to even more people. I've spoken to my contacts at Oxford, who are quietly searching for potentials of their own, but to train people will take time that we simply don't have."

As Henry moved to continue, there was a knock at the door, which Odette had closed behind her to conserve some of the heat. She opened it, and found Abigail standing on the other side.

"Lord Henry summoned me," the older woman explained, and Odette gave her a warm smile as she stepped aside to allow the maid in. Abigail looked a little surprised but comforted by the greeting, as if she'd been expecting a much cooler reception from the poor sap responsible for taking over her duties.

"Ah, Abigail. You've finished?"

As she closed the door behind her, Odette noticed that Abigail was holding a folded piece of cloth in her hands. It was beautifully though simply patterned with a check in various shades of watery blue. Odette could see that Abigail had made it as a sort of patchwork – each line and square of the check a separate piece. In her mind's eye, Odette could imagine the way she'd aligned everything, carefully folding the edges under to create neat seams.

The older woman nodded, and held out the cloth for Henry's inspection.

"No, let's have a demonstration!" he said with a smile, reaching for the sharp knife that Odette had brought up to slice the cake. "Would you open the cloth and hold it out?"

The sheet was too large for Abigail to hold on her own, so Odette took the other end and stepped backward until they'd extended the cloth between them as if preparing to fold it again. Henry approached and held the knife over the middle. Turning to his cousin, he offered a grin full of boyish glee.

"You'll not believe this," he said to Yasmin, before plunging the knife into the cloth. It shredded clean through, which seemed to surprise him so much that he stumbled, leaning against the bookcase for support. Abigail seemed equally stunned.

"I'm not sure what's so unbelievable about that," remarked Yasmin dryly.

Frowning, Henry reached for the half of the cloth closest to him. "Let me," he said, gathering it up in his hands.

Odette and Abigail released their ends and stepped backwards. Henry pushed the knife up against the cloth again – but this time, the material wouldn't budge, not even at the edges of the already-made tear.

Everyone in the room had become intrigued; even Yasmin had stood to examine the cloth closely.

"May I try?" she asked.

Henry handed her the cloth and knife, focusing his gaze on her as she attempted to damage it as had been done the first time.

"Goodness," Yasmin said after several failed attempts. "This is like trying to cut through a floorboard with a butter knife."

"I don't understand," said Abigail helplessly. Odette placed a comforting hand on her shoulder. "Why did it break before and not now?"

"I haven't the foggiest," said Henry, running his hand through his hair, still staring at the cloth.

Yasmin pursed her lips. "Ditty," she said slowly, holding out the fabric. "Would you mind trying? Perhaps I'm simply not strong enough."

Odette had the strongest suspicion that her mistress was lying, and that this was some sort of trick – but she wasn't about to refuse the request in front of others, certainly not one as simple as this, nor when the niggling feeling that she was missing something had begun to take hold of her. So she took the cloth, tucking one end between her knees and stretching it out to the middle, where the first tear still fluttered. She placed the knife in the centre, just as Henry had, and, noting with interest that it touched of the many seams, she plunged it cleanly through and out the other side.

"Ditty ..." whispered Yasmin, and suddenly realisation dawned. Robbie's unbreakable stick, Abigail's unbreakable cloth – both had faltered when she'd been holding them.

Dropping the cloth and knife in shock, Odette stumbled back against the bookcase, her hands pressed to her mouth. Her heart pounded in her ears and throat, and her legs began to buckle.

The four stood in silence for a moment, staring at the cloth on the floor. Carefully, Abigail knelt down, plucked the knife from her creation, and placed it back on the table before cradling ripped fabric to her chest. She shot an accusatory glare at a now trembling Odette.

"Oh," said Henry softly, his eyes locked on Odette again. "Now isn't that interesting?"

Time seemed to have slowed for Odette. She was distantly aware that Yasmin had taken her hands and led her to the lounge chair, and that her mistress now sat beside her. She could hear a soft, low voice – Henry? – speaking to her, but the words bounced off her mind as if she were deaf to their meaning. Her breathing became shallow, her face burned with embarrassment – or what it fear, or anger? – and hot tears rolled down her cheeks.

The pain in her chest from her air-deprived lungs brought her back to reality, where she found that she'd almost lost control; she was sobbing, shaking, and couldn't seem to stop. Her throat had swollen and every breath seemed harder to grasp. Yasmin's slender hands, clutched tightly around her own, steadied her.

As she tried to take in several desperate breaths, still deaf to the concerned voices around her, Odette recalled the last time she'd had one of her fits – three months ago, when she'd slipped and dropped a tray in the dining hall. Nothing had broken, but her embarrassment, and the laughter from those who'd watched her land on the ground, had driven her to hysterics once she'd fled the room.

Now, just as then, she was brought back to awareness by a sound that cut clearly across the incomprehensible din that otherwise surrounded her.

"Odette," said the voice, so familiar and so gentle. "It's all right, darling. I'm here – it's fine."

Through watery eyes, Odette lifted her head to see her mother's wrinkled face staring back at her. A fresh burst of sobs escaped her throat, but she leant into the cool hand that was placed on her cheek and began, somewhere in herself, to believe that it would be all right. Her mother enfolded her in her arms, and at length, she and Yasmin managed to soothe Odette's sobs to whimpers, and then her whimpers to silence.

When it was over, Odette's limbs felt heavy. She couldn't shake an overwhelming feeling of shame that so many people had seen her in such a state. Surely the room would now be filled with a tremendous awkwardness, and it would all be her fault. But slowly she began to realise that no one had left, and no one was looking at her as if she were mad. They were simply concerned, and gentle in their understanding. A final sigh fell from her lips, and she felt centred again.

"I'm s-so sorry," she said, wrapping her shaking hands around a glass of water that Abigail held out to her.

"Oh, hush," said her mother, giving her a final squeeze before releasing her. "You've had a shock. There's nothing to be sorry about – everyone just wants to know that you're all right."

"I am," Odette said, though there was a weakness in her voice that made it less convincing than she'd have wished. "I'm ever so sorry to be a bother."

A small chuckle ran through the room, but Yasmin ran her thumb over the back of Odette's hand as they laughed, so she knew it was not at her expense. "I thought you were going to faint," her mistress said, brushing a stray lock of hair out of Odette's eyes. "Are you are sure you're all right?"

"I feel ..." Odette struggled to find the right word. "Fragile."

A rustle of silk alerted her to Yasmin's moving to stand, and Odette looked up to see Henry gently ushering his cousin out of the way. Keeping hold of her hands, Yasmin knelt down in front of Odette, allowing Henry to sit on the chair next to her. She tried not to flinch – the near presence of so many unnerved her.

"Perhaps I can help," Henry said. "Close your eyes."

Odette complied, and felt suddenly relieved that she could no longer see everyone staring at her. Just as she began to wonder why her eyes were closed, Henry's voice came again – but this time in song, a lilting ballad, vaguely familiar. As before, the words were not English, but seemed even more impenetrable than had the Latin. Odette tried to place them, but could get no further than Welsh, Gaelic, or something of that ilk. And as she wrapped herself around the unfamiliar tongue, its comforting magic crept upon her. Only when Henry had finished, and she'd opened her eyes, did she realise that her hands had relaxed and her limbs felt lighter.

"Oh," she whispered softly, flashing Henry a shy smile, though meeting his gaze felt even harder than usual. "Thank you, m'lord. I'm sorry to have caused a fuss."

"Not at all," he said, clearing his throat. "I'm sorry to have startled you – and, indeed, not to have realised earlier what was happening. It would seem that my cousin's mind is sharper than my own."

"That would be because I've slept more than four hours a night," remarked Yasmin wryly.

Henry chuckled, and sitting so close to him Odette could appreciate just how deep a sound it was, a warm rumble that made her own stomach feel strange again.

"Now," he said, "we will need to talk about what's happened, of course – but not today. Get some rest, and come and see me first thing tomorrow morning. We'll work out what's happening, and then you'll feel much better."

"Thank you," Odette replied, not sure what else to say.

"I'll take her back to her room," her mother said, and everyone stood as Odette rose, steadier now. "Someone will be up to serve you, m'lady."

"Take your time," Yasmin replied with a smile, before astonishing Odette by pressing a soft kiss to her cheek. "Look after yourself, Ditty."

Flushing red, Odette allowed herself to be led out of the library and to her own bed, where she fell into a deep sleep, not waking until long after dinner.

9

Once they'd reassured Abigail that her powers existed, and that she'd done nothing wrong, Henry and Yasmin were left alone in the study. A dazed mood hung in the air between them. A dozen thoughts flooded Henry's mind, chief amongst them the notion that Odette's power – if it was indeed magical, and not some terrible fluke – could be precisely what the army had sent him to look for.

Several times he caught himself wanting to run after the young woman and pepper her with questions, but the image of her curled into a ball of terror filled him with immediate remorse.

"She has fits sometimes," explained Yasmin, clearly reading his thoughts. He sat back down on the lounge chair, and Yasmin took a place at his side. Her brow furrowed in deep concern. "It's ... very rare for her to have them in front of others. She does her best to hide them from everyone else."

"Is it a medical condition?"

This question gave Yasmin pause. "It must be," she said thoughtfully, "for it always happens in the same way, and I believe it's happened for as long as I've known her. Nancy – that's her mother, you know – and Robbie are usually the only people able to bring her out of them."

Henry mirrored his cousin's frown, and looked over at the

abandoned cloth and knife resting on the library table. "I hope we – I – didn't cause it."

"No, Henry," Yasmin said with conviction, resting her hand on his. "What happens to her is horrible, but it's certainly not your fault. If nothing else, you didn't know. And what you did for her afterwards … that was wonderful. No one's ever been able to help her after a fit before."

"What does she usually do?"

"Rest. Sometimes she reads, I think, to fill her mind with kinder thoughts. She's not spoken to me of what she experiences a great deal, but Nancy's told me that she sometimes feels trapped in her own mind. Like she's locked in a prison of thoughts, and can't focus on anything else."

Sighing, Henry tapped his fingers against his leg thoughtfully. "I can't imagine how difficult that must be," he said at length, shaking his head. "I hope she doesn't experience them often."

"I fear that she does – though, as I say, she doesn't often speak to me of it. I wouldn't wish to make assumptions."

Yasmin paused, and looking up at her Henry could see she'd adopted one of her more dangerous expressions. She was thinking furiously about something, eyes locked on him, and he felt rather like a great hunter's prey about to be caught and eaten.

When she spoke, it was in a low, warning tone. "Henry … I think you should know that Ditty is very important to me. She is my closest and dearest friend, though she may not know it, and if anything happened to her I should be incandescent."

He wanted to tell Yasmin that it would be perfectly fine; that none of them would ever be in danger or asked to do anything they were uncomfortable with. But he could not. He could no more promise Yasmin that Odette would be safe than he could promise Robbie that he'd not have to craft weapons, or Mary that she'd never be asked to hide poison in her cakes. He wanted to, desperately – but he couldn't. He was at his father's whim, and he knew it.

"She is perhaps the strongest person I know," continued Yasmin, just as Henry was about to reply. "In almost all other things, I'd have complete confidence in her ability to defend herself. But you must understand, she wants ever so much to *help*. And that's a dangerous thing, especially in this situation."

Henry frowned. "I can hardly stop a grown woman from putting herself in danger if it's her choice."

"Of course not. But you, and the others, can be there when she does it. Can watch out for her when she walks into the flames." Yasmin's concerned expression turned darker. "You may not be able to control what happens, Henry, but you *are* the one taking all of them into this. You know what they might have to do and you know you cannot stop it. You're responsible, whether you like it or not." Yasmin stood.

Sighing, Henry got to his feet and lifted his head to reply – but Yasmin had already begun to head for the door.

Over her shoulder, she murmured, "Henry, I'll never forgive you if anything happens to Ditty. Never."

The door clicked behind her as she left, and Henry collapsed into the chair in utter exhaustion. His thoughts warred with one another, half in support of Yasmin and the other half railing against her for blaming him for that which he couldn't possibly hope to control. He wasn't Braddock, after all. He'd not caused this. But there was still truth in what Yasmin was saying. A gnawing fear began to claw at his stomach, and he spent some time staring paralysed at the floor.

Eventually, he coaxed himself into action, drawing up a list of questions that he wished to ask Odette about her powers the next day. Though productive, it did nothing to calm him, and he eventually marched himself to dinner on time – a feat he'd not managed in the previous days – where he mutely sat and ate, only half-listening to the chatter of those around him.

When he finally dragged himself to bed, sleep eluded him, and it was late before dreams finally pulled him under.

10

Odette stirred, rubbing her eyes with the heels of her hands. A figure sat at the end of the bed – too large to be her mother. The shape shifted as she sat up.

"Morning, Det."

Blinking widely, Odette shuffled up and wrapped her arms around Robbie's waist. He held her tightly against him, resting his chin on the top of her head, and they sat there in silence for several minutes. With Robbie there, Odette felt the last of the tension in her body shift away, replaced by a gentle tickle of confusion and fear.

"What time is it? It can't be morning already."

"Hey, I'm kidding with you. It's fine – just after eleven," Robbie said. "Your mum and Abigail covered for you, and Mary's kept you some dinner back. You should eat."

"I'm not very hungry," replied Odette, but she knew he was right. "Someone should've woken me up sooner; Mum and Abigail shouldn't have done the evening all on their own – and Abigail's meant to be sewing ..."

"Don't worry about it."

Odette let go of Robbie and hugged her knees to her chest. "But I feel so silly," she said, immediately regretting having said so.

Letting out a soft laugh, Robbie brushed his hand over her

hair. "You're not silly, Det, and no one minds. I promise."

She was unconvinced, but felt that no matter how many times she apologised or tried to make up for it, she'd be told not to worry.

With Robbie's help she got out of bed and went down to the kitchens, where Mary clucked over her in a maternal fashion and heated up the soup that was left from dinner. The herb-filled bread to go with it tasted lovely, but didn't seem to have the same effect on Odette as it had everyone else – there were tales of how everyone had been overcome with fits of giggles upon eating it.

Once she was fed and watered, Robbie took her back upstairs and tucked her into bed, where he stayed by her side until she drifted off into a restful sleep.

In spite of her evening slumber, she slept through until the following morning. She dressed quickly and went downstairs, only to find that she'd been relieved of her duties and placed on Lord Henry's special list along with the others. She felt terribly guilty, but nevertheless was happy to be able to sit and have breakfast with Robbie. She took a seat next to him, and across from Isobel and Matthew.

Odette had never known Matthew terribly well – the stable folk tended to keep to themselves, and were often away from the house on the many riding events frequented by the countess. The countess had been a champion jumper in her youth, and still showed many of the horses at dressage events. All Odette knew was that Matthew was a few years older than her and Robbie, and that he was quite talkative – a fact that had been confirmed within moments of her sitting at the breakfast table.

"Oh, Odette! Robbie told us you'd be joining. Isn't it

exciting? I've never had so much fun in my life. I hardly know what to do with myself. But what is it that you can do? I didn't think you had any, you know, skills." This earned Matthew several glares, and he blushed deeply. Quickly backtracking, he went on, "I mean, like, Isobel here paints and Robbie does things with wood – hobbies. That sort of thing. I don't mean you don't have any skills – that was a stupid thing to say. I—"

"Matthew, it's all right," Odette said, cutting him off before he could dig himself any deeper. "I know what you meant – and I didn't think I had either. Nor did Lord Henry; at my interview he said it was generally an obvious skill or talent."

"Even people who know a lot about magic can miss it," said Isobel softly, smiling at Odette. "I've worked for the professor for years and he never noticed that my paintings were … odd. He'd even seen several of them."

Odette returned the smile gratefully. She'd always liked Isobel – though quiet, the tall girl was kind and caring, with wide blue eyes and jet-black hair that Odette envied terribly. It was not very often that Lord Henry came to stay, and having Isobel around was always one of the highlights, even if the two of them had never been very close – after all, they were usually run off their feet with work when the family was gathered together.

"I don't really know what it is I can do," said Odette, turning back to Matthew. "We know that I can do … something. Just not quite what it is."

"She managed to break one of my sticks, and could cut through Abigail's cloth," explained Robbie with a grin. "My bet's on super strength."

Laughing, Odette shook her head. "I'd like to think I'd

have noticed that by now." The last of the tension from the night before eased from Odette's mind, and she felt the world around her grow a little brighter. Buoyed, she went on, "Oh, but I want to know about what you've all been doing. What's using magic like?"

For each of them it seemed the experience was unique; they'd all been invited to explore and test the boundaries of their powers, and indeed to take the time to practise the skills that were the origin of their magic. For some, those skills were already finely honed, having been part of their jobs for a long time – Mary especially, though she was all too pleased to have an excuse to cook more. There seemed no limit to the enjoyment she could derive from feeding people. Others, like Robbie and Isobel, had finally found the opportunity to explore their skills at leisure – and with a significantly increased selection of tools at their disposal. It seemed that Lord Henry had spared no expense in equipping his cadre of mages, ensuring that their every need was catered for.

When they were not practising their crafts, Henry trained them. Though some seemed to think it was mostly hokum – Matthew especially – they'd each participated in meditation lessons designed to improve their ability to focus their powers when they were working. Abigail described this as something of a turning point – with the techniques Henry had taught her, she'd found herself able to sew at a significantly increased rate and with far greater effect. The impervious cloth was but one avenue that they'd explored – she was also working on garments that made the wearer significantly harder to see, and great gowns that would be impressive not only in appearance but presence, drawing the attention of all around in their majesty.

All this was fiercely interesting, but Odette couldn't see how much of it was likely to apply to her. So far, she seemed only to have undone the powers of the others – Abigail's cloth, Robbie's wand, and, now that she thought about it, Mary's bread too. She supposed it would take them some time to test whether this was all that she could do … but beyond that? What did she really have to practise?

After breakfast, she headed straight up to the study. Although she was off duty, she still felt uncomfortable dressing in her leisure clothes to walk around the house – not that she had many. It was bad enough that she was going upstairs and not working, though she supposed that this studying was a kind of work. The others seemed to have taken the same point of view to begin with, but eventually given in to a more relaxed state.

Lord Henry was waiting in the study for her when she arrived, and Odette suspected that he'd skipped breakfast entirely. The thought made her miss Yasmin – silly really, since not even a day had passed since she'd last seen her.

"Ah, good morning," said Henry, placing his paper down and flashing a genuine, if awkward smile. "I trust you're feeling better today?"

Odette felt her cheeks grow hot. "I am, thank you," she said, sitting down when gestured to. "I'm ever so sorry for causing a fuss. I'd – I thought I wasn't one of the people having to deal with all this, you see."

Henry's eyes twinkled with a mixture of amusement and understanding. "You're far from the first to be overwhelmed by it," he said. "And your case is, to me at least, very much unique – I've never met anyone whose magic didn't come from a demonstrable talent of some sort."

She supposed that was a compliment, though it seemed a rather strange way to put it. Shuffling awkwardly on the spot, she said, "I still don't understand what it is that I *can* do, m'lord."

"Ah!" laughed Henry. "Neither do I."

A look of confusion flashed across Odette's face before she caught the genuine smile in his eyes and joined him in laughing. It relieved some of the tension, and she flashed him an apologetic look. "I would like to know, though," she said with a little more calm and conviction, "where ought I begin to look?"

"Well, it's clear that you can interact with the magic of others in some manner. I'd like to begin by investigating that – how far it goes, whether it's only a negative thing … that's to say, whether you can only dampen magic, not whether it's a bad thing! … And after that, we may have more of an idea as to how to proceed." He pursed his lips in thought. "I understand from Robbie that you had a similar effect on his work to Miss Abigail's."

"Yes," said Odette, "but only when I was touching the things they'd made. I mean, I didn't stop you singing Miss Johanna to sleep or making me feel better yesterday afternoon."

Henry nodded. "Indeed, I'd made the same observation. Well, then, I'd like to begin with a few small experiments."

He moved over to a side table, where Odette noticed two large piles of objects – one of embroidered cloths, clearly Abigail's, and the other a selection of wooden carvings that were unmistakably Robbie's. Henry picked up several of them and brought them over, placing them on the coffee table before Odette. Chief amongst his choices were a set of engraved wooden rods similar to the one that Odette had broken previously.

"I had Robbie make these specially," he explained, "since they seemed easiest to use for testing. No faffing about with knives and similar. The cloths will come in useful later, however."

Nodding, Odette followed his instructions as he went on. First of all, he had her simply take a rod and snap it in two, after he'd attempted to break it himself. This went much as before, with Odette breaking it easily and Henry unable to shift it. This time, however, Henry took up one of the broken halves of the rod and attempted to break it further, to no avail. Odette, on the other hand, was able to snap it a second time.

Scribbling down the observation that her powers seemed only to function whilst she was holding the object, Henry next asked her to assist him in breaking one of the rods. With two of them holding one, it broke easily.

"Much as I expected," concluded Henry. "Now, for the next attempt – please take my hand."

For the first time, Odette's compliance faltered. Henry had spread his left hand out before her, palm up, and was politely waiting for her to acquiesce. A few stammered syllables fell from her lips as she struggled to comprehend what could possibly require her to hold hands with a nobleman, but after a slightly exasperated sigh from him she gave in. Surely, he'd not ask such a thing without very good reason, after all. She placed her hand in his, and his long, slender fingers wrapped around hers. His grip was warm and unexpectedly gentle.

"I wish to see whether your power can be transferred through a person," he explained, taking up another of the rods. Though it was tricky to do so with one hand, he made attempted to break it by holding one end and bending it against the table. Unlike the others, it did not snap – but it certainly bent a good deal more than the others had done. Eventually he ceased his attempts.

"Should I be ... doing something?" asked Odette, uncertain what precisely she could do, but wishing to be as useful as possible nonetheless.

Henry hummed under his breath in thought, and she felt a small tingle run through her hand, almost as if she'd had the briefest flash of pins and needles. "See if you can visualise your power running through your hand and into me," he said after a moment. "I think it's close to working."

Odette nodded, and closed her eyes. It was just daydreaming. She could do that.

She began to think of herself as a pillar of glowing liquid, and imagined pouring herself out through their linked hands, the golden glow rushing through Henry and into the rod. All of her focus went into the visualisation, until she'd lost track of time altogether, and it seemed as if nothing else—

Snap.

Her eyes flew open, and she let out a gasp of elation. "Oh!"

"Very interesting," said Henry, letting go of her hand and examining his own curiously. "Very interesting indeed. How did you do that, Odette?"

She explained a little of what she'd imagined, leaving out the fact that she'd learnt how to do it by daydreaming all the time – for that was hardly something she was about to tell the professor, even if he wasn't her employer.

They continued in the same vein for some time – Henry investigated all possible avenues, from precisely how much contact Odette needed – the more she had, the less focus required – to whether it was possible for her to have a partial effect – only when channelling her power through another person. He seemed obsessed with exhausting every possible permutation, and Odette became quite bored – especially when they'd tested almost the same thing a dozen times over.

By the time Henry was content with what they'd done, it was approaching lunchtime, and Odette was beginning to feel terribly weary. It was as if she'd worked all morning, yet really all that she'd done was spent a good deal of time in her head, and all of it sitting down.

It was possible that neither would've even stopped for lunch, were it not for Yasmin's interruption. She'd come, she explained, to ensure that the two of them weren't overworking themselves – and given that she'd found them surrounded by notes and broken rods, it was evident that they certainly would've done so without her intervention, which gave Yasmin a considerably smug air.

Odette was allowed to go back down to the kitchens for lunch, where she sat with Mary as the cook prepared the pastry for the evening's dessert. Although Odette offered to help – and ,oh, how she longed to do something that actually felt *useful* – Mary explained that Lord Henry had insisted upon her doing it all herself to ensure that she had as much practise as possible. Mary, like the others, had been taking meditation and visualisation classes, and was currently working on instilling a giddy sort of happiness into her creations – a task that, unsurprisingly, was being kept secret from the rest of the upstairs family. The degree to which the usually brusque old woman was excited by this amused Odette considerably; she'd never have guessed Mary to have such a mischievous streak.

After lunch, she joined all of the other potentials for a meditation class with Henry. Although it took her some time to settle, Odette found this relaxing; it had a good deal, she suspected, to do with Henry's voice, which was so low and gentle that it could've rocked her to sleep if she'd let it. This was of course only to be expected given that his own power came from his singing.

Her thoughts drifted from his instructions at one point, as she wondered whether she'd be able to negate Henry's power. With Mary, Abigail and Robbie it was more obvious as there was a clear object with which to interact. Henry, however, and perhaps Isobel, were more difficult. What would she touch in order to transfer her power?

She was still considering this as the session ended, and when she opened her eyes she found that she was not the only person who looked as though they'd been lulled into a gentle slumber. Out of the corner of her eye, she spotted Henry with a slightly amused look, and wondered whether he'd ever used this technique on his students whilst teaching at Oxford – or, indeed, a reversal of it, where he woke those slumbering students up during lectures.

There was a brief pause during which Henry explained Odette's powers to the others, and what they'd discovered that morning, whilst also catching up with their individual progress. Robbie had managed to make several dozen more testing rods, and had attempted to imbue them with different powers using the same visualisation techniques, though Odette suspected they weren't working so well for him – Robbie had an awful attention span. One batch, he claimed, would be much better for setting on fire than the others, despite all being of the same wood.

Once the others had gone, Odette felt a little of her nervousness begin to return as she and Henry were left alone together again. Though she often spent a long time upstairs, she was frequently back down below, and staying above for quite so long was beginning to make her feel as if she'd done something wrong, or gotten in the way. This pervading sense of guilt began to rest on her stomach as Henry announced that they would try something a little more adventurous.

Now that he'd drawn some conclusions about Odette's power, Henry was in a mood to experiment. He wanted to see whether her power could work in reverse – to enhance the powers of others, rather than negate it. It was quite a leap, but Henry told Odette excitedly of his gut feeling, explaining that it would enhance their understanding of her power. Still, he had to coax Odette into trying.

Eventually she acquiesced, and they began to prepare for this new trial.

This time, they weren't alone in the room – Yasmin had been brought in as a test subject, and she seemed eager to see her friend's talents put to work. She was seated before Henry and Odette, who stood in the middle of the room.

"I want you to try your visualisation again," he explained, "only this time ... change it. You said you thought about yourself being liquid – imagine now that we both are, and that your power is pouring into me." He held both of his hands out this time, and she took them with a little less hesitation than before. "Hopefully, we will see a result."

Odette worried at her bottom lip with her teeth. "What are you going to try and do?"

"I'm able to affect people's emotions a little. You've heard music that makes you sad, or joyous, yes?"

Odette nodded.

"I'll attempt to instil happiness in Yasmin. If I'm right, and your power works as I think it does, then this should be intensified." Henry gave Odette an encouraging smile, and she blushed. "Are you ready?"

"I think so," she said, and closed her eyes.

Odette took her vision upward, so that she was looking down on the two of them standing before Yasmin. In a single thought, she transformed her body and Henry's into humanoid pillars of glowing golden light, which swayed gelatinously. Distantly, she became aware that Henry had begun to sing – and imagined his power trailing out towards Yasmin, trickling in veins that slowly enveloped her in a glorious corona of light.

Once she was certain that she'd imagined the path of things, Odette looked down on herself and began to push the gold in her own form through their joined hands. As she did so, she felt herself being drawn towards Henry. Almost against her will, she watched her hands unclasp from his, and run up the inside of his arms until they were wrapped around his waist. Their golden forms began to mesh in her mind's eye, and a warm sensation grew at the base of her throat whilst butterflies danced in her stomach.

Her vision was no longer above – she couldn't help but imagine herself as herself, holding tightly onto Henry. Her head rested against his chest, which rose and fell as he sang – though she was so focused that she could barely place the words – and out of the corner of her eye she saw the corona around Yasmin begin to glow white hot. As she watched, she became aware of another sound at the periphery of her senses – a joyous peal of laughter. Focusing suddenly upon it, Odette saw white sparks shower from Yasmin's aura, and felt the knot in her own throat pulse with feeling.

Snapping her eyes open, she let in a sudden rush of breath, the world returning to her in a strangely disjointed order. First, she saw Yasmin holding her sides to contain her hysterical peals of laughter. Next, she became aware of just how warm she felt, wrapped in Henry's arms, and how that strange feeling in her stomach had not quite gone away.

Then she crashed down to reality and leapt backwards in shock.

"I – oh, gosh, I'm s-so sorry," she stammered, before realising that her legs were as wobbly as if she'd just run the length of the gardens. Flailing, she caught onto Henry's hands just as she stumbled.

With Henry's song ended, Yasmin had managed to regain some of her breath. "Are you all right?" she asked, shuffling up on the lounge chair so that Henry could guide Odette to sitting.

"I just feel a little tired," said Odette, her eyes flicking up to Henry's. His expression was full of curiosity, though a little tinged with embarrassment. "I'm ever so sorry, m'lord. I felt … I didn't feel like I had much control over what I was doing."

Clearing his throat, Henry shook his head. "It's quite all right. I'd much rather you … did as you needed to, and we discovered what does and doesn't work."

"It did seem to have quite the effect," said Yasmin, who was now able to breathe normally again. "I don't think I've laughed that much since the time Daniel made us balance chocolates on our foreheads and try to eat them without touching them."

A small chuckle escaped Odette, who'd shrunk back a little into the chair, face hot with the knowledge that both of them were looking at her intently. Every few moments, her mind flashed with the memory of Henry's embrace, as vivid as it had been in reality.

"You said you had no control," he began, pulling up a stool so that he could sit in front of her. "How do you mean?"

"When you're dreaming … do you always have control of things?" Odette asked rhetorically. "As I'm falling asleep, or as I'm waking up, sometimes I have dreams where I'm almost in control, but when I try and imagine changes, my mind won't let me. I try to imagine that I put a glass down, but every time I straighten back up in the dream, the glass is there in my hand again."

"As if you're being guided by it."

"Yes, exactly. Or it's just too stubborn to give in."

A slightly more comfortable silence fell over them, and Odette felt a little of her tension relax – though there were still butterflies in her stomach, and she couldn't bear to look up at Henry. A soft touch on her hand alerted her to Yasmin's continued presence, and she managed a small smile for her mistress, who'd always been able to read her better than Odette felt comfortable with. There was no hiding anything from her.

"At what point did you lose control?" asked Henry, breaking Odette out of her reverie. "I'm wondering if your power is guiding you to do something that it requires."

Blushing, Odette gathered her composure enough to answer. "When I … stepped closer to you, I felt pulled in."

"Then perhaps you need greater contact in order to transfer energy," Henry said thoughtfully, seeming either unaffected by the embarrassment or – more likely, Odette thought – breezing past it. "That makes it more difficult to utilise."

"There's something I don't understand," said Odette, the words falling from her before she realised she'd begun speaking. It was too late to retract it, however, so she continued. "Everyone else's powers – they're skills. Things that you can all do, that you're good at. But mine …"

"I've thought about this at length," said Henry, his voice settling into its usual gentle lilt. "And I'm afraid that I have no great answer for you."

Next to her, Odette felt Yasmin sit up with a start. "Oh, but isn't it obvious?" she said, chuckling softly.

"But I'm not … the others, they're terribly good at the things they do. I've never been like that with anything."

"Yes, you have," said Yasmin sharply, though she almost looked amused. "You've always found it easy to learn new things. You're exceptionally good at learning. Anything you try to do, you do effortlessly, and to a high standard. There are very few things that you're not good at if you put your mind to it."

Odette looked up rather helplessly at her, perplexed, as Henry let out a sudden sigh of understanding. "Oh, but of course!" he said, clucking at himself in disapproval. "You're very good at learning from others – and so, in a sense, you learn to control our powers. That's why you can enhance and negate them."

Understanding slowly dawned on her, too, though she shuffled on the spot. She'd never really thought a great deal about the fact that she was good at things – she'd just always tried to be a very good servant, and done her best, and that didn't seem strange to her at all. It simply … was. The idea that it was the thing that had influenced her magical power was both astonishing and disconcerting.

"Oh," she said softly. "Does that mean I can learn to … could I use your power?"

Henry blinked widely at her, and a brilliant smile suddenly unfurled. It made the seemingly permanent butterflies in her stomach do backflips. "Now that," he said, "is perhaps the most interesting question you've asked all day."

<h1 style="text-align:center">11</h1>

Unfortunately, Henry was to be disappointed. After a break for tea and cake at Yasmin's insistence, the three of them spent several hours testing Odette's ability – or lack of – to control Henry's power. But no matter how much she visualised the golden glow of his craft trickling into her body, she couldn't get her voice to carry the same power as his. She just felt overwhelmed by the embarrassment of singing in front of another person. And when Henry tried to sing with her, to see if that enhanced the power further, he only succeeded in bewitching Yasmin himself – leaving her with an uncontrollable fit of giggles that rendered her sides aching for the rest of the day.

Still, they'd achieved a great deal, and so when they called an end to things at dinner time – which Odette desperately tried to convince Yasmin to allow her to assist with, though to no avail – they didn't feel wholly disheartened. Odette ate dinner downstairs with Robbie and Isobel, who were excited to hear how Odette's training had gone. It was only at this point that she realised that none of the others had experienced so much individual training with Lord Henry as she had.

The thought made her butterflies return all over again, and she was certain that Robbie had spotted the way her cheeks burned as she looked away – there was certainly going to have to be some explaining about that later. But for the moment she was being packed off to bed by her mother and Abigail. Though it was still very early, Odette didn't protest too much; she felt drained – not tired so much as pulled too thin – and was more than happy to curl up in her bed and drift off to a restful sleep.

She dreamed of golden-formed people reaching out to touch one another with tendrils of happiness.

The next morning, when she was meant to be practising her visualisation – not that she really needed to, but Henry was working with some of the others and there was only so much time she could spend snapping rods – Odette snuck out to the orchard with Robbie. The two of them curled up on the bench, which was beginning to frost up as autumn turned to winter, and tucked into cinnamon pastries that Mary had made. Although they did nothing for Odette, they gave Robbie terrible pins and needles – he described feeling as if he'd sat on his hands and feet for hours on end. It was then that Odette found herself subject to her best friend's grilling.

"So what was all that about last night?" Robbie asked in a tone that would've been nonchalant were it not for the pointed look came with it. "You turned beet red when Roger was talking about how much time we'd each had with Lord Henry."

"Oh," said Odette, in what she hoped was an idle tone. "It's nothing, really. Just something that happened when we were practising."

The stare that she received in return made it clear that she wasn't going to get away with so simple an answer. Sighing, she pushed aside her embarrassment and continued – it was, after all, only Robbie, whom she could tell anything.

"The first time I tried to enhance his power," she began, "I got, I guess, carried away. When you've done the visualising thing – have you ever felt like you're being led by it, rather than leading?"

"Yeah, once," said Robbie thoughtfully. "When I was making all of those rods for you. I'd done so many that after a while I sort of zoned out, and I was just … watching it happen."

Nodding, Odette continued, "It was sort of like that. Only, when I went with it, I ended up … well, I sort of hugged him."

Robbie stared blankly at her for a moment before letting out a sudden burst of laughter. "Oh, God," he said, clutching his sides. "Only you would get this embarrassed over a hug."

"He's a *lord*, Robbie! Not to mention a professor, and a good deal older. And Yasmin was watching" – well, she'd been too busy laughing to really pay attention, but still – "and it was mortifying. God knows what I could've done if I hadn't stopped."

"It's an experiment, Det," he replied with an amused sigh. "He's not going to brand you a slattern just because you gave him a hug. It's not like you tore his clothes off or anything."

Even though she knew the last part was meant to further tease and inflame her already burning cheeks, Odette couldn't help but squirm with displeasure at the very idea that she'd lose such control of herself. It didn't bear thinking about – and the worst part was that she didn't think it was wholly impossible that she *could* lose that much control. She remembered how easily she'd given in to things earlier; how resisting the way her visualisation was going hadn't even entered her mind.

Her worries continued through the rest of the day, leaving her so distracted that she couldn't even focus on the simplest tasks. It wasn't, she realised, so much the embarrassment of the thing, or the fact that she'd manhandled one of her superiors, or even the suggestion that it was some sort of romantic advance on her part. It was the fact that, for a moment, Odette had had no control over what she was doing, had given over entirely to this power that she neither wanted nor understood.

The day went and another came, and she found herself grateful that Henry had not summoned her for further individual training. This was due to the return of his father, who upon his arrival late in the morning had holed himself up in the office with Lord Henry and refused to allow anyone entry. It had caused something of a commotion – the countess had been especially vocal about being barred from entering part of her own house – that in the ensuing hours had softened to a dull roar as lords, ladies and servants alike all murmured about what the two could possibly be discussing.

Odette was not surprised when, as the doors opened in the later afternoon, she and the rest of the potentials were immediately summoned. That much they'd expected. What came next, however, was quite beyond their anticipation.

"We're all being taken to Bristol early," explained Lord Henry. "Some of my colleagues have also gathered potential mages, and it's only logical that we gather together as soon as possible to share our knowledge and understanding."

"I've already secured temporary replacements for all of you," said the earl, who'd been called in an hour before the staff, and looked not at all surprised. "Obviously, the sooner we can have you back the better, but I'll not have it said that we refused to aid the country in its time of need."

With an approving nod, the major general took a step forward. "We've managed to keep it out of the papers thus far," he said, "but there've been four more murders. Two of the people killed are believed to have been mages, in the employ of one of my son's contacts."

Odette glanced at Henry, who had a grave look on his face. She thought she understood, then, why he looked so tired and worked himself so hard. If mages were in danger, then their lives and his were also on the line.

The discussion turned to logistics, matters of how they'd travel to Bristol and when – by carriage, at first light. And as Mary and Abigail began to query issues of lodging, Odette found herself tuning out. She'd just began to wonder how to explain the news to her mother when there was a soft rustling next to her.

"Miss Odette," murmured Henry, tucking his long fingers into the crook of her elbow and pulling her slightly away from the others. She felt Robbie's eyes on her, but didn't look back at him. "You should know that, to an extent, the army are aware of your powers and, well, believe that you especially might be in danger, should Braddock become aware of your ability."

"Why?" asked Odette, though she knew the answer already.

Henry sighed. "You could make him invulnerable. Imagine if you strengthened his already considerable power to repel us. There's no guarantee, of course, and I've emphasised to them that your powers are raw and untested – but that's the fear."

"Or I could be the only person who can take his power away," Odette whispered. And as Henry's grey eyes widened, she realised that he hadn't thought of this.

She could've sworn that Henry's fingers squeezed gently at her arm before he pulled away. The two of them turned their attention back to the conversation. Robbie shot Odette a searching look, and she shook her head. She'd tell him later, of course – but the longer he was ignorant of the danger, the better.

"Oh," said Henry softly, leaning so that she could just hear him. "And you'd best not mention that to anyone. My father would not be pleased to hear that I'd relayed the information."

Before she could consider the ramifications of that statement, Odette found herself whisked off with the rest of the staff to pack and prepare for their early departure the next morning.

As soon as she could find her, Odette rushed to tell her mother – who was both concerned for her wellbeing and proud that she was going to be doing something of such importance. True to Henry's request, Odette didn't mention the increased danger. Nor did she tell Robbie, instead saying that Henry had wanted to check that she was well enough to travel after her sickness earlier in the week.

In her matter-of-fact fashion, her mother channelled her mixed emotions into ensuring that Odette was packed neatly and had bathed, braiding her hair so that it would fall in gentle waves when taken out the next morning.

If Odette noticed the watery look in her mother's eyes as she wove her daughter's hair into neat plaits, she didn't comment – nor, of course, did her own eyes get a little thick with salty water.

Her clothes were pressed and folded into a battered suitcase that neither she nor her mother had used since they'd last visit her father and brothers.

Odette slept fitfully. Eventually she rose with the dawn, unable to spend another moment struggling to rest. She snuck silently out of the room and down to the kitchens, where she found Isobel sitting at the table, Mary watching over her like a brooding hen.

"Can't sleep?" asked the taller girl, holding out a chocolate-laden pastry, which Odette took gratefully.

Across the table, Mary let out a small chuckle. "You and the rest of the world," she said wryly, before gesturing to the pastry. "Don't worry about these. They're not, ah, intoxicating."

"Not that it would be a problem for you," said Isobel, giving her a small smile. "I think it's exciting."

"Exciting?"

"Your power. It's so – well, none of us are like you, are we?"

Odette blushed slightly, focusing her attention on picking apart her pastry. "Lord Henry says I'm …," she said a little helplessly, not sure how she could possibly explain it without sounding terribly headstrong. " … my skill is in learning things. Or so he thinks."

"Oh," said Isobel, looking a little chastened. "It's still exciting, though."

"Yes," said Odette, realising for the first time that she actually was. "And I'm excited about going to Bristol, too. The furthest I've been before is London, to visit my father.

He's a butler in another house up there; my brothers are valets, and my sister's a cook."

Mary pulled up a stool and poured the two girls glasses of cold milk before adding some to her own tea.

"I grew up in Bristol," she said thoughtfully.

Odette had never spoken to Mary a great deal about her youth, and leant forward in interest.

"It's changed now, o' course, and we ain't goin' int' city itself – there's a house no' far outside wha's puttin' us all up, Lord Henry said."

"Is there a family in residence?" Odette asked, and Mary shook her head.

"'S an army house," she explained, "given by t' last of a line, or some such. They use i' as a base out there for t' officers."

"I heard they're going to let us stay in *guest rooms*," said Isobel in a hushed whisper, as if the idea of it was too great a secret to be said at full volume – even though they were the only ones up this early, save for the stable hands, who were already tending to the horses. "What a lark!"

Though she was amused by the younger girl's reaction, Odette had to admit that the idea was exciting.

"I suppose we'll see when we get there," she said, secretly hoping that Isobel had not simply heard a fanciful rumour.

They devolved into excited chatter about the trip, interrupted only when the others began to rise to get breakfast ready.

All too soon, Odette was rushed into helping pack the carriages and prepare everything for their departure. She relished the chance to do some real work for a change.

Her mother had said goodbye to her earlier, knowing

it was unlikely that they'd get a chance to have a proper farewell as everyone left, what with all that had to be done. She'd pressed several coins into Odette's hands, despite her protests, and dropped a kiss on her daughter's perfectly curly head.

"Make me proud, darling," she'd said, before rushing to attend to her duties – which with the incoming staff had increased considerably.

Now Odette was dressed in her coat and holding the small holdall that contained her most precious possessions – her father's pocket watch, her grandmother's necklace, a small portrait of her mother and father from their wedding day, a hand mirror that Yasmin had given her for her eighteenth birthday, and several small wooden carvings that Robbie had made for her over the years. She stood lined up with the others before the carriages and waved to everyone before piling in. As Odette raised her hand to take hold of the rail, she heard a voice call out behind her.

"Ditty! I'll miss you!"

Yasmin was waving fiercely at her, a broad smile planted across her face. It was so infectious that Odette found herself smiling back, though she realised with a sudden pang just how much she'd feel the absence of her sunny mistress. They'd not had a chance to say goodbye properly, and Odette hadn't felt comfortable sneaking upstairs to see her – though she'd considered it, and now wished very dearly that she had. Although she opened her mouth to call out a goodbye, she found her throat thick with emotion, and instead, with a wave, turned to clamber into the carriage after Robbie.

They set off at a moderate pace, and Odette found herself quickly falling asleep on Abigail's shoulder, the restless night finally catching up with her as the carriage's movement gently rocked her into slumber.

As she slept, she dreamed of all her fellow potentials, standing in a circle, each of them a pillar of glowing golden energy, all linked through their hands and powers, becoming twined within one another into one blindingly bright circle that left lights dancing in the corners of her eyes when she finally woke and opened them.

The residents of each carriage shuffled about during the several stops to rest and change the horses. After their third break, Odette was summoned by a knocking at the door. A little confused and still somewhat sleepy, she glanced over at Robbie, who gave her a shrug, before climbing out of the carriage. It was much brighter outside than when they'd left, and Odette's eyes stung as they adjusted to the light.

The footman led her up several carriages to a much grander one than her own. This one was decked out in burgundy, with gold edging, and she couldn't help but swallow nervously as she eyed it. The footman reaching out with a gloved hand, opened the door for her, and helped her to climb in.

As her eyes adjusted to the dimness, Odette found herself looking into a calm, tired and familiar face. The professor's usually combed-back hair had escaped and now curled about his forehead and ears in an attractive fashion, framing his slate-grey eyes.

"Good afternoon, Odette," he said as she sat down on the seat opposite him, which was much comfier than the other carriage's.

"M'lord?"

"Thank you for joining me. I thought that now would be a good time for us to talk about … what's going to happen when we get to Bristol." He paused and looked at her with slight concern and anticipation. "I'm afraid I've rather lost control of the situation."

Blinking widely, Odette let out an "Um," of confusion before composing herself and replying. "Of what situation, m'lord?"

"Would you mind doing me a small favour, Odette?"

"What is it?"

A smile spread across his lips. "Call me Henry. I'd like, for a little while at least, to remember that I'm as much a person as you are."

The request stunned Odette somewhat, but she felt unable to refuse him – at that moment, he looked terribly small, despite being of above-average height, his shoulders hunched and worn.

"I shall try," she said slowly.

Nodding, Henry returned to her previous question. "I've fought for a very long time against my father's wish that all of your powers be used to assist the army in a more violent assault on Braddock. It was my hope, you see, that we'd find a peaceful resolution."

"But he's killed far too many people now to allow that," said Odette, remembering an early conversation with Yasmin about it.

"Indeed. I'm afraid that as a result it's quite likely that the others will be packed into rooms and forced to work on things such as, well, weaponry."

Odette grimaced. She'd promised Robbie that this wouldn't happen – a fool's promise, really, as she had little to no power over the situation at all, and since they were now on their way it was far too late to escape from it.

"The others?" she said suddenly, shuffling on the spot. "What about me?"

"I, ah – I believe I've managed to prevent your being misused … a little at least," Henry said, looking oddly uncomfortable. "It's involved a little bending of the truth."

"Lies," said Odette with a small smile.

"Lies," agreed Henry. "I mentioned that they know about your power – well, I've told them that you've only been able to augment my powers thus far, not any of the others'. And I've emphasised that you've not yet been able to stop active powers from working, like my own."

"But that's not wholly a lie, is it? I haven't tried it on people as they're working, so we don't know for sure that I can't, but …" She felt confused. "I don't understand what we gain from their thinking that, though. Are we not meant to be doing what they want?"

"Them thinking that means you'll not be whisked off by the army upon our arrival, never to be seen again," said Henry with a grave look that suggested that he'd seen this happen before. "If they don't think you're yet capable of taking down Braddock's defences, you're of less use to them – which means we can keep you safe with the rest of us, under the pretence of trying to expand the breadth of your powers."

Odette frowned. "You seem so sure that I'm capable of taking down someone's power as they're doing it, but we don't know that – we haven't tried it."

"I know," Henry said softly. "I made quite certain we never did."

Realisation dawned, and Odette felt a surge of gratefulness even as a knot began to form in her stomach. "I don't want to … kill anyone," she said softly, ducking her head. It was not a phrase that she'd ever thought she'd have to utter in any seriousness.

There was a soft touch on her chin as Henry leant forward and lifted her head up with the tips of his fingers. "I'll do my very best," he said, his voice resonating with usually hidden power, "to ensure that you don't have to."

"But you can't promise anything," Odette said with a sad smile, pushing his fingers away from her face with one gloved hand. "Though I know it's a phrase often said by children, I'm not a child, m' ... Henry." The name still tasted strange on her tongue. "I'll be fine. But thank you for looking out for me."

12

For the rest of the journey, the two of them fell into a comfortable silence, occasionally punctuated by discussions of what they could expect to happen – though Henry was quite in the dark for much of it, and wished he could give her more information. He didn't send her back to her own carriage, but couldn't explain to himself why this was so; instead, he periodically caught himself staring at her. What he must have looked like he did not know, but it earned him a rather confused look from the woman in front of him.

They arrived at Marston House at dinner time to find it a hive of activity. It was a much larger building than his family's estates, though a little less grand – as if the focus had been on making it as impressive from the outside as possible, rather than putting much consideration into the interior. Still, it was an imposing building, built entirely of a pale local stone and set in exceptionally green grounds – there were only a few flowers to be seen, a scant few honeysuckle bushes. It was a very matter-of-fact place, which Henry thought lent it an appropriately military charm.

It was heavily guarded, which surprised him, but then he supposed that any house containing quite so many high-ranking officers was likely to be a target for those wishing to attack the British Army's interests. And they were, after all, attempting to deal with an almost-invulnerable mage of seemingly incomparable power. Could one really be too cautious?

Once ushered in, Henry watched as his charges were shown to their rooms – an experience that was clearly more than a little disconcerting for them, so used as they were to being in the servants' quarters. Indeed, he saw Roger twitch a few times before managing, somewhat reluctantly, to enter via the front door. It amused Henry terribly, which was probably something of a comment on how tired he was.

As the last of them disappeared up the stairs, Henry was approached by an elderly woman he didn't recognise. She beckoned him into an adjoining room, explaining that the major general was there and wished to speak with him directly.

"Wonderful," he murmured under his breath, following her through the corridor to his father's temporary office. The name on the door was one he was unfamiliar with, and he could only imagine how the poor sot whose study it actually *was* had been treated when the major general had demanded somewhere to work.

Henry entered the room, stumbled and paused. His father was sitting behind the desk as he'd expected, but seated in front was another face he most decidedly recognised, and though he'd known the man would be here, the sight of him still shocked Henry terribly.

"Edward," he managed, rather stiffly. "It's ... good to see you."

Edward Morley was precisely as Henry remembered him; tall, elegant, handsome, and with a permanent sneer plastered across his face. Henry found himself wondering how he could ever have found that expression at all attractive, for surely it was the very definition of disdain.

"My goodness," drawled Edward, his voice as slow and condescending as Henry recalled it being. "Look what the cat dragged in."

"Yes, well," snapped the major general, clapping his hand down on the desk. "Come and have a seat, boy, and we'll be about it."

It was not often that Henry found himself grateful for his father's blustering mannerisms, but this was certainly one of those rare times. He had no idea whether his father was aware of his and Edward's history; it seemed unlikely that his father would've rescued him from the ensuing tension if he did, but it was nonetheless appreciated. Tearing his gaze away – but aware that Edward's own eyes did not leave him – Henry sat down in front of the desk and rested his hands on the arms of his chair.

"We've brought you here ahead of schedule because we've been disappointed by the lack of progress," Henry's father continued, before taking an unsettlingly large swig of whisky from his tumbler. "Since neither of you can evidently be trusted to work at an acceptable pace, you and your ... *potentials* ... shall work under our supervision. Furthermore, I've drafted in some assistance for you both from your respective establishments."

This was the best news Henry had heard all week. Additional help from the department at Oxford could mean only one person: his closest friend, Vivalda. The two of them practically *were* Oxford's magical studies department, and having her at his side in this hideous, awful situation – well, nothing would bring him more comfort.

"You've had plenty of time to train your people up," continued the major general. Morley let out a snort of disagreement. "So now we're really going to buckle down and focus on creating a plan. I don't need to remind you that I don't like this business of not knowing what we're doing."

"With respect, sir," said Edward, his voice a slither, "I can't speak for Henry, of course, but I at least do have a plan."

Henry's father let out a loud harrumph. "Well, why the bloody hell didn't you say so, man? Go on, then – spill the beans."

"I'll need a week to confirm that my theory's correct," Edward said with a smile. "Then I'm certain I'll have a way through Braddock's defences for you."

"Good. Excellent. Perhaps that girl of yours won't be needed after all, boy."

Bristling with indignation, Henry sat up a little straighter in his seat. "She is not a girl, sir," he replied as patiently as he could manage. It was one thing for his father to call him 'boy' – he was after all the man's son – but turning it on Odette sounded nothing short of derogatory. "Furthermore, I'd advise not leaping to conclusions before you've heard Edward's proposal. It would be foolish in the extreme to grasp at a potential solution too hastily, simply because it's the only one."

Slamming his glass down on the table and thrusting himself to his feet, the major general stalked towards the door. "One week, both of you," he bellowed over his shoulder as he marched out, leaving Henry unsure whether he'd won that point, or lost abysmally.

"I see your father never changes," Edward remarked as the door slammed shut.

Henry chuckled. "I do believe his changing would be the first sign of the apocalypse."

Edward stood up, and for a moment Henry thought he too was leaving – but then the taller man leant over to pluck the half-empty whisky decanter and two glasses from the sideboard. He returned to his seat, poured two generous fingers for each of them, and settled back.

"So, how many did you find?"

"Seven – four crafters, three actives," replied Henry. There was no need to hide it, after all – they'd all know soon enough. "Yourself?"

"You always were a show-off, Henry. I've four – there's no need for more than that, frankly. I'm surprised you've had the time to train yours at all." Edward took a composed sip of his drink. "Really, seven is far too many. What on earth are you planning to do with them all ?"

Blinking, Henry replied, "I didn't go out to select a specific number. I simply took all those who showed magical skill."

This seemed to confuse Edward, and for a long moment he sat back in his chair and examined Henry with a scrupulous gaze. "What a waste of time and effort. I found more, of course, but really there's only any point in spending time on the ones that will really *achieve* something. I'm sure you've a few duds in your pack."

Henry took several deep breaths. He knew very well that Edward was simply trying to get a rise out of him – it was how they'd been around one another, ever since ... well, the less thinking done about that the better. He'd been much younger and *much* stupider then.

"I suppose we shall see," he said once had steadied himself, and smiled slightly. "I'm very much looking forward to meeting all of your potentials. I daresay this is the most of our kind that have been gathered in one place for centuries."

"We should get our groups together tomorrow," agreed Edward, nodding. "We can see whether any of yours will be of use to me."

"Of use to y—" Henry began before catching himself and looking away. "No, you're not worth the effort. I'll see you tomorrow, Edward."

Henry was halfway to the door before Edward's laughter gave him pause. "Not tomorrow, dear friend. Have you not been told? There's to be a dance this evening – a feast to rouse the spirits of the troops."

There was a rustle of movement behind him, and Henry became aware that Edward was standing right behind him. A gentle pressure on the small of his back made his nerves jingle as a memory surfaced. He tilted his head to glance behind him.

"Of course, it's many years since you danced with anyone, isn't it," smirked Edward, a smug glint in his dark eyes. "In fact, I recall something you said – let me see, what was it ..."

"Edward ..."

Edward wrapped his fingers around Henry's left wrist, drawing his arm up and into position. "Yes, that was it. 'Edward, I do believe I shall never love to dance with someone as much as I love to dance with you.' Do you remember that night, Henry?"

He did.

Wrenching himself away, he turned on his heel to face Edward, rage surging within. "That's *enough*," he hissed. "I'm not your toy, Edward, not anymore. You don't get to *play* with me."

As soon as it was said, Henry realised he'd done nothing but rise to Edward in precisely the way the blasted man had intended – a fact made all the clearer by his wry chuckling as Henry fled the room, praying his retreat didn't look too much like cowardice.

He hated dancing.

13

As Odette was whisked away by one of the staff and shown up to her room – an experience that was more than a little disconcerting – a thought began to dance in her head. Had anyone actually considered what the origin of Braddock's power might be? If all powers manifested in skills, surely there must be some skill, talent or trait that was the origin of his. But she barely had time to think about it further before the maid opened the door to her new bedroom and took her breath away.

"Oh," said Odette a little dumbly. The maid gave her a curious look, then carried her diminutive suitcase through to the room. Odette had not been given simply a bedroom, but a whole suite; it left her slightly stunned.

It was an unexpectedly floral room given the sparse decoration in the rest of the house. The wallpaper was a mixture of pale-green and blue flowers accented with creams and whites that Odette found quite attractive – it reminded her very much of Johanna's room back home.

She'd not only her own living room and bedroom but her own bathroom, too, which smelt of lavender and rosemary.

If she was going to be forced into service to the army, Odette thought, it was kind of them to make it look like a holiday. Or, a little voice in the back of her mind murmured, it was simply tactical.

The maid showed her all the amenities, then explained that dinner would be at nine o'clock, a little later than usual to cater for their arrival, and that this would be accompanied by a dance to celebrate their progress and offer a small distraction.

This caused a flurry of panic to whirl in Odette's stomach. She'd never been to a dance – at least, not one that she wasn't working at – and she'd barely half an hour to prepare. Thanking the maid, Odette turned her attention to changing out of her travelling clothes and into her nicest dress – which was, as it happened, her only dress that was not her uniform. The idea of walking into the room wearing her old uniform made her stomach turn, and she quickly banished the unhelpfully vivid image from her mind.

The gown was an old dress of her mother's that Abigail had altered. Nancy was much taller than Odette, and a little slimmer, so the seamstress had widened the panel at the back and taken the skirt up so that it brushed just around the ankles rather than dragging along the floor. It was a pale mint-green colour, gathered underneath the bust, and with a gently scooping neckline that swept down from the furthest points of Odette's shoulders, exposing her collarbones and probably a little more of her chest than her mother would've liked.

About her neck she put a small chain that had been her grandmother's; it bore a wooden carving of a tiny rosebud that Robbie had made for her. It was her only item of jewellery, and the last time she'd worn it had been her eighteenth birthday, when the staff had put together a small party for her in the orchard. She took out her own modest collection of makeup and did her best to make herself look less like a servant and more like Yasmin.

Then, seeing that time had run away from her, she quickly made her way out to dinner.

Thankfully, over the years she'd honed her ability to navigate around houses as large as this, so it wasn't difficult to find her way. As she walked down the corridor she encountered Mary, who looked exceptionally awkward without her apron, and Abigail, who was unsurprisingly regal in a dress of her own creation. The two of them cooed approvingly over Odette's appearance, which she took to mean that she'd not disgraced herself, and perked her up considerably.

The three of them made their way to dinner, which turned out to be a much more extravagant affair than any of them had anticipated – more ball, in fact. Upon examination, however, it became clear why this buffet-style approach had been taken: there were almost fifty people in the room, a mixture of army officers and civilians, all milling about the various round tables that encircled a wood-panelled central space where, Odette noted with a little fondness, there were some couples dancing already.

At the door Odette found Isobel holding demurely onto Robbie's arm. She flashed her best friend an amused look, then made a point of giving Isobel a broad smile to ease the girl's nerves. Regardless of what anyone thought, she and Robbie had decided quite some time ago that they were simply not like that, and the quiet painter was a good fit for him – of course, Odette was sure she was jumping to conclusions far too early, but she'd always been something of a romantic.

Abigail, easily the most dashing amongst them, took Mary by the hand and led her in, whilst Matthew affected a great bow and offered his arm to Roger, whose moustache trembled as he laughed and accepted.

Odette was just about to follow them alone when there was a soft cough next to her. Turning, she looked up into Henry's face, which had lost a little of its tiredness. He gave her a soft smile and held his arm out, which she took with only a small blush.

"I must confess, I've always hated dances," he said to her in a low voice, "but we ought at least to try and enjoy ourselves whilst we're here. Shall we?"

Laughing softly, Odette nodded and fell into step with him. Henry was almost a foot taller than her, and she had to shuffle an extra step now and then to keep up as they followed the rest of their party. As they circled around the dancing couples, Robbie shot her a raised eyebrow over his shoulder, and Odette felt the blush in her cheeks deepening against her will. Thankfully, Henry seemed not to notice, instead waving over a young footman with a tray of punch glasses.

As he handed one to her, he cautioned, "The last time I was at an army function, two glasses of this stuff was putting most of the officers under the table. I'd nurse it carefully if I were you."

"Oh, gosh," she said, taking the glass cautiously. "I will. Thank you."

They were intercepted at that point by the major general, who looked exceptionally grand in his full military-dress uniform. He looked at Odette curiously for a moment, but was gracious when Henry properly introduced her, Mary and Roger. There was a period of polite chit-chat that Odette largely tuned out of, distracted as she was by the sight of so many new people. There were many more civilians than she'd expected, and not all of them looked to be military family. Several men and women were dressed in clothes that reminded her of Henry's, likely academics of some sort, and a handful of others who could've been anything from administrators to spies for all she knew.

Her reverie was startled when Henry's father suggested that they all avail themselves of the buffet, since it would likely be a long evening – a gathering of not only the usual residents but also several other branches of the forces and beyond who were all involved in working on dealing with Braddock.

"A bit of fun," he said brusquely, "to better help them deal with the realities of the situation tomorrow."

Odette couldn't help but smile at that. She knew that not every highborn family in the world was like the Oakleys – indeed, they were a rarity – but it nonetheless filled her with pleasure to observe their modern take on the wellbeing of those who worked for them. Evidently, the major general had managed to pass some of this Oakley thoughtfulness onto the army, or at least this portion of it.

Next to her, however, Henry's smile was tempered – he stared at his father intently, as if assessing him. If he noticed the scrutiny, the elder Oakley ignored it, and was quickly swept away by one of the other offices who simply *had* to introduce him to one of "Edward's young people".

"Edward Morley," murmured Henry in Odette's ear. His voice seemed oddly tense. "My ... equivalent from Cambridge. He was charged with gathering potential mages as well, but I fear he may have been a little less open-minded in his selection."

Odette chuckled softly. "Not everyone is as thoughtful

or inclusive as your family," she said, voicing her previous thoughts. "But I'm very glad that you all are."

"Yes, well," said Henry. "I suppose we ought to do as father says, and get our teeth into the buffet before the redcoats steal it all."

"You don't like the army very much," observed Odette, feeling an urge to clap her hand over her mouth; she seemed to be putting her foot in it more often than not lately.

Henry only laughed. "An astute observation," he said wryly, "almost worthy of my dear cousin. I'm sure she'll be pleased to hear that you've learnt from her. And speaking of my cousin, there's a feast here to satiate even her almighty appetite."

Odette had never eaten anything so grand, even when she'd stolen the leftovers from dinner back at the house. There were fruits and vegetables that she'd never even *seen* let alone tasted. She spotted the others looking as lost as she felt, eating things that only one or two of them were familiar with. She found particular amusement in watching Robbie attempt to eat lobster neatly. For some time, they simply gorged themselves on the exquisite food – though not so much so that they disgraced themselves, or looked particularly feral – until they were stuffed.

The conversation was light and idle, covering the sort of topics that were universal to all, but also communicated absolutely nothing of substance – the weather was discussed at length, some occasional forays into politics, but largely nonsensical things. Odette made sure to sip only genteelly at her punch, more out of fear that she'd fall victim to its considerable strength than a wish to be prim and proper. Just as she'd finished her last slither of cheesecake and taken a final sip of punch, Odette and Henry were approached by a grand-looking lady in an exquisite lavender ballgown.

"My dear!" she exclaimed, leaning down to plant a kiss on Henry's cheek. She was in her early forties, Odette thought, or perhaps a little more. There were laughter lines at her lips and eyes. "It's so good to see you. And these must be your potentials."

"Vivalda," said Henry with a warm smile, standing to greet her properly. He had a fond look on his face that reminded Odette of how one might look at a particularly favoured aunt. "I'm so, so glad you're here. It's wonderful to see you. And, yes, you're quite right."

"I didn't expect so many," replied Vivalda, looking at the Oakley party. "Even Edward has only managed to find four." She spoke his name as if she abhorred its very presence in her mouth. "You have ... let me see ..."

"Seven." Henry gestured to each of them in turn, not introducing them fully since so many were still engrossed in dinner and conversation. "Roger, my uncle's butler. He has an uncanny kinship with animals. Next to him is Mary, the cook, who can imbue her creations with such powerful emotions that you never know if eating them will make you giggle hysterically or sob with pain – occasionally both. Beside them is Matthew, a stable hand. You wouldn't know it to look at him, but he's quite adept at climbing. So adept, in fact, that he can scale a towering oak tree in a matter of moments. He's with Abigail, my youngest cousin's maid, a weaver of considerable skill. Then across at this table are Robbie and Isobel – she paints images of the future, and he's a dab hand with a whittling knife."

"And this lovely young lady?" asked Vivalda, flashing

Odette a warm smile. Odette couldn't remember the last time someone had called her lovely – it warmed her throughout and reddened her cheeks.

Henry held out his hand, needlessly assisting Odette to her feet. "This is Odette," he said, "my cousin Yasmin's maid. Her ability to interact with the powers of others is quite unique."

"It's a pleasure to meet you, m'lady," said Odette, bobbing into a small curtsey out of habit.

Vivalda let out a peal of laughter that sounded as melodic as windchimes, and gave Odette a firm kiss on the cheek. "Oh, how dear!" she exclaimed, somehow managing not to sound condescending. "I'm Vivalda Entwhistle, and the pleasure is – I assure you – entirely mine. And since Henry has been so kind as to explain all of your own powers, allow me to explain mine."

"Your power?" asked Odette, smiling. "Oh, what is it?"

"Vivalda," said Henry in a warning tone, though there was a smile playing across his lips.

"I shall not be uncouth," said Vivalda in a haughty tone. Turning back to Odette, she continued, "I have a knack with machinery, my dear."

"Forgive me, but I don't understand how that could be considered uncouth."

With a chuckle, Vivalda said, "Have you heard some of the mechanical terms for things? Goodness, you'd think they'd gone out of their way to give every invention a phallic reference of some kind. And if I like to throw out their names a little more often than I ought, well ..."

"Vivalda delights in tricking young men into thinking she has quite a different profession," Henry explained to Odette, looking a little uncomfortable himself.

Channelling some of Yasmin's insight, Odette grinned. "I see. *Young* men, you say?"

This comment evidently endeared her quickly to Vivalda, who let out the same ringing peal of laughter and linked her arm through Odette's. "Quite," she agreed, "and I see none of those here. Why, I believe Henry is fast approaching his thirtieth year. Not young at all. Now, Miss Odette, allow me to whisk you away from this font of boredom and introduce you to some of my friends."

Odette opened her mouth to protest that Henry really wasn't boring at all, but Vivalda had already launched into an appraisal of the gathering, pointing out so many names to Odette that she'd no hope of remembering any of them even if she could've worked out which faces Vivalda was gesturing towards. Some she was introduced to more fully, during which time she came to understand that Vivalda was a colleague of Henry's at Oxford. There were, it turned out, quite a few mages at both Oxford and Cambridge. This evening was apparently a rare thing, for they'd never before been gathered all at once.

She supposed that this was not really surprising, though the secrecy of it all still stunned her from time to time. Imagine if the whole world knew of these things that people could do!

In a scant hour, Odette was introduced to an artist who could copy any script so accurately that even the own author would swear they'd written it themselves, a farmer whose crops always grew perfectly, no matter the weather, and a silversmith who, like Robbie and Abigail, could craft things that never suffered wear or tear.

The sheer breadth of it stunned Odette, who until recently had possessed not even the slightest inkling of the truth of the world. And though she'd feared it greatly, now saw for the first time the amazement of this new reality.

More than that, however, she saw all of the people whose powers she could interfere with. By the time Vivalda had returned her in a flourish of triumph to Henry, Odette's mind was reeling with a mixture of giddy happiness, a sense of being terribly small, and a small tinge of fear.

"I return your lady unscathed," announced Vivalda, "but now I really must be getting back to Gerald. He does fret so without me, you know."

Kissing them both on the cheek, Vivalda disappeared as quickly as she'd arrived, the scent of jasmine lingering behind her. As Odette glanced over her shoulder after her, Henry brushed the tips of his fingers along her upper arm.

"What is it?" she asked, and looked about them. The major general was standing nearby, as were several of the high-ranking academics, and they were fixed on the two of them as if ready to pounce.

"Ah," said Henry as they began to approach. "Why don't we … ah …"

"Dance," said Odette brightly, spotting several couples in the centre of the room. "I haven't for so long."

She'd thought it a safe suggestion, but as soon as she said the words she recalled what Henry had said earlier about hating dancing. His face contorted in an unreadable expression, and she quickly babbled a retraction that he need not dance if he didn't wish to.

"No, it's … it's quite all right," he said softly, cutting off her panic. Odette's eyes flicked up to his and saw in them the gleam of a decision. "I would like to, very much. And it would be a very effective way of escaping our predators. Shall we?"

Henry offered her his arm and they joined the other swaying pairs. There was a brief moment of mutual embarrassment as he wrapped his arm around her waist and she placed hers on his shoulder, but once they began to move each discovered to their silent surprise that they were both quite acceptable dancers.

"Now," said Henry, "tell me what the matter is."

She thought this a strange opening, given that *he'd* been the one so wary of his father and the others, but perhaps it was simply his way of distracting himself from his own discomfort. And as she considered the question, the tension in her limbs began to reassert its presence in her awareness. Perhaps there had been something to notice after all. Before she could stop herself, the thoughts tumbled from her as they sprang into her head.

"It's nothing terribly bad," said Odette, worrying her bottom lip with her teeth. "It's just – there are so many of them. I didn't expect it, and ... well, isn't it just a matter of time before they discover all the things I can do? And ... will they resent me for it? I feel terribly greedy, you know."

Henry chuckled softly, and the vibration in his chest ran through to Odette and made her breath catch. "You're nothing of the sort," he said. "In fact, one could certainly argue that you're the most selfless of us all; your powers, after all, rely entirely on those of other people."

"I suppose," sighed Odette, glancing over at a large gathering of army officers. "When Vivalda was introducing me to people, all I could think of was how their powers might be abused. Did you know there's a silversmith? They've been trying to get him to work with other metals, and between him and Robbie ..."

"Yes," said Henry, mirroring her sigh. "They could all too easily be roped into manufacturing weaponry. It is, after all, what the army are used to – and they're hardly the type to start throwing off great traditions."

"Do you really think so?" asked Odette, blinking widely. "I don't. Look at us."

"At us?"

A wry smile spread across her lips. "Do you realise how much of a scandal we'd be causing usually? A servant dancing with a lord."

"Oh," said Henry, giving a small cough that indicated his embarrassment. "Yes, I suppose so. All of you being here is rather ... odd."

"Rather odd?" Odette couldn't help but laugh. "Did you not see Roger twitching to help serve people at the buffet? Or how Abigail and I keep straightening tablecloths when no one is looking? We're all creatures of habit, and we're used to the things we're used to. None of which involve dancing with handsome men in the middle of a house a hundred thousand times the size of anything we'd be likely to call our own, drinking expensive punch and eating food that's so exotic I've quite no idea where it comes from at all."

Finishing in a rush of breath, Odette's cheeks immediately coloured with embarrassment. Oh, if only she had control of her tongue!

But Henry made no reply save to look at her curiously, almost as if seeing her for the first time, and they fell into a comfortable silence.

Odette thought for a moment that his grip might have tightened on her; that he might've pulled her ever so slightly closer to him as they turned. Letting herself relax, she did her best to shed off the worries that weighed so heavily upon her – worries for herself, for Robbie, for all of the others and increasingly for Henry himself.

She'd just begun to feel content when she felt Henry stiffen and come to an abrupt stop. Turning to follow his gaze, she saw that a tall and incredibly handsome man had approached them, a brilliant smile upon his face. Despite his fair appearance, however, there was something about him that unsettled Odette.

"Well, well," he drawled in a deep voice that was at once enticing and condescending. "I see you've gotten over your distaste for dancing, Henry."

Though they'd stopped moving, Odette noticed that Henry had not let go of her. Indeed, if anything, he'd tightened his grip, almost painfully. Looking up at him, she noticed several lines of tension in his expression that had not been there before, and what almost looked like fear and pain in his eyes. When he spoke his voice was hard, unlike the silk that she was used to hearing.

"Not now, Edward."

Edward? That was the name of his counterpart at Cambridge, was it not? Odette knew there was something of a rivalry between the two establishments – many of Vivalda's introductions had made that clear – but the tension surrounding the two men felt like something else entirely.

"Such rudeness," Morley replied with an affronted look. "May I not be introduced to your lovely dancing partner?"

The grip around her waist tightened, and Odette became

convinced that Henry was indeed trying to shield her from this man for some reason. Then she remembered something that Yasmin had once said to her. "The quickest and simplest way to make someone leave, Ditty, is to give them what they want."

So Odette gave Henry's shoulder a squeeze, and as his grip faltered she turned and offered her hand to Morley. "It's a pleasure to meet you, sir," she said with as genuine a smile as she could muster. "My name is Odette."

"A beautiful name for a beautiful young lady," said Morley, kissing her hand. Odette thought it was quite the silliest line she'd ever heard, but she laughed nonetheless. "The pleasure is all mine."

"I must apologise," Odette went on, before Morley could react, "but I've never had the pleasure of dancing at so fine an event before, and Henry has been kind enough to indulge me."

Morley examined her for a moment, and it took all of Odette's willpower to continue to look him in the eyes. As she did, she realised how infrequently she held anyone's gaze; usually she'd look away in a matter of seconds.

"Then I shall not be so rude as to keep you from it," he said at length, dipping into a small bow. "Enjoy your evening."

As Morley disappeared into the crowds, Odette turned and placed a hand on Henry's arm. Her pulse was racing, and everything seemed to have become louder, but she was determined not to succumb to a fit when someone needed her.

"Are you all right?" she asked softly.

He shook his head, and Odette was not certain whether he was banishing a thought or answering her question. "I believe you handled that much better than I would've done – than I had begun to," he said softly. "Thank you. I – I think that I should like to continue dancing."

Odette's face broke into a smile, and she quickly stepped back into his arms, which though no longer vice-like still pulled her a little closer than might be proper. They resumed turning in slow circles in the centre of the ballroom, and she felt a surge of power for having shielded him from whatever pain Morley had brought forth in him. Indeed, despite the earlier tension, she no longer felt heavy at all.

Indeed, for the first time Odette began to realise just how powerful people were – not just the people looking out for her, but the people beyond. And though the thought scared her, both for what they could be called on to do and what they might have done to them, she felt lightened – because how could she be unhappy, or overcome with fear, or sullied by brief shadows in a world so brave and new as to have turned upside down?

She looked rather pretty, with her hair in curls and her special dress on, and she was dancing. She had a power that no one could take away from her, and it came from within some special part of herself that she could no longer deny. She was more than a servant. She was more than a silly girl who ran her mouth off at inopportune moments. And she was, above all, much more than her fears and her fits.

It was a good day.

14

When the night was coming to an end, Odette excused herself to bed. Henry watched her go with confusion swirling in his mind. She seemed at once to be both terrified and incredibly brave; she'd dealt with Edward so skilfully that he was still chuckling at the thought of it. It had been incredibly foolish too, of course – but she couldn't possibly have known that. Edward's power was in his voice, his words, his demeanour, his effortless pull that drew people to him.

"Whatever you're musing over, darling, it's far too dreary." Vivalda's voice carried to him as if from a distance, though when he turned she was right next to him. "You're frowning so deeply that your eyebrows are threatening to merge."

"Edward decided to make a scene after dinner," he confessed after glancing around to ensure no one was nearby. Most had left the ballroom already, and those who remained were clustered in small groups.

Rolling her eyes, Vivalda latched her arm into his and escorted him to a nearby table. "But of course he did," she said with a sigh. "That man is incapable of not making a scene. He makes a scene simply by entering the room. What happened?"

Henry explained, including the fact that Odette had rather saved him from anything worse. "I daren't think what might've happened if she hadn't been there."

"If she hadn't been there, I doubt he would've done it," observed Vivalda astutely, giving Henry a look that made him feel quite sheepish. "He's exhausted his existing ways of hurting you, darling. Don't give him more opportunities to do so. If he can use people you care about to hurt you, he will. You must trust me on that."

Her voice had softened with her last words, and Henry's gut roiled with as realisation dawned. "Did he ever ... you ..."

Vivalda tossed her hair. "Of course he *tried*, but you can imagine how far that got him, even with his powers. He's not wholly impossible to resist, you know; it's simply very difficult. Unfortunately for him I'm very, very stubborn."

This comforted him somewhat. "I only wish I'd been there to see it."

"You would've loved it, darling. He ran away with his tail between his legs."

"I'm afraid that Odette and the others don't quite possess your tenacity," Henry said. He sighed, shaking his head. "Even if they do, they don't know what he's capable of, and I ... I want to tell them, to warn them, but it involves—"

"Explaining some things you'd rather forget about."

He nodded. "It's so important to this whole process that they trust me, and if they knew I was capable of such weakness, how could they?"

A sharp blow to his arm made Henry jump in surprise. He'd barely seen Vivalda move her hand, let alone bring it down to slap him. She glared at him with a fury that he'd often seen her direct at others but incurred himself.

"Henry Oakley, you are not weak. Good grief! You've said

yourself in the past that he was different to begin with, and there's no reason for you to have known what he'd become. It's incredibly hard to see things when they're staring you right in the face, especially if they involve someone you love, and I daresay even the bravest and strongest person in the world would've done exactly the same as you."

Chastened, Henry reached for Vivalda's hands and squeezed them gratefully. "I'd still rather have made that mistake so that other people don't have to."

"Then find some way to tell them what his powers are – warn them that way, if you don't wish to tell them the whole story." She smiled at him and squeezed his hands in return. "And remember that they're perfectly capable of protecting themselves. I spoke with all of them this evening and they're wonderful people. You should be very proud to have found them."

"I am," Henry said with emphasis. "Telling them about his powers is a good start. It means they'll be warier."

Vivalda nodded. "Exactly. And if he so much as tries to get at you, Henry, dear ..." She looked at him squarely, and Henry realised that his expression must have given him away. Her lips pursed into a thin line. "What did he do?"

"Nothing," replied Henry quickly, before sighing. "My father left the two of us alone in his study earlier. Edward was just ... he was just trying to get me to react, that's all. He was just playing with me."

The breath rushed from Henry's lungs as Vivalda scooped him into a tight hug. "Darling," she murmured into his ear, "you tell me straight away the moment that monster of a man so much as looks at you in a way that makes you uncomfortable. You don't have to fight him on your own."

To his horror, Henry found that his throat had tightened and his eyes were threatening to spill over with tears. He buried his face in Vivalda's shoulder, and hugged her back for so long that they must surely have drawn stares. When he was certain that he'd not look like a fool, he drew back from her. She surreptitiously wiped the tear stains from his cheeks.

"I've missed you," Henry murmured, and their lips curved into mirrored smiles.

"Of course," remarked Vivalda, drawing them to their feet. "I'm eminently missable. But speaking of missing people, I really must get upstairs to Gerald. I'm sure he's fast asleep by now with nary a care for my whereabouts, and that simply will not do."

Henry chuckled. It was said amongst the Cambridge faculty that the term "long-suffering" had been invented on behalf of Mr Entwhistle. Vivalda's husband seemed to many to walk in her shadow – of course, most people around Vivalda seemed to walk in her shadow – but he knew that Gerald was utterly and passionately devoted to his whirlwind of a wife. The two of them made an odd pair, but they worked perfectly for one another, and Henry was very proud to call them his friends.

Kissing Vivalda on the cheek, he bade her goodnight and made his way to his own room for a better few hours of sleep than he'd managed in weeks.

15

The next day dawned with a piercingly cold light that crept in even through Odette's thick curtains. She woke early, as she normally would, only to find that there was no need for her to be up – she had nothing to prepare but herself. After a little more sleep, she crawled out of bed to find new clothes neatly laid out for her.

There was no maid to help her get ready – as if she needed one! – but someone had clearly been in to stoke the fire and bring her a pretty, periwinkle-blue dress. Examining it, she guessed it was of Abigail's making, for she recognised the faint flower pattern upon the material. It warmed her heart to know that there was no ill-will between them after the events of the past weeks. There was a matching coat hanging by the door, and Odette pulled on both of them quickly before wrestling her hair out of plaits and into some sort of order.

Breakfast, it seemed, was generally taken in their rooms – there was a continental-looking selection on the table in her sitting room, with an accompanying note saying that she and the others would be required to gather in the pearl lounge to meet the rest of the potentials and discuss the plan for going forward. Odette wasn't sure how she felt about the idea of a plan, but had begun to feel that it was probably better simply to get all of this done and out of the way – maybe, then, she could go home and begin to explore things for herself.

Once she'd eaten, she made her way downstairs, and promptly realised that she had no idea where to go. Luckily, there were several soldiers stationed in the entrance hall who were able to point her in the right direction. She reached the pearl lounge and found that she was not the first to arrive; Roger, Isobel and Robbie were all seated at one side of the room, chattering animatedly about the previous evening's entertainment. They were all wearing new creations of Abigail's, as if she'd endeavoured to kit them out in some sort of uniform. Odette noted with amusement that Robbie looked decidedly uncomfortable in his new outfit.

"Good morning," she said as she sat down next to him.

"Morning, Det. Sleep all right?"

Odette nodded. "I think the punch is mostly to blame for that. I was out like a light before my head touched the pillow."

"I couldn't sleep a wink," said Isobel, who was wringing her hands together in her lap. "I kept thinking of all the things that could happen. I didn't expect there to be so many guards here. Are we in danger?"

"Of course not," said Roger smoothly; he seemed quite convinced of the fact. "The earl and countess wouldn't have permitted us to come here if we were in any danger – nor, I'm sure, would your master have done so."

Odette couldn't help but wonder how much this was true, given what Henry had told her – the major general at least was clearly in on the plan to put them all forward as a solution. Still, she didn't want to worry Isobel further, and telling them would only mean revealing how she'd acquired the information in the first place. Breaking Henry's confidence was not something she wished to do, especially not when he was one of the few people she trusted to help her explore her powers without desiring to exploit them.

"Did you meet any of the other mages?" Odette asked the three of them. They shook their heads. "I met one of Lord Henry's colleagues from Oxford – Vivalda Entwhistle. She introduced me to quite a few of them, including some from Cambridge, but I'm not sure I could remember all their names if I tried."

"We all met Vivalda. She's quite something. Oh, and I heard one of them's an artist, like you," Robbie said to Isobel. "Or not quite the same, but her power comes from that sort of thing."

"She's a forger," said Odette with a smile. "I mean, she can copy things so perfectly that they're identical. I'm sure she's never done anything illegal."

"Oh!" said Isobel. "I should very much like to meet her."

Roger's lips twisted into a small, gruff smile. "I'm sure you will," he said before glancing over to the door. "Here's the professor."

As Roger stood, the others followed suit, all turning to watch as Henry entered. To Odette's dismay, he was accompanied by none other than Edward Morley.

She immediately searched Henry for signs of distress; he seemed tense, but Vivalda was at his side. With them were several other mages whom she was certain Vivalda had introduced her to, but she could barely remember their names.

"Ah, you're all here!" boomed Morley, whose voice was liquid silk even when enthused. "Good, good. Is this all of you?"

"No, there are three others," Henry replied, walking in several large strides to join his company. Odette wondered if he always walked like that, or whether he was trying put to put as much distance as possible between himself and Morley. "May I introduce Professor Edward Morley, coordinator of the Institute for Magical Studies at the University of Cambridge."

"The only university in the country to have pre-emptively formed such an Institute," said Morley proudly, inclining his head towards them. "Oxford's always been slow on the uptake."

"Not slow," remarked Vivalda smoothly, "so much as subtle. We don't feel the need to give things fancy titles and make great proclamations of our work; our work speaks for itself."

As Morley twitched his upper lip agitatedly, searching for a witty comeback, Vivalda smoothly introduced herself to everyone before gesturing to the four nervous-looking men and women hovering awkwardly behind Morley.

"This is Marie," she began, holding out a hand towards a tall woman dressed in deep purple. "An artist of some repute, whose ability to copy is uncanny. Next to her is Arnold" – an elderly-looking man in grey pinstripe – "trained as a silversmith, whose creations are unrivalled in beauty and construction. Then we have Lewis, a farmer from the fens, whose crops never fail." The farmer was a bulky man who looked as out of place as Odette and her fellow servants. He was accompanied by an effortlessly beautiful young man, the only member of the group who was not cowering. Gesturing last to him, Vivalda said, "Finally, this handsome young man is Peter, who is, well, I shall let you see for yourselves. He is ... quite unique."

Odette could have sworn that Vivalda's eyes passed over her as she finished speaking, and a nervous chill ran down her spine. At that point, Mary, Abigail and Matthew arrived, and were promptly introduced in turn to the newcomers along with the four already present.

Once everyone had been named and their powers explained, the company took seats in a large circle. Henry sat down to Odette's left, glancing cautiously at her as he did so, as if to warn her about some unknown danger.

"Now," said Morley, seated imperiously on the edge of his chair. The beautiful young man was on his right, almost mirroring his pose. "I think it's time we got right down to it. Oakley tells me that you've all explored the limitations of your powers. From here on, everyone shall be pushed further. There's no room for error."

Out of the corner of her eye, Odette saw Vivalda wrinkle her nose in distaste before interjecting. "What Edward is saying," she said calmly, "is that we're now subject to orders from the army, whose duty it is to ensure that no one else gets hurt. They've made certain requests that will need to be fulfilled, but they're also expecting us to come up with a solution."

"Wha' sor' of solution?" said Mary, narrowing her eyes at Vivalda.

"Whatever we believe will work," said Henry quickly, and Odette suspected that he was taking care to reply before Edward could. "This situation is unique, and ..."

Morley cleared his throat. "There's no need to search for a solution," he said in the idle tone of one assured of their own victory. He gestured to the boy beside him. "I've found one. Tell them, Peter."

"I'm able to control the powers of others," he said haughtily. "We simply need to get me close enough to Braddock to take down his shields – or whatever it is he's using – so that the army can *deal* with him."

There was an awkward pause during which Odette felt several pairs of eyes on her – those who knew what her own powers were.

"Really, Edward," said Henry with a sigh. "Don't you think we ought to find a solution that doesn't involve more death? The man's a murderer, yes, but we could learn from him too – God only knows what else he's done that we don't know about, for a start."

"Oh, and I suppose you've got a better idea."

They devolved into an argument that to Odette seemed less about the situation and more about their own distaste for one another. The tension from the previous evening was back in the air, and palpably uncomfortable. As they bickered, she glanced to her right at Robbie, who took her hand in his and squeezed it encouragingly.

"They don't know, do they?" he said softly to her. "What you can do."

"Not all of it," she admitted, gesturing over her shoulder to Henry. "He kept it secret. He thinks it's dangerous. That they might try and use me for ... things I'd rather not do."

A brief expression of concern flared in Robbie's eyes, but he did his best to school it away. "We won't let them," he said. "Besides, you can always refuse."

"I know," Odette said, looking over at her equivalent, who was examining his fingernails as if the ongoing argument was pointless. She wasn't sure she wholly disagreed with him – but suspected they disagreed for different reasons.

"I'm not sure it would work, anyway. The reversal, I mean. I've never tried it when the person is actually … manifesting. Using their power. Only on things that have been completed already."

"Maybe he has," said Robbie, jerking his head towards Peter. "Looks smug enough to be certain, anyway."

"That assumes his powers are the same as mine. And besides that … I still don't like the idea of killing someone." Odette ran her thumb over the back of Robbie's hand, though it was more for her own comfort than his. "And if I *helped* them with that plan, well, I'd feel like I'd done it myself, even if I didn't pull the trigger."

Vivalda finally lost patience with the bickering men, and slammed her hand down loudly on the table in front of her. Both Morley and Henry jumped in their chairs, the former looking slightly outraged, the latter decidedly embarrassed.

"That's quite enough," said Vivalda curtly. "There are people here with tasks to tend to, gentlemen. At least issue those orders and allow them to begin before descending into bickering about those left."

Looking only mildly chastened, Morley nodded. "Well, Professor Entwhistle, I suggest you take your charges with you then."

"Certainly. Robert, Arnold, Abigail, Mary – would you like to come with me? Our task is to craft armour that can be worn by those who'll need to get close to Braddock." Next to her, Odette felt Robbie exhale with relief. She squeezed his hand. "Since this is my area of expertise," Vivalda continued, "I shall be coordinating."

Their task assigned, the four crafters gathered themselves and departed, wishing the others luck as they left. The remaining company clustered closer together, drawing their chairs in.

"Now, let's try this again with less arguing," said Morley succinctly, clapping his hands on his thighs. "Surely you're not saying that it's not worth looking into this as a potential course of action. If we have no other options – and I believe that's the case – then we'd be shooting ourselves in the foot not to do so."

Henry's brow dipped and he wrinkled his nose, clearly unable to refute the argument. "Then those of us who remain," he said calmly, "should simply split into two groups – those attempting to aid you in your endeavours, and a second group to help me find a bloodless alternative."

"Hmph," Morley snorted, though he didn't oppose Henry.

They agreed to divide equally – which, with only a few of them left on each side already, was not too difficult. Henry retained Roger, Isobel, Matthew and Odette, whilst Morley took Peter, Lewis and Marie.

Once they'd separated, Henry led his group to another lounge. There seemed to be no end of living rooms in the expansive house, and Odette caught Roger murmuring under his breath about how much of a bugger it must be to keep clean.

16

"My apologies for your having to witness such a childish spat," said Henry, swishing his coat-tails out behind him as he sat in front of their now much smaller group. "Edward and I are ... old friends, or at least we were friends a long time ago. I've always found him too ... harsh, and I believe he's always seen me as far too soft. ... As a result, we've never quite managed to be fully in accord ... even when we agree on a subject."

There were too many pauses in his speech for him to be wholly believable, he knew. But it was better than nothing. "I should warn you, whilst we're on the subject, that Edward's magical powers lie in his charisma, his presence. He is exceptionally good at getting his way, and used to succeeding. Please be ... wary around him. I'll be sure to tell the others as well."

The group nodded, and an awkward tension floated in the air for some time.

"I think you were right to argue, m'lord," said Isobel suddenly, before looking a little sheepish for breaking the silence. "I don't want to kill anyone, even someone like him."

"Like Braddock, or like Edward?" asked Henry wryly, quickly flashing a small smile at Isobel when she looked appropriately scandalised. "Well, you all heard him. We have to come up with an alternative."

"He still needs his shields taken down to be stopped," said Roger thoughtfully. "That much I think is true."

Henry nodded. "Most probably."

His eyes lit on Odette just as realisation began to dawn on her. Her expression turned from worried to sudden comprehension, as if something that had been percolating had just clicked in her mind. "Oh," she said softly, drawing everyone else's attention to her. "I don't think their plan is going to work at all."

"Go on …"

"Is – is Peter's power the same as mine?" she asked. "If it is, then … well, you said my power comes from being able to learn things quickly. But you always learn in the manner that you're taught, right? Your teacher's style influences you."

"I suppose," said Henry thoughtfully. "And, yes, I believe his power to be similar to yours at least."

"Well, then, I think perhaps the style that influences me, or him, that's where your powers come from." She gestured to the rest of them with her hand. "I don't just make your powers stronger, or take them away. I make them stronger because two minds are better than one, or I turn them off because I know how to – but we've got to be thinking in the same way for me to do that."

"I think I know where you're going with this," said Roger, his bushy moustache twitching in excitement. "You're saying that this boy won't be able to do anything to Braddock's power if he doesn't understand where it comes from."

Odette nodded, and Henry felt a mixture of elation and dismay. She was right, he was certain of it – it went along with everything they'd ever managed to glean about how magical powers worked. They were intricately tied to a person's experiences and personality, just as their talents and skills were tied to what they'd done with them and what they associated them with.

"I'm worried," Odette began hesitantly, only continuing when encouraged to by the others. "Because that means we have to know him well – Braddock, I mean – for it to work. And I don't know if anyone has ... tried."

"The police and the army have both tried to speak to him," Henry said, "but no one seems to know much about him – beyond his followers, that is, who are loyal enough not to give anything away."

"I think," said Isobel quietly, "that he must be ever so scared." When everyone looked at her in confusion, she said simply, "Why else would he be so good at protecting himself? You wouldn't protect yourself if you weren't afraid."

With these realisations, the group sprang into action, purpose driving them to progress. It was clear that they needed to find out more about Braddock, to understand how his power had manifested so that it could be manipulated. They began also to think of ways in which he could be subdued once he'd been made vulnerable, though Isobel reminded them all that a desperate person could be driven to quite terrible things.

Henry found himself putting a great deal of thought into the dangers of Odette's own part in the plan – if Peter was unable to get through to Braddock, *she'd* have to, and her visualisation was far too slow a method to use in a situation that was potentially violent.

Later that afternoon, after speaking to the army officers

who'd witnessed Braddock's power, plus looking into his own history, Henry managed to catch a few moments alone with her.

He was seated in the same parlour they'd been in earlier, humming under his breath as he worked. A scrap of song had come to him, and he'd learned long ago that such moments of inspiration should never be ignored; they were often his mind providing him with precisely the strain of melody that he would soon be in need of. A page of manuscript paper rested before him, scrawled with pencil markings.

"I think I need to practise," Odette said, stepping into his field of vision. Henry snapped his head up in surprise, having been so deep in thought that he'd not seen her come in. "If I'm going to be the person who makes it possible for us to capture him, then I think I should know what I'm doing."

"I agree," he said, regaining some of his composure. "How can I help?"

Odette explained a theory about needing to find a faster way than visualisation, and Henry listened in silent agreement. Belatedly, he realised that at some point he'd ceased to be her teacher – that she was now some sort of colleague, approaching him for advice and help on an equal level. He was uncertain whether this pleased him or unsettled him. He'd been worried that his charges would never feel wholly comfortable around someone who until recently had been their superior, but Odette was not quite like the others.

"So, either I need to get close enough to him that he'll let me visualise," concluded Odette, "or I'll have to find another way."

They spent the rest of the day experimenting with various ways in which Odette could link with Henry's skills, both strengthening and weakening them, but to little avail. To test more widely, they had her attempt a similar thing with Roger and Isobel – which threw up yet another spanner in the works for their plan. Whilst Odette was able to enhance Roger's skills relatively easily, helping him calm several excitable guard dogs, she hit a stumbling block with Isobel's.

The issue was that Odette couldn't paint at all – every time she attempted to link with Isobel, she told him, it felt like there was a block in her visualisation. She simply couldn't imagine how Isobel would go about her task, since she didn't herself understand it. It was rare for Odette to be unable to pick up a skill, but Henry couldn't help but wonder if this was because she'd not painted much before. Some skills simply couldn't be picked up without a great degree of practise, even by Odette.

17

By dinner time, Odette was exhausted. Though she made a good show of sitting with the others, listening to how the crafting group's work had gone, and ate probably more than her fair share, she felt as weary in her mind as if she'd spent the entire day trying to do complicated sums. Though her fatigue didn't go unnoticed – both Isobel and Robbie shot her concerned looks – she didn't put voice to it, save to excuse herself as soon as the meal was done.

She pulled on an outdoor coat and slipped out of a side door into the grounds. Though they were nowhere near as grand as the Oakley estate, they were well kept, and the crunch of slightly frosty ground under her feet began to clear her mind somewhat as she walked.

Halfway around the garden, she heard the sound of someone else approaching on the gravel path. Turning, she saw Henry walking towards her, looking more than a little cold – he had no gloves on, appearing to have donned only his coat in haste, or perhaps absentmindedness.

"There you are," he said, sounding unexpectedly relieved. "I've been looking everywhere."

Blushing, Odette said, "I'm sorry. I didn't mean to cause a fuss – I just wanted to get away from, well, everyone. Clear my head a bit."

"You're not a fuss," Henry said softly, and Odette could almost swear there was fondness in his voice, though she was sure she must be imagining it; or perhaps it was real, but just a consequence of his decency.

"I am," she said matter of factly – then curled her lips into a small smile, "albeit with good reason. I'm not sure that we're any closer to finding a solution. It's not as if I can go wandering up to Braddock and convince him that I'm his dearest friend, someone he can trust implicitly."

Henry opened his mouth to reply, but then in a sudden burst of movement reached out and gripped her hands instead. "Ditty, that's brilliant!" He grinned impishly with the use of her nickname. "We can do precisely that. Did you know that I had Mary working on cakes that would make people more susceptible to emotions, rather than simply imbuing them with them? Or that Abigail can sew dresses so beautiful that they make the wearer shine above all others in a room? You'd not be able to wear them yourself, of course, but one of the others ..."

"Oh," said Odette softly, a strange combination of terror and relief dawning. "That way we could get close enough to him to find out where his power comes from."

"Yes," said Henry fiercely, and the two of them suddenly burst into victorious laughter.

It felt as if a huge weight had been lifted from her shoulders – there was a way for them to do this, a way that would not result in someone dying, or in Robbie being forced to make weapons.

As their laughter died, Odette's eyes flickered up to Henry's, and she found herself suddenly overcome with a desire to do something forbidden – a desire that flared up in one moment and was suddenly and unexpectedly quenched by the brushing of his lips against hers in the next. His fingers ran across the side of her face, pulling her hair askew, and her own hands had come to clutch the open front of his coat.

Time seemed to pass in slow motion, and Odette's overactive mind became blissfully silent. The world was no longer dark, or cold, or really anything at all – there was nothing except the two of them, waxing against one another like flames around kindling.

But the moment was over all too soon, as they pulled away, staring widely at one another, realising precisely what they'd just done.

Odette leapt away first, a sudden pain in her stomach. They stood there in stunned silence for several long moments during which Odette tried to resist the urge to worry her swollen bottom lip with her teeth.

"I'm sorry," they both said simultaneously when neither could bear the silence any longer.

Ducking her head shyly, Odette continued, "I – it won't happen again. I should ... well, we have things to plan, and—"

"Ditty," Henry said, something almost like pain in his voice. But whatever he'd been about to say he thought better of, instead offering only, "We shouldn't tell Edward and his people about this plan. They'll try and sabotage it. Or worse, they'll take it and use it to kill him."

If that wasn't a dismissal, Odette didn't know what was – though a small part of her was insisting that *he* had kissed *her*, and that she had nothing to be ashamed of – so she promised to keep the plan a secret and rushed back inside to hide her now roiling emotions.

What had she been *thinking*? This was not the world of her imagination, where she had control over everything, and nothing went wrong that could not be undone. She was a servant, and he was a nobleman. That they were working so closely together at all was scandalous enough in itself. That she'd kissed him, a man a dozen times her superior, was impossible. And yet she'd done it. She'd done it, and she couldn't take it back.

In Odette's hurried return to her bedroom she passed Robbie, who spotted the burning tears pouring down her cheeks, and promptly rushed towards her.

"Det? Det, what is it?"

He caught up with her as she pulled open the door to her room with an angry jerk. Though she didn't answer his question, she let him follow her into the room in flagrant ignorance of propriety, then began tearing her hair free of its pins and hurling them at the table before her.

He tried several times to get her attention, but eventually gave up – waiting until her fury was spent.

"We have a solution," she said eventually, flopping down onto the chair by the fire. "One that solves the problem with knowing how Braddock's power works."

"And ... this made you angry?" said Robbie cautiously, clearly sceptical. "What on earth is this idea?"

Shooting him a look of condescension, Odette sighed. "No, something else did. But it's not important. The idea is simply that we get close enough to Braddock to get to know him, understand him and his power."

"You're joking, right? Det, the man's killed at least half a dozen people. He's a loony!"

"He's scared," said Odette firmly, reiterating Isobel's

words because she had to believe that was the case. "And just because someone's done a terrible thing doesn't mean they're entirely terrible. People can atone for things, Robbie."

His brow furrowing with concern, Robbie knelt down in front of her and placed his hands on hers. It stilled her in a way that his urging had not. When she didn't flinch, he spoke to her softly. "I know. I know, all right? But that doesn't make him any less dangerous, Det, and you know it. You can't bring the dead back to life with compassion. Who came up with this idea, anyway?"

"I did," said Odette a little too quickly. "... Henry and I did."

If Robbie was at all surprised that she – usually scrupulous about addressing her superiors – had neglected to include Henry's title, he didn't show it. He tilted his head in thought. "He's the one who upset you, isn't he?"

"He ... yes," said Odette weakly, rubbing at the rapidly drying tears on her cheeks and blowing her nose loudly into a handkerchief. "I think he's just very tired. I'm not sure he knows what he's saying sometimes. Or doing. I'm not sure I do anymore, either."

Although he could tell she was still holding out on him, Robbie didn't press the issue further. "I don't want you to do it," he said instead, squeezing her hands gently. "But I think you're determined to, aren't you? And I don't think I've ever managed to talk you out of something that you were determined to do."

"I'll need help," Odette said, which was as good an affirmation as any. "I won't get close to him on my own; we'll need everyone to help."

"All right. What about the other group?"

"Morley's lot? We're not telling them. Henry thinks it – well, that they might try to sabotage what we're doing. Or that they'll take our idea and use it to allow the one who's like me, Peter, to make Braddock vulnerable so that he can be killed. And if we go partway, and then it all goes wrong … that could be the most dangerous thing of all."

Robbie's brow furrowed in confusion. "Why would they sabotage it? I mean, they might disagree, but we're all here to do the same thing, when it comes down to it. Like you said, they could just use the idea."

Odette bit her lip, wondering how much to say. "There's some sort of history between Henry and Morley," she said at length. "I don't know what it is, but Morley seems to have it in for him somehow."

"History? Like *history* history?"

This gave Odette pause. If they had some sort of romantic history, it would make a great deal of sense – the tension between them had that edge to it. And if it was not a good history then it would certainly explain their behaviour. She suddenly regretted telling Robbie anything at all, for it seemed she'd accidentally said more than she'd meant to.

"Maybe," she managed, knowing full well that Robbie could read her like an open book. "I don't know for sure."

"Doesn't seem right to try and guess," said Robbie, and Odette felt some of the tension ease from her shoulders. "Not really the sort of thing you'd want to tell a whole bunch of people, especially if you don't know them all that well. It'd explain why he was in a bad enough mood to upset you, too."

"He wasn't in a ba—" replied Odette automatically before realising precisely what she was saying. There was a pause peppered by her stuttering before Robbie took her by the hand and pulled her over to sit down.

"You might be excellent at lying to other people," he said with a smirk, "but you're terrible at lying to me. What happened?"

It took Odette some time to reply, for she was now considering what had happened in the context of Henry's past with Morley. Had she taken advantage of him? The idea was abhorrent to her, but that didn't mean it was untrue. Some of the worst things that people did to one another were done entirely by accident. But *he* had kissed *her*. It had just … happened. Her mind tied itself in knots trying to work out whether it had been a good idea or not, and eventually she felt Robbie tap her on the arm to get her attention.

"I … he kissed me," she said almost inaudibly. "I'd run out to get some air because I was feeling so overwhelmed, and I told him that I had no idea how we were going to work out where Braddock's powers came from, that I couldn't just walk up to him and become his best friend. And Henry said that was a brilliant idea, and then it just sort of … happened."

Odette stared down at their hands, unable to look into Robbie's face. "Oh, Det," he said, stroking her disarrayed hair. "Did you want to?"

"What?"

Chuckling, Robbie asked again, "Did you want to kiss him?"

She felt her cheeks turn bright red, answered his question. "I think so," she said hesitantly. "I hadn't really been thinking about it; but standing there, I just … I really wanted to."

"Then stop worrying. You didn't do anything wrong, and you certainly should never be ashamed for wanting the things or the people you want."

"But what about Morley? I ... I don't know if I was taking advantage of Henry, or if he's now afraid of being hurt again, or ..."

"Look, you said yourself that you don't know what happened between them. Don't tie yourself in knots around something you don't know. If you're that worried about it, ask him. He's probably feeling as confused as you are. It'll be good for both of you."

This calmed Odette a little, and she nodded. "I'll ... I'll talk to him tomorrow."

But Odette did not talk to Henry the next day, nor the day after. Indeed, a whole week passed before she dared even to consider it, so wrapped up were they all in working secretly on their own plan whilst pretending to try and come up with another.

And so her fears remained latched in her mind, and grew all the stronger for being neglected.

18

Eight days and fourteen long hours after he'd kissed Odette, Henry was summoned to his father's office for a progress report. As he'd both expected and feared, Edward was present, punctual as ever, waiting outside the major general's office.

"Ah," said Edward, closing the book in his hands and pocketing it. "There you are, Henry. I'm interested to hear what you've been up to. This segregation we've gone in for is so very dreary; I'd hoped to see a good deal more of your lovely young mages."

His skin prickling with wariness, Henry raised his hand and knocked on the office door. "I apologise for not giving you more opportunity to torment me, Edward," he murmured. "How unfair of me."

The major general's voice boomed, and Henry immediately forged onwards before Edward could make another witty comment.

"Good morning, Father," he said, taking a seat opposite the desk. He was somewhat relieved to note that there was no whisky present at this hour of the day.

Edward took the seat across from Henry, nodding to his father. "Major General."

"Good, you're both here. Now, I called you here to give

me an update on your progress, but Edward," he gestured with a thrust of his hand, "has told me some disappointing things about how you've all been working. I would like to remind you both that we did not bring you all here so that you could continue working in isolation. You will get over whatever spat it is the two of you have had and behave like damned adults, and get your people working *together* like they're bloody well meant to be."

"But, Father—"

"That's an order, boy," snapped the major general with a glare. "Starting as soon as you leave this room."

"And what shall we be working on?" drawled Edward, a faint smirk of victory on his lips. "I've confirmed this week that my dear Peter is quite capable of the powers necessary for my proposal. It will require some training to be successful every time, but he has managed to do it with several different mages on at least three occasions; he simply needs to learn to sustain it. Yet I note that, as of yet, I'm the only person to come up with a plan. Perhaps Henry's not been quite as lucky."

"Well, boy? You've had your week. More than, in fact."

Henry lowered his gaze. He was adept at lying to his father, but lying to Edward had always proven far more difficult. The man had a tendency to see straight through him; or, on the rare occasions that he couldn't, to coax the truth out of Henry through other means. Keeping their own plan secret hinged on two things: that Edward and his people never uncovered their scheme, and that they managed to stall Edward's strategy and give Odette time to get to Braddock.

He'd worried at length over whether this was the right thing to do. Edward's proposal guaranteed death, but theirs stood to cause even more loss if it went wrong. But he had no hope at all of convincing them to allow him the chance, did he? Hesitation crept in, and Henry found himself saying something quite contrary to his original plan.

"I have," he said at length, looking up at his father. "Whilst I don't have a detailed proposal of my own, I'm concerned that Edward's won't work."

His father merely raised his bushy eyebrows, which Henry took as permission to continue.

"Edward, am I correct in saying that Peter's powers come in part from being adept at picking up many varied talents to a naturally high level of skill?"

"Indeed," smirked Edward, puffing himself up slightly as he leapt upon the opportunity to proclaim his superiority. "He is brilliant, truly brilliant – why, I daresay he only has to try something once to excel at it. A true polymath."

Henry nodded. "A rare gift indeed. How is it that this translates to a power, exactly? I know you've mentioned his ability to take down the powers of others. That's quite a jump from being gifted at picking up new skills."

"Not at all." Edward waved a hand idly. "He simply observes one of us at work with our power, and then exerts his own upon us. Physical contact is required, but I'm sure that can be arranged; Braddock does like his rallies, and I'm sure he'd be more than happy to shake hands with an adoring fan."

He flashed the major general a smile, as if to demonstrate quite how perfect his strategy was, but failed entirely to notice that Henry too was smiling.

"Just to be clear, then – you're saying that Peter must understand how a person's power works in order to interact with it."

Edward nodded. "Precisely, though the nature of his ability is that he's a quick study."

Henry turned to his father, who appeared to be on the cusp of telling him to hurry the hell up, and spread his hands before him. "I've not met Braddock," he said thoughtfully, "but I've read the reports. He is, by all accounts, a very closed-off, private person – one who gives no outward sign of being more than a young man, save for his words. I cannot help but feel that, even for one as gifted as Peter, it would be difficult indeed to learn Braddock's inner workings in a brief encounter. A great deal would be risked upon this, and it could so easily end in failure. Do you think he'd allow people close to him again after that?"

The fact that his father did not reply immediately gave Henry hope, and he settled back in his chair, allowing the thought to hang in the room. He'd be deviating from the plan, but he was sure Odette would not have faulted him for it – she was just as desperate to ensure that this ended with as little loss of life as possible. Out of the corner of his eye, he could see Edward examining him calculatedly. It unsettled him, as Edward's gaze always did, but he found himself increasingly less concerned about being found out. For a start, he'd not yet lied.

"A valid concern," his father said at length, drumming his fingers on the table. "Is it not, Professor Morley?"

"Peter is a very quick study." Edward smiled. "I'm confident in his abilities, even if Henry isn't."

The disdain that flashed across his father's face told Henry that he certainly did not appreciate being dismissed, even in so smooth a manner. It gave him hope – but only for a fleeting moment. For in the next, his father was shaking his head and sighing.

"But we don't have any choice. I see your point, boy, and it concerns me – as it should concern all of us. Unless you have an alternative solution, however, I see no option but to go forward with Professor Morley's plan."

Henry opened his mouth to reply, but a cool pressure on his right wrist took his attention. He turned to regard Edward with what he hoped was a level stare, but could well have been abject horror at being touched. With unnatural grace and poise, which to him was as normal as breathing, Edward smiled at Henry and tilted his head.

"I fear Henry has no such plan, Major General," he said coolly. "He has just as much to lose by risking his charges; I'm sure he'd not do so on a fool's errand, and certainly not unless he was sure of their capabilities. Would you, Henry?"

To his father, it might well have sounded like a perfectly reasonable remark. To Henry, Edward's words dripped like cold poison trickling through his body. He might as well have held a knife to Odette's throat; and to his, to Vivalda's, to all those in his care. If he challenged Edward – and Edward clearly knew that he could – then he'd lose everything. Unbidden, the memory of the meeting in the garden sprung back into his mind, and Henry felt his heart clench in fear.

"Indeed," he said softly. "I'm afraid that Miss Odette does not possess the powers that I had hoped; she is not skilled in quite the same manner as young Peter."

It wasn't quite a lie, for he was certain Odette's powers were far superior to Peter's. Edward's eyes, still locked with his, gleamed with victory – but he moved his hand away, and Henry let out a breath he'd not known he was holding.

Turning to his father, he continued, hoping that he could salvage something from the situation.

"Though I can offer no alternative, I'd beg you to consider that once Braddock's defences are down he is *apprehended*, not slaughtered. There's too much to be lost by his death – the knowledge of any other victims whom we've not yet found, for example."

"I suppose we could use him for our research," mused Edward, and Henry breathed an inward sigh of relief. "Though it would take longer for Peter to negate Braddock's powers long enough to incarcerate him."

"This boy is dangerous," cautioned Henry's father, though he was clearly considering the point. "My men will not hesitate to shoot him if it seems that others are in danger. Furthermore, if it delays our moving upon him ..."

"With respect, sir, there haven't been any more deaths reported for over a week," said Edward.

"Our intelligence tells us that Braddock's caught us on his tail," the major general replied. "He's lying low as far as we can see. Working on his 'revolution'."

"Then – whilst there are of course no guarantees, and the risk is great – would it not be prudent to take the extra time and be certain of victory? With longer to prepare, we'll be far more likely to succeed, our people more prepared."

Henry nodded at Morley. "We'll only get one shot at this," he pointed out, unsettled to find himself agreeing with Edward. "If we do it wrong, he'll never let anyone close to him again. We must be as prepared as we can, even if it risks more deaths. I don't like it – it's horrible – but we cannot fail. If we fail he'll simply become even more desperate, more hostile."

There was a long silence whilst the major general considered the options. It was, Henry thought, rather fortuitous that Edward's strategy for convincing his father had not been that different to his own for convincing them both. He appeared to be on Edward's side, even though he most certainly wasn't. He was certain that Edward's seeming to agree with the idea of keeping Braddock alive was only a ruse to make him appear more open to compromise.

Eventually, the major general sighed. "We go with Professor Morley's plan," he said gruffly. "You can have as long as you need to prepare. I'll have my people keep the pressure on Braddock, keep him underground for as long as possible. But if it looks like he's coming out of hiding, you'd best be ready to go." He turned to look at Henry. "And the moment his powers are down, my men will shoot. You're right, boy. We've got one shot at this – we can't risk failure by being yellow-bellied."

Henry felt himself tense. He'd known the chance of convincing his father to capture Braddock was a long shot, but had hoped … Still, it was a victory on all other counts. Edward appeared to believe him, and they'd been given the extra time they needed to prepare their own plan – he only wished that they'd not been ordered to work together. Segregation gave them the cover they needed to work on it. It would be all the harder with Morley and his people breathing down their necks.

"Dismissed," his father snapped, pulling Henry out of his thoughts and to his feet.

"Thank you, sir," he and Edward said in tandem, and left the office.

They paused in the corridor. Henry turned to look at

Edward. The man had a decidedly smug air about him, his smirk seemingly permanently etched onto his perfect visage. Rather oddly, this only left Henry feeling relieved. A smug Edward was an Edward who believed he'd won, and that was precisely what Henry wanted. He did his best to look resigned as they discussed what the next order of business would be.

Unsurprisingly, Edward had a number of demands regarding what he and Peter would require in order to get close to Braddock. Henry did his best to balance disagreement with consent; the more Edward wanted, the longer it would take them to prepare, which from Henry's point of view was a very useful thing. But he was walking a fine line with his lies, and if he didn't put up any resistance then Edward would surely become suspicious.

Eventually, with a list of preparations that looked similar to those that Henry had been formulating for his own strategy, they gathered their potentials together in the largest study available. It had taken a little while to collect everyone from their disparate work, and Henry was quite out of breath by the time he'd marched back and forth throughout the house, finding all of his company.

Edward, of course, was standing smugly in the study when Henry returned with the last of his charges – having had only four people to collect rather than seven. He shot Henry a conceited smile and gestured for everyone to sit.

"I'm pleased to announce that we're finally ready to begin the preparations for our assault upon the rogue mage," proclaimed Edward, spreading his hands wide. Inwardly, Henry winced at his choice of words. "It's been decided that we shall indeed use Peter's unique skills to bring down Braddock's defences and allow the army to take their shot."

Murmurs rippled through the potentials. "They'll kill him, sir?" asked Arnold the silversmith, looking a little uncomfortable. A small, malicious part of Henry couldn't help but be rather pleased that there was dissent within Edward's ranks.

"We'll only get one chance at this," explained Edward with unexpected gentleness. "I'm afraid we can't risk it being wasted. If they're able to apprehend him then they will, but I don't think it's right to hold out hope of that possibility." He glanced disdainfully towards Henry. "For that reason, the rest of us shall be assisting Peter in getting close to the mage through any means possible. The armour you've already been working on will help protect him, and I believe our craftspeople should be capable of creating many other useful tools that will shield and assist Peter."

Henry's eyes drifted over to the boy in question, who was sitting bolt upright in his chair. He looked terribly proud, but Henry thought he saw a tension in the young man's shoulders, despite his haughty air. Thankfully, he didn't seem to be looking at Edward with the telltale signs of someone enraptured by his powers – there were small mercies left in the world, it seemed – but there was no question that Edward had obviously been driving the young man very hard. Henry only hoped that he'd never treat Odette in such a way, deliberately or accidentally. Neither of them deserved the weight placed upon their shoulders.

"Henry and I have drawn up a list of items that can be made," Edward continued, flashing Henry an unsettlingly vivid smile. "We'd also like to take you into different groups for additional training. At the major general's request, we'll be mixing your groups much more frequently. You'll all take classes with myself, Henry and Vivalda at varying points as needed—"

"I beg your pardon?" said Vivalda.

Henry sighed. He loved Vivalda dearly, but she did have something of a penchant for picking unnecessary fights – and interrupting Edward was a sure way to start one.

"My apologies, my dear," smiled Edward, tilting his head. "I was under the impression that you were here to instruct the potentials. Perhaps your skills were overestimated."

A chilly disdain settled across Vivalda's features. "I merely wished to observe that at no point have I been consulted about any of this." She rounded first on Edward, but then turned to Henry, who ran his hand through his hair sheepishly. "Neither of you have seen fit to so much as ask me for my opinion. Am I to infer that it's worthless to you?"

"This is not a democracy," Edward stated, seeming entirely unflustered by Vivalda's cold fury. "If you have a problem with that, then I'm sure we can find someone else to teach the crafters."

With slow, deliberate steps, Vivalda approached Edward. Henry was amused to see that in her heeled boots she loomed a couple of inches above him in height. "I'll not forget this, Edward Morley," she hissed. "You can send my crafters to me once you're done strutting about the place."

Out of the corner of his eye, Henry could see one or two of the staff hiding amused grins behind their hands as Vivalda departed.

Once she was gone, Edward launched into an explanation of the plan – which by and large was to prepare everything necessary to get Peter close to Braddock safely and successfully. Henry only infrequently interrupted. Thankfully, Edward seemed far too full of his victory to take note of much, so Henry's lack of general disagreement went unobserved.

It took so much of the afternoon to go through the preparations – from armour for Peter to paintings from Isobel that would help them glean Braddock's whereabouts – that there was no time left in the day to actually begin putting things in motion. Eventually, as they wrapped up the mundane task of scheduling their progress, Edward and Henry collectively declared that they'd begin work the next day.

As people began to filter out of the room, Henry took the opportunity to murmur to each of his mages in turn that they should gather back in one of the studies after dinner.

Then he sought out Vivalda and asked her to run interference – make an appearance elsewhere so that no one questioned their absence.

He found he could barely concentrate on the meal, though it was pleasant enough, and hoped that Edward and his people hadn't noticed how jittery he was – though, he supposed, there was no reason for them to believe he was plotting a secret deviation from their orders. If anything, Edward would probably attribute it to his own charm. It was not a blessing Henry was often grateful for, but in this instance it offered him some small comfort.

Once he'd given up on picking at his food, Henry excused himself and made his way to the study. He was quickly joined by Matthew, who began to chatter excitedly about how fun sneaking about was, which did little to assuage Henry's fears. He supposed it was a bit much to hope that Matthew would suddenly become a master of stealth and silence. One by one, the others filtered in, until they were gathered around the fireplace together in various degrees of nervousness.

"Before we begin," Henry said, settling back in his chair, "you should know that you're by no means obliged to be here. What we're planning to do goes against the orders we've been given and, frankly, some of it would probably be considered illegal. So if you don't wish to put yourself at risk, I understand completely, and would only ask that you respect those who remain by keeping our plans secret. I'll not be offended if anyone chooses to leave now."

As he allowed them a moment to consider this, Henry observed the staff glancing amongst one another as if communicating by some silent means. His eyes flickered over to Odette, who though looked nervous was gently smiling at him with such encouragement that a knot formed in his throat. He was broken from his reverie by a laugh akin to a cackle, and he turned to see Mary and Abigail with their heads together and a mischievous gleam in their eyes.

"As if we'd let 'em make murderers of us," said Mary, smirking and waving a hand at Henry dismissively. "You carry on, m'lord. We ain't going nowhere."

"Well, then." Henry smiled and let out a breath he hadn't known he was holding. Not for the first time he found himself marvelling at how so many of his supposed peers would possibly consider these incredible people inferior – or, more embarrassingly, how he'd done so himself. "We should begin by working out how to get close enough to Braddock to learn the source of his power."

Roger in derision. "Begging your pardon, m'lord, but I don't see the army letting us do that."

"We'll just have to do it without them, then," said Robbie with a faint grin. "How long's it going to take, though? I mean, do you need one conversation with him? A dozen?"

Henry noticed that it took Odette longer than expected to realise that Robbie's question was addressed to her.

"Oh!" She looked sheepish and shuffled on the spot. "I don't know. I mean, it could be obvious straight away, or it could not. I don't know enough about him to even guess."

"We'll need to plan for all eventualities then." He flashed Odette what he hoped was an encouraging smile, but then faltered. "That could mean being on the move for some time, and if we've gone without my father's permission ..."

Robbie frowned. "I don't see that we have much of a choice, Professor. The decision's been made – anything we do at this point is going to look like we're refusing an order. And, well, if you're going to refuse an order then you ought to do it in a way that's actually going to work."

Agreement rippled through the women and men around him, but Henry could only stare in astonishment. Somehow, this had escalated far beyond his intentions.

"You're suggesting that we ... leave?" he asked hesitantly. Robbie nodded. "But surely none of you would ..."

The blank, stubborn stares Henry received were enough to put him off the rest of his sentence. Even Odette had her chin up, and was looking at him with piercing intent. He wondered how it was that he'd arrived at this moment – scheming with servants to go against the wishes of not only his father but the entire army.

"I can't say you're wrong – my father's opinion is difficult to change at the best of times. And here we have so little control, but if we were ahead of them ..." His voice was as soft as a whisper when he spoke again. "Anything we do is going to involve leaving. But what to do once we have?"

There was a silence as they digested this, punctuated only

by the occasional murmur from the servants. It was broken by Isobel, who shifted forward hesitantly in her seat to ask, "What if we offered to protect him for a little while?"

"Protect Braddock? From the army?"

Isobel nodded. "It would be much easier than chasing after him. And we're not going to get to know him at all if he's running away from us. He … he needs to believe that we want to help him, otherwise he won't let us."

Her phrasing, Henry thought, was particularly interesting. Did Isobel think that they *weren't* trying to help him? He supposed they weren't, really, though they were certainly taking a stance more in Braddock's favour, ultimately trying to capture him and prevent him from hurting anyone else. There was at once both a world of and very little difference between their intention and the army's – they were disobeying the orders given to them, but only so they could twist them.

This thought had clearly occurred to the others as well; it was Abigail who sat forward and voiced the fear. "What is it that we're actually trying to do?" she asked. "I know we want to stop him being killed. But what do we want to happen to him after?"

If the silence before was tense, the pause that followed her words was worse.

"We want people to stop dying," murmured Robbie, the sound resounding through the room despite how softly he'd spoken. "If he's really intent on killing people, that means he has to be locked up somewhere, doesn't it?"

There was a ripple of agreement as some nodded their heads. Henry noticed that Odette, rather than nodding, reached over and laced her fingers through Robbie's. It tugged strangely on the knot in his throat, and he immediately berated himself. If they were anything other than friends, he'd seen no sign of it, though they were clearly incredibly close – and more to the point, this was not the time to be acting like a jealous teenager.

"It's still better than what they're offerin' him," Mary pointed out, pulling Henry out of his confusion.

Matthew was frowning. "I don't think he'll want us going on the run with him though. I mean, if it were me, and I were trying to run away from everyone – assuming that's what he's doing. I know we all think it is, but he could have some evil master plan or something – I'm not sure I'd want a bunch of strangers tagging along for the ride even if I thought they were there to be nice to me."

"That's a good point," said Roger, nodding. "We need something he wants. Something he'll stop and listen to."

"Respite." Everyone turned their heads to look at Abigail, who'd broken off from her ever-present embroidery. "Isobel's right. He's been running for weeks now. There's nothing he'd want more than sanctuary, surely. He must be exhausted."

It was one thing to suggest having occasional meetings with Braddock, quite another to offer to keep him safe.

"No," Henry said with a heavy sigh. "We might want to stop them killing him, but that doesn't change what he's done. He's killed over a dozen people. He's dangerous, and I'll not take all of you into a situation where he has that much of an opportunity to hurt you."

"But what other choice do we have? We can't just let them kill him!" said Odette, her voice rising in pitch. Her knuckles went white as they gripped Robbie's hand. "We don't even know how he killed those people, or why."

"You don't kill over a dozen people by accident, Det."

She shot Robbie a glare that Henry was rather glad not to be on the receiving end of. "But you could do it in self-defence, couldn't you? How many people do you think a soldier serving in a war kills?"

"Ain't no war goin' on here."

"Isn't there? Professor Entwhistle told me that Braddock has been holding rallies about mages. He's been trying to teach people about us and our powers. Isn't that how the first people died, at a rally? The people who drowned came after that."

Odette was looking at him for support, and Henry was forced to nod. "Even the army agree that the first deaths were self-defence, actually. Several people jumped him whilst he was giving the speech and he fought back; being possessed of the powers that he is, he defeated them easily. They died later from their injuries."

"And the others?"

"Less clear," Henry continued, recalling the reports he and Vivalda had read back in Oxford. "There were those who tried to apprehend him and killed in the ensuing struggle. The remaining deaths occurred in places that Braddock was known to have been, with similar injuries to his other victims – but no eyewitnesses."

"Oh, no." Isobel sighed, wringing her hands together in her lap. "They didn't bring us here to catch a murderer, not really. They think they did, but ... but he's just been attacked. Over and over and over again. He's just trying to make people understand, and they keep treating him like an animal that needs putting down."

Henry shook his head, resolute. "The why doesn't matter. It doesn't make him any the less dangerous."

"But it does matter!" Matthew's protest was so heartfelt that he leapt out of his seat. "If I go out into a city now and get beaten up for some reason, and use my powers to fight back – would you say I was dangerous?"

" It's not the sa—"

"And what if it happened more than once? Does that make it different? What if, when people start realising I'm not like them, they attack me more and more? Does that make it different?" He walked across the room to stand before Henry and faltered. "M–M'lord."

With the gentle strength of someone used to command, Roger eased Matthew back into his seat. "It doesn't," the older man said gruffly. "He's right, Professor. The only question is whether we believe Braddock was defending himself. If we do, we've good reason to help. If we don't, well, we might as well stop all this and help the major general."

Henry wanted to be back in Oxford. He wanted to be home, in his study, with a cup of coffee and a book. Hell, he'd even take marking at this point; dozens of essays on logic would be far preferable to actually having to apply ethics to real life. He leant forward, his elbows on his knees, and rubbed at his face, not caring when strands of his hair fell free and tumbled into his eyes.

A soft pressure on his shoulder alerted him to Isobel's presence. "Forget about us for a moment," she said quietly, so that only he could hear. "What do you think, m'lord? Really think."

"I …" he began, habitually moving to answer at once, but then pausing as he saw Isobel's face. Her watery eyes were wide and full of empathy, and support that he wasn't entirely sure he deserved. They were all counting on him. If what she wanted was for him to answer honestly, then he could do that. He would do that. "I think that the world doesn't understand us. I think it would be too easy for us to become like him. Perhaps not in the same way. Perhaps not so extreme. But we could."

"You think he's just defending himself?" prompted Isobel. It was a leading question, but he didn't care.

He found himself nodding, realising his own mind only as he expressed it out loud. "I do. God help me, I do."

"So do I," Odette said softly, and in chorus with Abigail; then a moment later Robbie was agreeing, and Roger, and Mary, until all of them were in accord with Matthew's impassioned speech. The knot that Odette's smile had formed in his stomach tightened with their support, with their conviction, and with the reverent gravity that shone in all of their faces.

"Then," Henry said, reaching up to place his hand on Isobel's in thanks, "we'll find a way to get close to him, and I'll find a place where we can offer him sanctuary. And after that ... well, we'll work it out from there. We've no time for anything else."

They made no more plans that evening; instead they simply basked in the wake of a decision made.

It was less cathartic than he'd hoped.

19

Sound returned to Odette's world in waves, crashing over her mind with gentle laps that brought her to waking against her will. As the noises carried her into consciousness, she curled into a ball, as if to cocoon herself against the world. The day lay before her, but she was not yet ready to face it; no, she wanted to remain here and walk in dreams of a world where everything was an adventure and she was never small, or weak, or stupid. She wanted to twist her mind into great feats of storytelling and explore the many lives she'd never get to live.

She succeeded in opening her eyes once or twice, but this only caused her to recoil from the light and curl deeper into her duvet. The grogginess of sleep still surrounded her, and she longed to walk back into its embrace, back to the safety of her daydreams where she could control everything and nothing would go wrong unless it suited her. Odette did not know how long she spent stuck in this desperate state, trying both to cling to her safe space and to convince herself to get out of bed, for there were things to do.

It was not the first day she'd experienced so difficult a waking, but it had certainly been happening with more frequency and greater difficulty lately. Whenever she thought about it, Odette was filled with a terrible shame. There was after all absolutely nothing difficult about getting out of bed; countless people did it every day, and none of them had a problem with it. She was simply being contrary and disappointing. She'd not even told Robbie about it, so desperate was she to keep the others from knowing how bad it had gotten.

To her great relief, the sun had risen enough that the heat of it warmed her skin to unpleasant degrees even as she curled away from it. The scent of freshly cooked bread coiled into her nose, and hunger overtook her, her body betraying her. With reticence, she released her grip on the daydream she'd been having, and opened her eyes. It was still some time before she hauled herself out of bed, but she'd at least accepted the inevitability of getting up, which was a far greater hurdle than she could make sense of.

Dressing in a pleasingly soft suit of sable grey that Abigail had sewn for her – these days, it seemed she was wearing a new outfit every week thanks to all the practice Abigail had been doing – Odette tamed her hair into a side plait and made her way down to breakfast. As she walked, the reality of the day that lay ahead of her began to sink in: she had a class with Morley first thing, to which she was most certainly not looking forward.

The man unsettled her, due largely, she knew, to whatever history he had with Henry. The two of them together oozed an awkwardness and tension that permeated everything around them. But that didn't help her push down the discomfort she felt from simply being around him. Still, it couldn't be helped. She'd have to work with him as part of their deception, she knew. Odette only hoped that she could lie well enough to be convincing.

The potentials with crafting powers were with Vivalda again, leaving the others to attend Morley's class. Odette was joined by Roger, Matthew, Isobel, Lewis and Peter. She was interested to note Isobel and Lewis's presence, since their powers involved making things. The only reason she could think of was that their powers did not make physical magical objects, but instead influenced what they touched – Isobel painting the future, and from what she'd heard of Lewis's power, it was a mixture of Roger and Vivalda's. He was wonderful with both farm animals and plants, just as they were with wild animals and machines.

They'd just begun to awkwardly reintroduce themselves to one another when Morley strode into the room. He seemed unnaturally graceful, as if he simply glided from one place to another, and when he smiled in greeting he lit up the room so brilliantly that everyone stared. Odette felt a gentle tugging at the base of her throat, like the deep throb of anticipation she felt before a dinner service or, her mind thought guiltily, whenever Henry locked eyes with her.

"Wonderful," Morley announced, leaning casually against one of the tables. "Wonderful that we're all together at last – we actives, that is."

"Actives, Professor?" asked Matthew, perched on the edge of his seat as if prepared to launch into a longer question. Odette was rather glad when he didn't.

A faint smile tugged at Morley's lips. "Ah." He sighed. "I see dear Henry has been remiss in his instruction. An active, my dear, is one whose powers do something in the moment; such as your climbing skill, or darling Henry's singing. Another type of mage is a crafter; those whose powers create something, or imbue an object with great power."

"Like Robbie, Mary and Abigail do," Matthew said, his enthusiasm for all things not dampened by Morley's slimy demeanour.

"Indeed."

Despite herself, Odette couldn't help but ask, "Are there other types of mage?"

The professor's smile turned into a smirk, and he took an almost predatory step towards Odette. She wondered, distantly, if the others could see just how constantly he stalked those he perceived as his prey.

"An excellent question, and one to which we don't yet know the answer. You see, there are some whose powers straddle both fields." He paused to reach a hand towards Isobel, who absentmindedly took it. In alarm, Odette realised that there was a glazed look in the young woman's eyes – and those of the others. "Some argue that they should be given a category unto themselves. Others feel they should be placed with one or the other."

Languidly, he released Isobel from his grip and drifted back to the centre of the room. That no one protested was, Odette thought, even more telling than their glazed looks. But she was fine. Of course, his power didn't work on her. Realising that her safety depended on not standing out, she did her best to outwardly mirror the others, whilst inwardly imagining that her glowing golden form was covered in a protective net that would repel even the strongest of Morley's assaults.

Clearly feeling that he now had a captive audience, Morley launched into an explanation of magical theory that Odette might have found fascinating had it been given by anyone else. Instead she could only half focus on it, so determined was she not to come under the sway of his power, and much of the detail escaped her.

He explained that magic as they knew it now had always existed, disguised as miracles or freak accidents. This was not news to them, of course – but Morley provided them with several examples throughout history of people who'd been proven to have magical powers, and the impact they could have on the world. He even spoke of a time in the medieval era when magic had in fact been known about by all … and the consequences that had fallen upon mages when the non-magical turned upon them. After that, magic had all but died out, until recently.

Even focused as she was on ignoring the silky-smooth timbre of his voice, and the fact that it made liquid heat trickle through her body – she was free of his dominion, but not his intoxication – Odette couldn't help but admit to herself that Morley was a very good teacher. He had a passion for his subject that was undeniable, and combined with his powers it made his lecturing a transfixing method of teaching.

"Interesting as this is, Professor, and with all due respect," interjected Roger, who seemed less affected by Morley's power than others, "is it really applicable to our present situation?"

"Why, very much so," replied Morley without a hint of discomfort. "After all, our success" – he turned a brilliant smile upon Peter, who swelled with pride – "depends upon our understanding of the murderer. And how can we understand him without understanding ourselves?"

Odette thought it strange that he could be so very correct and so very wrong all at once. Understanding magic, and themselves, would clearly offer some assistance – but only to an extent. It was like understanding the air around you and thinking that meant you understood the whole sky. The history of magic could have absolutely no bearing on Braddock at all; he might not even be aware of it.

Her disagreement clearly registered on her face – Morley zoned in on her again, sensing weakness, and flashed her a smile so discomfiting that she had to tighten her grip on her powers to keep from succumbing. But she was not touching him, and so as he put his full focus on her she found the net around her faltering – she couldn't help but let her thoughts spill from her lips as he probed her with his gaze. It was not the way she'd wanted to learn more of the limitations of her power.

"Does Braddock know this – all of the things you've been speaking of? It's just that they might not be relevant to him. He might have no idea, and all of the things weighing upon him could be entirely unrelated."

To her astonishment, Morley took one knee before her, resting his arms on the other. "My darling Odette," he replied silkily, "such a wit you've been bestowed with. Is she not quite the academic, dearest one?"

"Certainly, Professor," answered Peter so swiftly that it made Odette jump in her seat. "I'm very grateful for her insight."

Gritting her teeth, Odette pointed out, "You haven't answered my question, Professor."

"Oh?" Morley clutched a hand to his chest as if in astonishment. Others seemed to buy the gesture, for they laughed, and he got back to his feet. "Why, indeed I have not. And with good reason; your point is a fine one, and it leads me to what I truly wished to speak of today: motivation."

"Motivation, m'lord?"

"Indeed." With a flourish, he turned to Lewis. "My dear, how is it that you came to realise your powers?"

There was an awkward silence for a moment as all eyes turned to the farmer, and leaving Morley for the first time since the class had begun. Adjusting his tie nervously, Lewis composed himself before replying. His cheeks were permanently ruddy, but seemed to have flared all the brighter at the sudden attention, and with something more than just embarrassment.

"Well, it's like you said, m'lord. I weren't all that motivated t' do it afore me da went. An' even less before me brother did. Once I were the only one left, there weren't much of a choice aboot it."

His accent, which was unfamiliar to Odette, was so broad that she had to concentrate to process what he'd said. When she understood, she couldn't help but offer a baleful stare at Morley, who'd clearly known precisely what he was asking the man to admit in front of a room full of strangers. Thankfully the professor took no notice of her glare.

"You were spurred on by their deaths, then?" he prompted with all the gentleness of a hungry feline.

Lewis shook his head, and rubbed at the whiskery hair on the side of his cheek. "No, it were more – I en't never been *pushed* afore that. Wi' me da and Simon aboot, I were always the one tagging along. Wi'out them, it were just me. Ain't got nowhere to hide like tha'."

Odette sensed that it wasn't quite the answer Morley had wanted – as if he felt that a tale of sadness and woe would've been far more encouraging than the simple necessity of Lewis's story – but it was nonetheless effective. The glazed expressions throughout the room turned thoughtful, as each person began to consider what had pushed their powers to the fore. Most of them, Odette knew, were thinking of only a few weeks ago – she certainly was. Before then, they'd never really noticed their powers, since most of them had manifested simply as being good at their jobs. It was hardly the poetic tale of blossoming that Morley was looking for.

It was of little surprise to her then when he turned elsewhere for support – Matthew was his first target, but the young man's impassioned launch into how he realised now that he'd always had his powers but had not understood what they were was not what Morley was looking for. Nor was Peter's saccharin speech about how he owed all of his talents to the professor himself. Then, turning, he locked his eyes upon Odette, and she shivered from head to toe.

Ashamed relief flooded through her as Morley's gaze continued moving, settling on Roger. "And yourself?" he asked, silky smooth.

Decades of service had taught Roger to hide his emotions well. That was what made the flicker of fear and pain that flashed across his face all the more terrifying; Odette could practically feel Morley's magic pressing through the air on the normally composed man. And though Roger managed to conceal the discomfort on his face quickly, she could see that it echoed in the tension that ran up his spine.

"I was a stable boy in my youth, Professor," he replied in what Odette thought was an exceedingly polite tone given the circumstances. She wondered if Roger, under the full influence of Morley's powers, realised how inappropriate his probing was. "Always had an affinity for animals, I suppose. Even married the stable master."

The glint in Morley's eye suggested he knew he was onto something, and Odette didn't like it one bit.

"And how did your powers come about? Were they always there, like dear Matthew's?"

"No, no. I was an awful stable boy," said Roger, laughing as the power washing over him shifted, putting him more at ease. "It wasn't until my Sophia died that I really got the knack."

Triumphantly, Morley said, "Ah! So your powers were brought on by your wife's death. And what was your motivation? To cling to something of her?"

Disgust wrapped its slimy tendrils around Odette's throat, rendering her speechless in the face of Morley's questions. She put all her focus into hiding it, determined not to give herself away, and glanced either side of her. No one else looked as she felt; they were all listening intently, as if Morley were simply making a salient and interesting point on a relevant topic. Even Roger barely flinched, just nodding his head in agreement instead.

"I suppose that may have been my motivation, Professor. Though I wouldn't say it was what I was thinking."

The tension in the air lifted ever so slightly as Morley nodded and returned his attention to the room at large.

"Indeed!" he crowed, a grin that had no right to be as attractive as it was unfurling across his face. "Though we may not consciously think of these things, they *are* our motivations. But why do I mention this?"

Realising belatedly that this last question wasn't rhetorical, but was in fact directed at her, Odette sat up straighter in her seat. "Because it isn't a question of whether something weighs upon Braddock to motivate him – something must do, even if it's unconscious. It's just a question of what."

"Precisely." Morley was clearly taking her sluggish reply as proof that his powers were working, because his eyes flashed with that same triumph. "And motivation, my dear young lady, is the key to understanding how our powers work."

Odette couldn't help but wonder what Morley's motivation was. Did he think so little of himself that he felt it necessary to manipulate people into catering to his whims? Or was it the opposite? A genuine, deep-seated belief that he was better than everyone, and that the world was there to cater to do his bidding. She wasn't certain which option was more comforting than the other.

He was still scrutinising her, so she curled her lips into a smile and gushed, "Oh, I see."

It must have been enough, for Morley turned back to the rest of the class and spent the remainder of the session talking about how they could manipulate their own motivations and increase the strength of their powers. His own power did not let up on them throughout, even when he ceased to focus on them individually, and by the end of it Odette was exhausted – both from keeping his powers from working on her, and pretending that she was just as affected as everyone else.

Eventually, the class was over, and she was free.

Still, Odette could almost feel the silky-smooth timbre of Morley's voice sliding down her spine as she walked through the corridors. She shuddered, trying to throw the memory away, but it still echoed within her mind. And though she'd managed to keep much of his power from working on her, the attention required meant that she was all too aware of its touch upon her – even when he was speaking to the group. Though she was relieved to be out of the room, she couldn't shake the anger at being treated like a toy, and as these thoughts swirled in her mind she realised that she was unconsciously walking herself to the study Henry was using.

Unconscious motivation. What was hers?

She'd rapped gently on the door before she could stop herself, and pushing down the feelings that were choking her, she entered the study. Henry was seated at the desk, reading, and smiled up at her.

"Odette, I wasn't expec—" He examined her closely. "You're shaking."

As he stood and came over to her, Odette looked down at her hands with confusion, as if they were not her own. Indeed, they were trembling considerably, even when she clutched them together and tried to will them to calm. Henry's warm fingers closed over hers in a gentle gesture of support.

"Whatever's the matter?" he asked, and though she seemed to be made of terror Odette lifted her gaze to lock with his. The corners of his eyes were pinched with concern, and his lips were slightly parted. She was suddenly overcome with an intense anger, which bubbled up in so fiercely her that it made her start. The concern in Henry's expression deepened, but just as he began to ask again if she was all right, Odette found herself finally asking the question that had been churning in her stomach for so long.

"What did Morley do to you?"

The question hung in the air between them in a thick, tense silence. Henry released Odette's hands and became completely still. He stared at her, an unreadable expression clouding his features.

Odette stepped away, lowering her head ever so slightly in

shame; she'd hoped to word the question far more gently, but the anger running through her was too much to bear. She wanted to explain herself, to tell him why she needed so badly to know the answer, to excuse her demand to know something so private – but with some effort, she stopped herself and allowed Henry to answer in his own time if he so wished.

"I was very young when we met," he began softly. "Not just in age, but in maturity. Edward was … magnificent. He would walk into a room and people would stare at him, but he never seemed to exert himself to make that happen. I wanted him from the moment I saw him. Everyone did."

The knot in Odette's throat tightened. She'd wanted so very much not to be right. She'd wanted so dearly for there to be some other wrong between the two men; not out of jealousy, but because the scars left by love cut far deeper than most.

Henry turned away from her and sat on the nearby sofa, and with only a little hesitation Odette joined him.

"I was too scared to go near him, of course. But one day he came and found me. I thought my heart had stopped, so perfect was he. Before I knew it, he was everything, and I was … well, I was just holding onto his coat-tails." His face bore an expression of wistfulness and pain, and for a moment Odette almost wished she hadn't asked. "And somewhere along the way, I realised what he was doing, how he was manipulating me, using me. I realised that he wasn't the person I'd thought he was, not anymore; and perhaps he never had been. There wasn't any big event; he didn't beat me or anything of the sort. But once I'd realised, he sunk his claws in. He wouldn't let me go."

The desire to give him space warred with Odette's need to comfort Henry. He looked so tired, as if the story were one he'd told many times before and would tell many times again – without it ever becoming easier to explain.

"Eventually he had to go back to Cambridge, and I to Oxford, as our departments became real things for which we were responsible. The distance extricated me from his clutches." He shook his head. "I make more of it than I should. He never raised a hand to me, and he didn't destroy my life."

Odette felt a fresh lance of pain through her heart. "Never," she said with feeling, "never belittle how you felt. You can't compare one form of abuse to another, Henry. It doesn't work like that. He hurt you. He hurt you, and nothing excuses that."

The terrible silence hung between them again, and Odette pulled away from him as if ashamed. How had she come to this place, where she'd demand things of those born higher than her? She believed every word she'd said to him, of course, but that didn't make up for it. She'd behaved terribly, and there was certainly no reason for him to—

"I suppose," Henry said, cutting into Odette's harried thoughts. The sound of his voice was like a wash of calm slicing through the storm, and it pulled her eyes back to his. They were glassy with pain, but seemed somehow empty.

"What worse thing is there in this world," she said softly, "than taking away someone's free will? Nothing. And though it takes many forms – from killing a person to forcing them into doing something they would rather not – it's all the same in a way. Did you love him by choice?"

"At first. I mean, as much as anyone loves by choice. He didn't need to use his powers on me then; I was too besotted.

But somewhere along the way he did, and then when I started to suspect ...”

Odette sighed. “He used them to keep you with him.”

“Yes.” Henry looked down at his hands. His shoulders were hunched, as if he were a turtle trying to coil into its shell, either to shield himself from the world or hide from it. “Yes, he did.”

“I don’t think anything can excuse that, Henry. Not even that he loved you; people can do foolish things for love, but there’s a world of difference between foolish and terrible.” Moving slowly so as not to startle him, Odette reached out and wrapped her hands around his. Both were trembling. “Thank you for telling me. I’m ... I’m sorry I didn’t ask you in a kinder way.”

“I can’t help but feel,” Henry said after a moment, twining his fingers with hers, “that this must seem rather anticlimactic for you.”

Blinking in confusion, Odette shook her head. “I know that sometimes when you live with a feeling, the only way to cope with it is to make it smaller, to pretend it isn’t as big a problem. But, Henry, a horrible, traumatic thing happened to you. You may not think it’s that important, but he hurt you terribly. It’s all right to say that. It doesn’t mean you’ve let him win.”

As she lifted her head Odette realised, in a flurry of panic, that Henry was crying, but when she began to utter apologies, he reached up and brushed the pad of his thumb across her lips, silencing her. She felt tears welling in her own eyes, reflecting his, and realised that she had no idea if she’d said the right thing. What if she’d made it worse? But Henry trailed his thumb up along her cheekbone and tucked a stray lock of hair behind her ear.

"Ditty," he whispered in a honeyed voice, "I worry at what you must've endured to make you so wise. Sometimes I fear wisdom only comes from pain."

The statement made something deep within her hurt – the part that worried she was a bother, that she was demanding the attention of others with her weaknesses, that she'd dreamt up the whole notion of her fits and her worries simply to make her seem different or special. And yet, somehow, she found she couldn't answer with anything but the truth; as if a real, honest answer were being pulled from her and she could do nothing to stop it.

"There are days when I think it would be better if it had."

Henry frowned. "What do you mean?"

"Nothing bad happened to me, Henry. I was never mistreated – I have a wonderful family and I work for people who are truly, honestly good. I've always been loved and cared for, and given every opportunity – more opportunities than many people get." She paused, looking down at her hands, wondering if she was inventing their trembling. "And yet I'm ... like this. I wish something bad had happened, because then I'd have an explanation. Otherwise I have nothing but ... but bad luck. Ill fortune. The displeasure of some divine being."

Flustered, Odette ducked her head, feeling foolish tears trailing down her cheeks. "But even if it had," she said with a sigh, her voice shaking, "I would only pretend it was nothing, wouldn't I? Our hearts are only so big, but life can make them hold the whole sea."

She felt Henry gather her into his arms with slow, gentle movements, cradling her against him as if she were made of glass – or perhaps as if he were. One of his hands coiled about her waist, the other tangled in her hair, and Odette sighed as the last of her tears fell against his waistcoat. The anger that had brought her into the room coiled into a tight ball and nestled in her abdomen, and though she longed to hurl it at the person who'd hurt Henry so deeply, she forced herself to turn away from it. Instead she focused on the compassion blooming in her heart; anger would do nothing but give Morley attention he did not deserve, and the only person that deserved her focus right now was Henry.

She did her best not to listen to the voices in her mind that told her to flee.

20

The next day, Henry's class consisted of a mixture of crafters and actives; it was their turn to help test Peter's powers. Odette was present, though she wasn't practising quite as much – it would be too obvious that her powers were identical to Peter's if she did. Instead, Henry had set her to watching Peter, to see if his powers were indeed stymied by his inability to empathise

But there was little need to have enlisted her help, as it was apparent early on that Peter was struggling. Unlike Odette, he had some skill at painting, and so was able to engage with Isobel's skill; but he was so highly strung and impatient that it was impossible for him to adapt to Abigail's serene, almost meditative sewing – he could do nothing to her powers at all. And when he realised this, he only became all the more agitated.

It was a little difficult for Henry not to flash his people a small, hopeful smile. A few responded in kind: Abigail kept glancing at him with twinkling understanding, and once or twice he caught Isobel humming. Luckily, Peter was either far too engrossed in his frustration to notice their surreptitious interactions or passed them off as magic–inducing ritual, and by and large everything passed without incident.

As the class wound down and his students trailed out of

the study, Henry finally allowed himself to collapse into a chair and contemplate when it was that he'd last had a full night's sleep. Such a conundrum was it that he entirely failed to notice he was not alone in the room a throat cleared softly near him.

Jumping in his seat, Henry lifted his head to behold Robbie looking a little sheepish for having startled him. "Sorry, Professor," he said apologetically. "I was wondering if I could speak to you about something."

"Of course. Have a seat. What can I do for you?" As he regained some of his composure, Henry noticed with curiosity that Robbie seemed uncomfortable.

"Well, sir, it's like this – and I don't mean any disrespect by it, you should know," Robbie added quickly, wriggling in his seat. "Look, I'm afraid I'm going to be all stereotypical here and give you the talk."

Cocking an eyebrow, Henry remarked, "I believe my own father already subjected me to 'the talk' many years ago, Robbie, and I've not yet recovered from the embarrassment."

"Oh, gods," said Robbie with a cough, and turning beet red. "I don't mean *that* talk."

Henry's lips coiled into a wry grin, though he felt ever so slightly bad for teasing the younger man.

"I mean the 'hurt my friend and you'll have me to answer to' talk."

Now it was Henry's turn to blush. He opened his mouth to reply, but only succeeded in stammering several half-formed beginnings to sentences before Robbie waved a hand to quiet him.

"Look, just ... let me get this out, all right? I don't know all of what's going on with you two, nor is it my place to, but

Det's my best friend and I know what she's like, and ..." He sighed and pinched the bridge of his nose. "She's special, Professor. She doesn't do things by halves; it's part of who she is. But that means she – she opens herself up to things a lot more than most people. It leaves her vulnerable to being hurt."

"Robbie, I'm not going to—"

"I know you're not. I know that. You're clearly not a bad person. But just because you don't intend to do something doesn't mean you won't do it."

At that, Henry paused. It was certainly true. "To be honest," he said after a moment, "I'm not certain I understand how I feel about her yet."

Robbie frowned. "That's exactly what I mean. You're thinking one way and acting another, and that's what hurts people."

"I beg your pardon?"

"Well, if you don't have any feelings for her, why did you kiss her?" snapped Robbie, though he seemed immediately to regret losing his temper.

Henry couldn't fault him, though – it was a perfectly valid question, and one that he'd been struggling to answer since it had happened. "Because he'd wanted to" seemed so silly a reason, but he'd been unable to come up with anything better. "Because he'd simply gotten carried away" didn't do justice to the fact that he had in that moment – and several moments since – wanted very much to kiss her.

"Confusion is how people get hurt," Robbie said, sighing softly and pulling Henry out of his thoughts. "Yourself included, Professor. I'm not suggesting you walk over there right now and tell her how you feel – just that you do right by the both of you and work it out before anyone gets hurt."

Chuckling softly, Henry said, "I hope you didn't develop all this wisdom through painful lessons."

This drew a comfortable laugh from Robbie, who shook his head. "No, sir. I've always preferred to watch other people learn them for me."

"Call me Henry."

Robbie smirked. "I can certainly try to, but it's a sticky habit."

Henry smiled. Odette had said almost precisely the same thing.

21

Robbie's warnings lodged in Henry's mind and took root in the days that followed – but if anything, they simply made him *more* worried about getting something wrong, and certainly more aware of how conflicted his feelings were. The fact was that Henry had never been terribly good at relationships. He'd had a few since Edward, but he'd fallen into them somewhat accidentally. Much, if he was honest, as things seemed to be happening with Odette. And those relationships had either drifted or ended with someone getting hurt.

Really, it was a wonder anyone bothered risking relationships at all.

That they had work to do kept Henry from overly succumbing to his inner monologues. Now that they'd seen Peter's powers in action, and the difficulties he had with linking to others, Henry felt it was all the more necessary that they ensure Odette didn't suffer the same problem. Though he knew she'd hate to consider it, she was what would keep them safe from Braddock – because as genuinely as he believed that Braddock had been forced into this position and was defending himself, there was still no denying that he was capable of hurting them very badly.

And the only thing that could stand between that and them

was Odette's power.

Of course, now he needed to tell her his thoughts – if not all of them, at least that they needed to step up her practice regime. Which meant finding her. And if he knew her at all, she'd be holed up in the library with a book. His heels clicked on the floor as he made his way there, alternatively dragging his feet and skipping down the corridor. They hadn't been alone in the same place for some time. It was mostly by chance, but the absence left Henry with a flutter of panic in his gut.

He passed one of the living rooms, which spilled light and laughter out into the corridor; Vivalda was holding court on some tale of their student days, and her audience of both mages and soldiers were falling about themselves with mirth. Grinning despite his nerves, Henry lingered only a moment before rounding the corner to the library.

Odette was there, just as he'd suspected, so engrossed in her book that she'd completely failed to notice his appearance at the door. He opened his mouth to greet her, then paused. The firelight flickered on her face, lending it an otherworldly glow; stray curls that had sprung from behind her ears danced patterns on her cheeks. Not for the first time, Henry was struck by how beautiful she was. What a foolish idea it had been to think that she'd wish to be stuck with a wonky-nosed old academic. She was what? Nine years younger than him? Eight?

What, he thought with a stab of panic, if she didn't truly have feelings for him at all? What if she was simply getting caught up in everything, and reaching for him because she felt she ought to, or because she was confused? Gods. If he were there for any other reason, he'd have abandoned the library and returned to his room – but that would only postpone the inevitable. He'd still need to talk to her in the morning.

"Good, ah," he stumbled, clearing his throat. "Good evening."

If her face had been radiant before, the smile that lit it up when Odette looked at him was seraphic. "Hello."

He took a step into the room, rubbing his hands together as if trying to warm them – but really to channel some of his nervous energy away. "Do you mind if I interrupt you for a moment?"

"Not at all," Odette replied with the same awkward level of politeness, brow furrowing slightly in confusion. "Is everything all right?"

"Oh yes, yes of course." He sat down in the chair opposite her and ran a hand over his hair, attempting to smooth it back into place. "I just had a thought about your powers that I wanted to go through with you."

"Ahh," she said, understanding, then quirked her mouth into a sly grin. "For a moment I thought you might be here to talk about Robbie."

"Robbie?"

The raised pitch of his voice had certainly not escaped her. "I might have a best friend who's very protective of me, but I also have a best friend who's awful at lying to me. I don't know precisely what you talked about, but I do know that he … how did he put it? Had a talk with you. Which, to be honest, tells me everything I need to know."

"Oh."

Odette turned the corner of the page, placed the book aside and leant forward in her seat, resting her forearms on her crossed legs. "Henry," she said softly, "it's all right. You haven't done anything wrong. Now, what were you here to tell me?"

Despite himself, Henry chuckled. He wondered if Odette had any idea just how much she'd sounded like his cousin – her mistress – in that particular moment. Still, it soothed him in a way his own words could not, and he did his best to relax into the chair.

"I think that as well as preparing for our journey we need to ensure that you have as much control over your powers as possible. We need you to be better than Peter."

"We do?"

Odette had said that Robbie couldn't lie to her. Henry hoped he could. "Well, our numbers will be greatly reduced. We may need to defend ourselves, and in such an instance your ability to bolster our powers will be invaluable. Together you and I could send crowds to sleep; you and Roger could charm a forest full of animals; you could speed Abigail's sewing or Robbie's whittling to a supernatural pace."

When Odette's face lit up with pleasure, Henry did his best not to reveal his relief. Part of him felt terrible for manipulating her – for taking her into a situation where she might have to do something terrible – but he really did believe it was worth the risk.

Otherwise, he thought to himself, he wouldn't be taking any of them anywhere near Braddock.

"I've not been good at sustaining bolstering for terribly long." Odette sighed, her brow knitting in thought. "We should practise that."

"I think it would also help to practise dampening." Before she could protest, Henry raised a hand. "In my experience, those whose powers are multifaceted find that their skill with one facet plateaus if they don't also practise the others. When Vivalda and I were students, she spent hours working on fixing machines but was terrible at spending time studying the design side. Eventually she became stuck, until she was convinced to refocus."

Nodding, Odette said, "It makes sense. One helps you understand the other better."

Henry smiled. That had been easier than he'd feared – but, then, it should come as no surprise to find reality less terrible than all the things one could imagine, given free rein to fret.

"Then we have a plan. We'll need to do the dampening part in secret, of course, but there's no reason to hide that you're practising more with bolstering powers; indeed, my father and his people will likely be pleased to hear it. Shall we start now?"

22

Following Henry's suggestion, Odette had practiced bolstering the other mages' powers for longer. With Isobel, she still suffered a terrible block, but Abigail had managed to sew an entire waistcoat for Roger in a fraction of the normal time with Odette's help. The success of it left Odette buoyed with happiness and accomplishment for much of the day, and seemed to mark the last bit of mending needed on her relationship with Abigail.

But she couldn't practise her dampening powers in front of everyone. Her passive ability to break, or fail to make use of, the crafters' work was still in effect – and took some work to conceal. There'd been one or two close calls when Mary had brought food for everyone and Odette had been forced to watch others eat first to work out what emotion she was meant to perform . If nothing else, the whole experience had made her into something of a versatile actress.

So, once everyone had eaten dinner and retired for the evening or taken up more relaxing pursuits, Odette, Vivalda and Robbie stole into a secluded classroom. Vivalda had brought several of what she called her test machines – small but intricate clockwork creations with little function save to be practised upon. Meanwhile, Robbie had a selection of half-finished works that they could use.

"Now, darling," gushed Vivalda as she gathered them about the central table, "what I'd like to test today is whether you can block our powers whilst we're using them, rather than simply destroying our wonderful creations."

Coughing guiltily, Odette nodded. "I've never really tried this before."

"Which is precisely why we're here."

Patting her gently on the arm, Vivalda took a seat on the stool next to her. She picked up a thin screwdriver and gestured towards a complicated piece of clockwork. "I'm going to attempt to work on this little trinket here, channelling my powers to do so. I'll be using meditation techniques much like those I know Henry has taught. I'd like you to stop me."

"All right," Odette said, glancing over at Robbie. He gave her a supportive smile, and she reached to place her hand on Vivalda's shoulder, not wanting to physically get in the way of her work. Initially she simply watched, transfixed as the engineer began to tinker. Vivalda's skill was truly something else; she worked with the miniature metal parts as dexterously as a painter or a sculptor might, more art than science.

As Vivalda worked, Odette noticed that she swayed ever so slightly, and muttered under her breath. Odette closed her eyes to block out the rest of the room, trying to focus on what Vivalda was saying. The words were largely foreign to her; not literally, but in the manner of listening to someone talk about a highly technical subject of which one has absolutely no knowledge. The words were plosive and sibilant in equal measure – almost musical in their rhythm, like a chant.

This must be her form of meditation, Odette concluded;

and no sooner had she thought it than in her mind's eye Vivalda's shining golden figure appeared. Odette looked over at the woman's hands, gleaming with a radiant glow, like flares crackling around the sun. It was so beautiful that she let out a soft laugh, and saw the crafter look over towards her for a moment before returning to her work.

Unlike Henry's power, which was a pouring forth of golden light, Vivalda's was a weaving of it. The flares that danced about her hands knotted themselves into the machine beneath, and it was this that Odette was drawn to. She looked up at her own golden hand, resting on Vivalda's shoulder, and began to imagine that she was Rumpelstiltskin, spinning threads of gold into the older woman's power.

At first this served to give Vivalda *more* power; she began to work faster and faster, but this wasn't wholly unexpected. Odette remembered what Henry had said – that if she honed each side of her power equally, she'd better understand both.

Only once she'd become used to working with Vivalda's power did she try to unravel it. Rather than weaving, she unwove; rather than knotting, she untied; rather than pushing, she pulled – and bit by bit she began to slow Vivalda's movements, until they stilled entirely.

"Oh." The engineer sighed, astonished. "Do you know, I've quite forgotten what I was doing."

Laughter spilled from Odette's lips as she opened her eyes, returning to the real world. "It worked then?"

"I should say so." Quite contrary to looking dismayed at having briefly lost her own powers, Vivalda was alight with pride. "Though for a moment there, darling, I thought you were doing the opposite."

Robbie nodded. "She definitely was – you sped up at the

beginning.”

“It's all to do with what Henry told me,” Odette explained, ignoring Robbie's raised eyebrow. “In order to understand one side of my power, I need to understand the other. I didn't really know how to interact with your power, so I figured that if I learnt to bolster it first I'd learn how to pick it apart later. Just like learning to dampen will help me get better at bolstering, but in reverse, and quicker.”

“Marvellous!” chimed Vivalda, clapping her hands together. “But quite problematic.”

“A little, yes. It'd be awkward to want to do one thing but then achieve the opposite. Even just bolstering someone for a moment can make a big difference.”

Nodding in agreement, Vivalda hummed under her breath, clearly pondering the problem. Across from her, Robbie had picked up one of his half-finished carvings and begun absentmindedly to work on it. This caught the attention of the women across from him, who both let out small gasps of inspiration at precisely the same time.

“Darling, what if you – oh, do go first.”

Odette blushed. “No, please. Go ahead.”

“You utilise your power using visualisation, do you not? Would it be possible for you to visualise it *before* you made contact with the person?”

“So that I could think about bolstering their powers without actually doing it? Yes, that's exactly what I was going to say! Only ...” Odette frowned. “That rather relies on my powers working when it's just me, if you see what I mean.”

“Well, it does,” Robbie pointed out, holding up his carving by way of illustration. “You break things on your own, don't you?”

That was certainly true. As Robbie continued to whittle, Odette tilted her head in thought. His power was different still from both Vivalda and Henry's – where they wove and pushed, Robbie folded. He plucked golden light from the earth and the air around him, and pulled it into the carving beneath his knife. Watching him, Odette realised that she hadn't closed her eyes whilst visualising – she was imagining the golden light around the real Robbie in front of her.

Could she, then, do as Vivalda had suggested?

She looked down at her hands, and allowed herself to forget how normal they looked. Raising one aloft, she reached for a trail of golden light just like Robbie's and moved as if to push it towards him. It slipped from between her fingertips, but she seemed to know, to *feel* it would work. Was it enough? There was only one way to find out.

She moved around the bench in an almost dreamlike state, and reached out to place a hand on Robbie's shoulder. He jumped slightly in surprise, and in that moment she reached forward with her other hand and yanked the light he'd been enfolding from his grasp. For a brief second she thought it hadn't worked, but then he slipped with the knife and made an unsightly furrow in the beautiful carving.

"Hey! That – oh, was that you?"

Coming suddenly back to reality, Odette winced. "You almost cut your finger off," she said, reaching to check Robbie's hands. "I should've been more careful."

He grinned at her and pulled her into a one-armed hug. "S'all right, Det. *Almost,* not actually. Besides, that was pretty cool. You know you didn't even close your eyes?"

"I didn't need to," replied Odette, surprise creeping into her voice as she realised just how big a difference that had made. "And it's … getting faster? It certainly feels so. I'm never sure how much time I actually lose when I start thinking about using my powers."

"I suspect it's less than you think, my dear. Thoughts travel very fast, after all."

"You do it faster with some people than others, too," Robbie remarked thoughtfully. "I think you were slower with Professor Entwhistle's power because you're less familiar with it than mine."

"Darling, please do call me Vivalda. But you're quite right, and it fits with what we know of how these powers work." She gestured towards Odette. "You work well with the powers of others because you're excellent at picking up new skills. Those you already possess are therefore easier for you to reach for – it's hardly unsurprising."

Odette caught her bottom lip between her teeth. "Does that mean I'd get even better at using other people's powers if I … practised all sorts of other skills?"

Vivalda laughed. "I imagine it would. Your polymathy feeds your power, darling. The more wonderful you are, the stronger your power."

This made Odette blush with pride and embarrassment. She ducked her head against Robbie's shoulder and he squeezed her encouragingly about the waist – he, better than anyone, knew that she dealt almost as badly with compliments as with criticism.

"Now, why don't we try again. A good test is a thorough one, after all."

23

Odette had been so successful at working with Vivalda and Robbie's powers that she'd become curious about the limits of her own. She'd moved to working with several of the others, and it was Mary who, upon finding that she worked much faster with Odette's help, suggested that perhaps Odette might not just assist in their powers, but *use* them too. Of course, Mary had not witnessed Odette's initial attempts.

Henry could see that the very notion of trying again filled Odette with anxiety, but everyone else's excitement was so powerful that she made little attempt to dissuade them from helping her try once more. It had not, however, gone all that well. There were near-constant hints that it was possible, but never any achievement. On the fourth day, Henry began to see signs that Odette was giving up hope of success.

"I don't understand why it isn't working," she said, looking despondent. "No matter how hard I try, I can't get it to work. I've thought of all manner of images and none of them are helping."

Lost for an answer, Henry sat back and took in the image of her: perched on the edge of her seat, tense from head to toe, her eyes cast downwards. The tilt of her head failed to conceal the soft desperation and sheepishness in her expression. It was at that moment that it hit him – she was acting too much like a servant.

Leaning forward in his seat, he asked, "Have you ever been anywhere outside my aunt and uncle's house? Apart from here, I mean."

The young woman blinked, and jerked her head in a nod. "We lived in a different house before – in London, where my father works. When my mother was offered the job with the countess, she and I moved. I was very young, only four or five. I barely remember it."

Henry frowned. "But you were always with servants?"

"I've always been a servant, even when I was young," she replied, eyes glazing slightly with memory. "When I was very little, cook used to sit me at the kitchen table and have me help knead dough. I'm uncertain how much help I was, really, but—"

"Oh, well, that explains it."

She blinked again with wide eyes, her reply hesitant. "It does?"

Henry nodded. "You've always had to appear as you do for others. Even here, you feel you must do right by your employers – or worse, you're having to hide who you truly are for your own protection. Tell me, have you ever been somewhere where you didn't have to worry? Have you ever carried yourself without poise, without thought? Have you ever truly, well, let go? Let yourself do whatever you wanted, however you wanted, with whomever you wished?"

A blush coloured Odette's cheeks, and Henry's eyes were drawn to her lips as she caught one between her teeth. "I, um ..."

As the embarrassment flourished on Odette's face, Henry couldn't help but wonder what she could possibly be thinking of – a confusion that held him only for a moment, to be replaced quickly by a shared surge of shame and a furiously backpedalling stammer. What an idiot he was, to pick such awful leading words! Suddenly, there was a large elephant standing between the two of them, dominating the study, which now seemed far too small to accommodate two people. Robbie's talk leapt into his mind, and Henry felt a deep sense of guilt.

"Of course," he blustered, sitting back in his chair, "I don't mean, ah – I'm ever so sorry. That's not quite what I meant at all. I only meant …"

"It's all right," Odette said shyly. "I know you didn't mean … that. I suppose that, well, I haven't terribly much."

She shifted uncomfortably in her seat, as if her mind was flashing back to a time where she *had*, and that made Henry's stomach do a strange turn. His mind filled with the sudden image of the two of them dancing, the day they'd arrived in Bristol – after Edward had tried to accost them, when they'd finally relaxed. He became aware, rather slowly, that Odette was still talking.

"… just that I very much don't want to let your family down, as they've never been anything but kind to me, and certain things are expected of servants. Still, I … I can't help but think that you're wrong. Perhaps the problem is simply that I'm not terribly good at singing, and since I don't have the skill myself I can't use its magical properties."

At this Henry lost the last of his fluster and shook his head in vehement disagreement. "Not in the slightest – Odette, you have a wonderful voice. You know much of the technique of singing, even without the years of tuition that many have had." Her brow furrowed slightly at the compliment, as if she were unable to see any truth in it. "But what you're missing, what makes the difference, is *passion* – a passion that makes a strong connection with one's audience. If you can't command that, you can't possibly hope to influence others through song."

"Because they're not moved by passionless performances?"

"Precisely!" Henry exclaimed, beaming at her broadly. "That's the trick to my craft, and the craft of anyone whose magic is in performance. Have you ever been in a room and felt emotion so strong that it was almost tangible?"

Odette nodded. "Like when mobs riot, or crowds greet the queen and king as they arrive."

"It's that which magical performance commands," he said, pleased that she was beginning to understand. "But to take command of an audience, you must give a little of yourself – that way they'll believe it, and feel it. Only by convincing them of your own emotions can you pass them along."

"I suppose that makes sense," she replied slowly. Henry could practically see the cogs ticking in her mind at incredible speed. "Only ... I don't quite know how I'd begin to do that."

He gestured for her to stand, and brought her to the centre of the room. Quickly he made sure the doors were closed and that no one was in the hallways outside, which seemed to calm her somewhat. Once done, he returned and stood before her.

"What's your favourite song?" he asked. "Something that brings a fond memory for you."

Odette paused to consider this. "There's something my mother and father used to sing, to put us to sleep. It's from my favourite play." She frowned slightly. "The strangest thing happened, though – a year or so ago I was tidying in Lady Yasmin's bedroom and I heard her singing it."

"Then I think that's a perfect choice."

He noticed that Odette had deflated slightly, and wondered if she was missing his vibrant cousin. It was certainly true that Yasmin's presence in a room was impossible to miss, and he couldn't help but smile at the thought of her.

"Would you like me to sing it?" asked Odette hesitantly.

"Very much," said Henry, with a little more enthusiasm than he'd intended. Clearing his throat, he added, "But I'd like you to do something whilst you're singing – think of Yasmin, and of what she means to you. Could you do that?"

Nodding, Odette said, "I can certainly try."

Her eyes flickered briefly up to his, and Henry took a step back to give her space, and offered an encouraging smile.

It was several moments before she began to sing, and when she did her voice wavered slightly.

"Come unto these yellow sands, and then take hands: Curtsied when you have, and kiss'd the wild waves whist …"

As she sang, her eyes fluttered closed, and the faintest of smiles brushed across her lips. He could almost see Yasmin in his own mind now – the brightness that she radiated, and how it touched all around her. And as she fell deeper into her visualisation, Odette's voice grew stronger and fuller.

"Foot it featly here and there; and, sweet sprites, the burthen bear. Hark, hark! The watch-dogs bark. Hark, hark! I hear the strain of a strutting chanticleer cry, Cock a diddle dow."

The song, now that she was in the midst of it, was familiar to him, though he couldn't place it. Perhaps he too had heard

Yasmin singing it before, or knew it from reading. He thought perhaps that Odette was singing it a little slower than was usual, but that only served to empower her gentle, lilting voice. There was no great depth or power in her voice, but it was clear and soft-edged.

"Full fathom five thy father lies; of his bones are coral made; those are pearls that were his eyes: Nothing of him that doth fade, but doth suffer a sea-change into something rich and strange. Sea-nymphs hourly ring his knell: Ding dong. Hark! Now I hear them – ding, dong, bell."

Her eyes opened sleepily as she finished, and her face flushed with colour as if she'd entirely forgotten he was there. Almost absentmindedly, he reached over and took her hands in his. They were warm and slightly clammy, and even in her palms he could feel her pulse racing.

"See," he said with mirth. "You're more than capable of it if you just think of something important to you. Combine that with a little more eye contact and you'll do wonderfully."

A sadness edged her victorious smile that made Henry want to gather her in his arms and hold her – so much so that he found himself helplessly going along with his thoughts. She stumbled slightly in surprise, but within moments had gratefully slid her arms around his neck, burying her face in his shoulder. It was a marvel to him that she could ever have thought herself devoid of emotion; she was quite the opposite. Indeed, he thought he'd never met anyone quite so brimming over with feelings.

Quickly coming back to his senses, Henry released her and shuffled sheepishly on the spot. There was a brief moment of awkwardness before either spoke, but soon they'd resumed their attempt to extend Odette's powers; and now that she was able to use her visualisation and memory to strengthen her singing, success felt closer.

Henry, though, began to worry: the thought that he might have feelings for her made him almost as nervous as the concern that if he didn't, and didn't stop things sooner rather than later, he could so very easily hurt her. His confused emotions battled for ascendancy.

Pushing them down, he did his best to focus on their work. They did, after all, have a job to do.

24

At first it had been difficult to work with Edward's people. Not because they were anything like Morley – on the contrary, even Peter proved to be personable enough when removed from Edward's clutches. The problem was that Henry found himself truly wanting to help them explore and learn about their powers; but doing so was playing into Edward's hands, and out of his. The faster Peter learned to keep someone's powers down, the less time they had to prepare. But Edward would know if he was being a bad teacher – at least, that's what Henry told himself. He needed to be seen to push his students.

And how wonderful it was to see what they could *do*.

For almost two decades, magic had been commonplace for Henry. It was rare that he was struck by the incredible nature of it; with the awe that came from seeing it for the first time. With the new mages around, however, it was impossible *not* to feel it. All of them, young or old, lit up with joy when they managed to do something new – marvelling at the otherworldly power at their fingertips.

Such was the smile that turned Peter's beautiful mouth the morning he managed, for almost ten seconds, to prevent Henry from spelling one of the soldiers to sleep.

Henry broke off his song not long after, and silence hung

in the air between the three of them. The soldier, who'd snapped to waking as soon as Peter's powers took effect, yawned and blinked in astonishment at the men next to him. Looking at Peter, Henry noticed that though the young mage was smiling, there was no astonishment in his eyes; if anything, he looked quite afraid. Of himself, perhaps. Of what he'd have to do.

The thought of it made Henry's guts churn.

"You did it," he said softly, not quite wanting to believe it himself.

"I did it."

Clearing his throat, Henry tried to regain control of the situation. "You need to be sure you can do it reliably," he pointed out, tapping his watch. "In intense conditions, too. And ten seconds might not be enough for the army. They'll probably want more."

Peter nodded, but Henry could tell he wasn't really taking it in – and he could hardly blame the young man for it. They both knew that he was just making excuses at this point. Yes, it would need more practice and, yes, he wasn't quite there yet – but the turning point was hanging thick in the air between them.

"Congratulations," Henry added, with a sad smile that Peter didn't return.

Not for the first time, he wondered just how happy the mage was about being used in such a fashion. When Edward was around, Peter was all smiles, arrogance and poise – almost as if he used not only the powers of people around him but also their personalities. He was a homunculus, shaped by his company, uncertain of his own self. It made him impossible to read most of the time.

Surely, though, there was too much unspoken for Peter to be truly content with all that was happening. They should tell Edward. They should tell the major general. They should tell everyone. He should start practising more straight away. They should devise ways for him to practise taking powers down under pressure.

If any of these thoughts were swirling through Peter's mind, however, Henry couldn't see them. The young man had retreated to the seat next to the soldier, and sat down on the edge of it, slender fingers curled around the ends of the armrests. His eyes were fixed on a point somewhere in the middle of the rug, as if it might give him some comfort, or the answers to whatever weighed upon him.

He looked so utterly overwhelmed that Henry ceased caring that he wasn't meant to be helping.

"Look," he said, taking a nearby seat himself. "If you don't want to do this, you can say."

For a moment, a look of hope flashed across Peter's face, quickly replaced by a sneer that was so terribly Edward that Henry's throat tightened.

"Just because you're yellow-bellied, *Professor*," he replied in an icy tone, "doesn't mean the rest of us are."

Henry didn't need to look round to see what had brought this on. He sighed. Footsteps shuffled in the door behind him, clicking against the floorboards.

"Darling," enthused Edward, reaching out for Peter with open arms. The mage stood and clasped them, entirely different from the person who only moments ago had been trembling on the edge of his seat. "How's it going?"

"I just managed it, Professor. Ten seconds at least. I can sustain it!"

There was hope in his voice again, but not for salvation; hope for praise, for love. It was achingly familiar to the tone he'd used when talking to Edward not so many years ago.

Peter and Edward began to chatter delightedly about how wonderful this new development was, and Henry, now tired, stood. Beckoning to the soldier, who looked less sleepy and rather pleased to have been part of something so important, he turned to depart.

"Leaving so soon, my dear? But we have so much to celebrate!"

Henry paused on the threshold, and turned to look over his shoulder – not at Edward, but at the smiling man next to him. He knew there was little he could say; if Peter was under Edward's thrall –and the very thought made him nauseous – he'd not listen to anything that was said. He'd have to realise it and extricate himself. It was the only way to break Edward's power. But he couldn't just leave Peter there. Henry, of all people, knew what it was like.

"There's no situation," he said softly, "that you cannot get yourself out of. On your own, or with help. And there is always help."

Before either of them could reply, Henry turned on his heel and marched out of the room.

They didn't have much time left.

25

They were so nearly there.

The thought terrified Odette, whose nerves had been frayed ever since they'd arrived in Bristol. As the time for them to put their plan into action approached, she felt the knot in her stomach grow larger and tighter. It seemed now that she couldn't go more than a few minutes without her mind drifting back to the thought, and recoiling in fear.

More than one night she'd woken from a nightmare where she'd failed all of them by having one of her fits at an inopportune moment.

Her increased tension had not gone unnoticed, however, and more than once she'd been ordered to cease practising and rest. This time it had been Isobel, who though quiet was capable of being fiercely protective, and had ordered Odette to go somewhere calm. Too restless to sit, Odette chose to wander around the huge, sprawling manor and explore it a little better. She knew most of the main rooms now, and her way between places, but there always seemed to be more each time she explored.

A room she'd found several days earlier had reminded her greatly of her very first bedroom; high in the house, it rested snugly under the great beams of the roof. Anyone taller than her would have trouble fitting through the doorway, let alone into the room itself, and she'd found that comforting – as if the room had been made just for her. It had filled her with such a sense of nostalgia that she'd immediately felt compelled to write to her mother and tell her.

Almost unconsciously, Odette's feet led her to that corner of the house, though this time she passed by the tiny room and began to investigate those around it. She'd just begun to examine a rather gorgeously appointed reading room when a sound behind her made her jump out of her skin.

She clapped a hand to her chest. "Oh! You startled me."

A not-too-apologetic smile coiled across Edward Morley's face. "Please excuse me," he said softly. "It was not my intention; I thought you surely must've heard me, for I was not walking so quietly as you."

Blushing, Odette explained, "It's habit – the earl and countess hated it if the staff stomped around the house."

"An exceptionally useful habit," Morley drawled. It was at once the same as and entirely different from Henry's, Odette thought to herself. Silky smooth, but not soft and warm. There was no question that there was power in both their voices.

"I suppose it must be, if one wishes to sneak around the place."

Morley's eyes sparkled. "And is that what you're doing, Odette?"

She could feel her cheeks growing darker, and shook her head. There was a plush window seat surrounded by bookcases. She sat and folded her hands in her lap. Her legs felt wobbly again.

"Not intentionally, Professor. I was just stretching my legs." She was certainly not going to feel bad for taking a break, of all things. He was hardly within his rights to accuse her of slacking when he himself was clearly away from work too.

To her surprise, he did not attack her for it. Instead, he glided across the room and into the seat next to her. He was even more striking close up, and Odette had to swallow a nervous lump in her throat.

"As am I," he replied with an unsettlingly perfect smile. "I'm glad to have found you, in fact. I feel that we've not had the chance to get to know one another, and I think it's very important to the mission for all of us to know one another very well."

"Oh, well, we've all been very busy," stammered Odette, feeling suddenly pinned down by his overbearing presence. Her eyes darted towards the door, though she didn't know whether she was looking for an opportunity for escape or for an arriving saviour. "It's entirely understandable."

"Yet you've not been lacking in time to get to know dear Henry," Morley remarked casually. Odette's head snapped up abruptly and she stared openly at his knowing look. "Therefore I can hardly be blamed for wishing to occupy a little of that time myself."

The knot in her stomach doubled in size. Had Morley seen them, that time in the garden? Or when Henry had helped her work on the strength of her powers? The look in his eyes might suggest either or both. Worse still, she wondered, had he somehow heard Robbie confront Henry about the relationship between the two of them?

"I ..."

And a nagging voice began to whisper in her mind, sounding like a mixture of Henry and Vivalda, cautioning her against trusting Morley, reminding her that his power was in his voice and his presence. As she froze in place, imprisoned by her own rioting thoughts, Odette felt a cool hand brush her cheek. Her eyes locked with Morley's, bright with victory.

"I can hardly blame you," he murmured, leaning closer to her. "Henry is … lovely. I'd know, of course, but I'm sure that's not news to you. I'm certain he and that engineering lapdog of his have already warned you about me."

Her breath shallowed, and she became aware of the pull of his power on her; she couldn't understand why it was working to such an extent, now of all times, when it never had before. She'd felt it in their first class, but not so terribly as this. Even when he'd focused on her alone she'd endured. Then, the image of her golden shield had come to her immediately, without effort; now it was entirely absent. She wriggled against the side of the seat, but he only leaned closer – not improperly so, but just enough to make her feel as though she was pinned down. His arm slid along the windowsill, reaching for her.

"But I'm not so bad, my dear, not really. I know and I accept that I hurt Henry terribly, but … sometimes things are simply not as one remembers them. You'd hardly be able to live if you remembered yourself as the villain, after all. And desperate people – desperate, heartstruck people – can do things so very out of character."

The pad of his thumb ran across her cheekbone, sending lances of fire through her nerves, and Odette felt disgusted at herself for the reaction. An image came to her – of a mountain made of her feelings, devoid of footholds. As she focused on her disgust, however, a gripping point appeared, and she quickly grasped it. Placing all of her focus on her climb, Odette knew she was not replying to Morley, yet he did not seem to notice.

"I simply wished to explain myself," he continued, brushing a curl behind her ear. The tingling this caused gave her the strength to build one more handhold, his words yet another, and soon she was building stones from stubborn determination, from her duty to her friends, even from the tiny spark of burning hope within herself that lit up when Henry was near.

Bit by bit, piece by piece, as Morley continued to whisper poison into her ears she clambered to the top of the golden mountain, and as she reached the top she opened her eyes to find herself back in the room – staring at Morley, his wrist gripped in her hand like a vice, his eyes wide with shock.

"I know what you are," she murmured, pushing the mountain below her down and his power with it. "But you've no idea who you're dealing with, *Edward.* I'm far more than you could ever imagine."

As she yanked herself away from him and strode out of the room, she heard him say, "You most certainly are."

Her legs wobbled and her hands shook with the aftermath of having to push so very hard with her powers, but she felt in her heart the warm glow of victory – until, as she descended the stairs with no real thought as to where she was going, realisation hit her.

"Oh, gods," she whispered, clapping her hand to her mouth. She'd used her powers on Morley. The powers meant to be hidden from him. Replaying his last words in her mind, she saw in them the timbre of thoughtfulness, of understanding, and it made her sick to her stomach. She'd failed Henry. She'd failed all of them.

Terror fuelled her steps as she broke into a run, sprinting for the study where Henry had been working. She spared no time on her shame, so afraid was she of having ruined everything, and crashed into the room in a flurry of limbs. Tears had begun to pour down her cheeks. As she stumbled to a halt before Henry, who was mid-sentence, Odette noticed peripherally that Abigail and Vivalda were also in the room.

It was then that her legs chose to give way.

Henry was close enough to catch her as she fell, which only served to make Odette sob all the harder. She'd failed him; she did not deserve his arms, his embrace, his affection. She should've stayed in the room with Morley and let him ... let him do ...

She shuddered with the realisation of how close she'd come to being under Edward's thrall, and for a horrible moment she thought she was going to be sick. It was only the tightening of Henry's arms around her that kept her from losing her stomach. As if it had just then clicked that he was present, she turned into him and clasped her arms desperately around him. He murmured soothing words in her ear, but they only served to remind her of Morley's whispers, and she turned her head away until her sobs had subsided and the fit had passed.

As Henry pressed a handkerchief into her hands, Odette regained awareness enough to notice that Abigail and Vivalda had disappeared. She cleaned herself up with one shaking hand, the other clasped in Henry's like a lifeline.

"Ditty," he whispered, helping to brush tears from her cheeks. "What happened?"

She opened her mouth to form the words, but faltered. Heat welled in her eyes and she let out a noise of frustration at her own weakness. "I'm sorry," she spluttered, leaning into him.

Odette felt rather than saw as Henry shook his head. "You need never apologise to me," he said soothingly. "Never. You're safe here, and we can stay as long as you need." There was a pause, and he shuffled slightly on the spot. "Or at least until my legs go to sleep."

She realised then that she'd curled into his lap, and blushed. As she regained control of her breathing, he helped her into a seat and sat alongside her, still clasping her trembling hands. It was some minutes before she could form the words that she'd been repeating over and over in her mind, terrified of phrasing them badly.

"Morley tried to use his powers on me," she said finally. Henry tensed beside her, and she rushed on. "He found me on my own, and – I stopped him. Henry, I stopped him, he didn't manage to ..." She felt tears welling up again. "But now he knows what I can do. He knows, Henry. I'm so s-sorry."

Odette continued to splutter apologies, but Henry silenced them by pulling her roughly against him, practically back into his lap, his embrace so tight that she struggled to catch each shallow breath.

He fell entirely silent, which unsettled her further.

"I'm all right, Henry," she whispered, suddenly realising that he was cradling her in his arms as if to protect her, shield her. "I'm all right. He didn't do anything but scare me, Henry. I'm fine."

Shifting, she felt moisture on his cheeks, and noticed that she was no longer the only one shaking. Pushing the last of her fit aside, Odette ran her hand over Henry's head, stroking his hair soothingly. As she held him, she continued to murmur platitudes just as he'd done a few moments before, until the two of them had calmed. Even when the terror had ebbed from them, they remained entangled in one another, unwilling to let go.

"I can't believe …" Henry began hesitantly, "that he'd dare … that gods-damned bastard, he …"

He pulled back just enough to look Odette in the eyes. She darted away by instinct, but with difficulty forced herself to look back at him. As her eyes locked with his again, Henry leant forward and kissed her – but this time it had none of the gentle passion of their first kiss. It was desperate instead, as if he knew of no other way to express himself. Odette felt as if it pulled her back down to the ground from where she'd been floating in a cloud of panic.

"He didn't … hurt you?" Henry whispered after he'd rested his forehead against hers.

"No. No, he just scared me."

"That's all that matters," he replied with sudden fierceness, anger visibly set in his jaw. "We'll deal with the rest of it. All that matters is that you're all right."

Odette didn't know what to say; it made her chest tighten to hear it.

Worrying her bottom lip with her teeth, she found her voice. "I don't understand why his powers worked on me at all. I've never had to … push to stop powers working on me before."

There was a pause as Henry considered this, still running his hand over her curls. "But powers have worked on you before," he replied eventually. "When you first found out about what you could do, and I sang for you. You didn't stop me then."

"I was exhausted," Odette said automatically, shaking her

head.

"Are you exhausted now?"

Blinking, Odette nodded. "I've not been feeling right all day. My ... my limbs have been shaky, and I've been having trouble catching my breath. There's been so much going through my mind that I can barely concentrate sometimes."

Henry smiled softly at her, and pressed his lips to her forehead almost absentmindedly. "I think," he said, "your powers only work passively when you're ... wholly yourself, shall we say. If you're tired, or feeling unwell, then it requires some effort to put them into practice."

"I suppose that makes sense. I don't know what's wrong with me though – I've felt like this most of my life, but never this bad. Usually it's just on and off."

Henry opened his mouth to reply but then paused. Whether he'd thought better of what he was going to say, or had simply been unable to express himself, Odette couldn't tell. His eyes fell to their clasped hands.

"Odette, have you ever been to a physician about your fits or your nerves?"

She shook her head. It had never occurred to her to do such a thing. She'd wondered what was wrong with her, of course, but always put it down to personal weakness. She'd assumed that she couldn't cope with things like other people, that she was frail in a way that left her open to being overcome by thoughts and feelings. That was hardly the sort of thing one went to a doctor about. Indeed, some of the time she even thought she might be making it all up – though why, she didn't know.

"I think you should," Henry said gently, running his thumb over the back of her hand. "Not now, of course, but ... when this is all over. Would you do that for me? No, wait – don't do it for me. Do it for yourself. You don't deserve to be scared all the time, Ditty."

Shame filled Odette as her eyes welled with tears again, and she curled back into his arms in the vain hope that he'd not see her succumb to it again. "What if there's nothing wrong with me?"

"Wh–? Of course there's something wrong. I've seen you collapse, seen you struggle to breathe – these things are real. How could they not be?"

His voice was so full of genuine confusion that Odette couldn't bring herself to tell him the truth. It seemed obvious – her fits were nothing more than a manifestation of the time she spent in her own mind. Her imagination and her ability to visualise – the very key to her powers – could also send her spiralling into panic.

She wanted so badly to be the person people needed. She didn't want to disappoint anyone. How could she possibly tell him it was all in her head?

26

Whenever they gathered now, there was a tension in the air – the anticipation of knowing that soon, very soon, they were going to do something that couldn't be undone.

Henry hated it.

It was as if the fears in his mind had coalesced into a constant drone, echoing over and over that he was leading them into something terrible, that it would be his fault if they were hurt, that what they were doing went against reason. Though content with the decision they'd made as a group, he still felt overwhelmed by a sense of foreboding.

They'd taken to clustering together in the evenings And while the tension was still palpable, they found succour in each other's company – Henry could tell from the nervous, haunted looks in everyone's eyes that he was not alone in feeling doubt. It was a good sign, he hoped. A sign that they'd not forgotten that they were people. That they were not black and white in morality, but shades of grey, as were all things outside of fairy tales.

The door creaked open, and Matthew slipped in with the guilty air of one who'd been sneaking about.

"I, uh," he said in an unusual display of brevity and hesitation, "have something you should see."

Raising his eyebrows, Henry reached out to take the offered

sheaf of papers, and opened the thin vellum contained within. His father's regimental insignia gleamed at him from the top of the page, along with a pencil portrait of a young man and several paragraphs of notes: an assessment, Henry realised.

"Do I want to know how you got these, Matthew?"

The young climber's guilt was tempered by a bravado that made him stand tall whilst also wringing his hands together behind himself. "Probably best you don't ask, what with these notes having until recently been in your father's study and all. Though, of course, they couldn't have been taken, since his study is on the second floor and the door to it is locked, and he's the only one with the key."

Despite himself, Henry grinned. "Quite." Then he added idly, "There's a trellis on that wall of the house, isn't there? For climbing plants."

Matthew picked a stray petal from his trousers and tucked it in his pocket. "It's possible that there is, sir. I couldn't say for certain."

Out of the corner of his eye, Henry saw Mary fail to conceal a decidedly mischievous chuckle that made her eyes glint with near malevolence. Shaking his head fondly, he returned his attention to the paperwork. It didn't appear to be everything his father had on Braddock, but it was a good deal of it. There was a psychological assessment that Henry thought might be useful – until he read it and found it had been written by someone who'd entirely failed to be unbiased. Perhaps they'd lost someone to Braddock's attacks. Perhaps they were anti-mage. Either way, their assessment was relentless enough in its demonisation that it was near useless.

Doubt niggled in Henry's mind. Was it was possible that Braddock was simply a mindless killer stirring the masses toward a foolish revolution, with no end in mind but his own glory and powe?

"If nothing else," Henry said, plucking the portrait from the folder, "this will be useful. You should all see it."

He held it up and gestured for everyone to come over. With Robbie at his shoulder, Henry saw the sigh before it rushed from his lips. His eyes flickered to the younger man's face, which was lined with fatigue and worry. When had they all become so very old, these people who'd once bounced with excitement to learn of their powers?

"What is it?" he asked gently.

Robbie ran a hand through his hair. "He just looks so … normal. Like a normal kid. Like me, or Matthew. He's barely twenty."

All of them clustered a little closer around the portrait. Henry couldn't help but agree with Robbie's assessment – it seemed that Thomas Braddock was indeed a normal young man, with dark eyes and dark hair that ran straight to his chin. He was well dressed, but he a slightly rough look about him nonetheless. The portrait – done by one of the police sketchers – was uncannily realistic. Even the deep bags under the teen's eyes were perfectly replicated in pencil.

"There ain't no age requirement for murder," remarked Mary gruffly, but even she'd softened slightly with concern. "Looks t' me like he ain't well."

"I think that of all the things we might expect to find in Master Braddock, *well* is not one," agreed Henry, pushing the portrait away. "But there you are. This is what he looks like; this is who we have to find."

His charges nodded, each of them carefully taking in the image. Then they began slowly to return to their work.

But Henry's unease remained, wrapping itself around his throat and gut like a trembling vice.

27

Not since he was a much younger man had Henry been seized by such indecision over a relatively simple thing. He must look quite the picture, he thought: pacing back and forth before a closed door with a page of sheet music in his hand. But he had to be certain – it wasn't fair not to be.

A full fifteen minutes later, he raised his hand and knocked.

"H– oh, hello." A faint smile turned Odette's lips as she pulled the door open. "Did you need something?"

She fell back into the habit of servitude easily, leaving him struck suddenly with the worry that she'd never see him as an equal. He cleared his throat to push the thought aside, and held up the music by way of explanation. "I have something for you. Before we, ah …" His eyes darted back and forth to each side of the hallway. "Go."

Repeating his paranoid glance, Odette stepped backwards and gestured for him to come in. She'd changed since lunch, he noticed – the embroidered dress that Abigail had made for her abandoned in favour of a loose shirt and trousers. A faint blush on her cheeks betrayed that she was probably a little ashamed to be seen dressed so casually – and he could hardly be surprised, given how formally his aunt and uncle dressed their servants – which was, all things considered, rather adorable.

"Is that sheet music?"

"You can read it?"

She shook her head, then paused. "Well, a little." As she moved to sit on the small loveseat before the fire, she tucked a stray curl behind her ear. "Not enough to sight read."

Henry chuckled. "But enough to know what sight reading is."

The pink tint to her cheeks darkened. "Stop changing the subject. Can I see it? What's it for?"

"It's for you, actually."

Odette closed her fingers around the papers and looked at him with a confused expression. "For ... me? Did you – Henry, did you write this?"

The astonishment in her eyes made him wish he'd written her a thousand songs. "With all the preparation that the crafters have been doing ... none of it will work for you. Abigail's clothes, Mary's food, Robbie's carvings – they're wonderful for the rest of us, but they won't work for you. I wanted you to have something that would."

"But," Odette said, cradling the sheaf in her hands as if it were incredibly fragile and precious, "your songs don't work on me either. At least, not most of the time."

He smiled a languid, decidedly pleased smile at her. "This isn't magic in that sense. It could be if I were to sing it, but that's not the point of it."

"What is?"

"This is a much more mundane sort of magic." Twisting on the spot and reaching forward, Henry wrapped his hands around hers, running his thumbs over her knuckles. "The sort that you can remember when things are going wrong, to find some hope in dark places."

Odette stared blankly at him for a long moment, her eyes glistening. She looked down at the papers, and then back up at him – and Henry couldn't help but wonder what she was thinking. There was a dip in her brow, and her lips had parted slightly. Did she … was she thinking about kissing him? The notion consumed him.

But just as he tilted his head forward to turn the thought into action, Odette looked back at the pages and handed them to him. "Would you sing it for me?"

"I – oh." He hoped he didn't look as flustered as he felt. Gods, what was he, sixteen again? "Of course."

She smiled brilliantly at him, which did little to assuage the turmoil in his stomach, and he turned the pages round the right way. Lyrics had never been his strong point – melodies came far more naturally to him – so he'd decided to put a sonnet to music. After all, it was Shakespeare that Odette had chosen to sing when they'd been working on her powers together.

Taking a deep breath, he began to sing.

"When, in disgrace with fortune and men's eyes,
I all alone beweep my outcast state,
And trouble deaf heaven with my bootless cries,
And look upon myself, and curse my fate,
Wishing me like to one more rich in hope,
Featur'd like him, like him with friends possess'd,
Desiring this man's art and that man's scope,
With what I most enjoy contented least;
Yet in these thoughts myself almost despising,
Haply I think on thee, and then my state,
Like to the lark at break of day arising
From sullen earth, sings hymns at heaven's gate;

For thy sweet love remember'd such wealth brings

That then I scorn to change my state with kings."

It was not a melody that would rival those of the great composers, but he was – if he allowed himself a small moment of pride – rather pleased with it. Henry understood the power of his own voice well, and he hoped the years of practice would make him more adept at composition than he might otherwise have been. Even so, it was only when the last of his song had died away that he dared to look at Odette. And though he was used to making eye contact with his audience to ensure his powers had worked on them fully, he found himself rather nervous at that moment.

He needn't have been – her gaze was so enraptured that it made him stumble for words. "I, ah …"

He hadn't been certain what he was going to say, but it quickly became irrelevant: her lips were on his, soft and warm. Though it lasted but a moment, the kiss stole away the breath he'd only just regained, and left him staring at her as intently as she had at him only moments ago.

"I shouldn't have done that," she said at once, pulling back. "I'm sorry, I – I got carried away. It's just that … that was … no one has ever …"

Henry tipped his head forward and brushed his lips against hers again. He couldn't help himself. Then he sat back slightly, Odette's fingers still tangled in his hair.

"I, ah, take it you like it, then."

"Oh." She sighed, looking both sheepish and excited. "It was … Shakespeare? I've always loved – and it was so … did you really write that just for me?"

She sounded so utterly disbelieving that it made his heart ache. "I didn't want you to feel that you had nothing to take with you. When we leave, I mean. Everyone else has armour and food to invigorate them and ... I didn't want you to have nothing."

"It's perfect. Thank you. I wish I had something for you now ..."

"You don't need to do that." He chuckled, shaking his head. "You're the key to our plan, the one keeping us all safe. Without you we wouldn't dare go near Braddock, would we? With you there, we know that he can't hurt us."

As soon as the words were out of his mouth, Henry regretted them. Odette flinched and stood up, almost turning her back on him as she looked over at the fire. "Don't, please. I don't want to – to think that I could have to ... I don't want anyone to get hurt."

"I'm sorry," he said at once, standing and reaching for her hands. "That's not what I meant."

"It was."

"Yes, but I didn't mean—" He sighed. It was too late to take it back. "I'm truly sorry. Just remember that this way ... this way we're safe, and Braddock might be safe too. If he's been forced into this situation against his will, we might be able to help him in a way that no one else can."

A faint, relieved chuckle burst from Odette's lips. "Because no one else would dare consider that things might not be as they seem."

Henry shrugged. "Perhaps. People are scared, and when people are scared, they rarely think clearly."

But this seemed not to offer her the comfort he'd hoped it would; Odette simply squeezed his hands and let go of them, her eyes drifting towards the door. They were pinched in a mixture of thought and pain. One hand drifted to her chest as if to acknowledge some knot of feeling that had taken root there.

"Thank you for the song," she said. She wanted him to leave – but why? "I'll see you later."

He nodded, trying to ignore a faint wave of nausea and the voice in his head plaintively asking what he'd done wrong. He glanced at her as he left. Her brow was still dipped, her mouth twisted in an expression of confusion and hurt. He resolved to push it down. There was surely nothing he could do by worrying.

But when had that ever stopped him before?

28

Henry left the room and Odette's knees gave way – not because she was having a fit, but because they'd felt for some time as if they were made of jelly. Even as she'd leapt out of her seat, only adrenaline had kept her upright. Now alone, there was little enough left to buoy her. How strange it was that elation and fear felt quite so similar. And in her mind, confusion turned to realisation.

Odette stared at the scattered pages of Henry's song.

He loved her.

No – that was not the right word. It was not love, not yet. Though Odette had read dozens of stories that told of love at first sight, she knew in her heart that it was something that grew over time, not something that flourished from nothing. And yet it could grow very fast – that she did know. For though in some ways love was always eternal, for once you had loved someone you could never truly *unlove* them, not all loves were the same. Some were more fleeting than others; some came intertwined with other events, other feelings; very few were the once-and-forever loves of stories.

But that did not make love any the less precious, and so Odette was left gasping. For what could this song be if not proof that he loved her? He cared for several of the others very much, but he was not giving them songs. No, this was something he'd written for her and her alone.

And, a slightly smug voice in the back of her mind pointed out, he'd likely not gone around kissing the other mages.

Her lips tingled from the memory. She felt like a character in a melodrama.

One realisation came swift on the heels of another, however, and soon Odette was left with the horrible truth that she was at a crossroads. She could either choose to do nothing about their feelings for each other – push them down until they faded with time – or she could confront him. There was no middle ground to be had, not when they were about to undertake so risky a journey. She was unfocused enough as it was; carrying uncertainty on top of everything else could prove disastrous.

And she really didn't want anyone to get hurt.

So she reached for the pages of the song he'd written her, stacked them neatly upon the table, and began to do that which so rarely came to her. Closing her eyes, Odette began to daydream about her very own life. Not the lives of princesses and princes, kings and queens, knights, soldiers and dashing heroines ... but hers. She looked to each side of the junction at which she stood and told the story of each fork, over and over, until she thought she must surely have imagined every possibility.

When she opened her eyes, several hours later, she discovered she'd lulled herself to sleep. Robbie sat next to her, an amused smile on his lips.

"Strange time of day for a nap," he said, and held up a paper-wrapped sandwich. "You missed dinner. Mary made this for you."

Odette blushed as deeply as if Robbie had read her mind,

though why she was so embarrassed she wasn't quite sure. "Thank you."

"I saw the professor leaving here earlier." He spoke so nonchalantly that he might as well have been asking about the weather, but Odette paused halfway to a mouthful of sandwich, wondering whether her embarrassment was prescient. "Entertaining him in your bedroom now?"

Placing the food and plate aside, Odette sighed. Of all people, Robbie had the most right to tease her – and, being her best friend, the most skill at it – but as much as it drew a laugh from her it also served to remind her of her dilemma.

"I think," she began hesitantly, "I think he …"

She could feel Robbie's grin. "Yeah, he does." There was a long pause, before he added, "and you feel the same."

Odette wrapped her arms around her knees and drew them up to her chest, resting her heels on the edge of her seat. "I think I might."

"So?" Robbie said, perching next to her. "What are you going to do about it?"

Lifting her head to look at her best friend, Odette's face broke into a smile that lit up her eyes. She knew exactly what she was going to do.

29

For a moment, Odette thought she might be dreaming –
the rain was coming down in a fine mist that seemed to fog
the air, and the full moon's light was bright enough to cast a
silvery glow over the gardens. She walked in smooth, silent
steps close to the honeysuckle bushes, as if she were their
shadow. They seemed oddly silent without the bees busily
going about their work. The heady scent of the flowers filled
her senses as she brushed past them, and she prayed she
wouldn't sneeze and alert the guards to her presence.

She felt dizzy; her hands and face were clammy with rain
and nervous sweat, and it was all she could do to focus
on taking one step after another, carrying herself at what
seemed like great length to the sheltered bench where she'd
met Henry the afternoon they decided to go after Braddock.

As she sat, hidden by the perfectly trimmed hedges, Odette
became aware of a thumping sound. Could it be that Henry
was already here? She'd left early. More to the point, it didn't
sound like footsteps.

As the rhythm echoed in her mind, Odette realised that it
was the pulsing of her own heartbeat, skittering along like a
spider pursued by a playful kitten.

"Come on, Ditty," she whispered to herself. "There's
nothing to be afraid of. Far better to say it now than let it

fester."

But even the thought of rejection made her stomach clench with fear. Swallowing her queasiness, she drew her cloak closer about herself and waited, doing her best to ignore her doubts. It was no use – her mind was made up; and, besides, she couldn't think of an excuse for why she'd called Henry out here. There was no backing out.

More than that, she *wanted* to tell him. And it was very rare that Odette allowed herself to want something enough to leap for it. Until that moment they'd both been perfectly proper, doing nothing but shuffling shyly onwards, leaping away in the times they overstepped. But she was done, so very done with being proper. She'd show him, this man who'd give such impassioned lectures and sing with such earth-shattering emotion, but flee in the face of his own desire rather than acknowledge his own passion.

Her determination only served to make her hands shake all the more, and it was this she focused on concealing when Henry appeared.

"This is a very strange time to ask for a meeting," he said, his low voice mellifluous in the early-morning silence.

Henry stood at the edge of the shadowed arbour. Silhouetted by the light of the moon, he seemed taller and leaner. At Odette's beckoning, he stepped into the shelter and sat next to her, brushing ineffectually at the moisture on his coat.

"I'm sorry for waking you – or, or keeping you up, or – for the inconvenience," Odette stammered before pausing to compose herself. She was better than this. When she spoke again, her voice had lost its desperate edge. "It's just that there's something I'd like to discuss. A problem, you see, that I've noticed."

Henry's brow creased with concern. "A problem so great that it can't be discussed in the daytime?"

"A problem so delicate and secret," she corrected gently, taking comfort in formalities, "that I couldn't dare risk it being overheard by others."

She took a small measure of satisfaction in seeing his confusion deepen, and felt a touch of warmth flare at the realisation that, even in his confusion, his concern still shone through.

"I'm afraid I don't understand what you mean," he said, reaching up to swipe his hand over his hair, which, to Odette's dismay, was being kept well in place by the rain.

Steeling herself, she turned to face him. "I have a problem with – with you, my—" No, she couldn't call him that, not now. She was falling back on decorum out of panic. "I have a problem with you, and I'm afraid I've done my best to make it go away, but all I've succeeded in doing is discovering that it's not only my problem but your own."

"Good gods, woman," Henry said, now looking like a scared rabbit caught by a hunting hound. "Whatever have I done? If I've caused injury to you in any way—"

The gentle pressure of Odette's index finger on his lips was so unexpected that it silenced him immediately. Feeling a little heady from how daring she was being, Odette decided simply to plough onwards – in for a penny, in for a pound – though she got to her feet and paced restlessly as she continued.

"You've done nothing of the sort," she said, shaking her head. "On the contrary, many would consider this to be a rather positive problem, though it could so easily become otherwise – and I know that I'm rambling but I really think it's best if we broach the matter now."

She paused, and Henry stared at her, slightly dumbstruck. With only a little hesitation, Odette got to the heart of the matter.

"I'm afraid I've found that I like you a good deal, rather more than is appropriate." Her voice wavered only a little at the end, which she took some pride in. "I wouldn't have told you but for the fact that – and perhaps I'm about to make an utter fool of myself here – I'm becoming rather suspicious that you feel quite the same about me. I mean, ah. We have, um. We seem to keep – you know."

There – it was done. She couldn't undo the words any more than she'd been able to undo the feelings themselves. Breath trembling, she turned and watched Henry's reaction. First, shock blossomed across his face, his eyes widening and mouth dropping ever so slightly open. A muted look of disbelief followed, then a slightly apologetic smile, and finally a downward glance.

"Well," he said softly, "that's certainly not what I expected you to say. Though I'm not really sure what I did expect."

It was only then that Odette allowed the hope in her heart to bloom into something more fully recognised. Even by the moon's pale light she could see the colour in his cheeks, and noted the way his hands had begun to move with nervous energy. All of a sudden, a breathy laugh fled her lips, a great sense of relief overcoming her. Even still, she cast her eyes down in shame, for it was not at all the time to be laughing, but soon the sound of her laughter had company in her companion's own chuckling, which loosed in turn another giggle from Odette's own lips.

Hesitantly, she looked down at Henry, his eyes glittering

with smiles.

"I suppose it's my turn to address the ... problem, as you so put it."

"That would be both polite and appreciated," Odette replied, unable to keep herself from mirroring his smile. He rose with a formal grace and moved to stand before her, his eyes never leaving her for even a moment.

"I am – I've never been very skilled at this sort of thing," he said, his tone apologetic. "But you've been, well, I don't think brave quite covers it, for there's far more to be admired than simple bravery. But ..."

Odette realised with amusement that Henry was quite as nervous as she was. The thought made her own trembling abate a little, and she waited patiently for him to resume, though her eyes still darted about.

"What I mean to say is – I must honour the bravery and honesty you've shown me, for else I'd do you a great disservice." He reached over and took Odette's hands in his own, causing her heart to flutter. His were far softer, save for the index finger and thumb of his writing hand, and incredibly warm. "You're quite right, I think, to say that – that I've become fond of you."

Odette's breath fell from her in a rush, and it felt like the bottom had dropped out of her stomach. She let out a soft *oh*, the single sound articulating all her relief, surprise and overwhelming pleasure from knowing she'd not been wrong.

"You are ..." Henry said, and Odette glanced up at him. Her gaze made him pause and reach up to tuck a lock of hair behind her ear. His fingers brushed against her skin for only a moment, but it lanced through her nerves like lightning. "Odette, I think you're quite unlike anyone else I've ever met.

I couldn't do you justice by explaining all the things about you that are beautiful if I tried."

She stared back at him, too overwhelmed to look away, even when his eyes locked with hers and made her feel as if she was being pressed down into the floor. Quite unconsciously, she rested her free hand on his chest, running her thumb along the edge of his waistcoat. She remembered the day back at home, so long ago now, when he'd pulled her into his arms, and observed distantly that she was swaying up against him even now.

"The world is going so very fast," she said softly as Henry let go of her hand and slipped his arm around her waist. "I feel as though trying to keep up with it is a trap. I don't want to get pushed along so fast that we make mistakes, or trip, or ... I'm not explaining this very well."

Warmth flooded through Odette as Henry kissed her, so tenderly that it made her breath hitch. "If you don't want ..." he began, voice tensing in an echo of pain. "You should never do anything you don't want to. I don't expect you to, or desire it."

That almost made her pause – perhaps more than his rejection she'd feared the notion that she'd become anything like Morley; that unwittingly she might use however Henry felt about her against him, and become no better than if she'd manipulated him using superhuman powers. But she trusted him to tell her before that happened, she had to, otherwise there was no chance that this would ever work at all.

"It's not that I don't want to." Admitting it out loud made her squirm and blush, but somehow she only succeeded in wriggling closer. "I just – I don't want to get so caught up in flying that I forget what it's like to walk on the ground. And

I don't want you to either."

"Then we won't."

It was so simple a statement, but he made it so honestly that it sounded less like a promise and almost like a prayer. And suddenly she was kissing him again, unaware of who had started it, one hand tangling in his hair as if to keep him from escaping.

"It won't be that easy," she replied breathlessly. It was too late for her nerves to stop her now, but they could certainly interject and admonish at length. "People get things wrong, Henry. They mess them up. We'll do that too."

"No, it won't – yes, they do – and yes, we will." He punctuated each phrase with a kiss, finally catching her bottom lip between his teeth with a gentle ferocity that made Odette's toes curl. "And yet increasingly I find myself not caring."

This made her laugh, and even managed halt her further objections. So much of her tension, she realised, had come from the fact that Henry had always been a strange combination of passive and active. But now he was the one pulling her against him; he was the one catching her lips against his over and over; he was the one convincing her that whatever they had was worth it. That, more than anything else, helped the knot in her stomach to finally settle.

The butterflies of course were still doing backflips – doubly so since he was now tracing spirals up and down her spine with his fingertips. "Let's go inside," she said, before turning bright red and stammering, but not soon enough to stop Henry's lips turning in a devilish grin. "Not like that! I just mean, um, it's starting to rain."

It wasn't, but he was polite enough not to mention it.

Lacing his fingers through hers, Henry led Odette back up the winding path to the house and into his empty study, and the two of them curled up together on the sofa. Hours passed without their noticing, and even when the sun began to come up neither could quite bring themselves to leave; just for once, just for this one night, it would surely be all right to pretend that there was nothing else in the world but the two of them.

30

"Well, isn't this cosy."

Awareness came slowly to Henry; for a moment, the silky-smooth voice's intrusion made him wonder if he'd strayed back into one of his nightmares. But everything felt too real. For one thing, his right arm was numb, which probably had something to do with the head rested against his shoulder. So he opened his eyes and looked up into the face he least wanted to see.

"E–Edward," he said, instantly infuriated with himself for the sudden surge of shame and embarrassment. "I, ah ..."

The abrupt tension in Odette's body, which was impossible to miss given that her legs were curled across his lap, told Henry that she too had awoken at precisely the wrong moment. One instinct told him to move away from her as quickly as possible, whilst another of equal strength urged him to keep her close as long as Edward was around.

Whether that was for his benefit or hers, he didn't care to analyse.

"I suppose it was only a matter of time before your love for those beneath you landed you in a ... compromising position," Edward continued, raising one perfect eyebrow and sneering at them. "Really, Henry, a servant?"

His embarrassment quickly turning to fury, Henry tightened his grip around Odette, whose fingers were now digging hard into his arm. "I don't see what business it is of yours," she snapped in an unusually hard voice.

"Oh, my dear. But it's precisely my business. If you've manipulated dear Henry here into keeping your powers secret, well." Edward plucked a hair from his sleeve idly. "I should think it rather important to everyone. I can hardly blame you – he is, after all, so terribly … *malleable*."

"Get out," Henry said almost instinctively. "I don't care for your games, *Edward*. Get out and do with your supposed secrets what you will."

"Is this a game, my dear? You had best hope it's not, for it's not one that you'll win. I'll beat you, Henry. I'll beat you because I'm prepared to do what none of your little brats can muster. You try to emulate me, I know, but you fail – I imagine your father would be very interested to hear about the secrets you're keeping from him. Perhaps it would be better coming from you, yes? Wouldn't you like to tell him all the things you've done wrong?"

Henry knew what was happening, what Edward was doing, but he couldn't stop it. He felt the soft, crooning words wrap around him and lift his heart from his chest just like they had all those years ago. Perhaps … yes, perhaps it would be better. He could tell his father, and it would be kinder than coming from Edward. He should just tell his father everything. About Odette, about the plan, about all that they were doing. For what sort of son was he to keep such secrets?

"No."

Odette sprang from his lap with such strength that Henry was crushed against the chair. He blinked confusion and magic from his eyes to see her standing before him like a small, ferocious shield, one hand wrapped firmly around Edward's wrist. From his prone position he couldn't see the expression on her face, but her trembling form and icy tone made her fury clear.

"You will leave. You will not tell anyone what you've seen. You will leave us alone." There was something different about her voice: it was lower, smoother, more powerful. Eyes widening, Henry realised that she sounded like Edward. Was she ... using his power? "You will tell Peter that he needs to spend more time practising before he's ready to move on Braddock. Won't you ... my dear?"

Gods. She was using his power.

A faint shimmer had settled over Edward's eyes, and a dreamy smile curled his unfairly perfect lips. "Yes. Yes, I will. What wonderful ideas you have. Truly a gem amongst coal."

He turned and strolled from the room in a daze, leaving Henry staring dumbly at the place where he'd stood only moments ago.

Odette had used Edward's own powers on him. This, more than anything, allowed him to shake off the anxiety from having fallen prey to them himself again. His disquiet faded and he became aware that Odette was trembling even more.

"Ditty," he said, standing and scooping her into his arms just as she began to sway. Comforting her seemed to give him some equilibrium. "Here, come sit down. It's all right. He's gone."

There were tears rolling down her cheeks. "He was going to hurt you," she whispered, her voice thin and reedy in comparison to moments before. "He was going to hurt you."

"He didn't," Henry said, realising only moments later that

it was a lie – the anxiety was gone, but nausea still roiled his stomach from being under Edward's control again. He hadn't forgotten how insidious it was – he never would – but there was a piercing clarity to the experience that memories couldn't replicate. Doing his best to ignore it, he tightened his grip around Odette's waist and shoulders as she curled her head into his neck. "You kept me safe."

Sobs still shook her shoulders.

"I – I shouldn't have done that … I just wanted him to go away, but that power … that power is horrible, Henry. What sort of world would let such a power exist?"

He'd wondered the same thing for years. Sometimes he'd wanted to scream at the world, to demand why. Sometimes all of those frustrations coalesced into one simple question: why did bad things happen to people?

As if there were any purpose to things. The world did not work like that. He'd been raised to believe in higher powers, and perhaps there would always be a part of him that thought there was something more to the world.

But Henry had no answers; just more questions. If there were some greater force in the world, some deified being, surely he had no hope of ever comprehending its motives.

"It's not the power," he found himself saying, "but what he does with it. Otherwise he'd be no different to someone who's simply very good at getting their way in the most normal of senses."

Odette blew her nose loudly on her handkerchief, and the corner of Henry's lips twitched slightly. That she'd regained focus enough to notice that her nose was running seemed a good sign.

"It would be better if the power didn't exist. How easy

must it be to use accidentally? To be so carried away by how much you want something that you fail to notice what you're doing." She looked down at her trembling hands. She wasn't just talking about Edward. "I don't even understand how I—"

"It's not accidental." His voice was laden with pain and bitterness, the words biting, but he didn't care. "He does it on purpose. He knows what he's doing. His powers might not be inherently evil, but he chooses to use them that way."

"I didn't mean—"

"I know. But he's not a good person. You can't make him one by wishing."

Odette tucked her handkerchief into her sleeve and reached up to brush her palm across his cheek, where his stubble was beginning to shade his skin.

Henry tried to push aside the anger still surging within him, his nausea warring with the sudden drop in adrenaline. It was futile, though. She didn't know. She couldn't know. It wasn't her fault.

"Maybe that's not the point," she said, resting her forehead against his. "Maybe it's not about changing other people, but changing ourselves. Choosing to believe the world can be better, even if we can't make it so."

At any other point in time, Henry might've thought on this more; debated it, explored it. But now he was just too tired. Too wrung out from all that had happened. He couldn't even bring himself to be curious. They could talk about her powers another time, he decided, pressing his lips to the top of her head. It could wait.

They needed to prepare for the evening; for the point of no return.

"It's time."

Robbie's whisper cut through the silence of Odette's bedroom like a butcher's knife. Nodding, she hefted her bag onto her back and followed him silently from the room. She'd been waiting on edge for hours. In the distance, she could hear the heavy movement of boots – Roger's distraction must have kicked in. As she and Robbie descended the staircase, hearts pounding in their chests, alarm bells began to peal and the braying of horses and the barking of dogs rippled through the air.

Odette saw a flash of white out of the corner of her eye as her best friend grinned. "That's our cue. Come on – the door's already unlocked."

Together they stole through the now empty corridor, silently thanking Matthew's climbing skills for allowing him to get the details of the soldiers' defence drills and daily patrols. This was the route that was kept clear for escape, and soon it would be crammed – but right now it was empty, all the way to the door and beyond. Going as fast as they could without creating a ruckus, Odette and Robbie made it out of the door before the sound of boots came too near.

Almost everyone else was there waiting – only Roger and Matthew were absent, taking care of the distraction and keeping an eye out from the trees respectively. Once they'd left, Roger would take one of the horses, whilst Matthew was nimble enough to catch them on foot. Odette couldn't help worrying for them nonetheless – they might be possessed of magical powers, but they were still two men against trained soldiers.

"Everyone here?" asked Henry as they clustered together. He counted them quickly. "Good. Let's go. Isobel?"

The young woman nodded. She'd been up several nights in a row painting their route, and knew it clearly – though she still looked terrified as she led the group out of the grounds and into the fields that ran between the manor and the forest. Though there were one or two points where she had to pause to get her bearings, she proved an effective leader through the unfamiliar land.

It was hard work. For the first hour, they couldn't risk taking too slow a pace. With amusement, they discovered that it was Henry who struggled to keep up; though much older, Mary and Abigail were used to running up and down the stairs, as were all the servants. Henry, however, was used to standing in a lecture hall or working in a study – not the sort of lifestyle that prepared one for a march across the rolling hills of Wales.

The group fell into an easy camaraderie that just about assuaged their collective terror. Relief came when the clip-clop of hooves announced Roger's successful arrival. Though slick with sweat, he had an almost boyish grin concealed beneath his bushy moustache, and couldn't help but raise his hand in a silent cheer as he reached them. Swinging down from his horse, Roger murmured gently in its ear before sending it cantering off into the moonlight.

"She'll find her way home eventually," he explained to the curious faces. "Better this way – horses leave much clearer tracks."

It took Matthew a little longer to arrive, but in time he did, swinging down from the trees above. He too had a grin plastered across his sweaty face – it seemed that not even escaping from a heavily defended army base could do anything but excite him. They clapped him on the back, their group finally united, and allowed their pace to ease a little so that he could make his report.

"The dogs were brilliant!" he began loudly, earning him a stern shush from Abigail. Lowering his voice seemed to take him some effort, but he managed it nonetheless. "They did exactly what Roger told them to – led the soldiers off in completely the wrong direction. A couple did come this way, but on foot and without the dogs. I think it was just them doing a perimeter check rather than realising we'd gone this way."

"Do they know we've escaped, then?" asked Henry, hesitantly.

Matthew shook his head. "Not when I last heard them talking, at least. I mean they might've worked it out by now; it took me a little while to catch up with you and they've probably searched the whole house by this point, maybe even started to look this way. But we've got a massive head start, almost three hours. I think we'll be fine."

"They also have no idea where we're going, or why," Robbie pointed out when one or two people started to look nervous. "That's got to count for something."

Henry nodded, but his frown didn't abate. "Edward will work it out eventually."

"Right now, he's probably too busy complaining that they disturbed his beauty sleep," murmured Odette, slipping her hand into Henry's. This managed to pull a small smile from him, so she squeezed and pushed on. "Anyway, Vivalda's there. She'll have them running in circles." It was the part of the plan that the engineer had been most excited to take charge of.

Chuckling, Henry said, "I'm a little sad I won't get to see it."

Thus placated, Henry gestured for Isobel to continue leading them. The walk to the house they'd planned would take all night and most of the following day, but it would bring them right to where Braddock had last been sighted. He'd told Odette that it was a family building, and had been suggested as a good spot – it was only used in the summer, and they didn't keep so much as a housekeeper there in the off seasons. It was neither too large, nor too small, and was as conveniently placed as anywhere else. She was rather thankful for it, and pleased that they'd been afforded a little luck for once.

The journey was hard-going. None of them had slept well for a long time, and even those who were used to a good deal of physical exertion were running on empty before very long. But eventually they began to see gaps in the trees and the hills began to level. Abigail let out an excited gasp.

"There, look! On the horizon!" She pointed, and all eyes followed.

Sure enough, there was a glimpse of a chimney. Even without any smoke, the sight was inherently welcoming and gave the group the burst of hope and energy needed to push themselves the final stretch. It was still some time before they reached the house, but the last hour went much quicker for the sense of being almost there.

The building was set into a glade within the forest, where the river changed direction as it tumbled down the hills – or mountains, Odette suspected, though they were not quite as steep here. It was tranquil, with a comforting sense of being removed from all things. Even the path up to the house – which they'd not taken, since they'd travelled as indirectly as possible – was barely an excuse for one.

Odette came to a standstill before the building, watching as Matthew and Mary raced into the entrance hall to explore. A cold hand laced through hers and drew her attention from the brick archway.

"Well," Henry said, smiling tiredly down at her. "Here we are."

Odette turned and looked back around them, out into the forest, where Roger had already set to work, introducing himself to the local wildlife in order to enlist their help as lookouts. A part of her couldn't help but wonder if she felt too safe. Too content. Pushing the worries aside, she allowed herself just a few moments to bask in the idea that there was nothing else in the world but this house; nothing but her and the others, hidden and safe.

"Here we are."

Reaching up with a grass-stained hand, Henry tucked a stray lock of hair behind her ear with such gentleness that it made her shiver. They remained there for several moments before entering the house, neither wanting to discuss why they were there, the weight of the truth weighing down their tongues.

Once it was clear they'd not been followed, everyone began to settle. There were more than enough bedrooms, but Isobel, Abigail and Matthew rushed up the stairs to select theirs first. Odette chuckled – the novelty of not staying in the servants' quarters would clearly never leave them, or at least not for a very long time. She followed a little while after, selecting a modestly sized room in the middle of the long hallway that ran the length of the house.

Although it was late morning, everyone was too exhausted to do much with their day. There were some meagre provisions in the pantry, which some set about turning into an evening meal whilst the others dealt with the dust and disuse of a house that was traditionally only used in the summer.

Henry had said it was a family property, but she'd never been to it before. There were a few places like it, she knew; Yasmin had a house bequeathed to her out this way, so it was unsurprising that the family owned more land nearby.

Though they were all tired, the former servants derived a great deal of amusement from Henry's attempts to participate in the cleaning. He was eager to help and do his fair share – a fact that they all quickly had to become less uncomfortable with – but woefully lacking in experience or skill. After half an hour of watching him attempt to change the sheets on one of the beds, Odette and Robbie were laughing so much that they both had stitches in their sides.

Despite the danger, dinner was a relaxed and happy affair. It was as if they'd finally let out a collectively held breath, and could now take comfort in the success of the first stage of their task.

The house was well stocked with wine and, with no sign of outside threats, more than a few bottles cracked open. By the end of the evening Odette's limbs were warm and light from the alcohol and the company of her friends.

All but Odette and Henry excused themselves to their rooms, deeming tomorrow the day to begin planning and working on going forward. She put the last of the dishes away with Henry's help. A comfortable silence fell over them until it came time to go upstairs, at which point they lingered together in the middle of the hall, near the door to Odette's room.

"Well," said Henry, looking as awkward as Odette felt. "Goodnight."

There was a tense pause during which Odette was quite certain she wanted to kiss him, and had a strong suspicion that the feeling was mutual, but neither moved. Odette wriggled her fingers in Henry's hand, wondering if he could tell that her palms were slightly clammy. Which was silly, of course, because if anything the house was very cold.

But his eyes were burning into her skin.

"Goodnight," she said, turning towards her room. He surged towards her and wrapped her in his arms, but then paused, lips slightly parted as their noses bumped. He was, Odette realised, terribly tense. Perhaps it didn't matter that her heart was threatening to jump out of her ribcage.

His kiss, when it came, was unexpectedly gentle. She wondered idly how it was that sating the desire she'd felt for hours could do nothing but make her wish for more; and then he was stepping away from her, cheeks flushed and his hair falling into his eyes.

"Goodnight," he said again, moving past her with slow steps, as if he didn't wish to move away. In a rare display of bravado, Odette looked up to meet his gaze, and wondered if she was melting.

Moments later she felt the door click closed behind her, the light of the candles in the hallway fading. As she looked over the bedroom – which was now lit only by moonlight – she reflected on how quickly she'd become used to having someone to do things for her. Aside from the lack of light, there was no fire in the grate and the bed hadn't been turned down. In her mind's eye, she could imagine the servants who'd move quietly through the room to prepare it in the months when the house was used.

The thought was so vivid that she almost imagined she could see her former self knelt by the fire, carefully stacking kindling within it. She barely recognised the young woman who rested on her heels in her perfect – but not *too* perfect – uniform; she couldn't recall the pervasive dirt of soot on her hands, or the calluses of a scrubbing brush. It occurred to her in that moment how strange it was to be herself, and yet not be the same person as she'd once been.

Blinking the image away, she looked down at her hands, dismayed to find that they still trembled. If she'd truly changed so much, why had she not yet gotten hold of her fear?

She turned back towards the door and rested one hand

upon the centre panel. Suddenly, the weight of Henry's presence down the corridor began to weigh upon her; the heat of his last glance as she'd entered the bedroom warmed her again. Perhaps she'd not learned to shed her fear, but she had learned that it was all right to want things. Hadn't she?

Before she could catch up with her own thoughts, her hand had moved to the door handle. A chorus of voices, all her own, sounded in her mind – about propriety, and station, and impossibility. But Odette knew, deep down, that she was as stubborn as she was cowardly. Perhaps it was time to be one and not the other. Her hand twitched, pulling the door open, and she stepped back out into the light.

It was quickly evident that despite her frantic thoughts, very little time had passed – for Henry had not yet made it the whole way down the corridor to his room. He paused as she stepped into the hall, turning at the sound of the door opening. The candles behind him silhouetted his form and shrouded his face.

"What is it?" he asked, his voice low as he stepped back towards her.

Though her legs felt stiff and wobbly all at once, Odette closed the space between them and pinched hold of his lapels, gripping them tightly to hide her shaking limbs. She could barely look at his face; especially now, when there was a breath trembling in her throat and fire coursing through her limbs.

"I ..." His hands brushed against her sides, as if to hold her steady. "I think that in times of upheaval such as this, it's nonsensical to cling to social norms. Status, rank, decorum, that sort of thing."

The corners of Henry's lips quirked, but he didn't mock her sudden formality. "It could be argued that in times of upheaval, social norms and traditions offer comfort."

The light teasing in his tone gave her encouragement enough to flick her eyes up to his for a moment. "It could. But that would be counterproductive."

"Oh?"

His arms tensed, one hand splaying across her back to pull her gently closer to him, the other twisting so that his thumb ran down over her hipbone. Odette wondered if he could feel her heart beating; it seemed to be trying to escape her chest entirely.

"Henry," she said softly, adjusting her grip, "for God's sake, don't make me say it out loud."

Chuckling, he tilted his head and pressed his lips to her cheek, spreading warmth across her skin like ripples of water. "Perhaps," he replied, "I *want* to hear you say it out loud."

There was a melodic intonation to his voice that made her wonder, just for a moment, if he was using his powers on her – or whether she'd simply never appreciated the resonance of his voice when it was low in pitch and barely above a whisper.

"I don't want to go back to my room."

Henry tightened one arm around her and reached for his own door with the other. "I've never found Society's arbitrary constructs particularly comforting," he said casually, and then pulled her into the darkness of his chambers. He closed the door carefully, but the sound seemed to Odette to echo throughout the house, alerting everyone to what was happening. The idea made her heart skip.

Then his body was pressing hers against the wall, and her hands were tangled in his hair, pulling it askew – and, for a little while, Odette forgot that there was anything else in the world but the two of them.

33

No matter how hard she tried, Odette couldn't push down the knot in her stomach. She'd never dealt well with anticipation, often feeling overwhelmed by how desperately she wanted whatever she was waiting for to happen *now*. Sometimes this would be so bad that she'd not seek out things she wanted at all because she couldn't bear the time between wanting and getting. With things she didn't want, or was afraid of, the story was much the same.

If they could just be in the town, finding Braddock now, it would all be much better. At least, that was the hope.

The others had been working on last-minute adjustments, some more curious than others. Odette was certain that all the detailed embroidery Abigail was putting on their travelling clothes would be wasted on her, given that it would lose its power as soon as she touched it. Still, it would work on the others and it seemed to be calming the older woman somewhat.

Isobel had locked herself away all day painting, and Roger had been going over the maps for escape routes from the nearby town. Matthew had continued to take charge of the defence of the house, though it seemed they hadn't been followed.

Mostly they'd been scattered about, working individually.

This was both good and bad for Odette: being around people might've helped her forget a little of her panic, though at least on her own no one could see how much her hands were shaking. She could pass out the rest of the time quietly reading by the fire and no one would be any the wiser. At least, that had been her plan.

Much to her dismay, the sudden clattering of the door opening snapped her from her reading and destroyed all hopes for a worry-free evening. She lifted her head to see Matthew standing in the doorway, his hair askew and a broad grin on his face.

"Come on! Up! No one is to be hiding on their own this evening, Professor's orders."

Her attempts to protest fell on deaf ears, and eventually she was forced to lift herself out of the chair and after Matthew, who led her through to one of the adjoining living rooms. It was not wholly surprising that they were gathering – after all, they hadn't yet made an actual *plan*. It had been decided that they would sneak people into the town to work out where Braddock was and what he was doing, but that was the extent of it.

Sure enough, as soon as Odette entered the room – which was small enough to look overly full even though their group was hardly a large one – there was an animated discussion already in progress about what, precisely, they were going to do. She shuffled over to where Robbie was sitting and curled up in the small space between him and the arm of the loveseat, feeling Henry's eyes heavy on her back as she moved.

Since the previous night, she'd done her best not to look at him when there were other people around; the grin that would spill across her face would probably give everything away, and for now she wanted what they had to be a precious secret.

"But what are we going to tell him?" Robbie said, running his hand over his short hair. "He's not very well going to be all chummy with us if we explain who we are."

"Hmm," said Mary, eyes gleaming. "P'raps 'e would. Ain't no harm in tellin' the truth ... half of it, mind. Tell 'im we're on the run. Tell 'im the army's after us too. An' that we're all mages."

"And," Isobel added, smiling shyly at Mary, "that we have somewhere to hide that we think is safe – for now, at least."

No one, Henry included, could think of a better enticement for Braddock than this. It was risky – for if he worked out who they were he'd surely see it as a betrayal – but all things considered very little they were doing now was without hazard. It was simply a matter of working out which was the safest or most effective.

What Henry couldn't do was talk Odette out of being the one to make first contact with Braddock.

"I'm the one who has to know him best," she said for what was probably the third time. Everyone else had left the living room and scattered to their various bedrooms. "We don't want to hurt him, but he doesn't know that – he's dangerous, and I'm the only one who can make it possible for us to capture him. It makes sense for it to be me."

"Yes, but ..."

Henry had been pacing back and forth for some time. Odette stood directly in front of him, and placed her hands on her hips. Stubbornness lifted her chin as she glared at him. "But what?"

"But …" He sighed. "It's dangerous."

"Henry, just *being* here is dangerous. Please … please at least let me do something useful rather than just waiting to get caught. Everyone else has something to do – Matthew and Roger are being lookouts; Mary, Abigail and Robbie are making things to keep us safe; Isobel's making sure we're on the right track, and you're in charge of everything. What am I doing?"

Henry paused, staring at her as if seeing her for the first time. It struck her then that they didn't know one another well at all, for they were still capable of surprising one another considerably. Perhaps this should've made her uncomfortable, but Odette found that she did not mind. A small surge of pride rippled through her as his face softened in acquiescence – her logic had evidently defeated him.

But there was fear in his eyes too, so she reached out to pull his wringing hands apart from one another. "I'll be all right, Henry."

"You can't promise me that," he said, tugging her close enough to press his lips into her hair, "any more than I can promise you."

"But we can do things to make ourselves safer." She did her best to make her voice soothing, like his when he sang. Inwardly wincing, she admitted with hesitation, "And the best way to make us safe from him is for me to know him well enough to control his powers. It's ironic, but …"

He chuckled again and nodded. "But you're right."

34

Over the ensuing days, they sent out several reconnaissance teams. In groups of one or two they'd go into town on the pretence of purchasing food. Quietly and surreptitiously, they began to gather information on Braddock: how often he'd been seen, what people thought of him, how dangerous he truly was.

Mary proved to be the most skilled at such interrogations. She was adept at making people feel at ease around her, a combination of her broad but more local accent and cheerful demeanour. She'd discovered that Braddock was known to be within or around the town, that there were many people gathered there who were sympathetic to his cause, and that most of the townsfolk considered him to be a sort of anti-hero. Henry was uncertain whether this was a good thing or a bad one – either they'd all been taken in by his lies, or there was more to Braddock than they'd thought.

She'd also found out that Braddock would be holding a rally in the town square on the coming Saturday. It was not surprising – he'd spent the past several weeks, even months, gathering a following around him. Believers. Galvanised, they began to prepare for the opportunity to see him.

After some discussion, they decided that Odette would endeavour to invite him to a private meeting where she could learn more about him.

It was not a plan that Henry agreed to easily, but once again he was defeated by logic.

So there was nothing left to do but get into the rally – which would likely have a far larger army presence – safely.

Fortunately, the rally was attended well enough that it wasn't dangerous for a few of them to sneak in and watch. They'd decided to alternate who went into town where possible, so as not to be recognised by the locals – though Roger and Matthew were of course always close by. This time Henry went with Odette, Robbie and Mary, all of them dressed in cloaks Abigail had made to make them seem as inconsequential as possible.

Thomas Braddock, meanwhile, looked to be the very opposite.

Of all the things he'd thought Braddock might be, Henry hadn't considered charismatic. But the young man commanded the stage like a seasoned performer; his voice carried through the crowds with effortless clarity; there was a draw, a pull about him that was almost akin to Edward's. It was no wonder he'd managed to escape thus far, if he could rally so loyal a following.

The worst part was that he was saying an awful lot of things that Henry agreed with.

"It isn't their fault," Braddock continued, holding his hands high. "They don't know any better. But we do. And it's our responsibility to show them how wrong they are. Now, there are some people who'd have you believe that we should hide. That we should keep ourselves secret. That we're safer this way. To those people I say: what is a prison if not barriers? What are barriers if not restrictions? You would imprison yourselves for safety, and deny yourself free lives, *true* lives.”

He paced back and forth across the makeshift stage, and Henry could feel the tension in the enthralled crowd growing. “And, yes, if we revealed ourselves one by one, it would be dangerous. I stand before you blessed to be safe enough, thanks to my powers to reveal myself now, though I stand alone. But there can be no recriminations if we stand united, if we turn to the world as one and say: we’re here! We’re real! And we want you to see us for who we are at last!”

The crowd erupted into riotous cheer, many leaping to their feet and stamping as they clapped and shouted in agreement. Some even began to unleash their magic: one woman lifted her hands and hurled magically crafted concoctions into the air, creating sparks of light like miniature fireworks; a man across from her leapt into an somersault that sent him spiralling through the display; and a set of young twins whistled tunes that drove the audience into even wilder celebration. Where had Braddock found these people? Had he taught them about their magic or had they already known? It was so easy not to notice it, and yet …

“Wow,” said Robbie, loud enough for Henry to hear him but quiet enough to go unnoticed by the raucous crowd. “He’s good.”

Mary clicked her tongue. “Thought ’e was mean’ t’ be scared.”

Tilting his head upwards, Henry looked at the makeshift stage where Braddock was now greeting his supporters. He never shook their hands, Henry noticed, and he stood slightly aloof from them, even though he looked engaged. There was a tension in his stance, as if he were drawing people in and keeping them at arm's reach all at once.

"He *is* scared," Robbie replied, echoing Henry's own thoughts. "He's just good at not showing it – or he's using his fear to be good at this."

Braddock's ordinary appearance unsettled Henry. Certainly there was something off about his demeanour, and he'd definitely not stayed anywhere with more than the most basic hygiene facilities for some time … but no one around him seemed to notice or mind. And there were wanted posters and newspapers everywhere, splattered with his face. Surely everyone here knew who he was, what he'd done – and yet they accepted him. Him, a murderer.

But was this truly abnormal? No person was only one thing. Braddock was a killer, yes, but he was many other things as well – just as Henry was more than simply a professor, and his friends were more than just servants. His father, who'd served for decades in the army, had probably killed far more people than Braddock had. In the eyes of their society, though, that was legitimised by his membership of the army.

And what was this loyalty Braddock commanded if not a different form of legitimacy? If people believed in him, and what he was saying, then it was unsurprising that they'd see nothing wrong with what he'd done. They would turn the situation around and see a man who'd valiantly defended himself against an oppressive regime; just as Henry and the others had decided to see a scared man who was desperately in need of help.

Worse still was that Henry could see no right answer – each of these points of view was just as valid as the other, all possessed positives and negatives, and all anyone could do was weigh them up and decide what they thought was best.

Or, Henry thought, looking over the crowd, be caught up in whatever wave of activity happened to pass by.

No, the danger was not in thinking that yours was the only point of view, but in never choosing that point of view for yourself. Some would call it ignorance, others yielding, submissive, subservient. Whatever it was, it was dangerous. It was inescapable.

"Well," said Odette, who until that moment had been quite silent. She did not, Henry suspected, feel comfortable in crowds. "I should go and introduce myself."

Her statement was plaintive and followed by the inaction of someone lacking conviction.

"We'll be right near you, Det," murmured Robbie. "And if you don't want to do it, it's still not too late for one of us to."

Odette shook her head fiercely. "No, I'm doing it. It makes the most sense. I just, um … I need help getting through the crowd."

Nodding, Mary looped her arm tightly round Odette's. "I've got yeh, gel."

"We'll watch from nearby," Henry said, glancing hesitantly at Odette. He could see her hands shaking even from a few steps away. He should stop her – tell her to let him do it. But she was right. "You know the signal if you need us."

"Just drop my handkerchief." Odette placed her free hand in her pocket where the white silk rested. Then, to comfort herself as much as the others, she added, "I'll be fine."

Together, Henry and Robbie moved to one the side of the stage whilst Odette and Mary weaved round to the other. They pretended to be interested in one of the groups of magical performers who'd taken up position there, lingering at the edge of the circle that surrounded it. Though they had their backs to Braddock, Henry found he could quite clearly hear everything the young man was saying.

" ... isn't going to change overnight, we know this. But it has to start somewhere, and if we just keep hoping that something will change, nothing will happen. Revealing ourselves is a strong move – and make no mistake, it's going to have consequences – but it will make things start to happen. That's what's important."

Whomever he was talking to was clearly pleased; they thanked him in a rush of words and promised to spread the word until the next rally. Then there was the creaking of boards – the stage was rather a ramshackle affair – and the shuffling of soft, barely audible footsteps.

"Hello," he heard Odette say. Her voice, soft and hesitant as it was, was harder to hear than Braddock's. Henry rocked back slightly, giving the appearance of adjusting his standing position whilst actually moving closer to her. "Your speech was wonderful."

Braddock's reply was polite, if not warm. "Thank you."

"I was wondering, um, I'd like to talk to you. But not – not around this many people."

There was a pause. Was it too long a pause? Henry began to fret. He raised his hands in applause towards the performers he pretended to watch, hands shaking with fear.

"Why?" asked Braddock, this time with a little less civility and more suspicion.

To her credit, Odette sounded far more composed than Henry felt. "Because not all of us are ready to reveal ourselves. And not everyone's powers are ... quite so worthy of celebration. Or quite so normal."

"None of our powers are normal," Braddock said, though

Henry thought he could hear curiosity in his tone.

"No," chuckled Odette. "But mine is even less so. And I … I'm not fond of crowds."

Henry risked a brief glance behind him on the pretence of allowing a child to pass him for a better view. Braddock, Odette and Mary were alone on the centre of the stage now, his admirers having gathered to have a lively debate on the other side. Odette had her hands clasped together before her, nervously twisting the fabric of her gloves. Braddock's arms were folded, his brow furrowed.

"There's a place called Martha's," he said at length, floorboards creaking as he moved. "Be there at ten tomorrow."

Not until she was safely back with him did Henry hear Odette let out the breath she'd been holding. Her arm was back in Mary's, and it was unclear which of them was holding onto the other tighter – Odette for support or Mary to protect her.

"Ye did it, gel," the older woman said, fondly. "Now les ge' home."

Robbie and Henry nodded in agreement. It was done – it had worked, and they were all safe. Or they would be, assuming they got out of town without incident. The sooner they were gone from here the better, as they'd only be able to use the crowds for so long.

The three made their way swiftly through, splitting up at points so as not to draw attention. Fortune favoured them once more, however; they were as unimpeded on the way out as they'd been on the way in. Henry had expected to feel relief once they got back to the house, but found he could think of nothing but Odette's lone meeting with Braddock the next day.

It gnarled at him all night, echoing voices demanding to know what the hell he thought he was doing, leading all of them into this.

35

Abigail had insisted that Odette wear one of the dresses she'd sewn to meet Braddock, even though it would do absolutely nothing for her magically. It was made of a thin, soft wool that had been dyed a deep indigo, and covered in intricate silver embroidery. Such embellishments were fast becoming Abigail's trademark, and this dress was a particularly fine example of her skill. From a distance, it looked simply like scrollwork; close up, one could pick out tiny flowers in different stages of germination, laid deep within the twirling vines.

Thus dressed, Odette tried to hide both her nerves and a smile as Abigail insisted on doing her hair. The tension between them back at home had dissolved over time as Abigail's own powers had grown – a source of some relief to Odette, as she'd never been very good at confronting people about problems.

That she'd managed to tell Henry how she felt was something of a miracle, and one that had caused no small amount of distress.

Still, this achievement aside, heading into a town full of soldiers to meet a murderer seemed a terrible idea, all things considered.

But for all that Odette had been terrified of, even she had

to admit that she was generally just as stubborn as she was afraid – and there was nothing she hated more than being incapable, or letting people down. Not for the first time, she wondered to what degree their powers came from their personalities. Robbie was sturdy and grounded, just like the wood he worked with; Abigail was caring and something of a perfectionist; Isobel was easily distracted and prone to dreaming ... though perhaps she was simply finding what she was looking for and not *seeing* the others. Even still, she couldn't help but be curious.

Once Abigail had finished braiding her hair into an artfully dishevelled crown, Odette was drawn from her thoughts – and faced with the realisation that there was nothing to do now but leave. Matthew and Roger would be escorting her through the forest and hills, since between them they'd come to know the route reasonably well. They were waiting for her in the entrance hall as she descended the stairs. Henry was there, too, with so deep a frown knotting his brow that she had the sudden urge to brush it away with her fingertips.

But though their burgeoning relationship was hardly hidden from the others, they'd not quite progressed to displaying. So, instead, Odette reached out and squeezed his hand in what she hoped was an acceptably reassuring gesture. Henry seemed to understand and gently ran his thumb over her knuckles before releasing her.

"You'll be careful?" he asked, his voice so soft that it made something ache deep in her chest.

She nodded. They'd decided it was better for her to go into the town alone, lookouts excepted – they didn't want to spook Braddock and waste the trip. "I will."

It wasn't the goodbye she wanted, but it would have to do.

The journey was uneventful. Seeing Roger's care for the animals in his service or Matthew's gravity-defying feats of acrobatics usually cheered her, but Odette was too nervous to take delight in their powers. Roger had quickly picked up on her wish to remain silent, and even Matthew stopped trying to get her to talk after a while – he couldn't quite manage to stay silent himself, but there was something comforting about having him prattle on in the background. As they neared the town, this too died away.

She was less conspicuous entering on her own so Roger and Matthew bade her farewell on the edge of the forest. They'd be joining her in the town, to keep watch over her meeting, but she wouldn't see them – knowing where they or their agents were might give them away.

Following their directions, Odette made her way along the edge of a field towards the road from a nearby village that led to the town. It provided a logical explanation for where she'd come from, should anyone ask, and was a little easier to walk along than the path through the fields.

Reaching into her pocket, she checked her father's watch – she was right on time.

She made her way as quickly as she could, knowing that it would take a little while to find the small tea shop that Braddock had told her to meet him in. It was, he'd said, not far from the square where the rally had been.

The increased army presence since the rally was noticeable – though the side streets were largely free of redcoats, the main thoroughfares were littered with them.

Thankfully the weather was bad enough that Odette did not look out of place with her hood up, and, it being around lunchtime, the town was bustling with such life that it was easy to disappear within the crowd, magical cloak or not.

For once the large numbers of people served to comfort her rather than fill her with anxiety. No one gave her a second glance, and she was able to find the way to the shop rather easily.

It was a quaint building with a weather-beaten sign: Martha's Tea & Cake Shoppe. Through the window, Odette could see a scattering of people inside, though Braddock wasn't immediately obvious – which was intentional, she was certain. Glancing once more at her watch, she decided it would be better to be a few minutes early than to loiter in the much emptier side street, and pushed open the door. It chimed with the rattling of a bell as she entered, drawing the attention of the proprietor.

"Afternoon, dearie." The woman behind the counter smiled at Odette. She was missing several teeth, but had a reddish glow about her face that was welcoming. "I'm Martha. Take a seat. I'll have the boy get to you shortly."

Odette did her best to return the smile. "Actually, I'm meeting someone here." She glanced nervously over the room, but there was no sign of him. "Perhaps I'm a little early."

She looked back at Martha, and found that she was being examined with some scrutiny.

"Meeting a young man, perhaps?"

Odette blushed. "Oh. Yes, I suppose I am."

This seemed to earn Martha's approval in some way – the woman nodded, and gestured for Odette to follow her. "Just through here, dear."

At first, Odette thought she was being led to a backroom of some kind, but Martha only took her to the rear of the shop. They passed several tables filled with chattering men and women, most of whom were twice her age; none paid her more than a fleeting glance. It was reassuring, and she could see why Braddock had chosen this place. In contrast to the gossip and exposure from a tavern, here everyone seemed focused on their own business.

At the back of the room, a booth of upholstered benches curved to shield those seated from the view of most of the other tables. It was occupied.

Thomas Braddock was neither tall nor particularly short. He was certainly young, but unlike his portrait had a pervasive fatigue about his face that distorted any attempts to guess his age. There were deep purplish-blue bags under his eyes, and his hair had a greasy shine to it. That, along with the sheen of dirt on his clothes and skin, suggested he rarely got the opportunity to wash. Odette supposed there were few places he could stay, and winced at the voice in her head that told her this a good thing, given that part of their goal was to convince him to stay with them. He had unremarkable features, and was not especially handsome, but there was a confidence in his bearing that made up for it.

"Thank you, Martha," he said politely as they approached. The proprietor seemed to take this as a dismissal, but Odette noticed that she smiled and nodded at Braddock before departing.

Thus abandoned, Odette waited to be invited to sit, but Braddock simply stared at her with raised eyebrows, and she concluded that politeness did not necessarily correlate with upper-class codes of etiquette, and she seated herself. Only then did she pull her hood down. She did her best to smile in an encouraging fashion, and reached up to tuck a stray lock of hair behind her ear.

"Thank you for meeting me. It's, um, lovely to meet someone else who understands."

For a long moment Braddock scrutinised her. Her face heated up with embarrassment and she looked away. While this granted her a reprieve from his intense stare, it did nothing to help her gauge whether she'd met his approval. When he replied, his voice small in comparison to the loud preaching of the rally, it startled her so much that she practically jumped in her seat.

"It is," he agreed, though he sounded mildly unconvinced. "Assuming that the understanding goes both ways."

In a rush of breath, Odette found herself apologising. "I know I didn't explain much about why I wanted to meet you. I'm sorry for that. It's just, well, I was afraid you wouldn't agree to meet me. That you'd think it was silly."

This piqued his curiosity and Odette noticed the change in his demeanour. "Why would I think that?"

She chuckled despite herself. "Well," she said hesitantly, "my friends barely believe what I can do. Apparently it isn't a normal ... power, even amongst our kind. I suppose I thought you'd think the same."

It wasn't quite true – there was Peter, after all, but it seemed the two of them were unlike most of the other mages.

"And what is it that you can do?"

"I, um." Odette pushed away the same lock of hair that persisted in falling over her eyes, wishing that Abigail had braided it in a less distracting style. "Well, I can make people who have powers ... better at using them. Not forever, just, um, briefly. Whilst I'm helping."

Braddock drew so sharp a breath that it made Odette look

up in surprise. "You … that's …"

"I know."

"I've never heard of anyone being able to do that before."

Odette chuckled. "Neither has anyone I know, and a couple are academics who've been studying magic for years."

Braddock looked as if he were about to burst – like he wanted to ask a dozen questions simultaneously. At that moment, however, Martha returned to ask if Odette would like anything.

"Oh, I …" She realised she had no money on her. They'd pooled their limited resources to feed everyone – the house they were staying in had some provisions, but not enough to last long. Consequently, the money her mother had given her was all gone. "No, thank you. I can't – I ate before I came."

Martha accepted the obvious lie and departed with a tooth-less smile. Braddock, though, was having none of it. "You're too well dressed to be poor," he said, gesturing towards her. "So why don't you have any money?"

"I never said—"

He snorted. "Yeah, you did."

"Well," Odette said, trying to regain her composure, and figuring that it was as good a time as any to introduce a little more of the truth. "Actually, my friends and I are … on the run."

No acting was necessary – she was afraid enough of being caught out in her lies that she lowered her voice and looked about nervously without having to think about it.

"I think I would've remembered seeing you in the papers." Though there was scepticism in his voice, Braddock was leaning forward now, listening intently.

Odette shook her head and began to tell the story they'd

decided on. "We haven't done anything. I mean, not yet. The army had some lecturers from Oxford gather us together and train us up – we'd no idea we had powers until a few weeks ago, no idea what it was for, and we just ..." She caught her bottom lip between her teeth. "You know when you just have a sense that something very bad is happening? They started asking my best friend, who carves things out of wood, whether he'd make weapons. The woman who made the dress I'm wearing was asked to make armour."

"So you left?"

"We asked to. They said no – that we'd agreed to it and had to stay." She looked down, letting her fear show to try to make her performance all the more believable. "We ran away during the night. We've got a house not too far from here where we've been hiding."

Absorbing this with wide eyes, Braddock shook his head. "Of course they'd want to use us," he all but growled, banging his fist against the table so hard that a couple seated nearby looked over. "You're lucky you got away. How'd you manage to?"

Odette grinned despite the situation. "One of our group is good with animals. I mean, magically good. He asks them to do something and they just do it. He told the army's search dogs to lead the soldiers the wrong way, and had birds scouting for us. All sorts."

Braddock's glare turned to a grin of his own. "Bet they weren't expecting that."

"Not at all. Honestly, they might not even have worked it out yet."

It was hard not to look towards the window to see if Roger's lookouts were there. She was rather glad they'd come in separately; though it would've been reassuring to be able to see them, she would've given them away a dozen times over with her nervous glances. She simply had to trust that somewhere at the window was a pigeon keeping an eye on her, watching for her signal. It was rather a strange thing to wish for; the sort of thing she might've daydreamed about whilst working.

"Serves them right for trying to control all of you. You never found out what they were going to make you do?"

"No." She shook her head, suddenly overcome by the memory of Morley's hand running across her cheek. "To be honest, I don't want to know. It was … it was like they didn't even see us as people. Just potential."

"Don't know what else you expected from the army." Braddock's voice turned thin and full of anger; it seemed to not to fit with him somehow, despite being more in tune with the persona they'd been led to expect. "So what's your plan. Stay holed up forever? It doesn't work; I've tried it before."

"I'm not sure what we're going to do in the long term. It's all happened quite fast, to be honest. We've barely had a chance to think. Henry – he's one of the lecturers from Oxford – he's sort of our leader. And he says it's safe for now, and that's the main thing." Just thinking about the future made her tense up; she was sure Braddock could see that.

"Oakley?" he remarked with a thoughtful tone that was at odds with the jarring bolt of fear that ran through Odette at the damning question. How did he know Henry?

Braddock hummed, eyes darting towards the windows and the town outside. Whatever he was thinking, it took him some time to voice his conclusions. When he looked back at her he remarked simply, "I suppose with the animal world on your side, you'd be safer than most."

Odette nodded, unsure where this was going. "We've got Matthew, too, who's astonishingly good at climbing. Literally monkey-like. And we have a woman who can paint the future."

Doing nothing to hide his incredulity, Braddock raised his eyebrows. "Really?"

"Yes. It's difficult, of course; whatever she paints does come true, but she doesn't have a huge amount of control over what she paints. She can try to do a certain thing, but there's always an element of randomness to it. She's getting better and better every day, though, and she paints all the time – so I think if we were going to be attacked she'd have some indication."

His eyes dropped to the table and his hands clenched together in fists. "Whenever I've stayed in the same place before," he said quietly, "I've gotten people into trouble."

With that soft confession, Odette began to understand, and her heart leapt – if he thought coming with them was his idea, then he wouldn't suspect them of having lied. They could keep him safe from the army until they worked out what to do. Not for the first time, she wished she was better at talking people into things.

"We're already in trouble," she said gently. But this only served to make him narrow his eyes.

"Then why are you here? Do you want to bring them down on me, too? Because I'm in enough trouble as it is."

"No, I ..." Panic rose in Odette's throat. "I just don't want them to do to other people what they did to us. To you. I don't want a world where people get forced into terrible situations that make them do things they wish they hadn't."

Though she regretted saying it as soon as the words had left her mouth, it was too late to take it back. Her breath began to jump erratically.

"I just want us to understand each other more," she concluded a little helplessly, feeling as if the conversation was running away from her.

"You're right. It's good to understand one another," Braddock replied, staring at her intently.

Then he bowed his head, unknowingly tilting his face out of the view of Roger's lookouts, and murmured something that chilled her to the bone.

"You know, part of the reason people don't hurt one another more when they get into fights is that their own pain restricts them. You can't punch someone without hurting yourself. But I can. I never get hurt when I hit people. I never have to stop. They think I'm powerful, but they have no idea just how powerful I am … and neither do you."

Odette's fingers clutched tightly around the handkerchief in her pocket. She could pull it out and they would get her out of here. She'd be safe. They would go away, the army would find Braddock, and Peter would take down his powers. Eventually, anyway. All it would take was a twitch of her wrist, a stumbling apology, the silk thrown to the ground where her hidden reinforcements could see it.

But she didn't move a muscle. People were more than one thing. She had to believe that.

"No," she said instead. "I don't. But I don't doubt that if you wanted to you could kill me in a few seconds. You haven't, though."

"I haven't."

She didn't dare to look up at his face, lest she give away her terror, but it almost sounded as if Braddock approved of her in some way.

"Everyone underestimates us because they don't understand us. Sometimes you have to show them to make them understand. It's … it's not always something they force you to do."

Odette swallowed, her throat feeling thick with fear. "It's not always an accident. You're not just made by the world; there's always part of you that's just … you."

"Exactly."

Her eyes flickered up to meet his, and found a horrible smile on his lips that was at odds with the pained glimmer in his eyes. It made Odette's heart ache; was he really meant to be like this? They'd spun a story about what the army had forced them to do, but, whether Braddock believed it or not, he'd been turned into the person he was because they'd forced him to become so. And no, that didn't absolve him – it didn't change much, really … save for the fact that it could happen to any of them. Because it wasn't about becoming someone different … it was just about doing things that every single person was capable of.

The very thought made her feel sick.

But she didn't want to let them down. She couldn't let them down; they'd sent her here to do something and she was going to see it through. And Braddock? Well, she didn't want to let him down either. Despite what he'd done. Everyone, she suspected, had always let him down, and she wanted to prove to him that the world was better than that. That the things that had gone wrong before didn't have to repeat themselves.

That he could do things differently.

So she sighed, pulled her hand from the pocket and left the handkerchief behind. Then she told him why she was really there. "Would you like to come with me? Stay with us?"

Whatever he'd been expecting her to say, this wasn't it.

"I just threatened you," he pointed out, as if she were truly stupid. "And you want me to go with you."

"Yes."

He let out a horrible, empty laugh. "You're mad. You know that, right?"

"Maybe," she admitted with a chuckle of her own. It was certainly possible; she was here, alone with a murderer, trying to save his life. "But so is the world, sometimes. And as far as I can tell, you're one of the few people trying to do something about that. It's not your fault the world disagrees."

They fell silent. Braddock seemed deep in thought, and Odette tried to calm her breathing. The worst had passed. Her limbs had begun to feel heavy – she needed to leave soon or she'd become too tired to protect herself.

"I want to meet this lecturer of yours," Braddock stated with the conviction that comes from being used to people obeying. "Talk to him. Here, tomorrow, at the same time. Then I'll decide."

Odette felt her face light up in a brilliant smile, her fear of putting Henry in danger eclipsed for a moment by triumph. "I'll bring him."

36

The hours spent waiting for Odette to come back were some of the longest in Henry's life.

He was clearly not alone in feeling that way – they had, in unspoken agreement, gathered in one of the living rooms to take solace in one another's company. Abigail was curled up before the fire, sewing gloves that would offer even more protection from the cold; next to her, Mary was placing dough to prove and kneading more; Robbie and Isobel had taken up seats either side of Henry like some sort of honour guard, and were trying to teach him one of the servants' card games. Truth be told, he couldn't remember any of the rules – nor, he suspected, did they much care.

When it finally came, the click of the door echoed throughout the silent house, caused them to start. At once, Robbie dashed out towards the entrance; the rest hovered with bated breath.

How many pairs of footsteps could he hear? Were they all back? Roger and Matthew had hardly been in danger – that was the point of using animal lookouts – but the army would be everywhere now that Braddock was holding rallies.

"They're home!" yelled Robbie.

There was a collective sigh of relief. A few moments later he returned to the room, one hand gripping Odette's tightly. Matthew and Roger followed close behind. The three of them looked exhausted from the walk back, and were immediately fussed over. If Henry had noticed one thing about the servants, it was that they were very good at looking after each other.

He wanted to go to her, to smooth the dent in her brow and hold her until her hands stopped shaking, but he couldn't. So instead he sat nearby, keeping his gaze upon her in an attempt to analyse her every move, checking for any sign of distress. Only once refreshments had been brought in – Odette was, Henry noticed, tired enough to perk up at the taste of Mary's cakes – did they press any of them to speak.

"From our point of view it all went well," said Roger, clearly offering up the explanation before Matthew got the chance to do it with more verbosity. "There's definitely more soldiers in the area but they're just as predictable. It just means we have narrower windows in which to enter without being seen by patrols."

Leaping on the older man's pause, Matthew gushed, "And I made a map of all their new patrol loops so that when we go back we know who's going where, because I thought that would be useful. Oh, and I also left some markers for myself up in the trees so that it's easy for me to spot the best lookout spaces – I had one of Roger's birds tell me what spots I could sit in where people couldn't see me but I'd see as much as possible."

A small chuckle rippled through the room. "That's wonderful, Matthew," Henry said. "Hopefully that'll make us a lot safer in the future."

Then, because it could be postponed no longer, he looked over at Odette. The others did the same, so she placed her plate to one side and wrapped her fingers together in her lap. She'd taken a seat between Robbie and Roger, across from where Henry and Isobel were sitting. Mary and Abigail were still next to the fire, and Matthew had taken his customary perch on the windowsill.

"It went … well," she said, smiling faintly in surprise. "Really well. He believed me, which is the most important thing. As to what he's like – I think he *is* very scared. But he also really does believe what he's saying. I think the two are intertwined."

"You called it," remarked Robbie to Isobel, who smiled shyly.

With a fond glance towards the painter, Odette nodded and continued. "He seems to know quite a lot about magical theory. He'd heard of you, Henry."

This surprised Henry so much that he started in his seat. "He … he has?" he asked, knotting his brow in thought. "My position is hardly public."

"I don't know how he knows, but he does. In fact, he wants to meet you."

Henry chuckled, more out of bravado than anything else. "Well, then I suppose I shan't fret too much about how he knows of me, if his knowledge has proven useful. Did he say much else?"

There was, he noticed, a brief pause before Odette shook her head. "I think the place I met him – it's a tea shop – is somewhere he hides quite often. He seemed to know the proprietor very well. It's possible there are more people in the town sheltering him."

They spent a little while discussing this and their plans for the next meeting until it was time for dinner to be prepared.

Some helped Mary carry her risen dough to the kitchen, whilst others went for more firewood. Eventually, as they filtered out, Henry and Odette were left alone in the room. As soon as the door had clicked shut behind Matthew, Henry stepped across to her and wrapped his arms around her waist.

"Oh," she murmured in surprise, placing her arms around his neck as he rested his head on her shoulder. "I really am all right, you know. It wasn't all that bad."

But Henry knew better. The hesitation he'd heard in her voice earlier was back, and she was still trembling slightly. Drawing back, he brushed a stray lock of hair behind her ear and frowned at her.

"What is it that you didn't tell the others?"

Her face flushed with colour. "I don't know what you mean."

Henry became anxious. He *had* seen something. He looked her up and down, as if searching for wounds – but saw nothing to indicate that Braddock had hurt her. She wilted slightly under his gaze, eyes darting aside as if to avoid him.

"It's nothing bad," she said, this lie even more unconvincing than the previous one.

When he made no reply save to stare at her, she sighed and rubbed at her face with her hands. "I upset him at one point. It was my fault. I said something about ... not wanting people to be forced into terrible situations, where they had to do horrible things."

Henry winced and did his best to ignore the flare of anger at her words – what a foolish, foolish thing to say!

"But he didn't hurt you."

Odette shook her head at once, rocking back towards him. "No. No, he didn't touch me. He ... he threatened me, but that's all."

No sooner had he quenched his anger than it returned, fierce and kindled with the fuel of protectiveness. He wanted, suddenly, to shake some sense into her – to make her realise exactly how dangerous this man was, that he was not simply a tortured soul to be pitied. But Henry didn't want to become his father, so he turned aside and began to pace back and forth, hands clenched into fists.

"We should never have come here," he said, astonishing himself at how bitter, how alien his voice sounded. "This is too dangerous. He can kill us, all of us, in an instant. We're not the army; we're not meant to be dealing with this."

"I'm all right, Henry. It wasn't like that," Odette urged at once, reaching to grab hold of him in an attempt to ground him.

He looked down almost distantly at where her fingers rested at the crook of his elbow, unable to push away the realisation that the danger she was in was his fault. Still, the touch of her hand calmed him, and he ceased pacing.

"It's not an empty threat from him, Ditty." The words came slowly, as if he both had to say them and couldn't bear to. "He's killed people. If he's threatened you …"

Turning his gaze back to Odette, Henry sighed. Her eyes refused to meet his. It seemed a long while since she'd been so skittish with him. Thus unwatched, he looked at her, searching for a sign that she truly understood how dangerous Braddock was. He trailed the edge of his finger down the side of her face, but the skin was soft and dry. He let his thumb tug gently at her bottom lip, but it wasn't clutched between her teeth. And the hand at his elbow was trembling, but no more than usual.

"But it worked, Henry. It worked. He promised to talk to you." Her voice was soft and hesitant, and Henry's stomach churned for having seeded doubt in her. "Can't we concentrate on that?"

Part of him still wanted to shake her until she understood, but he knew it would be hypocritical. He'd sent her into the lion's den; he could hardly fault her for having been roared at. And he certainly didn't consider her defenceless, or even reckless. She was right, after all. It had worked. But he couldn't quite shake the idea that one day he might be right instead. That one day Braddock would go through with his threat, and she wouldn't come back to them. To him.

His thoughts must have shown in his face, for he was pulled from them by Odette nestling her body close against his. "I'm all right," she repeated, her breath warm against his neck.

"This time."

She didn't respond.

He tilted his chin forward and pressed his lips against the top of her head, smelling the lavender soap in her hair. He wrapped his arms around her. There were so many words poised on the tip of his tongue, but few, he suspected, would be helpful or welcomed; chastising her any more was clearly going to have no effect. If he'd learned anything about her over the past weeks, it was that she could be so terribly stubborn, especially when she thought she was doing the right thing.

No, perhaps words were not the best idea. But, then, he didn't have to tell her things in words.

He tangled his fingers in her hair, which was plaited into an artfully tousled crown – or had been some hours ago, before she'd walked to and from the town – and rubbed at the base of her head with his fingertips. She whimpered, and Henry knew without having to look that she was blushing into the crook of his neck. Grinning, he tightened the arm around her waist and half lifted her in the direction of the stairs, feeling much more confident than the last time they'd stumbled that way.

"Henry, it's not even dinnertime yet. Everyone else is awake," she mumbled shyly, feet scurrying to adjust to the sudden movement.

His eyes gleamed.

"Then we'll just have to be quiet."

37

Odette felt Henry's fingers tighten slightly around her own as they wove through the crowds – though whether it was for her benefit or his, she couldn't tell. Crowds had always made her nervous, but her place in life meant she rarely had to suffer them. Still, she couldn't blame Braddock for hiding in such a way. His was a face that many knew, and there was only so much a cowl would do. The worst part was having to be so hyper-aware of all the people; both she and Henry were nervously scanning about them to look for redcoats.

Eventually they made it to the side street where she'd met Braddock the day before, and the crowds died down. There was no sign of the army, nor even police officers, and so they moved towards the tea shop straight away.

Another tightening of Henry's grip made her pause. "Ditty … I'll be there with you, all right? He's not going to hurt you."

A knot wound itself in Odette's throat twice over: once for the fact that he cared enough to say it, and once for the memory of Braddock's threat. She opened her mouth to reply, but realised she had little to say. To claim she didn't need protecting would be a lie; to suggest that Henry's protection would do little to help would be pointless at best and offensive at worst; not to reply at all would be rude.

So instead she turned on the spot, rolled up onto her toes and caught Henry's lips with hers, her free hand caressing the growing stubble on his cheek – because it seemed, all things considered, the best response. The only response.

He pulled her against him, one hand in the small of her back, and held her there for a moment.

"We should go in," Odette murmured. "We don't want to keep him waiting."

Henry agreed, and they entered the largely deserted tea shop hand in hand.

Braddock was seated in an alcove towards the back that placed him out of view of those entering whilst ensuring that he had a clear view of all who came through the door. He didn't stand to meet them, but nodded his head, eyes darting about with their usual paranoia.

"Thomas, this is Henry. He's the one I—"

"Professor." So abrupt, and so revealing, was Braddock's interruption that both of them paused, perched on the edge of their seats. He really did know who Henry was. "Oh, you're quite famous in the magical world, you know."

"Then in many ways you have the advantage on me," replied Henry with more calm than Odette suspected he was feeling. "It's a pleasure to meet you."

"Piss off. You know as well as I do that this whole situation is fucked, and so is everything that happens in it."

Odette frowned. "Thomas, there's no need to be rude."

Both men turned to look at her as if she'd grown a third head. For a moment, Odette feared that her gamble – which, if she was honest, had been an accidental slip – had not paid off, but then Braddock chuckled.

"You know what?" he said, shaking his head. "Fine. Nice

to meet you too, Professor. Now what do you want? I don't, as it happens, have all day to sit around in public places."

Odette closely examined Braddock, now that his attention focused on Henry. The bags under his eyes were no worse, but certainly no better. His complexion remained pale and his appearance was no less bedraggled. But there remained a spark in his eyes: defiance, maybe, or perhaps hope. The latter made the knot in her throat grow. What if they couldn't save him?

Running his hand through his hair, Henry sighed. "I'll be blunt, then, as I think you'll appreciate it more than the alternatives. We want to offer you sanctuary. I have a place in the woods a couple of miles away that the army almost certainly doesn't know about. It's a place given to me by family, not on many maps, probably as safe as you can get without leaving the country. Which you could do, if you wanted, with our help."

Braddock stared at them with wide, dark eyes, almost as if trying to pierce the truth of the statement. His reply was blunt.

"Why?"

"Because we're mages too. Because you're not the only one on the run. There are more of us; I'm sure Odette's told you about them. Because we believe that all you want is to be free; just like we do."

There was a thick, tense pause. Odette didn't dare fill it lest she irritate Braddock – which, she'd learned last time, was all too easily done. Instead she twisted her hands together in her lap and, unbeknownst to herself, mirrored Braddock's darting gaze.

"I read a book you wrote," he stated. "You said something

in it. I don't remember the exact words. It was something like 'Maybe we will never get to live out in the open, but that doesn't mean we can't live as our true selves. Until the world at large understands us, we should make our own world.'"

Next to her, Odette heard Henry chuckle, and she looked up to see a nervous smile quirking the corners of his lips. "You read my thesis. My real thesis. How on earth did you get a copy? It was never published."

"Live underground for long enough and you get hold of plenty of illegal things."

"I'm pleased to hear that it's out there somewhere," Henry confessed. "I was always disappointed that it couldn't be shown to other mages."

Braddock nodded. "People listen to me, you know. Power makes people listen to you. So does intelligence. And people respect institutions. It's how the army and the police manage to keep control." At first it seemed like they'd finally coaxed him into conversation, but then he paused, narrowing his eyes. "All that influence you've got ... what have you done with it?"

Odette winced in sympathy, but Henry didn't flinch. If anything, his smile broadened. "Not enough," he confessed in a slightly sing-song voice that she could tell was laced with power. "Which, frankly, is why I'm here. To start doing more."

An indecipherable emotion gleamed in Braddock's eyes, and he nodded, then stiffened, his back straightening so much that it became clear he generally held himself hunched. "Did you hear that?"

As soon as he'd said it, Odette heard a scuffling in the distance; boots traipsed through the streets outside with unnerving strength and unity.

"Marching," she whispered in horror, and the three of them leapt from their seats.

Gripping her arm suddenly, Braddock all but growled, "You should get out of here."

His fingers crushed her skin painfully – that, even more than the realisation that they'd been followed, jarred her fully into the moment.

"Not without you."

That Odette and Henry spoke simultaneously seemed to lend their words power. Eyes gleaming again, Braddock nodded, and gestured behind them. "There's a back exit. Through that door – go." Over his shoulder, he said to the woman behind the counter, "Sorry, Martha."

Henry put his fingers to his lips, letting out an ear-splitting whistle: the signal to Roger's lookouts.

And then all hell broke loose.

They were barely through the back door when the army burst into the shop, demanding to know where the fugitive was hiding. The three of them took off at a run, impeded by the twisting corridors that led through past the kitchens and out into the alleyway behind. So loud was the clattering of the door behind them that the army must surely have been in pursuit. Odette's heart was thudding in her ears, beating out a tattoo to accompany the rattling terror in her mind. She didn't want to die. Gods, but she didn't want to die.

They sprinted down the backstreet behind the shop, following Braddock's lead. He was faster, which was hardly surprising, and Henry's lack of conditioning made it hard-going. But there was no sign of pursuit behind them as they rounded corner after corner, and for a moment ... just a moment … Odette began to think they'd escaped …

Until half a dozen soldiers rounded the corner, cutting into their path.

They raised guns to their shoulders and aimed. She and Henry skidded to a halt, but Braddock continued to charge.

Flaring his power, he kicked one leg into the ankles of the first soldier, who clattered to the ground hard as Braddock used her momentum against her. He hurled a punch at the second soldier with supernaturally enhanced skill. The bullets fired at him bounced off his skin as if it were stone.

Odette had never seen a truly violent fight before, and she was struck by the sounds so rarely described in the books she read and that had never featured in her daydreams. She heard the breath rush from the soldiers' chests and the cracking of bones.

It was self-defence. She had to remember that.

But there was little time to dwell on it: two more soldiers had made it past Braddock and were heading towards them. Not thinking, she stepped in front of Henry, who'd immediately raised his voice in song – if she could just give him long enough, perhaps he'd be able to put them to sleep.

Odette braced herself, but exhaled with relief when they collapsed to the ground before reaching her.

"You'll need to help me," Henry called, grabbing her hand and pulling her towards Braddock, who was struggling to fight off reinforcements. Though supernaturally invulnerable, he could still be felled by enough people pinning him to the ground.

"There are too many of them for me handle alone. And if we don't help, he'll kill them. We'll do it together, just like we practised."

Nodding, Odette closed her eyes and desperately tried to clear her mind of distractions as Henry began to sing again. She shut off her exterior senses one by one: first the sounds of battle, then the smells. Her sense of touch she reduced to her hand clenched within Henry's. Their palms were sweaty, and she could feel their pulses jumping in their nestled-together wrists.

Only then did visualise the two of them. The glowing golden power within Henry refracted onto the soldiers, but only grazed them. Odette noticed that it bounced cleanly off Braddock, whose power glowed even brighter than Henry's song. Then, with all of her mind's might she pushed – sending the light within herself cascading over Henry. His back arched with the strain, propelling his song all the louder towards the soldiers …

Who, one after the other, began to collapse to the ground.

When Odette opened her eyes, she and Henry were leaning heavily against one another, exhausted.

Braddock had fared no better – though entirely unharmed, sweat ran down his temples. He stood and stared at them with renewed astonishment.

"Well," he said, "I guess you'd better show me where that house of yours is."

38

They ran from the town. Henry wrestled with the distant voice shrieking in his mind. He recalled the blood pooling beneath some of the soldiers – those he hadn't managed to put to sleep in time. Odette's power had worked faster than ever before, but not fast enough to stop Braddock from cracking several of the soldiers' heads against the stone.

He could only hope that when this was all over, if it ever was, they'd be able to do something for the families.

His side began to burn as they ran. Odette and even Braddock seemed to struggle too – the fight had taken its toll on all of them. But they were unimpeded as they made their way out of the town, where the forests and hills offered far better cover and, more importantly, reinforcements of their own.

Henry whistled, as sharply and as loudly as he could, and not long after they'd entered the forest a nimble body swung down from the trees.

"Professor! Are you all right? What happened? Is that – oh, gosh, you're covered in – emergency?"

Grateful that Matthew had curbed his usual rambling, Henry nodded. "Where's Roger?"

"He was waiting for his lookouts. If you gave the signal, he'll have scrambled the interference. Are they following you?"

"Always." Braddock said, still trying to catch his breath. "We lost them coming out of the town but they'll be after us. We don't have time to stand around fucking dawdling."

Matthew looked slightly taken aback, and his eyes flickered to Henry's as if looking for support. "Let's use the alternative route just to be sure," he said, and the young climber gestured to the three of them to follow. Glancing at Braddock, he explained, "It'll make sure we've definitely lost them."

Silence was their companion for much of the ensuing hike. At Matthew's suggestion – and to Henry's great relief – they ceased running and instead walked the meandering path through the woods, though still at a brutal pace. Though the house was but three miles from the town, the journey took longer on foot, even more so on horseback. There was one reasonably quick route, but they couldn't risk exposing the house.

Instead they took a route that wound around the hills and through a decidedly boggy marsh that neatly covered their tracks. A pigeon alighted on Henry's shoulder, a small note in its beak.

Opposing forces approx. 1.5 miles behind. Have found initial trail but my allies are confusing further tracks – they should lose you. See you at dinner. Regards, R.

Henry couldn't help but laugh at Roger's polite sign-off. "Looks like we're going to be fine, if we can keep this pace up." He read the note out loud and tucked it into his pocket.

"Allies?" Braddock asked. It was the first time he'd spoken since they'd met up with Matthew, and his voice was scratchy with exertion.

"Roger's really good with animals," explained Matthew

excitedly. "I mean really good. When we escaped from the army base he had their own dogs lead them on a wild goose chase; it was brilliant. And he has the house watched day and night by an army of birds. *And* he's got a load of deer running around after us to stomp all over our trails."

"That's … amazing."

Braddock's genuine awe relaxed the atmosphere for the rest of the hike. Though all four had cramps in their legs and sides halfway through, their discomfort was eased by the fact that they were now talking. Much of the discussion revolved around their various powers: they explained their different skills and talents to Braddock, and how they'd all discovered them.

Henry had been a little nervous about explaining Odette's power, but she did so very cleverly. She told the truth, but explained only half of her power, just as she'd done back in Bristol. And while she'd already told him some of what she could do, now of course Braddock had seen her power in action.

Of note, however, was that Braddock revealed absolutely nothing about himself. When Matthew asked him about it, he said simply that all he was capable of had been reported in the papers. None of them pressed him further; and Henry suspected that to have done so would not have been welcomed.

By the time they reached the house they were exhausted, and grateful for the restorative food and drink that Mary forced upon them the moment they entered. Robbie took Henry and Odette's bloodied coats, quiet as he did so, save for the intent glare of disapproval that Henry couldn't have missed even if he were blind.

As they rested, Braddock was introduced. Unlike Matthew, most were decidedly nervous around him. None offered him a hand to shake; most skittered away within moments of being introduced, and the dialogue that followed was largely monosyllabic.

And, much to his later shame, Henry was so busy trying to make up for this that he entirely failed to notice the effect it was having on Odette.

<h1 align="center">39</h1>

She hadn't felt right since they'd returned, and it wasn't just because her body was so worn out from the hiking and the running. It was as if someone had taken all of her emotions and drawn them to the front of her mind in one fell swoop. The knot in her throat had moved down, and now rested behind her sternum. It felt heavy. She dared not focus on it, because then she'd ...

No – not here. Not in front of *him*.

But it was too late. Sometimes, if she spotted them coming early enough, Odette could work herself out of her fits before they began. But there was a point of no return. If her fear of losing control began to feed into itself then she had no chance of stopping it. Her breathing would shorten, making her so afraid that it would become even shallower. And now her breath was ragged. Perhaps it was relief rearing a queer head, or the during the escape from the army wearing off. Whatever the reason, Odette's legs gave way and everyone – Braddock included – was staring at her.

"Det, it's all right. I'm here." Robbie was at her side in an instant, one arm around her shoulders and the other holding her arms to keep her from curling into herself. It felt like handfuls of freezing water were being thrown at her, and Robbie's voice was the only thing she could catch to parch her overwhelming thirst.

Through her panic she could feel Braddock's dark eyes boring a hole in the back of her neck. Her body was wracked by a heavy sob, and Robbie pulled her against him.

"Deep breaths. That's all that's important, Det. Just take deep breaths. You can do it; you've done it before. You remember how. You're safe here, and nothing's going to hurt you. You're safe."

With each word, Odette fought for purchase on her breathing, each inhalation a little stronger than the one before. When she faltered and began to snatch air again, Robbie repeated the mantra, until there was nothing left but snivels and sighs. Isobel was at her side with a handkerchief then, delicately moving to conceal the mess Odette's face had become. As she regained her awareness, she realised that Henry had moved to sit next to her, taking Braddock's place.

"I'm s-so sorry." The others leapt at once to tell her there was no need to apologise, but Odette couldn't help but feel that she'd distracted them from making Braddock feel at home, which given how flighty he was should surely be more important than her fits. Curling up against Robbie, she clutched her shaking hands together on her knees and tried to ignore everyone's focus on her.

"Why don't I show you where you'll be staying?" Abigail said to Braddock, breaking the silence. "There are more bedrooms than we know what to do with, so you can have your pick."

Gratitude swelled in Odette's chest as Abigail – who a few moments earlier had been so nervous of Braddock – led him upstairs to select his room. With him gone, the room relaxed and Odette found it easier to draw each shaking breath. Robbie drew her against his shoulder and held her there as the others began to question Henry about what had gone wrong.

"I think it was just a patrol that happened to catch us," he said, running a hand through his hair and shaking it askew. "There were … a dozen of them, maybe. Perhaps eighteen."

Robbie raised his eyebrows. "That's an awful lot for a patrol."

"My father doubled the patrol sizes in the area before we left. I don't know the exact numbers, but they ended up as more than you'd expect. If they'd actually tracked Braddock down and this was their attack, they would've sent a lot more men."

"They weren't … organised," Odette mumbled. "Like they would've been if it was premeditated. Braddock surprised them."

Henry nodded, a grim expression on his face. "He did."

"Did 'e …"

Odette tensed in Robbie's arms, and saw Henry sigh heavily. "Yes," he said. "I'm not sure how many. Two or three, perhaps. Odette and I managed to put the rest to sleep before … before things got out of hand."

"For what it's worth, they attacked him first."

"Very much so. But his reply was not of equal force. When he fights, it's … it's truly something else." Henry sounded almost awestruck, but his expression was one of disgust. "I've never seen such incredible power."

"It's because he doesn't feel pain." Odette sat up and out of Robbie's arms, instead taking his hand for support. "When they fight, most people hold back so that they don't hurt themselves. Thomas … doesn't have to."

She hoped that none of the others could see the tension in her spine, and that Robbie couldn't feel the shake in her hands. It was not an idea that had occurred to her without prompting, after all. When she blinked, Odette imagined that she could see Braddock's eyes as they'd been when he'd threatened her – cold, dark, detached.

Nervously, she looked at the others to check they'd not noticed. Most were simply sighing and shaking their heads, and Robbie seemed concerned for her in general rather than curious about what she'd said.

Henry, though, had not missed the inference – and she could see an angry vein jumping in his neck. She'd have to explain this later.

But for now, all she wanted to do was rest; everything felt just so heavy.

40

When Odette woke several hours later, she felt a little more herself – though pulling herself out of dreams was no easy feat. She'd dreamt of wandering through the world, meeting other people with powers; helping them learn to use and bolster them. Whether any of the powers she'd imagined existed she had absolutely no idea – many were based on myths, legends or books she'd read – but that didn't seem to be the point. She knew now that magic was real. It wasn't about how it manifested, but rather the sense of amazement at remembering it. It was a comforting balm over the wounds of the day.

Not quite willing to come back to the real world yet, Odette decided to make her way down to the library. It reminded her a great deal of the library back home, which seemed like so far and so long ago now. It was comforting to walk between the shelves, searching for something she'd never read before. This was harder than she'd expected, for though she'd never thought of herself as particularly well read, the Oakley family library was well stocked and she'd read all of it over the years – even the dry tomes on botany.

Eventually something caught her eye, and she curled up in the chair by the unlit fire. It was comfortable and quiet, and the book didn't ask her how she was – a question that she doubted she could answer at that moment. The words on the page wrapped around her like a warm embrace.

"I've never met anyone who had attacks like mine before."

The voice was so sudden that it startled Odette from her chair. She turned; Braddock was behind her – though how long he'd been there, she had no idea. Her mind had been so full of daydreams that she'd hardly been present herself.

Composing herself, she said, "Attack? Oh – *oh*." Empathy flashed through her on the heels of realisation. "I ... I haven't, either."

His arms were folded as usual, and he'd barely come into the room, but at least he was talking. "D'you know what they are?"

"No." She sighed, shaking her head, and took to her a seat again. She didn't bother to gesture to the chair across from her – if he wanted to, he'd sit, and she wasn't going to make the mistake of pressuring him into anything. "I wish I did, but I don't."

"My mother took me to see a doctor about it once." He took a step forward that looked more like an exaggerated scuffing of his boots. "He said I was making it up. That it was a tantrum."

It sounded painfully like something she'd told herself many times. "That's awful, Tom."

He almost laughed. "Yeah, well. Didn't have one for a while, did I? And then I did. And it was worse, since I hadn't had one for so long."

There was a pause, and then Odette nodded. "I get that too. Sometimes I can tell why they happen. I dropped a tray once in front of everyone at home, and I was so embarrassed that I had a fit as soon as I got out of the dining room. But then another time I didn't have one for a few weeks, and then out of the blue there one was. I couldn't really tell why."

"I don't get them so much now." He was almost at the chair, but hadn't sat down. She considered it a partial victory. "Not since – well, I wouldn't have lasted this long if I did, would I? I mean I get them, but … like you just did. Afterwards."

He laughed again, but Odette didn't. There was nothing funny about knowing how close he'd come to dying at the army's hands – especially now that she was beginning to understand him. A deep frown knitted across her brow. Were they the same? Was this what she could've become had things gone differently?

"When did you start having them?" she asked, hoping that he'd relaxed enough to answer rather than deflect the question.

Finally, Braddock sat down. "When I was fifteen. Maybe a bit older. My parents had money, so they sent me to the local school. And kids are – they can be …" He slumped back into the chair, arms still folded. "Teachers said it was normal. Or that if I stopped being weird maybe the other kids wouldn't do it."

"Do what?"

"Kick me. Throw me in the pond. Chase me back to my house some days. I almost preferred it when they hit me. That was easier than the stuff they'd say." He rubbed roughly at the side of his stubble-peppered face. "My parents tried to stop it, but that just made it worse. And then eventually I started having attacks."

Odette caught her bottom lip between her teeth. "Were they linked? Your attacks and the … what the children did to you?"

"First one I had, I was in class. French. I loved languages." For a moment, an almost dreamy look mixed with boyish glee lit up his face. "It's just really cool to be able to understand what they're saying, and hold conversations that no one else can ... anyway, I was in class, and I guess they didn't like how I answered a question or something. Maybe my magic was starting to show again – it did that sometimes. They started calling me names, and the teacher did nothing, so I ran out of the room. Then ... that happened."

He gestured vaguely towards her and fell quiet, as if realising how long he'd been talking and how much he'd revealed.

There were so many questions Odette wanted to ask, but she didn't dare push him. He'd already taken such a big risk telling her this much; she owed it to him to let him respond at his own pace. She'd had to when she'd first told her mother and Robbie – she'd tried to hide it from them for months.

But the silence was somehow more terrible, and so she carefully selected the easiest of her questions, the one least likely to cause him discomfort.

"Why do you call them attacks?"

"Because," he replied with the same bitter, empty laugh, "that's what they feel like. Like you're being attacked."

A knot wrenched in Odette's throat and gut, and she looked at the floor. He was right.

41

"He's not a bad person."

Odette's voice drifted over towards him so gently that for a moment Henry thought he might be dreaming. Looking up, he found her standing in the door, leaning against the frame. Her eyes were focused on a spot where the wallpaper was beginning to fray, even more so as she worried at the paper with her fingers.

"Braddock?"

Her brow knitted. "Isn't it strange that we call people by their surnames both to demean them and as a mark of friendship?" she remarked tangentially, and smoothed down the wallpaper with her thumb.

"You should be resting," Henry said, placing his book aside and rising from the chair to take a step towards her. "It's not safe for you to be tired with Br–, Thomas around. You need your strength so your powers can protect you."

Odette's lips parted several times, as if there were something she wanted to say but could not. Eventually she said, "I'm not going to need to use my powers against him," though Henry was uncertain it was the answer she'd originally intended.

He was tired, he reasoned with himself. He, too, had endured the attack – an attack for which he'd been wholly unprepared. He'd seen men brutally crushed to the ground by a boy who seemed devoid of remorse. And worst of all, he'd thought it was a good thing. And then he'd taken that murderer into a home with his friends, the people for whom he was responsible.

It was only understandable that it would've all become too much.

"Yes, you are!" he snapped, so loudly that Odette jumped away from him in shock and, he noticed with guilt, a certain amount of fear. But even that was not enough to repair the dam within him. "He's a *murderer*, Ditty. How many men did we watch him kill today? How long did it take him?"

"They *shot* at him! At us!"

"Of course they did. They were defending the country from him, like they're meant to, because it's their job." He'd been wrong. They'd all been wrong. "Gods above, what have we done? There's a killer in this house and we brought him here."

Odette folded her arms across her chest and glared at him. "Yes, we did. Because we believe he can be more than a killer."

"How naive are we?"

Henry's voice dropped suddenly to a soft murmur. Horror gripped his heart in a vice. "We should have stayed at Marston. We should've done as my father said—"

"For heaven's sake, Henry!" snapped Odette, causing him to leap with surprise from his desperate reverie. "You believed, just like we did. You believed people could be rainbows, not just black and white and shades of grey. You believed *we* could be better, too. You promised us you'd make sure that we didn't become tools, weapons."

Her hands clutched his shirt now, as if trying to shake the thoughts out of him. He stared at her unblinkingly, frozen, his mind completely blank and the vice around his heart turning him numb.

More softly, she continued. "You *promised*, Henry – we ran away and worked behind everyone's backs because we didn't want them to use us like that – and now … now you doubt us? You're not like them, I know you're not. You still believe."

"I'm trying to help you," stammered Henry, though he seemed increasingly unconvinced – but of what, he was unsure. It felt like something was tearing open inside him. And he was so, so tired.

When he closed his eyes he could still see the blood, smell it, taste the copper on his tongue. He let out a shaky breath close to a sob. "What if we're wrong?"

His voice came out smaller than he'd hoped, barely more than a whisper. Odette's eyes flicked up to meet his in an unusual moment of contact.

"You know we're not," she said with conviction.

Through her fury, Odette seemed to forget all of her fear, and looked up into Henry's eyes. They swam with a confused medley of emotions, and though he tried several times to form a reply to her, words abandoned him.

Odette leaned onto the tips of her toes, placed her hands on his cheeks, and ran her thumbs across his cheekbones.

"You still believe. You do." Her voice was softer, though with no less emphasis. "I know inside that there's a man as angry as I am, as determined as I am not to be used in this way. To not give up on people, even when it seems like they've fallen so far. Someone who knows who they are and what they believe, and will fight for it."

"I wish the world was like that, but—"

Her hands slipped down to the lapels of his jacket, and she shook Henry towards her in frustration. "Why can't it be?" she said, half-sobbing, eyes gleaming with moisture. "I know it's scary, believe me I do. But if you're going to give up on everything after one moment of doubt, then how will you ever make the world the one you want to live in?"

He blinked, surprised by the tears running down his cheeks. "He killed so many of them, Ditty."

Odette reached up and stroked into place the hair that had fallen into his eyes. "He did. And you're not wrong. He is a killer, and we did bring him into this house. And, yes, maybe, one day I'll have to use my powers to stop him." Her voice broke into a sob on the last words. "But if we let the chance of failure stop us from even trying ... well, then no one will win. Not Thomas, not your father ... not anyone."

Only in the silence that followed did Henry feel the last of the anger leave him, as if there were nothing more trapped within him, all his emotions spent.

"I ... I'm so sorry," he said, finding the statement wholly insufficient.

Letting out a deep, quivering breath, Odette shook her head and gently guided him towards the door.

She wrapped her fingers around his. "I'm not the only one who's been through a lot and needs to rest."

He let her lead him upstairs to his room. He knew that both of them had been right, but this offered him little comfort – so he took what solace he could in her presence, the solidarity of her fear.

When he woke the next day, he came downstairs to find Braddock sitting at the dining table between Robbie and Abigail, both holding items of their own creation, demonstrating to him their indestructible nature.

They were also demonstrating the power of Abigail's crafting in other, unseen ways – wearing clothes that she'd sewn to make them approachable. He found his eye drawn to them the moment he entered, even though his attention should have been fully on Braddock.

Mary entered a moment later, carrying a tray of breakfast goods that made their faces light up with interest – and as he watched them, in that moment and in the days that followed, Henry found that his pride in these brave and generous people renewed with every passing moment.

<h1 style="text-align:center">42</h1>

It had been too much to hope for – having time to work out what their next steps would be. Three days after Braddock had arrived, the forest erupted with a loud crack. It wasn't the rumble of distant hunting; it wasn't the snap of a horse master's whip; it was the crack of a gun, barely a few miles away from their sanctuary.

At once, everyone gathered in the hallway – even Braddock, who hung in Odette's shadow like a cat unsure of whether to pounce.

"They're too close," announced Roger grimly. "Matthew's gone to check how far, but you can tell from the sound."

Isobel was tugging on Henry's sleeve. "Will Abigail and Robbie be all right? It sounded like it came from that way, from the town."

"Maybe they were spotted. But I can't imagine my father's men would shoot at them." Henry's brow knitted in a deep frown. "Either way, it was far too close."

"I think," Roger said, giving voice to everyone's thoughts, "we might be running out of time."

Not that they'd had much to begin with.

Henry couldn't help but feel they'd been lulled into a false sense of security – the problem was that they all come to like Braddock, far more than they'd expected, and despite their doubts and having known him for so short a time.

They agreed with what he wished to do, even if not with how he was doing it, and that had complicated things. But, then, had they ever really had an end goal? They could hardly have expected to keep him here forever.

Not for the first time, Henry found himself sighing and running his hands through his hair. He'd gravely miscalculated. They'd spent so much time thinking about why they wanted to do things that they'd neglected to consider the *what* and been distracted by the *how*.

The treacherous part of him that had invoked Odette's ire the previous day wondered whether it would not be a good thing if the army came. He did his best to push the thought down. She was right; it was too late to turn back now. If he'd had doubts, he should've voiced them before earlier – before he'd dragged all of them into this mess. Now they had no choice but to run, and that meant leaving the house that had been their sanctuary.

With great fatigue, he said as much to the others and they began to gather their things. Braddock, who had nothing to pack, watched them all with a sad, angry smirk – as if he'd known this would happen, and for that reason had never truly invested in it.

"You should come with us," Henry said to him several hours later as he brought his pack downstairs. "We're going to head northeast; Roger says that's the clearest way."

Braddock simply shrugged at first. Only when Henry remained standing expectantly did he add, "Thanks for the heads-up."

He said nothing more.

As Henry continued to help the others prepare for their

time on the run, he began to fear that they'd fail after all – that Braddock wouldn't come with them, that they'd not have the time they needed to ... what? Convince him to turn over a new leaf? Get him to repent his sins?

It was dark by the time they were ready. On Roger's advisement, they decided not to leave until the following morning – it was clear now, and if they needed to leave in a hurry they could. They'd get much further for having had a night's sleep.

When everyone else had gone to bed, Henry lingered in Odette's room and finally voiced his fears from day before, bereft of anger and frustration.

"I don't think," he said, looking down at their intertwined hands, "that this is going to end how we want it to."

Odette turned her head downwards, and Henry noticed that her cheeks had taken on a glossy sheen. Without thinking, he reached out to brush at the tear tracks, the sudden movement causing her to flinch. Her wide eyes darted up to meet his.

"I can't do it," she whispered, and he heard the sadness in her voice. "He's just scared, so very scared. He doesn't ... he doesn't know what else to do."

"He killed people, Ditty."

"I know that! I know, and so does he. His insides are all torn up from it, and I don't think he'll ever have a day where it doesn't hurt him – but Henry, if I let them in they'll *kill* him, and then ..." Odette's voice tapered to silence. When she spoke again, it was barely a whisper. "Then I'll be torn up too. I'll be just like him."

There was no pain like the one that had Henry's heart in a vice. He wanted so badly to tell Odette that she didn't have to do it – that they could find another way to capture

Braddock, to arrest him safely and securely, without any need for violence. But Edward's words rang in his mind. *I'll beat you, Henry. I'll beat you because I'm prepared to do what none of your little brats can muster.*

If Odette didn't do it, Peter would one day find the key to Braddock's power, and that would surely be a worse fate for them all. Then they'd know they'd not tried; that they'd condemned a man to death through their inaction.

There was no choice, at least none that was good, and it chilled Henry to the bone.

"One chance," she whispered, pulling Henry from his thoughts. Her cool hands came to rest on his face. "Give me one chance, Henry. Let me try to convince him to come willingly."

"If you fail, he'll know you're more than you're pretending to be."

Odette's eyes filled with tears, and she nodded. "I know. But I can't do it, Henry. I'm not what they need me to be. I – I don't want to be what they need. I'm not going to strip him of his power just so they can shoot him."

Henry opened his lips to draw breath. His chest and throat had constricted. Swallowing, he felt hot rivulets trail down his cheeks and onto Odette's hands.

"If you fail," he said again, barely able to give sound to the words, "he could kill you."

She brushed the tears from his cheeks this time, and drew him close to her, cradling him in her arms as if to shield him from the world. As his head came to rest against her chin, he felt her face shift into a smile, which she pressed into his hair.

"You asked me how I could manage to tap into his power,"

she whispered. "The truth is that I know it like the back of my hand. I know it because my mind is, and always has been, just like his. I'm afraid, Henry, afraid of everything. I carry my fear around with me like a pilgrim's burden. Yes, he might kill me. But I live in fear of dying every day. I know this fear – I'm as comforted by its presence as terrified."

"Just because you're capable of facing your fear doesn't mean you should have to."

To his surprise, Odette laughed, a pealing melody that made his breath catch.

"No," she agreed, "but if I don't face it, I can never conquer it – and neither can he. He deserves the chance to master his fear, Henry, just as I deserve mine."

A thousand thoughts wove through Henry's mind – but no words came. They swirled in his head like desperate fragments – how incredible she was to him, how proud he was, that she'd be safe, that she'd have all the things in the world that she wanted … even if reaching for those things was dangerous.

Instead he simply said, "I love you." The words slipped from his lips with an easy honesty and not a little desperation, and he prayed she'd understand.

43

When he was certain that Odette was fast asleep, curled up against the pillow next to him, Henry slipped from the room. He wasn't anywhere near as skilled in subterfuge as the others, but one didn't grow up with a major general for a father without gaining the ability to be quiet when needed.

As silently as possible, he made his way down the corridor to Isobel's room, praying she'd be awake.

The gentle flicker of candlelight under her door brought him relief, and softly he knocked. There was a slight clatter-ing – he'd likely startled her – and a few moments later the young woman's tired face appeared in the door.

"Oh, sir," she murmured. "It's so late. Is everything all right? Do we need to go?"

"No, it's – I'm sorry. Everything is fine. May I come in?"

It occurred to Henry as he stepped into his maid's bedroom that doing so in his pyjamas and dressing gown was excep-tionally improper, but then a lot of traditional propriety had gone out of the window of late. Isobel thankfully seemed to think nothing of it, gesturing for him to take a seat on the one chair not covered in makeshift canvases.

"Is something wrong?" she asked, looking at him with concern.

He rested his elbow on the arm of the chair and leant his

head against his hand. "I need you to paint something for me. I need it painted now, in secret. And then I need you to forget what you've seen."

Part of him hated himself for even asking. Isobel trusted him – had served him loyally for years, since he'd left his parents' household – and he was asking her to keep secrets from her friends. Secrets that could get them hurt, or be seen as a betrayal. It might be nothing of the sort, of course, but he had no way of knowing. Not until she'd painted it. If she even could.

And Isobel, dear Isobel, barely hesitated before replying. "All right," she said, taking a half-finished canvas from her easel and replacing it with a fresh one. "What is it? What should I focus on?"

Her instant agreement wrenched something in Henry's heart, and forgetting himself he leapt up to hug her. Though clearly surprised, Isobel wrapped her arms around his shoulders and sighed softly – as if that very gesture had answered her question. With the gentle patience and wisdom of someone much older than her years, she patted him on the back and released him.

"What about her?"

Isobel had always known him too well. The best servants did. He made no attempt to hide the emotion that thickened his voice as he replied, "She's going to confront Braddock. I need to know that she comes out of it alive."

This gave the young woman pause, and her eyes pinched. Henry saw it in her face as she realised precisely what he was asking her to do – and what he was asking her to be part of. To his relief, she didn't answer or move straight away. She stood there, looking at him carefully, visibly weighing up the situation.

Then, as he'd taught her to, she closed her eyes and focused.

Henry had no artistic skill, and marvelled at the way Isobel layered the painting, turning what looked to him like unformed masses of darkness into trees, grass, bodies. Two people began to form: one resting on the roots of the foremost tree, the other standing just above, or perhaps kneeling. Clarity began to emerge ... and Henry felt creeping suspicion claw at his stomach. But he found it impossible to look away. Even as the arms of the larger figure became defined, even as their hands began to take shape around the throat of the other, he looked on. The horror of what Isobel was painting held him transfixed.

Just as he thought she was finished – that she'd concluded painting his nightmares – Isobel paused. She reached for a different colour; a pasty white tinged with grey. And she took the colour to Odette's painted face, and mixed it with her skin, giving it a corpse-like sheen.

Corpse-like.

He was going to be sick.

Whatever force had kept his eyes upon the painting faded, and Henry turned away with a chill in his heart. Did Isobel always paint the future? No. Perhaps this one wasn't the future. Perhaps it was ... but no. He'd seen the glazed look in her eyes when she focused. Gritting his teeth, he tried to will the nausea to leave, but it continued to gnaw at his insides in painful empathy.

Then there was a scrape of a stool, and Henry turned to see Isobel reach for another canvas, swapping it with the still-wet painting of Odette's death. He asked what she was doing, but she seemed not to hear him – the glazed, meditative focus still shone in her face, as if it had never left. His curiosity took hold enough to distract him from his tormented heart, and he sat down to watch as Isobel began to paint again.

At first it seemed to be the same painting; she blacked out the shadows of trees before dressing them in their bark, each placed in precisely the same spot as before. But this time she drew not two figures, but one – prone on the floor. It was indistinguishable at first, but soon Henry saw to his ashamed relief that the hair was the wrong colour to be Odette's. Spread across the floor, there was an unnatural crookedness to the way Braddock's body was positioned, one that made a similar sense of foreboding rise in Henry's throat.

This time Isobel didn't reach for the pasty white – instead, she took red, brown and black, and splattered streaks of blood across the young man's form. When she'd finished, she stumbled back, brushes dropping to the floor as she snapped out of her meditative state.

"It's all right," Henry said at once, leaping over to her and guiding her to a seat. She looked as pale as he felt, and shame rushed through him. "Isobel, I'm sorry, I shouldn't have—"

"No," she said at once, shaking her head. "I'm all right, m'lord, I just wasn't … sometimes, when I'm painting, I don't really *see* the painting until I'm done. Does that make sense? At least, I don't think about it. I don't really take in what it is or what it means."

He nodded and began to collect the scattered brushes to allow her a moment to compose herself. Then he stood, looking back at the painting that still rested on the easel. Though rushed and slightly blurred, it was a stark representation of Braddock with what looked like a gunshot wound to the chest:

his ribs had burst open in a spray of gore. If the first painting was his worst nightmare, then this was surely Odette's.

"What does it mean? Why are there two of them?"

The question pulled Henry from his thoughts, and he returned to Isobel's side, trying to offer her a stability he barely felt. Tearing his eyes from the images, he asked gently, "You've never painted two like this before?"

Shaking her head, Isobel replied, "No. I've painted some in succession, but I've always stopped between each one. I didn't realise I'd made two just now until I'd finished."

"Then they must be linked somehow." He frowned deeply, mirroring her expression. "But they're not the same painting; one isn't an extension of the other. They can't be – the backgrounds are precisely the same."

"I don't think they are." Isobel pressed shaking fingers against her lips in horror. "I think they're ... alternatives."

His mind was so foggy with fear that it was hard to think, let alone speak. "Alternatives?"

It took Isobel a moment to speak, and as Henry looked over at her he saw certainty. Her voice, when she replied, was soft – born half out of gentleness and half out of pain. "Two possible futures that are as likely as each other."

To this Henry could make no reply, for he was sure that Isobel was correct. Standing once again, he began to pace back and forth across the room, barely noticing the trail of paint he was treading through the carpet as he stepped on the discarded brushes. Yasmin would've had his head for it.

As a student at Oxford, he'd studied classical philosophy. Historically, philosophy had been intrinsically had been intertwined with spirituality – not just religion, but magic too. Henry was in little doubt that many of the ancient figures of legend had indeed had magic, even if not in the way that stories told. It was difficult to believe otherwise; he knew there was magic in the world.

Consequently, he'd always taken the lessons of the past a little more seriously – and there were certain warnings that now played in the forefront of his mind: the dangers of seeing the future, the madness of the sibyl and other ancient prophets. He thought that now, perhaps, he could understand them a little better … and with that understanding came the regret that he'd asked Isobel to paint what was to come.

Perhaps ignorance was bliss.

It was many minutes before either spoke again, both reeling from the images before them – but when they did, they turned to one another and said simultaneously: "We shouldn't do anything."

Relief welling in his heart, Henry added quickly, "Forgive me, Isobel. I should never have asked you to …"

"Sir." She reached out and took his hand. Hers were cold and covered in flecks of paint. "You don't need to apologise. I could've said no if I'd wanted to, and I would've done. You were – you are – scared about someone who means a great deal to you. Of course you wanted to do anything you could to keep her safe. I wanted that, too, for my friend."

"How can I go back to her, knowing tomorrow that she'll either be dead, or her worst nightmare will have come true?"

Isobel stared up at him with wide eyes, clearly wishing she had an answer, but possessing nothing that could begin to comfort him. "There is a chance that neither will come true," she said, but neither of them took heart from it. Her powers had never failed before.

"Isobel, I—"

"I won't say anything, sir. It's all right." She swallowed, and Henry imagined that there was a lump in her throat almost identical to his own. "You should go back to her."

In case it was his last chance to.

He was grateful to Isobel for not saying it out loud.

"Yes," he agreed, squeezing her hands with his. "I'm ... truly sorry that I ... Goodnight, Isobel."

The walk back to his room felt as long as the day they'd brought Braddock to the house. He wished now so very much that they'd never come. That all those weeks ago he'd simply refused to be part of his father's plan, and that he'd never dragged Odette, or Isobel, or any of them into this mess. It might not be his fault, but it *was* his responsibility – and he'd failed all of them. No matter which of the paintings came true, he'd failed.

And the worst part was that he couldn't help but wish Braddock dead.

The intellectual part of him knew this to be logical: Braddock was not to him what Odette was; Braddock was a murderer; Braddock's death would mean the rest of them would be safe. But he was still just a young man, and a young man whom any of them could so very easily have become. What would Henry himself have been if he'd not been privileged enough to have been born into wealth and the security that came with it? What might the others have been if their powers had been discovered in other circumstances?

He was a terrible person to wish anyone dead – no matter the situation. And yet he couldn't help but wish it with every part of himself.

He couldn't lose her. Not like this; not at all. And the pain that the fear of it caused shook him to the core.

He froze at his door, trembling in a way that he hadn't since the day he'd escaped Edward for the final time. He could only pray that Odette was still asleep – for if she was awake he'd not be able to hide it from her. Several deep breaths later, he stole in as quietly as he could, and was relieved to find her sound asleep.

In his absence she'd sprawled over most of the bed, burrowing into the covers like a hibernating animal.

He'd never imagined that loving someone could hurt this much – and he did love her, had loved her before, and seemed to love her most painfully now that the possibility of losing her loomed before him. Even he, who'd known what it was to love a man who viewed him as a possession.

He slipped into the bed beside her and gently brushed a knot of curls out of her eyes. Her breathing was slow and shallow, and he allowed himself to listen until it lulled him into a restless sleep, all the while trying desperately not to imagine a time when it would be silenced.

44

It took Odette a long time to tear herself from Henry's arms. It was like the days when she couldn't get out of bed; she knew the world was there, waiting for her, and that she had to go, but it just felt like too much. Staying with him, in the bed they'd eventually stumbled into, would've been so much safer. So much easier. But she couldn't. The army was coming.

Even with her determination hanging heavy inside her, Odette still felt as if she had to rip herself from the room. She washed and dressed almost in a daze, paying no attention to her growling stomach, and after a quick word with Roger slipped away quietly through the house to Braddock's room. He was curled up on the sofa just inside, looking terribly small.

"Huh," Braddock said, surprise evident in his voice. "I thought you were all leaving me here. Who are you looking for?"

It made Odette's heart break just a little. "You," she said, smiling gently. "Are you all right? I'm sorry you were left on your own."

He wrinkled his nose up. "None of the others seem to mind."

She didn't have much of an answer to that. It was certainly

true that the others had at times kept their distance from him. Liking someone didn't always help you forget that they were a murderer.

"Would you like to go for a walk?"

This seemed to confuse Braddock, and he opened and closed his mouth several times as if searching for words.

Odette laughed gently and placed her hand on his shoulder. He flinched but did not pull away from her touch.

"Why?"

Odette lifted her shoulders in a gentle shrug. "Because it's a nice day, and Roger said the foxes couldn't find any of the army nearby. We'll be safe. It might be our last chance to, you know, relax. Be free of them."

He still seemed hesitant, but nodded and followed her out of the side door.

The holiday house gave way to the woods almost instantly, and the uneven ground helped Odette to forget for a moment just how much her legs were shaking. If this went wrong ... no. No, she wouldn't think about it like that. She'd talk to him and, at worst nothing, would change. She had to believe that or she'd never get out the words.

"It's quieter out here," Braddock remarked as they reached an area where the woods became thicker.

Odette nodded. "I've come out here a few times, whenever Roger and Matthew have said it's fine to. The others are wonderful, but ... well, it gets a bit crowded. It feels like such a small house sometimes, even when it isn't."

"Smaller when people stare at you every time you walk in the room."

"I know." She sighed and shook her head. "I'm sorry. But you can understand why it happens."

A snort escaped Braddock's lips. "Yeah, sure. They're scared of me. You all are. And you should be."

Dropping her head, Odette stopped walking. It took Braddock some moments to realise, and when he turned round she lifted her head to look at him. "That can't be what you want," she said softly. "Just to make people scared of you? People are scary, Tom, but they're also wonderful. But if you push everyone away, how will you ever find that out?"

"You're the most scared of the lot of them." He raised his eyebrows and folded his arms. "Who're you to talk?"

She smiled at that. "You're wrong. I don't think I'm the most scared, Tom. I think you are." When he blustered and tried to walk away, she took a step towards him. "You deflect anything that's difficult whenever I talk to you. Whenever anyone talks to you. And you do it to yourself as well, don't you? You bury your feelings so that you'll never have to face them, because they terrify you."

"How would you know?" Braddock yelled, rounding on Odette with such fury that it made her flinch.

"Because I do it too," she said simply, wringing her trembling hands together in front of her. "I do it every day. I don't know how to process all the things I'm feeling, so I push them down. But I can't do that forever. Eventually they build up too much for me to cope with."

He hesitated, though she could still feel the anger bristling off him. "And then what? You're not the same as me. You know what I've done."

"I do. When it builds up too much, we both explode; that explosion just takes different forms. I have fits. My legs give out, and I can't breathe, and I cry like the world is about to end. Like you used to. But now you … sometimes when you explode, you hurt the people around you. I don't know why that changed for you, but it did."

Braddock frowned. "That's not it. I don't hurt people because I *want* to. I do it because they make me. Have you ever had a gun pulled on you?"

"Before this week? No." Odette shook her head. "But I'm sorry. I didn't mean to suggest you did it on purpose."

"But that's what you'll never understand, none of you! It's not about whether you do it on purpose or not; it's not about what the world makes you do; it's that … that things are a certain way and they shouldn't be," Braddock snapped. "We're not the same. We never will be."

Odette sighed. "No, we won't, and you're right that I can't understand truly. Even if we were exactly the same I'd never claim to know precisely how you feel. But we are similar – and we don't have to be the same for me to understand."

This gave him pause. "So what if you do? What does that get me?"

"A friend. Someone who wants to help you."

He scoffed. "I don't need friends." He folded his arms again and moved as if to turn away, but didn't quite put his back to her. "They always bring more harm than hurt."

"They can do," she said softly. "I'm not going to deny that. But you've been running from people, fighting people for so long, Tom. Wouldn't you like to stop?"

"And do what?" he asked, though his voice had lost its hard edge. "I've killed people. There's nowhere to go back to but a prison cell, or worse."

"Certainty."

Braddock stared at Odette as if she'd grown a third head.

"Certainty?"

She smiled. "You can keep running. But one day you'll get caught. One day they'll find you, and they'll kill you, Tom." She took a single, brave step forward and placed a hand on his arm. This time he didn't flinch. "Yes, if you hand yourself in, you'll go to jail. But you won't die. Would you really rather die?"

Odette could almost see the thoughts as they whirled in his mind. She wished she had something more to offer him – a place to escape to, a different future, a world for him where there'd be no more death. But even as she thought this a voice in her mind whispered that some things – like taking away a person's free will, taking away their lives – could not be forgiven. There were consequences for every action, and though she believed with all her heart that death should never be replied to with more death, she knew it would be wrong to deny the consequences entirely.

"I don't want to die," Braddock said after a long silence, and Odette squeezed his arm in reassurance. Then his brow furrowed. "But if I keep running, there's a chance. There's a chance that, one day, we'll be able to live out in the world, unashamed, like we should do. I'd rather die than have to hide who I am."

Panic smothered Odette's, and her gentle squeeze of his arm turned to a desperate grip. "But the world doesn't work like that. I wish it did, but it doesn't – there are more of them and even you can't run forever!" she said, though she knew her words were futile.

His eyes narrowed in anger, and time seemed to still for a moment. Odette realised, with painful clarity, that something within him had snapped. Something in what she'd said had pushed him – and too far, so that he broke, just like the world had done.

She was no better than anyone else. He wasn't the monster; she was.

When the thought faded and the world rushed back into motion, Braddock seized her by the arms and hurled her roughly against a nearby tree. The bark tore at her skin and she shrieked in pain, all the air knocked out of her.

"You're just as bad as the rest of them!" he yelled in a painful echo of her own thoughts, dragging Odette to the ground and wrapping his hands around her throat. "Only you're worse, aren't you? You lie and pretend to help when all you want to do is control me!"

"Tom ... please ..." she spluttered, trying to reach for his wrists – but his power had flared into a protective coating around him, and she couldn't get purchase. The world began to spin, and blur, and shadows crept towards her. Perhaps she might've stopped to consider whether she was going to die, but in that moment all she could think of was how she'd failed. She'd failed to get through to him, and now no one ever would.

Tears streamed down her cheeks, but the pain from her starving lungs bloomed so fiercely that it consumed her.

And then, in the distance, like a lighthouse on the edge of a choppy sea, she heard a scrap of song. A gentle, lilting melody, full of hope and joy. Henry. The song Henry had written for her. She sobbed with relief and in her mind a familiar voice murmured, "Come on now, Det. You can do it. Just a little bit at a time." Robbie. Yes, she could do this. She could. She had to.

For though she could barely see now, and though there was

no breath left in her, the world had become a golden blur, and like little grains of sand she saw her power flow into Braddock's shield – no, the grains *were* his shield, flying out towards her and sticking to her like an aura. They danced forth like waves of sound in time to Henry's song, with Robbie's gentle encouragement, and little by little she saw Braddock's strength falter and hers increase, until her flailing limbs finally took purchase and threw him from her with stolen magic.

Air came to her lungs like life-giving fire, and Odette stumbled to sit, gasping and coughing in equal measure. The strength she'd stolen faded, leaving her weak and trembling, the golden aura gone from around her. As Odette looked up, Braddock leapt for her again, his face now contorted with a hideous fury. She drew a deep breath, held her hands up in front of her like a shield, and …

Crack.

Warmth splattered across Odette's hands and arms, some reaching her face. Braddock fell to the ground in front of her, and she blinked in confusion, her eyes becoming clouded by something. She touched her fingertips to her sleeve, and her brain finally registered the colour. Crimson. There was a coppery taste on her tongue, in her nose, and the world had become so loud that it felt as if a gale was blowing in her ears.

She looked up at the blur of the empty forest, then down at the blood on her hands, and at Braddock's body – and felt the world splinter into a thousand pieces.

<h1 style="text-align:center">45</h1>

"Det?"

Warm arms enveloped her. Her breath came in fits and starts and her nose was blocked. She began to panic. She raised a hand to her face to wipe the tears away, but her fingers brushed against blood – Braddock's – and her chest seized up entirely.

"Det, it's all right. I'm here. Here, let me get that for you." Then soft silk brushed against her face, wiping away the blood and tears. "It's all right. Everything's going to be all right."

And just like that, Robbie's voice finally cut through the din in her mind. He wrapped his arms around her again and she clung to his coat.

"He's dead," she spluttered through a fresh wave of tears, her throat still aching and raw from Braddock's crushing grip. "He's dead."

"I know," Robbie said, brushing her hair out of her face. "Just take a deep breath for me now. That's it. Just keep taking deep breaths. You can do it."

The world became nothing but Robbie's coaxing voice, until her breathing steadied and the black began to recede. When she'd calmed, she felt the rest of the world trickle back into her senses – the noise of people moving around them, the way her body was shaking from head to toe, and the metallic scent in the air singed with gunpowder.

"The two of you need to come with us, son," said a voice that Odette didn't recognise. She clung closer to Robbie's coat, burying her face against his shoulder.

Robbie shook his head firmly. "We're not going anywhere until she's well enough to walk, and you're sure as hell not rushing that."

"I'm sorry, son, I wasn't giving you the option. You and the young lady are under arrest."

Robbie tensed, but just as he began to speak the ground near them cracked with someone's approach.

"She most certainly is not," said a voice that was cold it took Odette several stunned moments to realise whom it belonged to. "I don't know what happened here, Corporal, but there's no way you're taking her into custody in this state. If you have a problem with that, I suggest you speak to my father."

She curled tighter against Robbie, even more ashamed of what had happened and how she was reacting. She didn't deserve Henry's defence, not now, not when she'd helped them kill Braddock. Her chest heaved in a fresh sob, and Robbie pressed a kiss to the top of her head. The undergrowth cracked as the soldier walked away, and Odette felt Henry kneel next to her.

"What happened, Ditty?" he asked so softly that it made her eyes heat with tears again.

She thought of all the ways she could say it. Words leapt to the front of her mind, but none so strongly as the horrible, painful truth. And though the explanation sat heavy on her tongue, she couldn't give it sound. Saying things aloud always made them real. If she told Henry what she'd done, he'd never forgive her – and why should he? Why should he want anything to do with her ever again?

"It's fine, Det, you don't have to tell us."

Odette frowned. "No, Robbie," she mumbled into his chest. "I failed. I made Thomas angry. It was my fault. I had to take his powers down, and they … they … I got him killed, Henry. I might as well have shot him myself."

Silence hung thick between them, broken only by the sound of Braddock's body being lifted onto a stretcher. Odette knew it was only a matter of time before Henry walked away from her. She was surprised that Robbie was still holding her. She wanted nothing to do with herself.

"Ditty …" Henry sighed, his voice cracking. "No. No, darling, you didn't – it wasn't your fault. The person who shot him is the one who killed him."

"Which he couldn't have done if I hadn't taken his powers down!" Odette yelled, turning to look at Henry. His face was thick with pity, and it made her feel sick to her stomach. "I stole his power. I took it and used it so that *he* couldn't! Don't try to placate me, Henry. I know what I did. It's my fault. Mine."

Though Robbie tried to stop her, Odette scrambled shakily to her feet and began walking off into the forest. She had little idea what she was doing. People shouted at her to come back – perhaps Henry, or Robbie, or some of the soldiers. She found that she didn't particularly care. There was a permanent knot sitting on her chest, as if all of the things she was feeling – and there were so many of them – had coiled up into a ball, ready to strike. But at the same time, ice trickled through her body, numbing her entirely until she felt as if she were underwater. Everything was slow and distant.

A part of her knew that this was a warning sign, something she should be concerned about. Something she should tell people. But there was nothing around her save for water, and she suspected it was the only thing holding her up. The only thing standing between her and the horrible truth that lay on the other side.

46

With some difficulty, Henry and Robbie had managed to coax Odette into a carriage. The army had insisted on taking them back to the manor – though Henry was pleased that none of the soldiers dared to mention arresting anyone again. Even still, he worried deeply about what would happen when they reached Bristol.

And, yet, he couldn't help but feel relief. Burning, treacherous relief.

She was alive.

He and Robbie had fought to be allowed to travel with Odette, though she barely reacted to them. Most of the time she seemed not to notice that anyone was there, and simply stared off into the distance – and she'd not spoken a single word since storming off into the forest.

Whether she was lost in thought, or something worse had happened, Henry couldn't tell – but from the looks Robbie had been exchanging with him, this was not something she'd done before.

Finally, Odette had curled up with her head in his lap. In sleep, her breathing calmed, and the furrow in her brow softened a little.

"I've never seen her like this," said Robbie softly, breaking the silence. His face was pinched with concern and fear, and

Henry suspected his own expression was the same. "I don't know what to do."

Henry sighed. "I shouldn't have forced her to talk about it."

"No, I was going to do the same." Robbie shook his head. "I don't think anything we could've said would've helped. Hey, at least you got angry. I wanted to be angry at them for taking advantage of her like this. Or at Roger and Matthew for not seeing this coming. But ... I don't know. I've never seen her like this. It's hard to be angry when she looks like she's ..."

With gentle brushes of his fingertips, Henry smoothed down Odette's hair as best he could. It had become matted with blood and the detritus of the forest floor, a painful reminder of what had occurred.

"Like she's not really there," he whispered, and Robbie nodded. "I won't let them hurt her. You must know that. I would never allow them to punish her for what was my idea in the first place."

Incongruously, Robbie chuckled. "She'd hit you if she were herself. It was her idea to do this, Henry. She knows it, deep down, even if she can't find that bit of herself right now. But ... I'm glad. She needs help, not a cell."

"There are doctors at the manor."

Robbie shook his head. "A doctor's just going to say she's in shock. You know it's more than that. She ... she's had problems all her life. And I don't mean she's weaker for it. Hell, if anything she's stronger. But this sort of thing, it's going to affect her differently to people without ... whatever this is."

"There are specialists," Henry said thoughtfully, looking

down at her again. "I've no experience with this sort of thing, but I know there are people at Oxford who study nervous disorders."

Robbie sighed. "There's no way they'll let us take her to Oxford right now. But I don't know what we can do."

Henry frowned. "You've been her best friend for years, Robbie. I've seen you with her when she has her fits. You might not think it, but you know exactly what to do, even when it feels like you don't. I don't think there is a right answer, or a right thing to do, not really. You just do your best."

Initially Henry's statement simply made Robbie blush – but within a few moments, his eyes had become glassy and he turned his head away out of shame.

Leaning forward as best he could, Henry took the younger man's hand in his own, knowing that there was little he could offer but solidarity.

Part of him felt as if his mind should be focused what they'd do next – but it was difficult when most of their options lay in the army's hands. Whether they'd be punished for deviating from their orders, he simply didn't know. None of them were soldiers, so they couldn't be discharged. Handing them over to the police was certainly a possibility, for they'd harboured and aided a felon – but somehow Henry couldn't quite see that happening. He knew there were members of the police force who were aware of the existence of magic, but arrests like this would not be a secret from the public. No, whatever was to be done with them, it would be done privately – and that in many ways unnerved him more than the idea of being sent to jail.

A private punishment was far more likely to take an

unsavoury form. His father and the rest of the army might be honourable men, but it would be all too easy for them to convince themselves to exact a more insidious penalty. Ordering the university to shut down his department, for example, or exiling them from the country altogether. He didn't want to consider what that would do to all of them – to be suddenly ripped away from everything they'd ever known, sent to a strange country for trying to do what was right.

It struck Henry again that he'd done all of them a great disservice. He was their mentor, and he'd been so obsessed with the idea of saving a single life that he'd omitted to think about the others that would be ruined if he failed. And now that he had, the foolishness of that hurt him deeply. He'd played a risky hand with all of their futures, and it had backfired. If only Odette hadn't insisted on talking to Braddock! But no – he couldn't be angry with her, not when she'd taken so great a risk. Their last conversation together was still fresh in his mind, as was the determination in her face as she'd fought for her chance to face her fears.

As he brushed Odette's hair gently behind her ear, he wondered whether it would be worth it for even one day. Of course, she'd measure it by Braddock's death – how could she not? He'd been shot in front of her, a death made possible only by her powers. But that was not her fault, not really. Light fell across her sleeping form, and Henry saw in sharp relief the bruises that had begun to bloom across her neck, the grazes that ran down her spine – traces of precisely the eventuality that Isobel had painted for him.

Just for a moment, he wasn't just glad that she was alive; a terrible part of him was happy that someone had been there to kill Braddock so that she'd live.

A broken laugh must have escaped his lips, for Robbie looked up at him sharply. "I don't even know who killed him. Who saved her."

"It – it wasn't the army?"

"They weren't there. They arrived afterwards – whoever shot him was there already. Had known ..." Henry traced Odette's bruises with his fingertips, unable to finish the sentence. Isobel had known. Isobel had known what Odette was going to do. But surely she'd never ...

"You were with me when it happened," Robbie said, his voice hardening suddenly.

Henry frowned. "I was in my room when I heard the ... No one was—"

"You were with me," Robbie repeated. "We were in your room, talking about the route we were going to take when we left."

Just for a moment, Henry wondered. He looked up at the younger man opposite, who was tense from head to toe, as though preparing to pounce upon some unsuspecting prey. If Isobel had told Robbie ...

"You – you didn't ..."

Robbie shook his head and sighed heavily. "I didn't. Maybe I would've, if I'd known. But I had no idea. I was with you, remember?"

"In my room."

"Yes." Robbie's eyes followed the movement of Henry's hand as it left Odette's neck, and a grim expression clouded his features. "The ground was pretty roughed up around her when I got there. I think they had quite a fight before she managed to take his powers down. And she said she managed to steal his power ... I didn't even know she could do that."

"It's a wonder she managed it at all," marvelled Henry, even as he remembered the last time that Odette had been able to use someone else's magic. "She's never been able even to dampen someone's powers when she's feeling overwhelmed before. As for *using* someone else's, she's only ever done it once, and that was only for a moment."

He decided not to mention when, or how. Things were bad enough.

An incongruous smile twitched at Robbie's lips. "That's our Det," he said, chuckling softly. "Stronger than she realises. Stronger than any of us realise."

Henry nodded. "She'll be all right."

He must have sounded unconvinced, though, because Robbie reached over and patted him on the arm.

"She will," Robbie repeated, but Henry could hear the same uncertainty wobbling in his voice. "It might take a while, but she will."

47

They were marched into Marston House with a larger guard than Henry thought was necessary. He and Robbie had managed to get Odette to walk with them, though her acquiescence made him uneasy. She did as they asked so quickly and pliantly that he was eerily reminded of telling a well-trained dog to sit or stay.

His father awaited them in the foyer, and locked him at once with so piercing a stare that Henry's stomach turned. He'd disappointed his father before and knew what that face looked like, but that wasn't the one he wore. No, this was something far deeper; he looked ashamed. Henry was certain that they'd done the right thing, and always would be, but seeing the destitution in the major general's eyes was more painful than he'd expected.

He was flanked by several high-ranking officers, a woman in a police uniform whom Henry didn't recognise, and Edward and Vivalda.

"I'd ask you to explain yourself, boy," said his father in a voice so soft and cold that it made him shiver, "but you can't possibly have anything to say that would undo what you've done."

The policewoman cleared her throat and took a step forward. "I apologise for not coming to meet you personally," she said. She was not excessively kind in her tone, but next to his father she seemed the epitome of a warm welcome. "Due to the sensitive nature of the situation, I felt it was best to conduct the investigation here."

"Ma'am?" inquired Roger when she was finished speaking. He stepped forward and removed his hat, inclining his head. "Regrettably the major general's men have thus far been unable to inform us precisely what it is we've been arrested for, or indeed if we've truly been arrested at all. Might I inquire as to the nature of our supposed crimes?"

He asked this so casually, so politely, that Henry had to suppress a proud chuckle. To her credit, the policewoman listened to his question and sighed apologetically. "You're presently charged with aiding and abetting a murderer, and are the prime suspects in the murder of one Thomas Braddock. Further charges may be applied as the investigation continues. Until then, I'm placing you under house arrest, and—"

The sudden intrusion of a crowd of people in the hallway made Odette leap against Henry, and he wrapped an arm around her.

"It's all right," he murmured, holding her tightly. "It's just the other mages. I'm not going to let anyone hurt you."

It didn't seem to do much to calm her, likely because the group were so loud in their sudden rush of questions, and Henry realised to his discomfort, congratulations. They rushed up to their fellow mages and began to shake their hands and ask them what had happened.

Henry saw his father begin to shake with anger, and glare over at Edward – who, he noticed with some satisfaction, was also looking quite uncomfortable.

"That's quite enough," Edward said, his voice cutting cleanly and powerfully over the din, causing everyone at once to cease their chattering. "I did not teach you to be an unruly mob."

Only in the silence did the other mages notice Odette curled up into Henry's side. He released his death grip upon her, but she barely moved a muscle; she was shaking so much that everyone nearby could see it.

Robbie reached over and placed a steadying hand on her shoulder, but it seemed to offer little solace – especially as more eyes fell upon her. Whispers rippled through the mages. They knew, it seemed, what had happened. Then a slender figure stepped out from within them.

Though his instinct was to protect Odette no matter what, Henry allowed Peter to step close enough to her to see the condition she was in. Somehow, he felt like someone needed to see it – to take notice of it. He watched as the young man turned to his mentor, staring emptily up at him as if unable to comprehend something terribly profound.

"This is what you'd have done to me," he said, his voice as soft as ice. "If we'd succeeded – this would've been me. I would've been ..."

He turned away, and Henry found he couldn't blame him.

Vivalda stepped forward, reached out and placed a protective arm around Peter, pulling him away from Edward. A faint swell of pride surged within Henry as he saw not only his group move to shield the young man, but all of Edward's too. Indeed, they'd all taken several steps away from their mentor, who was now left adrift in the centre of the room, the subject of a throng of deadly stares.

As he was ushered into safety, Peter looked up to the major

general on his way past. "Sir," he said, straightening his back, "is this … is this what you really wanted?"

"A vigilante on the loose? No, it bloody well is not," Henry's father replied gruffly, his face like a storm cloud. "Whoever did this has no respect, no respect at all for the police or the army – the people trained to do this job, to make sure no one else has to. The only comfort, boy, is that Braddock is dead. That he can't kill anyone else."

"I know. And I don't want to demean how important it is that people are safe," said Peter, clearly beginning to lose some of his bravado. "I just thought … I thought that victory was meant to be sweeter."

Before any further commotion occurred, they were ushered away to their rooms.

Peter's words rang painfully in Henry's ears, echoing his own thoughts. He'd thought that once they rescued Braddock everything would be clearer. But it hadn't been, and now someone was dead as a result – and he had no idea at all who'd done it.

As he walked through the corridors under guard, he realised that this made him feel sad – not simply that someone had died, but that he'd not gotten the chance to know Braddock better. His glimpses of the man had suggested that his philosophy was not wholly different from Henry's own – and a large part of Henry began to wonder whether, perhaps, Braddock had been right. That they needed the world to know who and what they were. Wasn't that what he'd always wanted, really? What he'd always hoped for?

When they reached Odette's room, she extricated herself from his arms and reached for the handle. It was the first action he'd seen her take of her own volition for some time, and made him blink in surprise.

"You don't have to be on your own," he murmured, stepping closer to her so that the soldiers couldn't hear. "I'll tell them to let you stay with me."

Odette looked up at him then. Her face was pale but blemished with the redness of tears; her eyes were watery and bloodshot, and deep, sickly bags hung beneath them. The light from the thin windows at the end of the hall made the bruises on her neck stand out in painful clarity.

She shook her head. "No."

It was the first thing she'd said since they'd arrived back at Marston. It made his heart leap with hope until she continued, "I want to be on my own."

Then she stepped into the bedroom and closed the door in his face.

Henry stood, dazed, as one of the soldiers in their group took up position to the right of the door. The others urged him to continue on to his room, but he felt unable to move. What had he done wrong? Had he said something to upset her? Why was she turning him away now of all times? And so coldly, as if he meant nothing to her. Only a gentle touch on his arm stirred him from his painful thoughts.

"She'll be all right," Matthew said. "She's probably just worried that she's bothering people. I'd want to be on my own, I think, if ..."

It wasn't comforting, but Henry nodded nonetheless. He'd have to trust her, and respect her wishes – even though part of him wondered, perhaps unkindly, if she was capable of making decisions for herself in her state. The problem was that he had no idea what to do, what to say or even what to feel. Nothing about the situation was right.

So he sighed and allowed the soldiers to lead him the rest of the way to his room, where he fell into a restless slumber.

48

Several days passed. They were subjected to interrogation upon interrogation by the inspector, the major general, anyone, it seemed, who thought they could get the truth out of them.

Part of Henry desperately wanted to talk to Isobel, to ask her what had happened. He found it impossible to believe that the gentle young woman who'd been in his employ would ever have killed someone, shot them in the back. Where would she have acquired a gun?

But they'd all changed so much that to his dismay, he found he was no longer certain.

Odette still wouldn't speak to anyone but him and Robbie, and she said little enough even to them. And as time went on, they became increasingly concerned. Sometimes it seemed that she wished to be on her own; sometimes she'd cling to them as if they were buoys on choppy water. Something had to change – and Henry was convinced that they had to get her out of Marston. That they had to get her home.

But his father would have none of it. He refused to let them leave until the killer had been found, and was convinced that Odette's testimony was the key to discovering the person's identity.

Odette couldn't testify though; she could barely speak.

Henry had shouted himself hoarse in the small office, until Vivalda had pulled him away and negotiated a compromise; Yasmin and Odette's mother would be sent for in the hope that it would help Odette to open up.

They arrived late in the afternoon, accompanied by a dreary grey sky and drizzling rain that looked about as cheery as Henry felt. He met them in the entrance hall along with Robbie and Mary, who scooped Nancy into their arms as soon as she entered.

"Henry," said Yasmin, who looked just as tired. "Are you all right? What *happened*? They told us hardly anything."

Across the hall, Henry could see the others explaining to Odette's mother what had happened, so he took Yasmin's hands in his and began to explain. "We found Braddock. He came to stay with us, but the army got too close. We were about to move on but Odette was scared that we'd spook him, that he wouldn't trust us anymore. So she ... confronted him. He attacked her. She took his powers down, and – someone shot him. We don't know who."

"Is she ..."

"She's alive." It was the best he could manage. "She's ... she's very sick."

He couldn't hide the crack of his voice, and Yasmin's eyes flew wide with concern and understanding. "Oh, Henry."

He took a deep breath and did his best to recount the whole story in detail. As he stammered his way through it, distantly hearing Robbie do the same, Yasmin's hands tightened around his. By the time he was done she'd pulled him into a fierce hug that made his eyes water. If his cousin noticed she made nothing of it, instead pulling back and looking at him with determination.

"She'll be all right," Yasmin urged. "May we see her?"

"She doesn't know you're here, actually." Robbie joined the conversation, Nancy's arm tucked into his. The older woman looked drawn and worried, but she flashed Henry a small smile as he looked at her. Mary stood at her other side like an honour guard. "I'd like to tell her beforehand. If that's all right, m'lady."

Yasmin nodded, and let go of Henry's hands to place one on Robbie's shoulder. "Of course. How are you?"

"I'm ... I'm all right. Just worried about Det."

"Why don't you go and tell her that we're here? Perhaps we might see her one at a time. That might be easier." She glanced over at Nancy, who nodded. "We'll wait here."

Patting Nancy comfortingly on the hand, Robbie excused himself to the other room, where they'd left Odette with Isobel. The four of them waited in silence until he returned, looking slightly hopeful but still tired.

"She'll see you, m'lady. Or, at least, she didn't say she wouldn't see you, which is ..." He glanced over at Nancy. "It's as much as we're getting at the moment."

"Worse than when her grandfather died?" Nancy asked quietly. Robbie nodded. "She curled up into herself for months after that. They were very close. I'll wait here whilst you go in, m'lady."

"You should come as well, H–, er, Professor," said Robbie, stumbling, Henry suspected, because Yasmin was there. "I think it would help if we were both there."

Wrapping an arm around the woman next to her, Mary said, "I'll stay wi' Nancy."

Silence fell as the three of them walked down the corridor to the small living room. Henry's eyes fell to where Odette was curled up in a small ball on the sofa, and he drew a shaking breath and looked up at Yasmin. He watched a series of conflicting emotions wash across his cousin's face in painful clarity. At first she contorted in horror, looking down at the small form of her best friend; then her eyes pinched with pain and narrowed in anger; then her whole expression softened in a mixture of compassion and relief.

"Ditty, darling." She sighed and knelt down on the rug next to the sofa. "Oh, my darling."

Quietly, he and Robbie moved away from Odette and Yasmin. In a silent agreement, they chose not to leave the room – knowing that Odette's mood was too changeable, and that they were often the only anchors that she had to the real world, the only way to escape all of the things that flew around in her head.

It took Yasmin several minutes of gentle coaxing to pull Odette out of her turtle-like pose, finally managing to clutch the younger woman against her in a protective embrace. She seemed not to mind that Odette said nothing back to her, instead resolutely murmuring platitudes and encouragements into her ear. Only when Odette had shifted to allow Yasmin to sit next to her did Henry's cousin look up at him – or, rather, at Robbie.

"Would you get Nancy?"

Henry saw Odette tense from head to toe, and her knuckles turned white where her fingers were wrapped around Yasmin's arm. Frantically, she began to shake her head against Yasmin's shoulder, still coiling in as if to hide herself from the world.

"What?" asked Yasmin softly, tilting her head as if to hear something. "No – no, darling. She loves you. She loves you, and you've nothing to be ashamed about. You don't have to hide, not from her, not from me, not from any of us."

Only then did Henry realise to his great relief that Odette was speaking to Yasmin – quietly and in broken shards of sentences, but she was *speaking.* Robbie had noticed too, for he hesitated instead of following out Yasmin's order, seemingly waiting for Odette's permission to go and fetch her mother.

With a small quirk of a smile, Yasmin said, "You know as well as I do that she'll come into this room whether invited or not."

Next to him, Henry felt Robbie chuckle and nod in agreement. When a barely audible agreement came from Odette, he slipped quietly from the room to fetch Nancy. Several minutes passed in his absence, during which Henry took a seat across from Yasmin and Odette, leaving room next to them for Odette's mother when she arrived. It seemed that Odette had fallen silent again, but he felt lifted nonetheless by the fact that she'd finally spoken.

What Nancy said to her when she came in Henry didn't hear; close as he was, he couldn't hear the woman's gently murmured words. He saw none of the same ripple of emotions in her face as he'd seen in Yasmin's – Nancy, instead, was pure determination. Only afterwards, when Yasmin took an overwhelmed Odette to her room to sit somewhere quieter, did Henry see Nancy break down. Her shaking sobs served to remind him of how afraid he was, of how empty he'd felt since Braddock had died.

And as Mary and Robbie moved to soothe her, Henry found no comfort in their empathy. He turned and left the room.

49

Isobel had not been allowed out of her quarters. The army were keeping most of them under lock and key unless the major general felt it necessary to make exceptions – Henry suspected that he'd allowed them to greet Yasmin and Nancy only because it might get Odette talking. So in order to get the conversation he wanted, Henry was going to have to lie.

"My father," he said, turning to the soldier who was preparing to escort him back to his room, "has *instructed* me to speak with the others. Apparently, he believes I'm capable of making them cooperate."

He put on his best beleaguered-son voice, which was apparently convincing enough to lead the young soldier to ask him where he'd like to go first. She accepted his gruff response without issue, and led him up to Isobel's room. Henry could hardly believe his luck – something was going right for once – and struggled to hide his smile as they ascended the stairs. Then he remembered why he wanted to speak to Isobel, and it faded from his face.

After a few quick words with the comrade on guard, the soldier opened the door to Isobel's room. Thanking them both in as perfunctory a manner as he could muster, Henry entered the room and took a deep breath.

"Professor," Isobel said, getting up from where she'd been

sitting by the window, "I didn't think we were allowed ... are you all right?"

Henry opened his mouth to reply but found he could not. Not yet. Not until he knew. He glanced over his shoulder at the door closing behind him and strode across the room to the window where Isobel was now tentatively sitting back down. The chair opposite her was empty, and he sat in it without looking at her.

"No one else knew where she was going," he said, his voice barely carrying to Isobel, let alone beyond. "No one else knew what she was doing. Except us."

The painter froze awkwardly on the edge of her seat, her unusually clean hands clutched around the wooden arms. "I haven't told them. About the paintings. I destroyed them as soon as you left."

"Isobel, you – you didn't ..."

All this effort to speak to her, and he couldn't ask her if she'd done it, if those small hands that he'd watched paint masterpieces had pulled the trigger of a gun and killed Braddock to save Odette.

A broken laugh, so brief as to sound like a sob, parted Isobel's lips. "Professor – Henry – I thought ... I thought *you* ..."

He blinked. "No," he replied, wondering if he'd have ever done it. "Not me. But if you didn't, then who did?"

"I didn't tell anyone else. I haven't spoken to anyone about it at all – I thought, well, I thought I was covering for you." Colour filled her cheeks. "I'm sorry, sir."

Reaching out, Henry took her hands in his and squeezed them, looking her in the eye for the first time. "You must never feel you have to do something like that for me, Isobel.

Please. I'd never want you to be put in danger on my behalf. We're both innocent; we can tell them the truth and know that we're safe."

"I didn't do it because I had to," replied Isobel with such matter-of-factness that he found himself redefining his perception of her. "Who else knew she was going?"

"I didn't think anyone knew."

"Well *someone* must've known. She must've told someone – but I suppose she wouldn't tell us who it was even if we asked."

Henry sighed. Odette had only just begun to speak; he couldn't put her through this, not now, not when her grip on the world was so tenuous. And who would they be leading to prison as a result? It had to be one of them. It wasn't the army, and yet the soldiers were the only other people who'd known where they were. Someone he trusted had killed Braddock, and was hiding it from all of them.

And he had no idea whether he wanted to damn them or protect them.

Every day since their arrival, the group had been invited to make or amend their statements to the inspector, a process that was neither pleasant nor an invitation. Henry felt as if he'd recited the same things a hundred times. After talking to Isobel, however, he had new reason to accept the invitation.

"I understand that you have something you wish to add to your statement," said the inspector, leaning back in the major general's chair and placing her hands in her lap.

"You've asked me previously about my knowledge of Odette's intent to speak with Braddock."

The inspector perked up. "And you've declined to comment."

"I have. I was concerned that you'd make assumptions based on what I had to say." When she gave no reply, Henry took a deep breath and continued. "Odette told me of her intention to speak with Braddock. She wished to convince him to hand himself over to the authorities."

"Did she tell you when she'd be doing this?"

"Not at that precise moment, but I was aware that it would be soon after our conversation – the next day, as it happened."

"And," the inspector asked, her voice cutting through the scratching sound of the stenographer, "do you know if she told anyone else?"

Henry shook his head, but then sighed. "No, but I did."

"You did?"

"I told someone else. My maid, Isobel. I requested that she paint the outcome of Odette's conversation with Braddock." He forged onwards, determined to get the story out in one fell swoop. "She created not one but two paintings. In one, Braddock was dead, shot, as would be his fate. In the other, Odette was dead. Isobel has never created two paintings for one future before. We surmised that both futures were equally likely."

A dozen questions contorted the policewoman's face – not least amongst them, he was sure, whether it was possible to paint the future – but she schooled them away. "Do these paintings still exist?"

"No. Isobel burned them."

"And what did you do as a result?"

"We decided it would be wrong to intervene. I went back to bed and told Isobel to do so as well." It sounded so terrible now he'd said it out loud; Henry all but winced. "The next morning, when Odette got up, I made no attempt to stop her from speaking with him."

There was a tense silence that became all the quieter as the stenographer's frantic note-taking ceased. Henry felt it important that he not look away – it seemed to be a telling sign of deception, when in fact he was finally revealing the whole truth.

Then the inspector asked the questions he'd been bracing himself for since leaving Isobel's room.

"Did you kill Thomas Braddock?"

"No."

"Where were you at the time of his death?"

"In the house, with Robbie."

"To your knowledge, did Isobel Sterling kill Thomas Braddock?"

"It's my belief that she did not. I understand that she was with Matthew and Abigail when it happened."

Another hour passed as the inspector hit him with a barrage of questions: what had the paintings looked like? Was anyone else aware that Isobel had painted them? Why had they chosen to destroy them? Why had he chosen not to intervene? By the time they were done, Henry felt as if each answer had been pulled from him by a fish hook.

He was escorted back to his room, where he sat in the certainty that Isobel was about to be subjected to the same scrutiny.

The sudden onset of new information caused a resurgence in the inspector's investigation. Others were suddenly pulled in and questioned about Isobel's paintings, about their knowledge of Henry and Isobel's conversation. He'd no way of knowing how they'd responded, gleaning only that they'd been questioned from a scant snippets of conversation. He was grateful that Odette was still not speaking to the inspector; he was not sure he wanted her to know what they'd done, not now.

Then, three days later, the inspector gathered them together. One by one, they filed into the study they'd used when planning their escape from the army – a poetic touch that Henry was certain was unintentional, but nonetheless made him chuckle hoarsely under his breath. He took the seat next to Odette and reached out to take her hand in his – grateful beyond words when she did not pull away.

Then Yasmin entered the room with the inspector, and he frowned. Something was going on here. Something had changed, though he was uncertain what. The policewoman gestured for silence, and the room quietened.

"It has become clear that this investigation cannot continue without some form of intervention. The public are demanding an explanation for Thomas Braddock's – from their point of view – disappearance, and it's becoming increasingly difficult to keep a lid on the story."

Henry couldn't help but feel that this was hardly their problem.

"To this end, I have no option but to escort you all to London, where you'll be placed behind bars until such time as a decision can be made."

There was a sudden and total silence in the room – the statement so abrupt that it left an echo of astonishment.

"I beg your pardon?" Henry found himself saying, tightening his grip on Odette's hand. "What precisely are we being charged with?"

"I would remind you, Professor Oakley, that you're already under house arrest, and only by virtue of the army's generosity. More importantly, you're all suspects in a murder investigation."

"But *you* were going to kill him anyway!" snapped Matthew, who was quickly pressed back into his seat by Mary as he moved to get up.

"This is *your* doing, isn't it, Uncle?" demanded Yasmin, her face stern. "You do realise that the army cannot simply ignore the law because they find it inconvenient."

Henry's father bristled. "We're doing no such thing."

"It's precisely what you're doing," Yasmin replied, now on

the edge of her seat, as if about to pounce. "If they're under arrest, why have they not been permitted bail? If you're placing them into jail, why are they not being charged? You cannot hold them indefinitely without cause and you know it."

"This would all be dealt with if that snivelling chit would just tell us what she saw."

His father had always been ruthless, but he'd never been cold. Never like this. Never so dismissive of the wellbeing of another person. Rage surged within Henry, and he sat up to attention at once, opening his mouth to demand an explanation.

He was beaten to it.

"How *dare* you," Yasmin snarled, rounding on her uncle with now incandescent fury. "Look at her! Really look, Uncle!"

Henry saw his father's eyes glance briefly at Odette's shaking form, and for the briefest of moments, he thought he saw something in his soldier's mask crack. Yasmin must have seen it too, for she leapt at it like a lioness who realises her prey has finally succumbed.

"Too many people have died already," she continued. "Do you really want to kill another person? Because if you take her to jail, if you take any of them to jail, that's what you'll do. And not one of us will ever forgive you – not me, not Henry, none of us. And I hope to all the heavens that you'd never forgive yourself."

Though Odette curled closer against him, Henry had to conceal a smile; Yasmin had made his father stumble for words. She was a far better orator than he could ever hope to be – and that, right now, was exactly what they needed. Now she was rounding on the inspector, and as Henry ran his hand gently over Odette's hair to soothe her, Yasmin took a step towards the increasingly uncomfortable-looking woman.

"And you. Given your previous statements, I imagine that in order to justify taking them anywhere, you must surely charging these people for something – what is it? Aiding a felon? Being party to a criminal act?"

"Traditionally, your ladyship," the inspector said, "a sentence for aiding or abetting a crime would accord with committing the crime personally. And since we're certain that someone in this room murdered Thomas Braddock, these people have committed that crime twice over – aiding both Braddock and the person who killed him."

"I see. And if I understand the law correctly, that can be applied to all those who offered aid, even if they weren't with the felon?"

"It would, yes."

A brilliant smile lit up Yasmin's face, and Henry felt suddenly nervous. What was she doing? Odette also tensed, and lifted her head just enough to make eye contact with him. He wished he had something reassuring to say, but could do nothing but mirror her worried frown.

"Well, then," said Yasmin summarily. "Inspector, please place me under arrest."

"What?" bellowed the major general, causing everyone but Yasmin to jump in surprise.

"I really must apologise for not coming forward before," Yasmin continued with a sigh. "You see, Henry and I have been in almost constant contact since he went away, the period wherein they were absent from Marston notwithstanding – have we not, dear?"

Henry's frown deepened; there was nothing he could do at this point but tell the truth, though he feared he could see where Yasmin was going. "We have, yes."

"And would you be so kind as to tell the major general and the inspector whose house it was that you sought refuge in whilst Thomas Braddock was with you?"

The floor disappeared from Henry's stomach. She was doing it. "Yasmin, no—"

"Answer the question, boy!" his father snapped, though it looked like he too had begun to fear where Yasmin's speech was going.

With a deep sigh, Henry lowered his head and answered. "It was your house, Yasmin. One of many holiday lodges owned by our family. This one was given to you by your mother when you came of age."

The broad, triumphant smile was still shining on Yasmin's face as she turned to the inspector.

"Ma'am," she said politely, "I'm afraid I must confess to having given Henry permission to use my house for illegal purposes. And" – she held up a hand as the inspector moved to interrupt – "yes, I was indeed in full knowledge of what he intended to use it for. Indeed, I insisted that he use it, despite his attempt to refuse my offer. I have his letters back in Brighton, if you'd like proof, as I imagine he has mine. By your reckoning, I've knowingly given sanctuary to not one but two murderers."

Beneath the combination of exasperation and gratitude he was feeling for Yasmin, Henry couldn't help but experience a pang of empathy for the inspector. As much as he hated the inherent prejudice, the notion of having to justify placing one member of the aristocracy under arrest without being able to give a proper explanation to the public was bad enough; two would cause an outcry without a doubt.

It was rather genius of Yasmin; he had no doubt that she was well aware of this and had done it very much on purpose.

"Well, then," the harassed policewoman said with a sigh, "Yasmin Oakley, you're under arrest for two counts of aiding and abetting a felon. Constable, please escort her and the rest of the accused to their rooms. Major General, my office."

51

Henry's father flatly refused to allow them to stay in Marston House. He was not quite the same around them after Yasmin's assault upon him. Odette felt badly for him. He had, after all, only been doing what he felt was right – and they'd yanked everything out from beneath him with the finesse of a servant pulling a tablecloth from under a full setting. In the end, it was decided that they'd return home and continue their house arrest there – the countess apparently insisted upon it, which Odette thought rather worrying.

Everyone was expecting her to click back into normality the moment she walked through the door. They all watched her as her feet touched the floorboards of the ancestral Oakley estate, desperately searching her face for some sort of change.

But she felt nothing.

There was no lifting of burdens, no unfurling of the knot in her chest, no breath released in sweet relief. There was just a long, arduous journey and a sense of having disappointed everyone. Barely minutes after arriving, she quietly asked her assigned guard to escort her to bed, ignoring the concerned queries of those around her. They tried to encourage her towards one of the guest rooms, but Odette followed a desperate thread of longing, letting it carry her to the room she'd shared with her mother since she was small.

And there she stayed, nights and days blurring. Sometimes she'd find blissful sleep; others she'd lie awake, tossing and turning, trying not to think. People came and went; there was almost always someone sitting with her. But it made no difference, even when Henry curled up on the tiny cot with her and cradled her in his arms. Even when Yasmin snuck into the servants' quarters and brushed her hair, as Odette had done for her every day for years. Even when Robbie came and told her about all the gossip they'd missed, the scant bits of information he'd managed to glean despite his imprisonment.

But then came Tuesday.

Later, Odette would find herself unable to explain precisely what it had been about that Tuesday morning that had made everything align just right. The day before, she'd barely stirred from her bed save to relieve herself, and even then she'd scurried back in fear that someone other than her nameless, omnipresent guard would see her in the corridor and look at her with hope – or worse, pity. There was nothing to indicate that Tuesday would be any different.

But that morning, the sun rose and Odette got out of bed. Not because she needed to, but because she wanted to. And though she still felt as if her insides were tearing her apart, and everything still served to remind her of Braddock and what had happened to him, she put on the clothes that had been lying next to her bed for so long that they'd gathered dust, and asked the guard's permission to go to the library.

As she walked, Odette silently prayed that the room would be empty – and to her relief it was. It was late in the morning though, and everyone else was likely busy with ... well, she didn't know what really. She could imagine it – Yasmin holding force against the army, Mary returning happily to her own kitchen, Abigail reunited with her young charge. It comforted her to be able to daydream again at last.

In the days since Braddock's death, she'd been almost unable to daydream. What had once offered her salvation from the hectic pace of her mind became impossible to access. She could do it, a little at a time, but the shadows in the back of her head always reasserted themselves. A fanciful daydream about being a noble archer riding through the forest to rescue a village would be quickly sundered by the violent crack of a bullet and the bitter taste of gunpowder.

After several such experiences, she'd all but given up on being able to daydream anymore. But now she felt a little more in control, and so for some time she simply sat on a chair in the library, letting her mind drift. When she felt her nerves begin to jangle again and concentration became more difficult, she reached blindly behind her for the shelves and picked up the first book that came to hand.

It was how she'd picked books to read when she was younger. Thus armed by random chance and Yasmin's tendency to steal from the library for her benefit, Odette had whiled away much of her childhood with her nose in a book, and she doubted that there was much in the library she hadn't read – it amused her no end, therefore, that the book she selected was her favourite play.

As she opened it and began to read, she couldn't help but think of the day Henry had asked her to sing from this very text – or of the time she'd caught Yasmin singing that same song. As she turned the pages, she hummed the tune quietly underneath her breath, and perhaps it was this that drew the attention of Isobel as she passed the study.

"You're up!" the young painter exclaimed as she poked her head in the room. At first Odette cringed in shame, but then quickly realised that there was no malice in Isobel's tone, simply genuine pleasure. "How are you feeling? Would you mind if I joined you? Ah – is it all right if I join her? Please?"

The last questions were clearly not directed at her but at the two guards who conferred by the doorway before reluctantly allowing Isobel to enter. Odette watched the young woman's feet as they shuffled into the library and stood before the chair in front of her. Her shame was gone now, replaced by a painfully sharp gratitude that Isobel would think to ask *her* if it were all right to come in. Was she really that fragile? The answer, she knew, was quite obvious.

"I'm – here," she said eventually, feeling neither able to lie nor up to answering the question fully. "And … yes, I'd like that."

With a warm smile that Odette could see even out of the corner of her eye, Isobel sat down opposite her. It was funny, she thought, how much they'd all changed . Or perhaps funny wasn't quite the right word.

"Odette, I …" Isobel's pause was thick with a need to speak and a fear of wounding. "I want to apologise to you."

Whatever she'd been expecting Isobel to say, that was not it. It confused and intrigued her so much that she actually lifted her head to look at the woman in front of her. Now Isobel was the one who had her head cast down, looking at her perpetually paint-stained hands. There was a tension in her body that Odette hadn't noticed at first – largely because she hadn't looked up long enough – and seeing it made her start to worry.

"Whatever for?"

Isobel took a deep breath as if composing herself. "When we were in the forest, the night before Thomas died, I painted you."

Everyone else who'd mentioned Braddock in front of her had trodden carefully, as if afraid of breaking her with the words. Even the inspector had been tentative in her questioning – asking her simply, again and again, if Odette had seen the person who'd killed Braddock.

Isobel did no such thing; she passed over it smoothly, cleanly, and Odette found this far more comforting and easy to hear than the awkward discussions with the others.

So wrapped up in this observation was Odette, that she barely took in what Isobel had actually said. When she did, she frowned in confusion.

"You painted me? Why?"

"Henry asked me to. He was ... scared for you. I've never seen him like it. He said he knew it was awful to do it without asking you, and that I didn't have to, but he needed to know you'd be safe."

In the past few days Odette hadn't thought much about Henry, despite his frequent visits. Frankly she hadn't thought all that much about anything – it had been safer that way. But Isobel's answer made her chest tighten with a mixture of emotions that were too strong and intertwined to be distinguishable or bearable. She found herself hitching for breath, and hoped Isobel hadn't noticed.

"The painting came so easily," Isobel continued. "I just closed my eyes and started to see it. It happens sometimes; some things are harder than others. It didn't take long at all. But when I was done ... when I was done, I knew I wasn't finished. The painting was, but it wasn't the whole story. So then I painted another."

"Has that ever happened before?" asked Odette.

Isobel shook her head. "No. And it hasn't since. I think it could do though. I think … sometimes there are things in life that could very easily go different ways. So easily that one outcome is as likely as the other; normally the things I paint are lopsided – I mean, they're more likely than others."

Sometimes Odette wondered whether Isobel's power was surely the most terrifying of all. She nodded, allowing her friend to continue at her own pace – the nervousness still hadn't left the small painter's form.

"One of the paintings was of what ended up happening," said Isobel, and Odette began to understand why she'd been so reticent. "I had to destroy them so that the army wouldn't find them, but … it was of Thomas, with his hands around your throat."

Though there was clearly more to be said, Isobel paused, and when Odette's breathing began to hitch again she was at her side in a moment. Her small, soft hands wrapped around Odette's and grounded her, drawing her back a little from the panic that had started to bloom.

"It's all right," Isobel said, looking at Odette with gentle earnestness. "I'm not going to let anything happen to you."

Odette wanted to explain that it was too late – that it had already happened – but the words got stuck in her throat. The throat that he'd crushed. Instead, she did her best to focus on Isobel's cool, steadying grip, not wanting to ruin everything by having another attack.

"I'll be all right," she assured Isobel once she was certain she could speak without her voice cracking. "What – what did the other painting look like?"

The reply was so simple it felt like a blow to Odette's chest. "It was of Thomas's body."

Pain and confusion swept across Odette's mind in equal measure. "But you said you'd painted two different futures," she said aloud, quite without thinking. "Those were both true. Both of those things – they happened. I don't understand."

"There's something else you should know about the first one," Isobel said, casting her eyes away. "Odette, in the first one, you were dead."

In the silence that followed, Odette ran her fingertips along her throat, where the bruises had faded to yellow and pale green. She'd thought about it, of course – how close she'd come to dying. More than a few times, she'd wished it had happened. She hadn't told anyone as much … she'd put them through enough without adding to their list of worries. She knew it wasn't a good thing to think, but that hadn't stopped her from thinking it, nor had it made the wish any the less genuine.

It felt disjointed from her; as if she were thinking not about herself but of someone else. That same distant feeling came over her as she heard Isobel's softly spoken words, and her mind conjured at once what the painting might've looked like.

Odette was so swept up in her thoughts that she completely failed to realise that she hadn't replied, and that Isobel was looking increasingly worried.

"Odette?"

Blinking, she looked up. "Yes. Sorry, I'm …" She sighed softly, and shook her head. "If that's what it was, then I'm surprised neither of you stopped me going."

The thought formed in her mind as she spoke it aloud, giving her no time to worry about the consequences, nor warning her that saying it would feed the knot of emotion still lodged heavy in her stomach.

"I thought about it," Isobel admitted quietly. "I'd be surprised if Henry hadn't too."

Henry.

Henry, who'd barely left her side since Braddock had died. Henry, who'd raged in her defence with a fury worthy of Yasmin. Henry, who'd tried so desperately to stop her from going. Henry, who loved her.

It made her toes curl with shame. What was she doing to him? To all of them, every person who loved her. They were afraid and she was coiling in on herself, thinking of no one else, listening only to the thoughts in her head. She was letting them down. All of them. With every breath she took.

Because she had no idea who'd killed Braddock. They were trapped here, desperate for the words from her lips that would free them, but she'd not seen anyone. There'd been so much pain, and the images of her power had been too strong for her to see beyond them; the shot had come from so far away that she couldn't even recall spotting more than a flutter of movement.

It made no sense, she thought, staring blankly into the fireplace. None of the others would've followed her. Most of them hadn't even known where she'd been going, what her intentions were, or how dangerous it was. Except ...

"Isobel," A vice closed fully around Odette's heart. "Isobel, tell me he didn't—"

"He didn't. Neither did I. We – we did nothing, Odette. We did nothing, and I'm so sorry."

Odette wanted to be sick. She wished she'd been the one who'd died, not Braddock, that she'd never ended up in this situation at all. Because she remembered. She knew. There was only one person she'd told apart from Henry, only one other person who'd known where she was going.

She knew who'd killed Braddock.

She couldn't move, couldn't speak. Isobel was talking to her, but she heard none of the words – they bounced off her as cleanly as if she was wearing Braddock's shield again.

She could tell she was crying because her face was wet, knew that she was having an attack because she couldn't breathe, but it seemed to be happening to someone else.

52

"Ditty," Henry said, pulling his handkerchief from his pocket and brushing it over her cheeks, "take a deep breath. It's all right. Everything's going to be all right."

Her eyes were wide and staring at him piercingly, as if trying to look through him. Little by little her breathing calmed, as she began to follow his quiet instructions. The policemen who'd brought him there were standing just inside the door, several feet away. Isobel was seated across from them, her face contorted into worry. But all Henry saw was the pale woman shaking in front of him, as if they were had the room all to themselves.

Odette surged forwards, throwing her arms around his neck and burying her face in his neck. The movement seemed strange and sudden; he'd thought that she was settling down, but now her hands were grasping at him as desperately as if she were drowning and he the only buoyancy, and she was hissing in his ear so softly that he struggled to hear what she was saying.

"Isobel told me about the paintings. I know who did it, Henry."

He tensed from head to toe, wrapping his arms around her waist and tilting his head so that he faced away from the policemen. "It wasn't—"

"I know. I know it wasn't you, or her. I told someone else. I told someone else where I was going."

And now Henry understood what had happened. Why the policeman on guard had come bursting into his room to tell him that Odette had succumbed to a fit so severe that no one could rouse her from it. He understood why there was vomit in her hair and why Isobel looked like she was watching herself paint death.

"What do I do, Henry? What do I do?"

Henry screwed his eyes shut and wished desperately that he'd never heard the name Thomas Braddock.

"Was it one of us?" he asked – it was not the question he wanted to ask. He wanted to know who'd done it, so that he could kiss them and throttle them in equal measure. But he couldn't ask her; not that, not now. "One of our group?"

"Yes."

"All right. Everything's going to be all right." He smoothed her greasy, matted hair down with one hand and pulled back from her, pressing his handkerchief into her hand. She stared at it, crying with renewed fervour, and he turned to look up at the policemen. "She isn't well. I'd like to take her back to her room, and I'd like to speak to the inspector."

"The inspector is currently with the major general, your lordship."

"Then I'll speak with her when she's free."

The guard nodded. "I'll escort you to the servants' quarters."

Turning back to Odette, Henry twisted her in his arms, looping one under her knees and the other around her shoulders. "I'm not going to make you do anything you don't want to. I'm not going to do anything for you unless you ask me to," he said carefully.

"I trust you." She leant against his chest, screwing his handkerchief up in his hands. "I just ... I just want this to be over. Is that terrible? I just want it all to stop."

Henry summoned strength he didn't know he possessed and got to his feet. "It's not terrible," he said, moving towards the door as the guards stood aside to let them through. The rest of his words were hushed. "You can't protect people from themselves."

He carried Odette silently though to her room, where he placed her in her bed and refused to leave her side, instead sending out a flurry of requests. Their guards, seemingly overwhelmed by events, did precisely as he asked without question – and soon Isobel and Robbie were with them as well, the inspector not far behind.

To her credit, the policewoman was quiet and unimposing as she stepped into the room, taking a seat opposite them on Nancy's bed. She folded her hands together in her lap and frowned.

"I understand this morning has been difficult," she said, looking across at where Odette was curled between Henry and Robbie. "Is there anything I can do?"

Yasmin, Henry thought, would've told the inspector that she could've been this accommodating from the start. But he was not his cousin, and he'd seen better than most the special treatment that they'd tried to give Odette. She alone had been allowed visits from the others; she was much of the reason that he and Robbie had been permitted to leave their rooms at all.

"We're concerned that the ongoing investigation is causing Odette's ill health to worsen. It's bringing up again and again the details of her assault such that it's impossible for her to see any improvement until she's no longer exposed to this environment."

"I cannot cease my investigation until I've uncovered the truth, Professor. I'm sorry."

Henry nodded, believing her wholeheartedly. "You've been placed in a difficult position, and I recognise that we've not been the most forthcoming. I'd like to help you. You believe that it's one of our number responsible for Thomas Braddock's death. These people are my charge, and my responsibility."

"You cannot take responsibility for their actions," the inspector replied, shaking her head. "Not in this way."

"I don't intend to. I'd like to speak with all of them, to encourage them to cooperate with you so that we can find a resolution. Would you allow me to do so?"

There was a pause as the inspector contemplated the request. Henry tightened his grip on Odette's hand, praying silently that his plan would work.

"Very well. But you'll speak to all of them at once, and both I and the major general will be present."

Henry nodded. It would have to do. You couldn't protect people from themselves – but what you could do was offer them the opportunity to protect others.

53

"I've gathered all of you here in the hope of moving the investigation forward," Henry stated, pacing back and forth in front of the group. Everyone had gathered, even Yasmin. They sat in a semi-circle, their guards standing behind like shadows. "We've been here quite long enough. We know what we've done, and I hope that none of us would've done what we did if we were not willing to accept the consequences."

Odette looked fastidiously at the floor. Her hands were in the laps either side of her – one held by Robbie, the other by Yasmin – and it was not for lack of bravery that she looked down. It was because she'd not been in the same place as … that person … since they'd been moved back home. She couldn't look. If she did she was certain she'd be sick again. She could already taste the echoes of Braddock's blood on her tongue.

"We must remember," Henry continued, "that our actions have consequences not only for ourselves, but also for those around us. And if we don't accept the consequences, then it's those around us who suffer."

Not for the first time since she'd realised the truth, Odette wondered why Braddock had been killed. The killer had not seen what Isobel and Henry had seen, didn't know what she'd been going to speak with Braddock about. Had they followed her as she'd walked with him, and shot him in her defence? Had they done it out of a wish to fulfil the army's original intentions? Every time she thought she knew the answer another question popped up in its wake, leaving her lost in limbo.

It was too much. She lifted her eyes, looking for the first time at the people gathered around her, allowing her gaze to travel from one side of the line to the other. Abigail was furthest left, her skin sallow, her fingers fiddling incessantly with the indestructible hem of one sleeve; beside her, Mary, whose face was stern and hardened by the bags under her eyes. Yasmin sat tall but turned towards her in concern; Robbie was hunched against her protectively. To the right were Isobel, Roger and Matthew. The painter was on the edge of her seat, long fingers wrapped around the cushion; Roger was as stoic as always, standing stiffly; Matthew chewed relentlessly at the side of his thumbnail.

Odette looked last at Henry, who seemed in the midst of a thunderstorm. She remembered the day she'd come into the study and seen him after days without sleep, and wondered how she'd ever thought him exhausted then; for now he looked as tired as she felt, as drawn out, as lost for what to do.

She bit the inside of her mouth, and decided that she no longer wanted to let them down. She was not the only one who needed this to be over.

"I think I know who killed Thomas Braddock," she said, her voice ringing clearly into the silence. Across from her, Henry froze, still but for the slow movement of his head as he turned to look at her. She kept going, propelled by the inability to take her words back. "I told someone that I was going to speak with him. They didn't know why, but I told them that I was going out with him alone. I asked them to make sure it was safe."

"Who was it?" snapped the major general, asking the question visible in the faces of every single person in the room – even the police who'd been their guards every moment since their arrest. Even the inspector, who was so good at hiding her thoughts.

All of the faces, except one.

Odette took a deep breath and focused on the strength in Yasmin and Robbie's grips. "I'm not going to tell you."

"Then you will be charged with impeding a murder investigation," the inspector pointed out, though there was no accusation in her tone.

"I know," Odette said, her breath hitching. She could tell, and then it would be over. It would be done. But she'd never be able to live with herself. "I wish they hadn't done it. I wish Thomas was alive. But I wouldn't be if it weren't for them. They saved my life. I'm not going to end theirs."

Tears rolled down her cheeks. Yasmin had put her arm around her shoulders, and Henry stared at her like she was the sun and he couldn't look away. The major general fumed, and the inspector watched in cool contemplation.

But Odette saw none of these things. They were there in front of her eyes, but a moment after they'd registered all she could do was hear.

"You don't have to."

She felt him stand up on her right, tall and proud amidst the horror etched on their faces. He stepped in front of her and knelt down. Odette looked at him, sight returning to her consciousness, and saw the lines in his face as if for the first time. Gone was his expressionless mask, replaced by a look of determination and sorrow. Odette twisted her right hand free of Robbie's, and reached out to press it to Roger's cheek.

"I killed Thomas Braddock," he stated, directing the words towards her but saying them loud enough for everyone to hear. "The rifle I used is buried half a mile from where he died. I had the rabbits take it into their tunnels. None of these people assisted me in what I did."

In one fell swoop the weight that had pressed upon Odette lifted. She'd been right. She'd been right, and it felt terrible.

"Thank you," she whispered. She wasn't sure if she meant it – or, indeed, why she'd said it at all.

Seconds later the room became a flurry of activity: policemen moved to flank Roger and placed him into handcuffs whilst voices criss-crossed over one another in a rising cacophony. Yasmin had risen to her feet and released Odette's hands, charging over to her uncle. The inspector was giving quiet orders to those around her. Henry stood on the spot, hands hanging limply at his sides, looking at nothing at all.

Odette's focus narrowed again, moving to encompass only the parting words from the man who'd saved her life.

"He's dead – but you get to live. Live, child."

54

In the days that followed, Odette was not privy to much of the fallout from Roger's arrest. She knew only that he'd been taken away, the major general with him. Indeed, it seemed that the army were sated by the arrest of Braddock's killer, for soon the charges had been dropped, and the inspector had departed the house with polite thanks for their cooperation. This resolution seemed to Odette to be the strangest irony, but she didn't doubt that it owed much of its neatness to their desire to keep the truth of magic as hidden from the world as possible – and to the political machinations of the countess.

Of the details, however, Odette knew little. She spent the ensuing days in Henry's room, the two of them saying and doing nothing as they processed all that had happened. And though she'd lost the mindless state that had encompassed her since Braddock had died, she wasn't overwhelmed with flurries of thought. She was too exhausted to think on what had happened at any great length – and too concerned for Henry, who'd collapsed into bed the day after Roger had been taken to London and barely risen for the next two days.

They were visited often by the others, most of all Yasmin, who'd taken to coming in each day and reading to them from the most dreary and tedious books she could find in the library. These texts she read in a variety of incongruous voices, the comedic production serving to draw Odette and Henry out of themselves when it seemed that they were on the verge of disappearing again.

No one made mention of the impropriety of her staying in Henry's room. Even the countess all but insisted on it, and had Odette's things moved out of her old room without a word, as if proclaiming that the arrangement was tolerated by her and therefore was to be tolerated by all. It was strange, but it functioned – and, besides, it was not as if Odette had a job to return to. She'd been gone so long that Yasmin had been assigned a new maid who was now on permanent staff.

Then, one morning, a letter arrived for her, and Odette was forced to remember that the future was an uncertainty gifted to her by a well-timed gunshot. Henry had gone to see Isobel, and Odette found herself quite alone in his room as she reached for the missive.

It was made of exceptionally fine paper and had been sealed with a stamp that she didn't recognise. It seemed, curiously, to have been hand-delivered – at least, there was no address on the front. She picked up a knife and, careful not to spoil it, slid it underneath the wax, allowing her to pull out the creamy parchment within.

It was not one sheet but three, and all were marked proudly with the heraldry of the University of Oxford. She devoured the words in barely any time at all. Then she paused. Surely she'd misread it. Disbelieving, she read it again. It offering her a place in the university's department for magical studies. A full scholarship, in fact, in return for her services to the country, and on the condition that she didn't mind being a test subject for their new curriculum. It seemed they were expanding the research centre into a full teaching department.

It was signed – of course – V. Entwhistle, and a postscript read: *Darling, Henry doesn't know about this. I thought you'd wish to make the decision yourself. Love, V.*

The additional sheets detailed the course, what she could expect to learn and to help with, information about where she could live within the college, and all manner of details that, in that moment, escaped Odette's focus entirely. For she'd dreamt of going to university when she was little. There'd been no chance of it, though; she lived on a servant's wage, and had never been formally schooled. There wasn't a university in the country that would take her.

Apparently things were different when you were famous, or when you had magical powers. She wasn't quite sure how she felt about that; she knew that many of the others had been sent their own offers, for though the truth of Braddock's death had been covered up there were enough people in the know to cause outside interest. She'd never expected one for herself though.

So many thoughts began to wage war in her mind that she became quite paralysed, unable do anything save stare down at the letter and read it over and over again, still expecting it to disappear or for her to wake up from what must surely be a strange dream.

She was still cradling the letter in her hands when there was the soft shuffle of footsteps behind her. She turned and held the parchment to her back.

"Oh, m'lady. I'm sorry. I was worried for a moment that you were Henry," she said, her panic deflating.

"The last I checked I was not," remarked Yasmin with dry fondness, hugging Odette gently. "And don't call me that, Ditty, not anymore. But why would you not want to see Henry? Did he do something? I shall box his ears, I swear—"

"No, no. It's ..." Odette's eyes darted back to the letter, and she pulled Yasmin towards the sofa in front of the fireplace. "Here – read it."

A gentle frown dipped Yasmin's brow as she took the letter and saw at once where it was from. Within moments, however, her confusion was washed away by a fervent delight that lit up her face. She practically squealed as she returned the letter.

"But that's wonderful news!" said Yasmin.

And Odette couldn't help but smile. It *was* wonderful ... but it was also terrible at the same time.

"Come, now, you cannot tell me that you don't want to go."

"I do," said Odette with an honesty that surprised her considering how confused she still felt. "But Henry—"

"Will be as delighted as I am," replied Yasmin, though she clearly knew there was more to it than that. "Why would he not?"

"I don't know what he wants to happen now. I can't just insert myself into his life."

"Henry does not have the monopoly on that part of the world, Ditty."

Odette couldn't help chuckling. "I know that," she said, though she felt a little sheepish. "But it's his department. I'd be coming into his world – he might not own it, but I'd be the one intruding. I'm not sure that's fair."

"Do you not want to go?"

"No, I do!" Odette nodded her head fiercely. "I do, I really want to. I want to find out where these things we can do come from, and work out what they could do – imagine how many people there must be who don't know about their powers. Think of what a difference it could make to the world if they knew about them."

The impassioned speech rushed from her almost in a single breath, and when it was over Odette looked up to see Yasmin smirking. "Then don't you think you should talk to Henry about it, rather than assuming what he might or might not want?"

A far worse thought flashed into Odette's mind. "What if he *does* want me to go? Or he feels like he has to let me, and then gets stuck with me for years when he doesn't really want—"

"Ditty, if you're for a moment suggesting that my dear cousin doesn't love you, then I'm going to give serious thought to asking Nancy whether you were dropped repeatedly on your head as a child."

Anger overwhelmed Odette, and it shocked her; Yasmin's sarcasm and humour had never affected her in this way. "That's not what I mean and you know it!" she snapped, forgetting who she was and whom she was talking to, and that the possibility of Henry not feeling the same about her *had* crossed her mind. "I don't want to be with him just because we feel like that's what we ought to do, Yasmin."

Though at first her mistress looked affronted, it quickly soften to a mixture of approval and something akin to pride.

"Then tell him that, darling. Tell him. There's nothing worse than not knowing, even though it feels sometimes like the answer might be worse. It isn't. There's nothing worse than the things our minds can concoct when we don't have all the answers."

Yasmin's softly spoken statement was so painfully true that it made Odette's eyes well with tears. She turned to hide them, but was too late for her perceptive friend, and was quickly gathered into a warm embrace. Not for the first time, Odette wondered how different life might have been if she'd not ended up with the Oakley family.

55

Henry felt uneasy. For the past few weeks he'd known more or less what was going on ... had been able to decide what to do about everything. Now ... now he just felt lost. Was he expected to go back to Oxford and pretend that nothing had happened?

Vivalda found him in the study where they'd first decided to seek out Braddock. He was perched on the edge of his seat, deep in thought as he stared into the empty fireplace, and entirely failed to notice that she'd entered until she sat down next to him.

Raising an eyebrow, she said, "It's a wise man who realises he may not shoulder the world's burdens alone."

"Viv – you're here, my gods." He threw his arms around her at once, not caring what he must look like. "You're here."

"I'm so sorry I couldn't come earlier. They kept us at Marston for a while with all of their twittering questions. By the time we escaped there was so much more to be done. Darling ..." She pulled back and placed her hands either side of his cheeks, examining him sternly. "I heard about Roger."

Henry swallowed a lump in his throat.

"It's all right to be grateful," Vivalda continued, still holding him in place.

In the weeks that had passed since he'd first heard the

name Thomas Braddock, Henry had learned what it was to cry. Whether it was his own emotion brimming to the surface, or those of others – Odette's hitching, breath-stealing sobs – he'd come to understand it in a way that he'd not before. But as Vivalda's words washed over him, and the gasps welled up in his chest, he finally knew what it was to weep with relief.

She released his cheeks and pulled him against her, holding him there until he came back to himself, snuffling in remorse. "I never asked you how you were, or what happened whilst we were gone."

"Oh, pish." She waved a hand idly. "I'm sure you can guess. After a while, Edward was awful, as usual – crowing with delight about how he'd defeated you, or some such nonsense. Though I daresay he was also a little afraid that you'd gone off to beat him."

"Only after a while?"

"Strangest thing. For the first day or two he wouldn't talk about you at all. Kept changing the subject whenever I brought it up – it was quite hilarious, really. I may have done it with some frequency just to bask in his discomfort."

Henry chuckled again, and then suddenly remembered what had happened to Edward the day before they'd left. "I suspect," he said, "it has something to do with Odette. He threatened the two of us so she – well, she used his powers on him."

"I've always liked her," Vivalda replied cheerfully, though she also flashed him a look of concern. "But that, I think, is not what concerns you."

"No." He sighed and rubbed his face with the palms of his hands. "I suppose I'm trying to decide what happens next. What I want to do."

Vivalda narrowed her eyes. "I've known you a very long time, darling, and in my experience whenever you're agonising over a decision it's not that you don't know what to do. It's that you know precisely what you want to do but are struggling to justify it to yourself."

Was that what was happening? Perhaps. For so long, all he'd been worried about was Odette – whether she'd be all right, or forgiven him for what he'd taken her into; whether they'd escape imprisonment or worse. Then Roger had spoken four words that had turned his world upside down – *I killed Thomas Braddock* – and he'd found himself drowning in a thousand new thoughts and feelings.

Because all he'd been able to think about was Thomas Braddock. Or, more specifically, the last thing Braddock had said to him.

He'd not told anyone about the conversation. It had hardly been a conversation, after all – rather, a short exchange of thoughts. But as he'd turned to leave, Braddock had said something that Henry still couldn't get out of his mind.

"Your problem, Professor, is that you've bought into the idea that you bring shame on the world. That you should be hidden, kept secret, never spoken of. You still think you're worth less, just because you're a mage. You're not."

He recounted the words to Vivalda, and she frowned. The joviality drained from her, to be replaced by a long, solemn silence.

"It troubles you that he was right?"

Henry nodded. "That's the problem, Viv. He ... he was so very right. And now he's dead and the change he was bringing about can't happen."

"Why not?"

But it wasn't Vivalda who'd replied – it was Yasmin, who was stood just inside the room with arms folded. An apologetic smile turned her lips. "I didn't mean to eavesdrop but, Henry, you're more than capable of changing things. You might even be better at it than Thomas Braddock could've been."

She moved into the room and sat down adjacent to the two of them, smiling at Vivalda and taking her hand briefly in greeting. Henry was filled with a sense of foreboding that juxtaposed with his wonderment at these two women, who together were a force of nature.

"What is it that you want to change?" Vivalda asked, looking thoughtful.

"I don't think we can go from where we are now to the whole world knowing about us – not so quickly. We need provisions in place to protect us first ... to ensure we don't reveal ourselves only to be regarded as second-class citizens. I think that's where he went wrong. In part, at least." He frowned. "But I know nothing about law."

Vivalda, however, was clearly still focused on something else. "Yasmin is right; you're certainly capable of changing things. We both are. But Henry, darling, we've been doing that for years. Why does the how need to change? Why are you *really* doing this?"

Clearly, he needed to surround himself by people who were far less perceptive. It felt lately as if everyone he knew could see right through him – read his thoughts and feelings as if he were a book, open for all to see. But it was too late to escape now, so, sighing, he lowered his head and told her.

"So that none of this ever happens again. So that no more mages die because the world made them believe that they were abnormal, or unwanted, or hated. So that no one has to kill one mage to protect another ever, ever again."

At once, the two of them reached out to him; Yasmin took his hands and Vivalda placed hers on his shoulder. They sat there in silence until Henry began to speak.

It felt as if the words were being torn from him, as if he couldn't help but say them. He told them about the rally, and how he'd believed in what Braddock was saying; the hope in his eyes when they'd brought him back to the house; the way he'd lit up when he spoke of what could be – the possibilities of magic; how he wished, so very much, that he'd come to know him better. And about how every day he woke up glad that Braddock was dead, because it meant that Odette was alive. And how every time someone mentioned Roger's name, he felt proud – proud of the man who'd done what was necessary to shield her, in a way that he himself could not.

It felt like an exorcism. When he was done, he was as drained, as if he'd spent an hour sobbing. He wondered briefly if this was how Odette felt after one of her fits. The presence of his two dear friends seemed to be all that kept him from collapsing.

"I want to do it," he said softly at last. "I want to go to London, and I'm going to try and give him the world he wanted. But—"

"No buts," Vivalda chastised, brushing his hair out of his eyes. "You're quite capable of doing anything you put your mind to."

Henry frowned. "Odette—"

"Would be incredibly proud of you for trying and you bloody well know it." Yasmin spoke with such conviction that he wondered what it was that gave her so strong a certainty. Then she frowned. "They're going to destroy you in the city."

Feeling his pride slightly bruised, Henry replied, "I'm sure I can manage a few difficult conversations. Academic careers do involve a lot of debating, you know."

"Don't be silly, Henry," his cousin rebuffed, jabbing her finger into his chest pointedly. "You don't know the first thing about politics. You're far cleverer than I could ever hope to be, but that alone won't get you what you want. You need contacts, and cunning, and someone who can shout over the cacophony of that city."

That he couldn't find argument with.

Yasmin spotted his hesitation at once, and seized upon it with the glee of a triumphant predator. "Then it's settled. I'll tell Mother that we want to stay in the London house – it's certainly big enough – and we'll formulate a plan of action."

On any other day Henry might've felt a little overwhelmed by Yasmin's enthusiasm, but now he simply found himself utterly relieved that he'd not be doing this on his own. He let the two of them draw him into a lively discussion about Yasmin's various contacts within the city and who'd be most amenable to their plans. It lasted far into the night.

Somehow, though, he couldn't quite regret the tiredness he'd surely feel the next morning. A tentative smile had settled on his lips; he'd spent so much time worrying about the others that he'd forgotten, until that moment, to remind himself that *he* was going to be all right as well.

56

He couldn't put off telling her any longer. The words had sat heavy on the tip of his tongue for hours, since they'd retreated to his rooms after an early supper. It was a relatively frequent occurrence now, not just for them but for many of the recovering mages. The countess and earl were wonderful hosts, but sometimes they were a little too interested in how well everyone was doing – a little too strong in their attempt to push people towards getting back to their lives.

They were settled on the long lounge chair in his sitting room, in front of the unlit fireplace. Both with their heads in books, of course; it seemed there was no end to Odette's love for reading, and he was hardly called a light reader himself. It was a comfortable routine that had the added benefit of allowing them some time to escape their thoughts – which, though often appeared to be largely for Odette's sake, was something he too was grateful for.

It stopped him worrying – usually. That evening, he couldn't focus on the words at all; every time he tried to read a sentence, the words transformed into the conversation he and Vivalda had had earlier in the day. And now he could postpone it no longer. Sighing, he took a deep breath that drew Odette's attention from her novel.

"I need to tell you something." He'd tried to keep the

nerves out of his voice but failed miserably. Panicked, he looked across at Odette's expression – only to find that she too looked anxious. The two of them placed their books aside.

"Me too. But – you go first."

He nodded, and reached up to run a hand over his hair as it escaped and fell askew. "We need to talk about, ah, what we want to do now. With this." He gestured vaguely between the two of them, and then laced his fingers through hers.

"Oh." Odette sighed and offered a brief chuckle that made him relax and fret all at once. "Henry, that's exactly what I was going to say."

"It is?"

She shifted to curl her legs underneath her, shuffling closer to him in the process. "Yes. I think … look, everyone expects us to just, I don't know, run away together or something. I don't think that's the best idea." She was blushing, but seemed to be willing herself to keep talking. "We just went through something horrible, and I think … it would be too easy to just cling to one another in the wake of that. And I don't think that's healthy. Or rather, I think it's a perfectly logical thing to do in this situation, b–but – I don't think it's a good basis for a relationship."

Whatever he'd expected her to say, that wasn't it – but it was precisely what he'd been thinking. Precisely what he and Vivalda had talked about. A breath that he'd not known he was holding left his lips, and he looped his free hand around Odette's waist, pulling her in to press his lips into her hair.

"It's not that I don't love you," she urged at once, misinterpreting his gesture. "I do, Henry. That's the problem. I love you so much that—"

Just as she'd done to him all those weeks ago, Henry cut

her off with a gentle press of his fingers against her lips. "I know," he murmured softly. "And I love you – enough that I don't want to lean too heavily on you. But it would be so easy to. I have been, I think, these past days."

Odette blinked in confusion. "You, rely on me?"

"Of course." He felt himself smiling despite the seriousness of the conversation. "Sometimes it feels like you're the only thing that makes sense in the world anymore."

Her eyes turned glassy, but there was a radiant smile in them that was echoed by her quiet laughter – ever so slightly disbelieving, but entirely without malice. "Do you know what I think?"

He shook his head, though it clearly wasn't a question that merited an answer.

"I think that you can't build a house without bricks. But if you tried to make it only from bricks, it would fall down – imagine a roof, made only of bricks! – so you have to use other things, no matter how much it looks like bricks are what you need."

"What are we building?" he asked, drawing her closer. He caught a glimpse of a smile on her face as she rested her head against his shoulder and looked up at him.

"Our lives. Again."

An echo of Roger's words sprung unbidden into his mind. *You get to live.*

"I want to go to London. I want to go to the Houses, to the army, to everyone, and convince them that people like us don't need to be hidden away. That it's good to explain to the world who and what we are. That it will help everyone to be safer and happier."

She went very still, and he worried for a moment that she'd

retreated into herself – but he could do nothing but wait to see if that was the case. Then a few moments later she whispered, "I think Thomas would've liked that very much."

Of course Odette would understand – how could she not? Henry tilted his head downwards and caught her lips against his, not knowing quite how to else to express what he was feeling. "I hope so," he replied, voice as soft as a prayer.

Their faces were close enough for him to see the anticipation that flashed into her expression before she said, "I got offered a place at Oxford. I want to go."

"You did?" he exclaimed, forgetting that they were close enough that he needn't raise his voice. When she nodded, he scooped her into his lap and hugged her tightly, squeezing a surprised giggle from her. "You'll love it there. I can't think of anywhere else that would suit you more."

Dazed astonishment shone from Odette's face as she curled up against him, fingers tugging at his collar as her arms rested on his chest. "I wasn't sure how to tell you. I didn't want you to think you were stuck with me forever. Or that I wanted to leave you."

"Do you?" He asked the question gently.

"No. No, Henry, I ..." She leant in and kissed him so tenderly that it made his breath hitch. Then, in an echo of so many weeks ago, she said, "I love you. I couldn't tell you all the things I love about you if I tried. But I don't think that's a problem. I think the point is knowing that, and trying anyway."

"Trying what?"

She smiled so radiantly that it seemed to light up the room. "To tell you what all of those things are. To show you. I want to do that, too, as well as going to Oxford. As well as you going to London. I want us to do all of it."

The last shreds of fear that had knotted in his gut fell away, replaced by a tightness in his chest and throat. For a long time he simply held her against him, marvelling that even after everything she'd been through the hope in her heart still shone so brightly.

"You could stay in my house in Oxford. I could come back there each weekend … if you'd like."

Offering this, he felt as hesitant, as if he were a schoolboy inviting a classmate to a dance, and he knew he looked and sounded so.

But Odette pressed her lips to his cheek, quelling his diffidence in an instant. "I'd like that very much."

"Then," he said, leaning his forehead against hers, "we can build our lives with wood and stone as well as brick. That way they won't collapse in on themselves. And we can be sure to measure things carefully, and—"

"Henry."

"Yes?"

She smiled against his lips. "I'm afraid you've rather run away with that poor metaphor."

He cleared his throat, and made to try again, but before he got the chance, Odette caught his mouth against hers in a kiss that was anything but gentle; and whatever he'd been about to say became lost in an instant.

The countryside rushed by in a blur of green and brown as the carriage clattered along at full speed. Summer was ending, and the world was becoming tinted with gold as autumn drew near, but Odette was slightly too warm in the coat that Abigail had made for her. She picked at the lace on the cuffs, leaning against the side of the carriage, her feet drawn up underneath her. There was a gentle tickle of anxiety in her belly, as there had been for days now, but she found she didn't mind it much. It was there just as the press of her shoes on the sides and heels of her feet was; it had become part of the background.

It wasn't that she no longer had her attacks, or that she didn't feel her heart leap into her throat whenever someone strange spoke to her. She still walked through her day afraid of all the things that could go wrong, sometimes so much that it was paralysing. But since Roger had told her to live again, since he'd given her the chance, little by little Odette had felt the fear begin to lessen. It would always be there – she knew that now – but that realisation had begun to weigh on her less and less.

In an hour, she'd be arriving in Oxford, where Vivalda was waiting for her at Henry's house. On Monday her first classes would begin. A year ago, the idea of studying with people she'd never met, in a city she'd never been to, would've sent Odette straight into an attack. And though her pulse was racing, and her breath sometimes hopped and skipped, it was no longer because she was overcome with fear – no, this time it was excitement. She thought it rather funny that the feelings that had tormented her so would come to have so bright a meaning.

Time passed so slowly that, on occasion, she thought she couldn't bear a moment longer. But eventually the countryside gave way to scattered buildings, and they to bustling city streets.

As she grew closer to her destination her carriage's pace slowed, and Odette's stomach fluttered with anticipation.

Finally they arrived, just as the sky was beginning to turn dusky pink. The carriage pulled to a halt on a street just past what she presumed was the college, and as she stepped out Vivalda rushed down the steps of the large but modest building to greet her with a broad grin and open arms.

"Darling!" Vivalda pulled Odette into so fierce a hug that her toes lifted off the ground. "You made it. How was your journey?"

"Not as long as I expected, but longer than I would've liked!" Odette said, and smiled, unable to tear her eyes away from the beautiful sights around her. The house was one of a row of tall buildings that ran one into the other. Each had their own marble staircase, and the stone shone brightly.

Vivalda laughed and linked arms with Odette as the footman began to unload her belongings and carry them up the stairs.

"Henry gave you the key, I hope? If he didn't, I can leave you mine. There are staff here most of the time, but not always.”

As they followed the footman into the house, Odette reached into her pocket and plucked out the thin strip of silk from which hung the key.

Henry’s house had a bright reception room dominated by a spiral staircase that ran directly upwards. To her right, she could see a warmly appointed room with a fireplace, and to her left was the familiar sight and scent of books. The corridor continued past the stairs before them, running back a way and ending in a door that shone with the green of the garden beyond.

Though the footman tried to insist otherwise, Odette took her suitcase in one hand and her hatbox in the other and carried them up the staircase. The wooden chest would be awkward enough; they didn’t need yet more to add to their trouble. Vivalda took the hatbox from her as they ascended, not questioning whether it was necessary.

“Now, you simply *must* explore – you’re going to love it, my dear, I’m sure. But I don’t want you to be overwhelmed. If you need anything, anything at all, I’m just within the college itself. You’ll be absolutely no bother. Why don’t we go out together, take a wander around the city?”

A smile like the cresting dawn lit up Odette’s face. “You know,” she replied, tilting her head, “I think I’ll be all right on my own.”

Thanks

Mundane Magic would not have been possible without the support and love of a huge number of people. Thank you to everyone who has helped me along the way, but especially...

To Team Alpha – Martin, Steph, James and Joanna, who saw a fragment of the novel in its most nascent days. To Team Beta – Huw, Matt, Rich, Nina and my wonderful mother. Thank you all for your feedback and encouragement even when it wasn't quite there yet.

To my incredible, wonderful, amazing editor Louise. You not only made *Mundane Magic* as close to flawless as I could have hoped, you did so with care and generosity for which I will be eternally grateful. I hope that I can continue to absorb your lessons in future writing.

To Stephanie Selander, who many months ago sat me down and talked me into getting published, first in journals and then as a novelist. This book is dedicated to you because it simply would not exist without you; proof that a single conversation can change many things.

Lastly and certainly not least to my ever-suffering, ever-perfect fiancé, who lifted me up when I was down and was always there to remind me that sometimes the things that scare you the most are the things that you want most in the world.

www.ingramcontent.com/pod-product-compliance
Lightning Source LLC
Chambersburg PA
CBHW070234200726
48293CB00005B/1610